It was a game Clare had played all her life. *What if? What if...?*

Now, in the shimmering tarmacadam heat of a mid-summer afternoon, inching her red Fiat forward in the endless line of motorway traffic, she played it again. She was approaching the divide. Which way should she go? Direct to London, and risk the jam? Or peel off to Bristol?

But what if she could do both? What then...?

Parallel Lives, Elizabeth Gibson's fourth novel, following her award-winning *Old Photographs*, is a deeply satisfying story of family, relationships, love... The fascination of this double-stranded story lies in the fact that the main character, impulsive journalist Clare Hogarth, has both her choices.

ELIZABETH GIBSON is married with two children and lives in Maidstone, Kent—the setting of her historical novel, *Sons and Brothers*. She is a professional editor and writer. *Parallel Lives* and *Old Photographs* form part of a sequence of novels, each of which has character-links with the others.

For Bodie and Keith, my friends—
You were there at the beginning.
Thanks for all your encouragement.

PARALLEL LIVES

Elizabeth Gibson

A LION PAPERBACK
Oxford · Batavia · Sydney

Published by
Lion Publishing plc
Sandy Lane West, Oxford, England
ISBN 0 7459 2243 0
Albatross Books Pty Ltd
PO Box 320, Sutherland, NSW 2232, Australia
ISBN 0 7324 0603 X

First edition 1992

Acknowledgements
Lines from 'Stopping by Woods on a Snowy Evening'
and 'The Road Not Taken', by Robert Frost, *The
Complete Poems of Robert Frost*, edited by E.C. Lathem
(Jonathan Cape: London, 1951 and 1967) are used by
permission of Random Century, Ltd, London, and the
literary estate of Robert Frost.

A catalogue record for this book is available
from the British Library

Printed and bound in Great Britain
by Cox & Wyman, Reading

Author's Acknowledgements

I have always hated the custom of listing everyone including Auntie Mary and her pet canary in the bread-and-butter 'thank-you's' at the beginning of a book, but this time I cannot do without. As writers inevitably say at such moments, this book would certainly never have come into being without the help of many people in Britain and one or two in the United States.

Thanks go to my family for putting up with my daily disappearing act. To my patient editor, Pat. To former colleagues and dear friends in Eastbourne, who in their inimitable way gave me the time to write the book in the first place.

Thanks also to many members of the Kent County Constabulary, especially PC John Blackman, SOCO Margaret Sidaway, Press Officer Frances Edwards, Sgt Andrew Gent and his wife WPC Judy Gent, among others—who explained many things about careful police work that I'd never understood. Also to Chief Constable Robin Oake, of the Isle of Man. Thanks to Karen Barnes of *Woman's Own* magazine, a cheerful mine of information on the magazine world. To Fr Brian Purfield of the Franciscan Study Centre in Canterbury. To John and Joan Archer for their Bostonian encouragement. To Tony Collins, fisherman and friend. To MCS Fiat Dealers in Maidstone. To the Vice-Consulate of the US Embassy in London. And finally to Coventry Tourist Information Centre. Thank you, one and all.

Elizabeth Gibson

The characters shown on these family trees appear in four different novels: *The Water is Wide*, *Old Photographs*, *Parallel Lives* and a new novel in preparation.

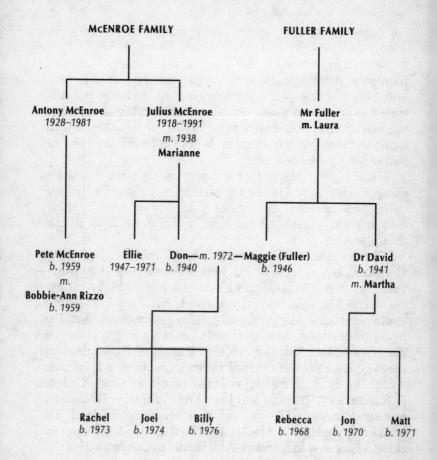

McENROE FAMILY

Antony McEnroe
1928–1981

Julius McEnroe
1918–1991
m. 1938
Marianne

Pete McEnroe
b. 1959
m.
Bobbie-Ann Rizzo
b. 1959

Ellie
1947–1971

Don—m. 1972—**Maggie (Fuller)**
b. 1940   *b. 1946*

Rachel
b. 1973

Joel
b. 1974

Billy
b. 1976

FULLER FAMILY

Mr Fuller
m. Laura

Dr David
b. 1941
m. **Martha**

Rebecca
b. 1968

Jon
b. 1970

Matt
b. 1971

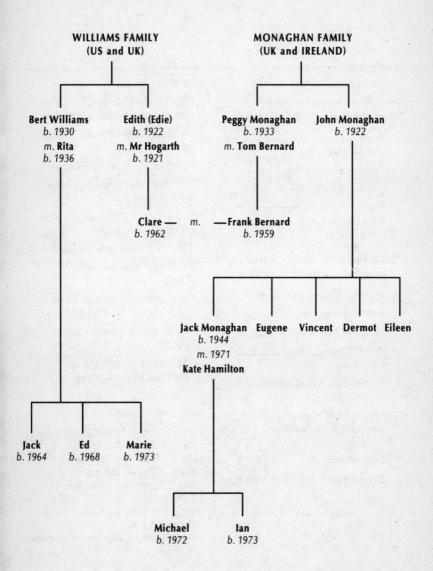

WILLIAMS FAMILY
(US and UK)

MONAGHAN FAMILY
(UK and IRELAND)

Bert Williams
b. 1930
m. **Rita**
b. 1936

Edith (Edie)
b. 1922
m. **Mr Hogarth**
b. 1921

Peggy Monaghan
b. 1933
m. **Tom Bernard**

John Monaghan
b. 1922

Clare — *m.* — **Frank Bernard**
b. 1962　　　　　*b. 1959*

Jack Monaghan　**Eugene**　**Vincent**　**Dermot**　**Eileen**
b. 1944
m. 1971
Kate Hamilton

Jack　**Ed**　**Marie**
b. 1964　*b. 1968*　*b. 1973*

Michael　　**Ian**
b. 1972　　*b. 1973*

Dramatis Personae

In London

Clare Hogarth

Edith Hogarth, her mother

Nina Cottham, fellow staff writer

Andy, editor of *Women Today* and Clare's boss

Dave, features editor

Sandy, Clare's flatmate

Danny, Suzanne, Valerie: other friends/colleagues

In Boston

Clare Hogarth

Bert Williams, her uncle

Rita Williams, her aunt

Jack, Ed, Marie: her cousins

Pete McEnroe, editor of *Citizen* and Clare's boss

Bobbie-Ann Rizzo, magazine photographer

Julius and Marianne McEnroe: Pete's uncle and aunt

Virginia, Kathy: other staff at *Citizen*

Angel Avalon, American rock star

In Bristol

DI Frank Bernard

DS Charlie Hotchkiss, administrator; Frank's friend

DI Nigel Sands, Frank's colleague and friend

WDC Jill Peterson, Nigel's girlfriend

Det. Supt. Bill Longley, Senior Investigating Officer

Sally, John, PC McGavran: other colleagues of Frank's

Tim, Richard: Frank's housemates

Tom and Peggy Bernard: Frank's parents

Lucy; Emily and Susie: one of Frank's sisters, and his nieces

Mrs Drury: mother of missing child Jennifer

(DI Joe Cafferty, Frank's counterpart in Coventry)

Abbreviations

SIO   Senior Investigating Officer
DI   Detective Inspector
DS   Detective Sergeant
WDC Woman Detective Constable
DC   Detective Constable
SOCO Scenes of Crime Officer
PC   Police Constable
H.O.L.M.E.S.
Home Office Large Major Enquiry System

Two roads diverged in a yellow wood,
And sorry I could not travel both
And be one traveller, long I stood
And looked down one as far as I could
To where it bent in the undergrowth;
Then took the other, as just as fair,
And having perhaps the better claim,
Because it was grassy and wanted wear;
Though as for that the passing there
Had worn them really about the same,
And both that morning equally lay
In leaves no step had trodden black.
Oh, I kept the first for another day!
Yet knowing how way leads on to way,
I doubted if I should ever come back.
I shall be telling this with a sigh
Somewhere ages and ages hence:
Two roads diverged in a wood, and I—
I took the one less travelled by,
And that has made all the difference.

The woods are lovely, dark and deep,
But I have promises to keep,
And miles to go before I sleep,
And miles to go before I sleep.

PART ONE

Two roads diverged in a yellow wood,
And sorry I could not travel both
And be one traveller . . .

Coming towards her was a woman very like herself: pale with fatigue, eyes huge from the surprise of lights so harsh, the dark pupils accentuated by the dark suit. She smiled vaguely, and the woman smiled back—a brittle, fixed smile. Hesitating, resting her flight bag on the ledge, she leaned forward over a basin. Then she groaned, shut her eyes, and stood still for an instant.

When she opened her eyes, the same woman looked back at her, grey eyes clear and unblinking, this time unsmiling. They looked at each other for perhaps twenty seconds; then Clare dropped her eyes and reached to turn on the taps.

Plunging her hands into lukewarm water, she felt a surge of relief.

What if he were waiting for me at the airport? she thought fancifully. *No, of course he won't be. But next time, when he's well, he'll be there for me.*

Thoughtfully, careful not to catch the other woman's eyes again, she dried her hands and retrieved the bag.

She turned away just as the woman on the other side of the line of basins turned away also. For a moment, her eyes betrayed her. The other woman was not now dressed as she was—in a simple navy suit—but in a garish jacket and skirt, American style. It was just a trick of the light. She frowned back at her, over her right shoulder, walking away from her, away through a door on the far side of the room.

Blinking, she turned her head again and moved forward. When she went out into the main concourse, she did not see that other woman again.

1

Always her life was in transit between one place and another. As a child she had sailed out of Liverpool and Southampton, wherever her father had wanted her to go. Later she flew out of London to California, Australia, or New York—wherever the magazine wanted her to go.

It was a game she had played all her life: on board ship, later on planes, and now on the motorway. *What if?*

Where the motorway branched like a tree—cars shooting left and right on separate journeys—as she drove parallel to another car she would watch herself draw away from it at the junction; watch herself separate, see herself pulling away. But what if she had sat in that other car? What if that car's driver had sat beside her? Where might they have gone together?

It was a game she had always played, and she played it now, sitting under the pall of exhaust in the middle of the M6, southbound. Above her loomed the great Y of the road sign, sending half the world to the relative heaven of the West Country and half to the relative hell of the M1 and London. In the shimmering tarmacadam heat of a mid-summer afternoon, no cars moved.

'The South-West, 1 mile,' announced the blue road sign. It told her nothing about where she was now. And where in the South-West did the motorway go? To Exeter and Plymouth? Or along the dreaming North Devon coast to Watersmeet, Lynton and Lynmouth? She was not sure. Or did it span the Severn and arch up and away into the clouds like a soaring DC9, to land somewhere in the Azores, or Texas? She was getting fanciful now!

In the window of a passing car she caught a glimpse of herself—saw the small, wry smile that twitched at her lips.

Then she noticed the amused face of the driver behind her. He flashed his lights, and she looked ahead, startled, to see a hundred yards of empty road between her Fiat and the car in front. The travellers had moved on, and she was left behind, at the head of the endless line of cars that tailed back and over the rise behind her.

Horns honked, and the driver behind her flashed his lights again. With a groan of annoyance and embarrassment she let out the clutch and jolted forward.

A few moments later all three lanes of snarled cars and snarling drivers were at a standstill again. Meanwhile, cars cruising north on the other side of the crash barrier slowed to stare at the jam: some smug, others sympathetic.

Behind her, in the middle lane, the same driver was laughing at her, but she wouldn't turn and share the joke. They inched forward, bonnet to bumper, windows rolled down, the smoky sunlight slithering and twisting off the roofs of the cars ahead.

Somewhere around Stafford, the Fiat's old radio had died. She'd thought the overhead power lines were to blame, but even when she had left them far behind there was only the hiss of static. Now, as she switched it on again, there was no sound at all. She looked around hopelessly—if only someone were travelling with her! She thought for the first time in several days of Danny, realizing that she hadn't missed him, even if she wanted company now. No, she was glad he wasn't with her. Once again she caught the eye of the driver behind her in his comfortable grey Sierra.

She sighed. *What a journey*. A thousand drivers on the glaring ribbon of the road, each alone, yet confining one another by their closeness.

Suddenly she reached a decision. Let the rest steam and stew their way to London. *She* would not go that way! Somewhere ahead—half a mile perhaps, or a mile—lay that M5 escape to the South-West. She began to play the *what if* game again. Let her more determined self drive on to London through the M6 maze with gritted teeth and thirsty mouth.

16

Let her do it! But *she* would not! No, even if the journey took her until dark, she would find another way. Any road—even the long motorway route on the M5 and M4—was better than this.

To her left, the slow lane began to move again. Two lorries passed her, then a stream of cars and vans accelerating enough to blow a rush of hot air around her. She craned sideways to see if the end of the jam were visible ahead, but instead saw only the second sign announcing that South-West divide. Meanwhile, the queue in the right lane remained stationary.

The middle lane crept forward once more. She passed a glossy American car. The driver smiled idly at her as she crawled by. He was smoking, at ease behind the wheel, fair hair ruffling backwards. He winked at her. She felt herself colouring and looked away.

The man behind her flashed his lights for the third time. Tutting with mild exasperation, she saw that the left lane had opened up, leaving a gap between her own car and the exit to the M5. The man behind her was signalling left, but waiting for her, giving her the chance to make the break first if she wanted to.

As she pulled out and changed gear, a breeze burst against her face and sent her hair fluttering out of the window. For the first time in an hour, the stink of exhaust fell behind her. *Escape, escape!* She reached the divide in less than a minute, then hesitated again. Farther along the M6, police lights flashed; but beyond them, for all she knew, traffic might be moving freely. She could keep going after all, just as she had planned, direct down the M6 and M1 to her flat in London. Unconsciously, she eased her foot off the accelerator. *Decide,* her brain told her. *Go on, or split here, now, while you've got the chance.*

She chose the M5. A red Fiat like her own was the last she saw separating from her, and out of the corner of her eye she saw a flash of hair as red as her own. A lone driver like herself. Then she drove up the ramp for Worcester and Gloucester.

Almost immediately, the air seemed cooler. She leaned back, extending her arms in the cramped space, and wished she could sleep while someone else drove. Now that concentration was less important, she had lost the will to concentrate at all. *Soon it'll be time to stop.* She checked her watch. *At this rate I'll be in Bristol by late evening and back in London by midnight.*

2

I'd had enough of the motorway. I decided to stop. The fact that the Fiat ahead of me was also pulling into the M5 service station had something to do with it, I admit. After following her for so long, I was curious to see the driver's face. She drove erratically: tired, no doubt, as I was. I guessed that unless she'd been heading west anyway, she'd heard the reports about what lay ahead on the M6. Even Radio 4— usually so pithy about lorries shedding their loads, and about cones and contraflows drawing lines into next year—warned of severe delays. 'Avoid the M6 if you possibly can.' No hint of sarcasm there.

Well, I could avoid it, and I did. I would get a coffee and take it easy—and let the other drivers go. *Life's too short,* I told myself, *to get in a stew over motorway traffic.* And there were other things to think of . . .

The tightness between my shoulder blades and the hollow ache in my stomach reminded me that the first meetings in West Midlands had taken their toll. But I wouldn't think of that now. There was still too much road between me and Bristol, and I wanted to get back.

The needle on the petrol gauge suddenly caught my eye. Almost empty. So I swung into the entrance marked 'fuel'. The red Fiat disappeared into the 'food' lane, and for a while I thought no more about the driver, except that—out of habit, I suppose—I noticed the registration plate. A London number.

When eventually I made my way inside the service complex, both restaurants were packed, the air thick with cigarette smoke and the floor sticky with discarded wrappings. At first, seeing nowhere to sit, I hesitated. A prickle of sweat broke out under the back of my shirt, but I was too hungry now to care about where or what I ate.

I hadn't, however, entirely forgotten my curiosity about that woman, and there she was: sitting at a table with a family that looked Italian. It was the hair that gave her away—waving red hair. Pretty. The same hair I'd seen tossed through her car windows by the breeze.

Her head was down, and she was studying the dessert menu as if it were some sort of scholarly work—utterly oblivious of all around her. The Italians talked fast and looked at her covertly because she wasn't looking at them. I'm sure they were thinking the same as I was: *She's pretty*. I thought of all the auburn-haired girls I'd met at parties and dances. This one was unusual.

One of the Italians felt me staring and looked up, but I kept moving and found a space a couple of tables away. Then the baby set up a howl and the whole family began clucking over it. I watched, and she looked up at last, watching the baby with a funny puckered line in her forehead: not quite a frown. She had stopped eating and was following the conversation around her, eyes jumping from one to the other as if any minute she'd leap up and offer in fluent Italian to hold the baby for a while. But then she went back to her salad and to the dessert menu with that same concentration, like a new constable filling in his first working sheet.

I let my eyes wander away. I hadn't meant to be rude. It was just that hair of hers.

Motorway food never has much appeal: like trying to chew cotton wool—and too much salt to mask the blandness. It looks OK under the glass cases and clever lighting, until it's right in front of you. I chewed away dutifully and then looked up again. She was gone, and I felt as if I had lost a pleasure I had postponed too long. The Italians were talking loudly, and I followed their eyes to the far side of the cafeteria, just in time to see her turn out into the walkway and disappear.

Abandoning what was left of the unsavoury savouries, I got up, gathered my newspaper, and followed her. Looking back now, I'm not exactly sure what my motives were; I certainly had no idea what I would say if I caught up with her. That she was travelling alone, I knew. That she drove a red Panda Fiat with a London 'X' registration, I also knew. That she was beautiful, but not in a conventional way, I needed no police training to notice.

I didn't find her. She found me, standing on the bridge over the M5 motorway, watching the Rovers and Toyotas breaking the speed limit down below.

She came and stood right beside me, hesitating, but looking directly into my face. It seemed an altogether improbable thing for her to be doing, but I wasn't going to miss my chance. I searched my mind for something—any-thing—to say. A rather hesitant 'hello' was all I managed at first, and I wanted to laugh at myself. *This isn't like you, Frank lad! Where's all the charm?*

She smiled. 'Hello.'

'I was the one who was following you just now on the motorway,' I told her. My mouth had gone dry, and my lips felt stiff as I spoke.

'Yes.' She smiled again in acknowledgement. 'I saw you a few times in the mirror. Sorry about the hold-ups.'

'That's OK.' I couldn't help grinning.

'I'm glad you found my driving entertaining.' There was a slight edge to her voice.

I could see this line was getting us nowhere. 'Didn't anyone ever tell you how unwise it is to chat with strangers who know you're alone?'

'Yes, of course. But I'm not.'

I bit back the impulse to ask her what she meant—that she wasn't unwise, or that she wasn't alone? I looked around but could see no one with her. Then I examined her face more closely. Perhaps she wasn't all there. Her grey eyes did look rather distant, but she'd turned away now, seeming as absorbed as I had been in watching the traffic.

'It certainly makes you wonder,' I began determinedly, 'whether people read the papers and listen to the news. Just yesterday there was a pile-up not far from here. It was all cleared by 6.30 this morning, and you'd never know it except for the flowers by the side of the road. But just look at them go, even though there's obviously been a smash-up today on the M6.' I heard my voice going on and on. Why on earth was I talking like that? The speed of the cars was the last thing on my mind once we'd begun to talk.

'Mmm, yes,' she murmured vaguely, 'but I wasn't thinking about the speed. I was thinking—'

'Yes?' I hoped my face would encourage her.

She assessed me for a moment, the way the detective chief superintendent did when he was trying to decide whether I was to be the investigating officer on the current case. Then she said, 'I know this sounds strange—but don't you ever wonder why you're up here and those other drivers are down there?' She paused again.

'Not really,' I answered drily. 'I've never thought about it, to be honest.'

'I mean, surely there's more to me than what's standing here in these shoes, size six-and-a-half?'

Ten out of ten, I thought, for an original opener. *Size six-and-a-half*. I would have to remember that, useless information though it was. I wanted to laugh.

She frowned again. I had never seen anyone else who looked beautiful with a furrowed brow. 'Don't you ever wonder about personality? Where do the edges come? The boundaries?'

She was like a university lecturer warming to her subject. Why had she chosen me for this little lecture in philosophy, or was it psychology? I hadn't a clue what she meant. I muttered something incoherent about 'motorway philosophers', but she ignored me and went on, more to herself than to me.

'And if there's more to me than what's wrapped up in my skin—' she hugged herself '—then who's to say that I'm not driving some other red Fiat down there, as well as standing up here with you—going in some other direction. Another me.'

I blinked, liking the way she'd said 'standing up here with you', but struggling to keep up. 'A sort of alternative existence, you mean? But wouldn't life get a bit complicated?'

All the lights in the dim walkway lit up suddenly. Or perhaps it was her smile. I couldn't help smiling back.

'Yes, it would be complicated. But don't you think it might be interesting?'

'I must be a very pedestrian chap,' I said, shaking my head and laughing. 'Unless of course you're a criminal who'd love to be in two places at once for the sake of good alibis.' I stared at her. *In my line of work,* I thought, *I know plenty of people who'd love to be in two places at once!* 'But it sounds like a nightmare to me.'

We fell into a companionable silence, standing a few feet apart, leaning against the wooden rail and pressing our faces against the glass. Her nose came about four inches below mine, so I now knew her height as well as the size of her feet—about five-foot-nine. More useless information!

Below us, the cars and lorries hurtled past. Even through the thick glazing the sound was mesmerizingly steady. Everything around me was real: the traffic, the dull glass, the scuffed floor, the airless walkway. But my conversation with this disarming, pretty woman was unsettling.

So much so that it suddenly occurred to me she might be psychotic. There was something strange about her. Something slightly fey, though there was nothing unreal in that radiant smile of hers, nothing clouded in those grey eyes now questioning mine.

Feeling uneasy, I tried to restore a note of normality. 'Going far?' I asked

'A long way, I hope.' I might have known I'd get that sort of answer. Her eyes were full of laughter. 'Bristol?' I knew I was pushing my luck.

'No, London.'

Hence the London numberplate, but why the M5? 'You're on the wrong road,' I told her. 'The M5's miles out of your way.'

'Thanks for telling me, but the M6 was blocked, as you know, and I didn't fancy the roads over the Cotswolds.'

I shook my head in disbelief, and we stood smiling at each other. If ever I wrote anything more creative than police reports, I promised myself, it would be a description of this woman's serene face and her light-up-the-world smile. Or a tale of how we met and what she'd said to me—if anyone would believe it. I did not want to forget her, and so stared longer than I should have done.

Her forehead creased again as it had in the restaurant, though she was not looking at me in the way that she had looked at the Italian baby—or in the way that I was probably looking at her. She wanted to say something, but was stuck. I also wanted to say something, though I knew it was bound to come out sounding wrong.

I offered her my right hand. 'You're right. It *would* be interesting if there were two of you. But just this one would suit me fine. My name's Frank Bernard.'

She shook my hand with the same hesitancy I had noticed at first but had seen none of since. I was surprised to see her cheeks suddenly flaming, and for a moment the laughter died out of her eyes. I forgot completely any ideas I had about mental unbalance. Unconventional, yes, but not psychotic.

'In fact,' I stumbled on, 'you were quite safe talking to me.' *Safe? Was she really? What are your intentions, Frank Bernard?* I pulled out my warrant card and showed it to her. 'Avon and Somerset Constabulary. Detective Inspector Frank Bernard,' I recited.

'Ah,' she said, 'Now I understand why you were talking about criminals and alibis.'

'Glad you do,' I parried. 'Though I'm not sure I have much clue what you were talking about just now.'

'Very honest of you,' she said. The laughter returned to her eyes. 'Perhaps I didn't know myself. But in any case, I'm not alone. So you don't need to worry about me.'

I saw her hesitate, as if she'd thought of saying more but then decided against. I waited, then finally said, 'I'll take your word for it. Meanwhile, if ever you're in Bristol, look me up. We could talk philosophy over a cup of coffee.'

I saw her throw a quick glance at my ringless left hand and decided it was a bit late for me to do the same. Had I been too casual in that invitation, or too quick? For a few seconds I was in suspense. 'I'd like that, thanks, Mr Bernard.'

I winced at the 'mister' but did not correct her. How could she call me 'Mr Bernard' after a conversation like that? Worse, she was not even going to give me her own name, I realized. It was time to go, though I would gladly have stayed.

3

Clare chose after all to stay on the M6. A red Fiat like her own was the last she saw separating from her as she deliberately followed the line of cars into the traffic jam beyond the parting of the motorways. Out of the corner of her eye she saw a flash of hair as red as her own. A lone driver like herself, but branching off onto the other motorway. *Her choice,* she thought. *But I'm going this way.*

She would resign herself and let the M6 traffic and the long journey take their course. There was no point in getting angry or feeling sorry for herself.

Later she thought she remembered deciding to turn off onto the M5 and take the long way back through Bristol; but she was well and truly stuck now. If she had gone the other way, she consoled herself, the journey would probably have taken far more time. In the end, the jam was bound to clear.

Blue police lights flashed pitilessly. Even from a quarter of a mile away, they hurt her eyes. She was glad that it was not yet dark, or the contrast would have been unbearable. She did not want to watch them, but their searing intensity drew her eyes anyway, and she had to force herself to look away.

Only a few cars passed in the opposite direction, accelerating, glad to have escaped the mêlée. Police in luminous green jackets were directing drivers to move on smartly, and over the roofs of cars lined up seemingly all the way to London she could see rescue vehicles being manoeuvred into place. Heavy lifting gear glinted in the fierce sun, and she wondered whether anyone were hurt. Automatically, she reached to switch on the radio. If only she could find out what was going on, how long she would be held up. But then she remembered: no radio.

She sighed. Around her most of the other drivers had

switched off their engines. One woman steered high onto the grass verge, stepped out and locked her car. Suitcase in hand, she walked past Clare and back towards the last exit. Clare smiled. What next?

The driver of an ice-cream van started his musical chimes. Cars honked in answer, and laughter broke out from open car windows all around. Doors slammed, and Clare heard children's voices. The ice-cream man was shouting and waving his arms. 'It's all going to melt unless I keep the engine on all day. We'll be here for hours. Come and eat it before you're parked in an ice-cream lake.'

She wasn't going to wait for a second invitation. Throwing a passing look at the woman still plodding along the hard shoulder with her suitcase, Clare joined the queue of women and children that had formed by the van. Around them, others got out and stood on the soft tarmac to stretch and commiserate. 'Anyone got a newspaper?' someone called. 'How about a game of bridge?' someone else rejoined, and Clare laughed. She thought of Danny. He would have found everything so funny, and he might have made the long wait pass more cheerfully. But then she realized that he would have talked all the time and got on her nerves before they'd gone a hundred miles; he wasn't always the good company he thought he was.

An hour later, no one was laughing. The ice-cream man had withdrawn into the relative coolness of his van. Men grumbled, and more and more drivers abandoned their cars, either to follow the first trekker towards the exit, or to walk ahead and complain to the police.

Growing thirst made Clare's tongue feel swollen in her mouth, and she knew she'd need to get to a toilet before long.

Now she thought of her mother. Always so practical. What would Mum do now? A few gorse bushes on the parched verge hardly afforded the dignified cover her mother would be on the look-out for, but her mother would also have made light of the whole situation. She would harumph about how hard it had been in London in the blitz: what did Clare know about discomfort? Nothing whatsoever!

She stood with the car door open and her face tilted up to the sunlight, one foot on the motorway and the other just inside the car. For a while, she forgot where she was and thought instead of her mother.

Guilt was the first emotion that assailed her. She knew she did not go to see her mother often enough. Barking wasn't the easiest place for anyone who worked in Blackfriars and lived in Ealing, but she knew how much she was missed. It wasn't just the geographical distance, though. There was a much wider gulf between them. A distance of language, of likes and dislikes—of lifestyle. A distance of age, too: her mother had been almost forty when she was born. But she couldn't explain those distances to her mother. Even though they shared one important thing—a certainty that they were loved—they had little else in common now.

Mum had always encouraged her into 'something better', something as far away from her cramped East London childhood as possible. 'You can do better than this, Clare, love. Blimey, look at them marks you get at school! You'll do something to make us all proud. Pity your dad won't ever see it, but never mind, eh? I'll see it—I'll see what you get up to.' And when she had come back with news of her first job: 'Magazines! Fancy that, Clare. Who'd have thought any kid of mine would be *writing*? Oh, that's something, that is! Clare 'Ogarth. What'll the neighbours think? They'll say we've gone all toffee-nosed, I shouldn't wonder. But there you are—never know, with God, do you, where you'll land up.'

Her mother's voice echoed in her head, sometimes rolling out like cream and bathing her in warmth, at other times rising into a shriek. Then she would end up cackling like the old crones Clare sometimes saw in the Portobello Road market on a Saturday. She gritted her teeth, just remembering the sound.

'But even if you do talk proper now,' her mother would say, 'I know you're just the same little kiddie, inside, what turned the skipping-rope like all the others up this street and sang those silly songs when your dad got home. Till you drove us all mad and 'e came out and gave you a clip round the ear. Poor old chap, 'e needed 'is sleep when 'e got 'ome, 'e did. D'you remember?' And she would go off into another cackle.

Of course she remembered. It was a past that half of her wanted to run from, felt ashamed about. No one in the office would understand the tangle of contradictory feelings that knotted her inside whenever anyone innocently asked about where she'd grown up. Guilt, embarrassment, amusement, and bewilderment. No doubt people assumed she was from Kingston or Windsor. Or if she mentioned her father's work, they might have thought she was from the right side of Southampton or the better side of Liverpool. The voice of East London had left her at university, and she wouldn't revert to it now. She had fought too long and hard to fit in with everyone else at Cambridge. And social battles were as hard as any tussles she and the other children had fought on the streets and playgrounds of Barking.

What if I stay at Mum's tonight? She knew she should go and see her mother. It wasn't as if she had any excuse now, not even the traffic jam. It would be simple enough to get to Blackfriars from Barking in the morning, certainly no more difficult than making her way past Heathrow and back into Ealing tonight. And there would be a limit to how long she would have to stay—there would be no need to explain why she had to go first thing in the morning.

Guilt, embarrassment, and bewilderment. All three had kept her away ... but what about the amusement her mother always afforded?

Her mother always made her laugh—sometimes on purpose, at other times quite unconsciously. If she missed anything about her mother, it was that sense of humour. But even that brought a niggle of guilt. Why was she doomed, now that she'd been away from home so long, always to be the self-conscious outsider, wryly observing her mother's life in Barking as if it were life on another planet? Was that why she so often took refuge in the old game of *What if?*

29

What if she had stayed in Barking and married that grammar school sweetheart of hers, perhaps come back from college to teach in Barking, to have children there much like herself but without the feeling of not belonging? What if her father had not been a first mate in the merchant navy and taken or sent her half way round the world and back again by the time she was sixteen, so that from the very beginning she was destined to be different, the outsider? What if, having got to know her well-to-do American cousins, she hadn't begun to dream of a more permanent way out of her surroundings? ('A way to better yourself,' her mother had called it.)

The Williams relatives had been attracted, she supposed, by her naive English ways. They had plied her with invitations to visit them again, invitations which she eventually took up the summer after she left university, six years ago now. She would go and see them again, some day, she knew. While she was still at school, those respectable exam results at school, those journeys abroad—had all marked her out as different. At Cambridge she had enjoyed knowing that she was different while she appeared to be a clone like everyone else, right down to the cut of the hair, the vintage of the bike, and the fake-faded denims.

But for six years now she had belonged to a world even more foreign to her mother than that of the Backs and punts on the River Cam. It was a world of copy deadlines, shrilling telephones, frantic interviews, rushed overseas trips, movable lunchtimes, and late departures out of the concrete-and-glass tower by the river where her office was housed.

Still standing there in the sun, she forgot her mother's voice for a while and heard the very different, cultured tones of Andy, her boss.

'If you're really going to make it here as senior staff writer,' he had told her the day he promoted her, 'you can't afford to lose sight of what really matters in this place. We have to get the copy to bed and the magazines out in the shops and stalls every week. That's the bottom line, Clare. It's *all* that matters, even if you have to climb over everyone else to achieve it.'

Yes, she remembered thinking at the time, *and 'everyone else' is not just other magazines. Sometimes he means other journalists in-house, as well.* The staff turnover figures and divorce rates among her colleagues told the tale of sacrifices made to the printed word.

She had told her mother what Andy had said, certain that, viewed from her mother's perspective, his outlook was chilling.

'It'll be dead hard to be a warm 'uman bein' there, love,' her mother had said.

'Somehow I'll have to be,' she had answered.

And somehow she still was; on a day-to-day basis the good relationships she had built up with the features editor and other writers made everything worthwhile. Worthwhile, but still impossible to explain to her mother out there in Planet Barking.

Suddenly, her mother and Barking and Andy in Black-friars disappeared as she saw that the cars ahead of her were starting up and filing forwards at last. She checked her watch. *At this rate,* she thought, *I'll be in Barking by ten or so.* Her mother's happy face when she arrived unexpectedly would at least be a little consolation after her long wait on the motorway. It was too long since she'd seen her.

4

Usually Clare would not have said much to someone she did not know. Not that she was shy like Nina, the junior writer who worked most closely with her, but she would rather wait until the other person had spoken to her. In a sense, though, Frank Bernard had been speaking to her for some time before they began to talk on that bridge. After all, he had flashed his lights at her three times, grinned at her more than once, and had waited for her to leave the M6 in front of him if she wanted to. So it wasn't as if he hadn't been 'talking' to her for a long time already. A long time.

She wished now that she'd given him her name. He had gentle eyes and a nice mouth. A slow, crinkly smile partly hidden in a dark beard. But once she had got herself into the conversation, something in her had held back—even though curiosity and the strange abstractedness of travelling away from home had drawn her on to say such unusual things.

She wondered where he was now. In the end, after showing her his identity card, he had gone on his way quite abruptly. Was he, too, puzzled and distracted by their meeting? Probably not, she admitted to herself. No doubt he was by now already hot on the trail of Bristol criminals, solving the West Country's woes. Superman in a Sierra with the sun on his dark hair. No Mr Plod. No Dixon of Dock Green, this one. And she'd certainly never see him again. Well, it would be a good tale to tell Nina on Friday. She laughed to herself as she imagined Nina's interested face. In her confusion she had forgotten to check on fuel, so she stopped again at a service station near Dursley, half-hoping she might see him, make amends, and tell him her name. As she filled up the petrol tank and checked the tyre pressure, realizing with a sigh how far it was still to London, she thought what she would say to him. Then she realized he might easily walk right past her and not recognize her. One face in thousands. It was no use thinking about him.

She drove past fields and farms that would normally be green in June. This summer was turning hot and unEnglish, and she wasn't sure she liked it. To her left the sky was streaked with lines of smoke; and on her right the sun, dipping red and angry into the haze, reflected on every metal and glass surface she passed. In a moment she would turn east and have the glare in her mirrors instead. More lights flashing in her eyes, only this time no Frank Bernard smiling at her from behind them.

As she slowed to leave the M5 for the M4, she noticed that the car was losing too much speed. Frowning, she pressed experimentally on the accelerator. The engine did not respond, and a frantic lift of her head told her that the car behind her was uncomfortably close. Swallowing hard, she tried again, then switched on the hazard lights and edged out towards the shoulder.

Now cruising at about fifteen miles an hour, seemingly without the power to go faster, she checked the fuel gauge and sniffed to see if anything smelled hot. Finally, with complete dignity but absolute decision, the car hesitated, stuttered briefly, and came to a standstill. Other drivers whooshed past, horns blaring.

Now what? She sat still, trying to think against the rumble of traffic, the click of cooling metal, and the beginnings of a headache. It was almost dusk, and she still had over a hundred miles to go before she could sleep. Typically, she had run out of money just when the AA membership reminder came, so there wasn't even that resort. She gave voice to a heartfelt prayer. 'Lord,' she said aloud, 'please help me think straight.' She remembered now how she had told Frank Bernard she wasn't alone. She should think of that again, and stay calm.

Her mother would have known what to do. *Why not start by putting up the bonnet?* she heard common sense telling her.

She pulled the catch under the dashboard and, watching

the buses and cars roaring past, got out carefully. She didn't expect to recognize the problem among the wires, pipes, and coils of metal and plastic—nor did she. There was, however, a curl of something very like steam coming from the radiator.

Tyres, petrol, and—oh, no, water! she groaned to herself. How could she have forgotten, in this heat? But would that account for the loss of power in the engine? Surely not?

She did not want to risk a scalding, knew enough to wait for help, even though there had been too many ugly stories in past months of predators on the motorway. Wistfully, and quite absurdly, she thought again of Frank. But he would be home now, duty done (whatever it was), and wouldn't welcome a call-out.

What was it he had said? 'If ever you're in Bristol, look me up.' Well, here was her excuse.

No, it would sound fabricated, feeble—and female in the worst way.

Leaving the bonnet up and the hazard lights on, she decided to risk a walk to the nearest call box. She had driven past a box only a few hundred yards from the M4 entrance, and she set off resolutely, ignoring catcalls from open cars and wishing hopelessly for the sight of a police car. An unmarked Sierra would be ideal, but any police car would do.

She telephoned from the orange box, but the surly man in the operations room told her that, since she was no longer an AA member, she might have to wait over an hour, or even two, for a garage driver to come out to her. She was to stay by the car, preferably inside it, and wait. Tiredness took over. The thought of sitting at her desk in Blackfriars by 9.30 a.m. the next day made her feel weak. What if she had gone home by the M6 after all? Having waited out the jam, she might even be back by now, soaking in the bath. Grit stung her eyes, and the hot wind blasted at her by passing traffic made her feel dirty. She slid into the car again, shutting her own door but leaving the passenger door open for air—it would be less conspicuous—and once again resigned herself to waiting. A yellow motorway maintenance van slowed briefly but passed her; after that the traffic ignored her. One by one the lights of Bristol punctured the softening sky but made little impression on the shadows stretching endlessly across Clare's view.

Twilight. At this edge of day, anything seemed possible. Arching over the motorway and the city, the sky poised like a girl about to dive into the lake of night. Under it, veiled in cobalt and as resigned as Clare herself, the more prosaic landscape lay waiting for dark.

During that long summer in Boston—1983—Clare had debated with her American cousins (Jack especially) the meaning of the words 'Celtic twilight'. Now, watching sky and earth tilt towards each other, she felt she half understood. Twilight was every time and no time. It was time and space between times and worlds. It lasted only minutes, but it promised eternity. It was at once azure and emerald, luminous rose and amethyst. It was full of mystery and, in spite of the roar of the traffic, it spoke silence to her.

With her heart half-way between earth and heaven, she belonged to neither. Here there were no promises to keep, no decisions to make: she had only to wait.

The wait was shorter than she'd expected. She gasped, seeing a grey Sierra brake and pull up behind her, thinking for a foolish moment that Frank Bernard had somehow found her.

A man and a woman opened the doors of the Sierra and came to stand on either side of the Fiat. The man bent down to her window, his glasses gleaming in the light of passing cars. Fleetingly she thought of rapists and muggers.

'Problems with the car, then?' he shouted.

She opened the window fully; he looked safe enough. 'Yes, not sure what.'

The man reached into his pocket in a gesture that reminded Clare of something or someone. 'Detective Inspector Nigel Sands—Avon and Somerset police,' he said, and showed her the second warrant card she'd seen in one day. In the darkness she didn't see his name, but it was immaterial this time.

She couldn't help grinning. 'Oh, I'm so glad to see you!'

'Just going in to work. This is my colleague, Jill Peterson—' And he indicated the woman. 'We'll see if we can get you started again. Did you ring for help, or what?'

She told him all that had happened. The inspector went for water and a torch, then gingerly unscrewed the radiator cap with his handkerchief. Clare watched him, fairly certain that he had no more idea than she did what was wrong with the car.

'A bit low on the old water, but there's something else, I reckon.'

'I was afraid so.' She got out and stood beside them, shivering. Now that the sun was gone, a wind had come up and pricked her skin with goose pimples.

'You may have some dirt in the carburettor. You sure you have enough petrol?'

'I've just filled it up.'

'Four star?'

'Yes, so there shouldn't have been any water in it, or anything.'

He looked at her sharply, eyebrows raised in surprise, then said, 'Or the cam belt might have died—that would cut the engine all right . . . Try starting her up again and see.'

The engine wouldn't even turn over, and he slammed the bonnet.

'Doesn't sound good. I'll radio the station that we'll be late, and we'll wait with you until the garage gets here.'

'Are you sure?' Now that the worst of her vigil was over, she felt childishly relieved.

'Of course. You sit in there and keep warm. Haven't you got a jacket? Miss Peterson will stay with you.'

The policewoman apparently felt more inclined to chat than Clare. 'Where are you going?' she began.

'London.'

'Ah, still a long journey.'

'Yes,' Clare said gloomily. 'It's more like "was" going, by the look of it.'

'I'm afraid so.' The policewoman paused. 'Do you come this way often?'

36

Clare wanted to laugh. 'Never. I decided to avoid a jam on the M6—I'm sure you heard about the accident and the queues of traffic up there—but I didn't really want to drive cross-country.' She knew that in spite of the jam it sounded ridiculous to drive from the north to London via Bristol. *That's what I'm doing, anyway,* she thought defensively.

The woman was unruffled. 'Not a good idea to go over the Cotswolds on your own, in any case.'

If Clare were to say this time—as she had to Frank Bernard—that she wasn't alone, she really might be locked up; so she decided to let the policewoman talk on if she wanted to. While it had seemed natural to her to refer indirectly to God when she'd been talking with Frank, she felt much less at ease with this policewoman. Once again she reached for the radio, and once again remembered: no radio.

'Looks as if you might not get to London tonight, Miss, er—'

'Hogarth. But I have to.'

'Work?'

'Yes, like yourself.'

'You could find a place to stay and ring in the morning.'

She shook her head. 'It wouldn't make me any friends, I can tell you. They're expecting a story from me.' She knew what was coming next, and it did.

'What sort of a job is it, then?'

'I'm a journalist with a magazine.'

A spark of interest kindled in the other woman's eyes. 'Oh—which?'

'No,' Clare laughed (it was an old joke), 'not *Which*—it's *Women Today*. But it's not as glamorous as it sounds, I'm afraid. I should have been back at home hours ago, with the copy typed up ready for tomorrow.'

The policewoman either missed or ignored the joke and clucked sympathetically. 'I've been in that sort of situation myself. I know how you feel. Well, never mind, you must have contacts in Bristol you can stay with—if you've come all this distance out of your way.'

37

It was a question rather than a statement, and Clare knew she should try to answer civilly, but by now she could hardly bear to talk at all. She wished the recovery vehicle would arrive. How long it seemed since that conversation on the bridge over the M5.

She licked her lips. 'No, I don't have anyone here. At least—I didn't. There's—' She stopped, too weary to want to explain.

'We could ring someone for you if you're here much longer.'

Yes, of course it would be easy for them to ring Frank Bernard for her. She would probably not even need to give them his telephone number. She smiled to herself and felt warmer.

5

I parked the car at the back of the station and sat there, thinking. All the way down the motorway I'd been looking for that red Fiat, though I knew I must have left it behind long before. I kept seeing her smile and the little frown over her eyes, and more than once I'd rewritten our conversation in my head. *Why didn't I ask her name? Why?*

Even if I couldn't make sense of all that stuff about personality boundaries, I did know one thing quite clearly: wherever that woman was, she hadn't taken all her personality with her. Something of her was left with me, and something of me went with her—wherever I went. It was like looking too long at a blue light: blue after-images flashing across your brain, fields of bluebells leapfrogging across the motorway. Her smile was the same, still incandescent behind my eyes. It lit up the dark car-park.

I'm going crazy, I thought, and her face was suddenly blotted out by the sobering RAC slogan: 'You're driving HOW far?' All right, so I had probably tried to cover far too much ground in the past few days. I wasn't used to all the driving. But distance wouldn't make me hallucinate, would it?

Suddenly I knew what I had to do.

In the glove box I found the notebook where I'd written her registration number, and tore off the top page. Now I'd know where to find her and probably her name as well—unless she'd borrowed or stolen the car.

I got out and walked to the side entrance. I put the numbers into the lock until the door clunked and I could go through. It was strange coming in at this time of the day. I'd often stayed late, but rarely arrived late. I checked my watch as I went up the stairs. *Just after ten.* The typists' rooms were empty, though I could hear one person talking into the phone through a half-open door—the only light falling into the corridor before I passed into CID. 'Nice to see you,' Sally called. 'Why aren't you out solving crimes, Frank?'

In CID the phone was ringing as usual, and John was shouting into another phone, to an old woman who often telephoned at this time of the evening to report a break-in. As regular as clockwork just after ten—the call coinciding with the end of *Crimewatch*. Her calls were generally dealt with in the front office, but that night someone new must have been been on shift and put the call through to John. Mrs Brownlow was the station mascot for my colleagues on late shift and for new PCs. As far as we knew, her house had never actually been burgled. The front office had taken to sending the newest PC on attachment to her every evening at the same time. Heaven help the old dear if ever there was a real break-in.

'Yes, Mrs Brownlow. Yes, I understand. Number twenty-two. Yes, we'll have PC McGavran round to you right away. Yes, goodnight for now, Mrs Brownlow.' John rang off and raised his eyes first to an exotic picture of rock star Angel Avalon, who adorned the wall, then to the ceiling. 'Hello, Frank. Gorgeous, isn't she?' He leered at the poster.

'Who, Mrs Brownlow?' I asked, straightfaced.

John looked at me properly, his face registering surprise. 'Didn't expect to see you till tomorrow. We've saved some real doozies for you. Useful trip?'

'Yes, useful,' I told him. Then I pushed the door to my office wider. Someone had drawn a garish poster on A3 paper proclaiming in day-glo colours that Frank Bernard was on his honeymoon in Birmingham until Friday at the earliest and was not to be disturbed. 'Fat chance. Honeymoon, indeed!' I ripped it down, balled it, and threw it at John. 'Look, I'll tell you all about it tomorrow if I get the chance. But there's something I want to see on screen.'

'Right. I'll leave you to it. Cup of tea, if I can find the kettle? Or something stronger? It's quiet in here for a change.'

I laughed at him. 'That your guilty conscience apologizing for the poster? Tea—thanks, yes. I'll be back in a few minutes. Cheers.'

Going downstairs to the control room, I noticed Nigel Sands was late tonight. Now what was he up to? I also felt a stab of unease. I shouldn't be looking up information on the PNC for my own private use. Shouldn't, but how else would I ever find her?

In any case, I told myself righteously, knowing you can justify almost anything if you think about it long enough, if she *was* psychotic, someone ought to know about her and protect her.

But I didn't for a minute think she was.

The front office was frantic, every phone in use or ringing. Trays of papers overflowing onto the desks, and a smell of sweat, cigarettes and stale coffee. I punched in the access code and the Fiat's 'X' registration number and waited. There it was. *Fiat Panda, Red, 3-door. Clare Hogarth, 192 Raleigh Road, Barking, Essex IG11 ... Keeper since 22-9-83.*

Barking. I stared, double-checking against the slip of paper at my elbow that I'd called up the right registration number. *Barking*. I wasn't sure I believed the address.

I went back upstairs for the Barking area phone-book. I had the right directory in my hand when Sally waylaid me with a cup of strong tea.

'Sit down and take it like a man,' she ordered. 'You look shattered, Frank.'

'Thanks, I am.' She looked at me curiously as I slumped into her chair. 'I thought you weren't in until tomorrow,' she said.

'I shouldn't be.' The tea was scalding, and I heard myself wince. 'Just checking something.'

Sally's phone rang, and she took it. 'Yes. Yes, I see. He's waiting with Jill at a breakdown? Right, when shall I tell Bill they'll both be in? He wants to get off home before midnight ... OK.' She was putting down the receiver when a shout at the other end of the line stopped her.

'Hold on a minute, Sal,' I said.

'What?' She put the receiver back to her ear. 'For Frank? Yes, he's here. No, I know he wasn't, but he came in anyway. He wants him . . . what?' Her eyebrows went up, and she pulled a face in my direction.

I reached to take the telephone, but she turned away. 'Uhuh. Oh, very funny. I'll tell him. What's that supposed to mean? Jill Peterson's been missing Frank, has she?' Sally laughed, and I was too tired to appreciate the teasing sound of her laugh.

'What's going on, Sally?'

She dropped the phone back into the cradle and faced me again. 'Coded radio message from the front office for our man Bernard.'

'Don't be daft, woman,' I said, laughing all the same.

'No, seriously. It's from "the M5 philosopher". Nigel Sands and Jill Peterson are with her now. They've just radioed in. Even philosophers' cars break down, apparently.'

Light was dawning slowly in my brain, but I wasn't going to let Sally see it. Anyway she seemed too preoccupied with the fascinating fact that WDC Peterson was quite openly coming in to work tonight with Nigel Sands to be interested in any insane reasons I might have for wanting to hear the message.

'Fine, I'm with you now. So what's the news?' I asked, pausing long enough to conceal my interest.

'Just greetings.'

I hesitated, not wanting too many enquiries. Sally didn't miss many tricks. On my lap the Barking phone directory felt hotter than the mug of tea. I tried to sound nonchalant. 'OK, thanks. I'll talk to Nigel and Jill when they get in.'

Sally leaned over and looked closely into my face. 'No, Frank, you need to go home.' She whisked the phone-book off my lap and marched away, calling infuriatingly over her shoulder, 'You're turning into a workaholic. You're mad! Go on, out!'

I drove off, feeling frustrated. Tim and Richard, who

shared the house with me, had gone to bed by the time I hefted my luggage into the front hall. All the lights were out, and I felt bleak.

In the kitchen I poured myself the one remaining can of lager (one out of a case I had bought to last the week) and sat leaning on the kitchen worktop. My father came to mind then, as he often did when I wanted someone to talk to. *It'll be no use pumping Nigel and Jill,* I thought. *That'll start the gossip all right!* It was too late to ring Dad over in Weston, so instead I held one of my internal debates with him.

'She's not the kind of woman I usually sit up and take note of, Dad,' I heard myself saying.

'Oh,' he'd grunt, his mouth twisting in faint mockery, 'and what kind of girls *do* you sit up and take note of? Enlighten me.'

I laughed. 'Don't you remember the last one you met? Full of fun—dark-haired, with mischievous dark eyes.'

'Hmm. I don't remember her looks, Frank. But I do remember she messed you about. A bit more than you bargained for, wasn't she?'

'Beautiful, but fiercely independent.' I did not add that she had proved greedy, thoughtless, and unkind; had made me feel as boring as Policeman Plod.

Dad coughed sarcastically and twinkled at me. 'Independent? Huh! What you need, Frank—'

'Here we go again.'

'What you need is a *real* woman to love. A wife, not a girlfriend.'

'Like "Old MacDonald", eh? "The farmer wants a wife. The farmer wants a wife!" Right!'

'And why not? You're coming up to thirty, aren't you?'

'Yes, and getting a bit old for teeny-boppers in discos.'

'Heaven help us—I should think so,' he groaned. Then he winked. 'Mind you, even at thirty, a bit young for a specimen like that Angel Avalon woman your sisters can't abide.'

'I think I rather fancy her,' I said, just to wind him up.

'D'you want my advice, or don't you? All the best women

43

seem to have been snapped up, is that it? Well, you're obviously wife-hunting in the wrong places. Parties and discos? Come on, Frank! Time you came to a parish evening and met some *real* women.'

That's exactly what he would have said. I knew that, as I sat sipping the cold lager—because he'd said it so many times before. The trouble was, I couldn't decide what I *did* want. I didn't think, somehow, that I'd find it in my parents' parish church, even though the people there had been kinder than I thought anyone could be when my young brother Damian had died of leukemia.

'Ah well,' I said aloud to no one in particular, 'I don't suppose I'll find the woman I love by sitting here moping.'

I took myself off to bed, then, to dream about a woman in a red Fiat on the M5: a woman with waving auburn hair and a smile I might not see again but would remember for a long time.

6

'Clare. Clare!'

A woman was calling her name harshly, over and over again from the other side of a door. She rolled over, confused, not remembering where she was. Her eyes were sticky with sleep and her head groggy.

'*Clare!*'

Then the house began to shake. A train was rolling past. She remembered everything. 'Oh—yes, Mum.'

'When was it you wanted to get up for work?'

She groaned, faint anxiety bubbling up. 'Half-six. Listen, come in, can't you?'

Her mother's slippers shuffled outside the door, then her head appeared, grey hair twisted into curlers and her face innocent of make-up except for the shine of nightcream. Clare felt uncomfortable seeing her that way. Why couldn't her mother care how she looked, even first thing in the morning? Was it a hangover from World War Two? Sometimes the age difference between them was even more perplexing than the divisions thrown up by the gulf between Cambridge and Barking.

She tossed back the bedclothes and turned away to pull open the curtains. Staring through the film of grime on the window into the next-door garden, she stretched hugely and pushed her fingers into her hair. The room where she had slept—where she had in fact slept as she grew up—felt close and stale.

Her mother seemed to guess her thoughts. 'Yeah, Clare, I know. If I'd known you was coming I'd've cleaned up a bit. Sorry, love. 'Ere, let's get this open.' She came and flipped the catch on the sash and hauled at the window, but it jammed only part-way up and slid down again. 'Sorry, dear,' her mother kept saying. 'Sorry.'

'Mum, that's OK. I shouldn't have landed on you last night.'

'No, it's very nice, Clare.' Her mother hovered, looking anxious. 'Anyway, I made you a nice cup of tea, love. I 'spect you want to get on to work now.'

It suddenly struck Clare, even through the dirty windows, that the light was too bright for early morning. 'You did say it was 6.30, didn't you?'

Her mother grimaced. 'No, sorry. You said you wanted to get up then. But I overslept, myself. Sorry, Clare.'

Unreasonable anger flooded her. The repeated 'sorry, sorry' grated on her nerves. 'Well then,' she snapped, 'what *is* the time?'

Backing towards the narrow doorway, her mother looked more and more unhappy. 'I think it's a bit after nine.' Then, as Clare sucked in her breath in exasperation and dismay, she rallied. 'But don't you go blaming me, now. You were that late last night. Done in proper when you got in. *And* I bet you sat up 'alf the night doing that flippin' writing you said you 'ad to.'

Clare fell onto the side of the bed. 'Done in, yes, but I had to finish the story last night. Now it's too late anyway. The deadline was nine today, Mum. I've missed it.'

Her mother opened her mouth to answer, her face at once pleading patience and showing irritation. 'Nine today? That don't make no sense to me.'

Clare groaned. She knew she sounded faintly hysterical, but she persisted anyway, unable to overcome the twist of bitterness in her voice. 'No, it wouldn't. Oh, this is typical! Nine o'clock—'

'Well, it might be nearer 'alf nine by now.'

'Worse and worse.' She thumped her hand on the mattress, but even her anger was futile. At last she looked up and heard herself say coldly, 'That's it, then. No point in going in today. I'll see if I can sort it all out on Monday. Might as well go back to the flat, I suppose.' She looked up to see what effect these jibes were having, and found that she'd hit the mark.

Then she felt mean for spoiling her mother's simple delight in having her home overnight.

Somewhere another train clattered along the line, and the house shook again. A few sparrows chirped tunelessly from the slate tiles next door, and she came to a sudden decision.

'No, Mum, maybe I won't.' She stood up and went to give her a hug. It was like hugging a tired old armchair; her mother's shapeless body bulged and sagged but felt warm and familiar. 'I'm sorry. I'm sure it can wait till Monday if it has to. My hours have been so long this week anyway. So let's take advantage of this sunshine and do something special. D'you want to?' She took a quick breath. 'I'll take the day off.'

Her mother gave an unconvincing scowl and looked at her sideways. 'Clare 'Ogarth, you tryin' to get round me for something?' But her eyebrows lifted hopefully.

Clare grinned. 'If I am, I haven't decided what it is yet.'

The smile she got in return was forgiving. 'All right, then.'

'All right what?'

'Let's go off for the day. Nice treat.' *Nice, nice,* Clare thought irritably; everything was 'nice'. 'You're not too busy, Mum?'

Her mother cackled—the laugh that had always embarrassed Clare as a child. She winced, remembering how she had tried to pretend to her schoolfriends (out of discomfort) that her mother was her grandmother. 'I shouldn't think so! The telly's on the blink. The window-boxes—well, I done them last week. The grass ain't so long in all this 'eat. Friday's not my day to 'elp them old ladies with their meals on wheels, so I ain't too busy, Clare.' She beamed, her dentures artificially bright in her sleepy face.

Clare ran a bath and lay soaking in it. She knew she ought to phone Nina and tell her where she was, but somehow the office seemed remote and irrelevant. Downstairs the phone rang as she was drying herself. *They've caught me skiving,* she thought, but felt no real anxiety. No one in the office knew her mother's number anyway. She would call Nina later, or ask her mother to do so, before they went out.

'Clare?' her mother was shuffling up the stairs again. Her voice sounded surprised. 'Clare, there's a bloke wants to talk to you.'

She wrapped herself in a towel. 'I'm coming, Mum.' *It must be Danny,* she thought, though she couldn't remember having given him the Barking number, either.

''Urry up, then.'

The phone lay on the front-room table where it had always been: right by the front door. There had never been any privacy, and even now her mother planted herself in the nearest chair, tea in hand, pretending to take out her rollers but with an expression of undisguised inquisitiveness. Clare hesitated and covered the mouthpiece. 'Who is it?'

Her mother sniffed. 'Prince Charles, I shouldn't wonder. Talks like a toff, anyway.'

Clare was determined not to rise to the bait. 'Well, I'll soon find out . . . hello, yes, this is Clare Hogarth.' She assumed her office voice.

The voice at the other end of the line sounded warm but unfamiliar to her.

'Hi, this is Frank Bernard. Remember?' He didn't wait for her to answer but rushed straight on. He sounded tense. 'I gather you got held up again yesterday. Sorry to hear that.'

Clare could feel her face creasing into a frown. *Who's Frank Bernard?* Someone she was supposed to know? 'Er, yes, the M6 was bad news altogether.'

'And your car?'

'What?'

'I said, what about your car?' She could hear laughter in his voice. 'You know, the red Fiat on four wheels—at least it was when I last saw it. You've had it repaired, have you?'

Repaired? Clare pushed wet hair out of her eyes. What was he talking about? She did not recognize the voice at all, and his words seemed increasingly bizarre. She felt as if some of the gears in her brain had slipped. She must be more tired than she thought, so she decided she would play along until she woke up sufficiently to remember who Frank Bernard was. 'The car's fine,' she said non-committally, then added as an afterthought, 'Fine—thanks.'

'Good—good.' He spoke almost too fast. Whoever he was, something was definitely bothering him. 'Look,' he continued, 'I wished I'd got your name yesterday. But it was two of my colleagues you met last night—Jill Peterson and Nigel Sands. And I found out where you were.'

She stood shaking her head, watching her mother's face change from mild interest to rabid curiosity. She drew her mouth down at the corners and raised her eyes, gesturing with her free hand by way of explanation to her mother that the man was mad. 'Well, it's unusual to catch me here. I'm generally at the office.'

There was a pause. 'But I thought—'

She decided to join him in this absurd game, whatever it was. 'Yes, you know. I must have told you, surely?' She winked at her mother. '*Women Today*. You remember?'

A longer pause. 'You didn't tell me. No. But I was wondering—'

'Mr Bernard.' Clare collected her wits. 'Forgive me, but my mother and I are just going out—' She looked down at her legs, bare under the towel, and at the damp trail of footmarks she had left on the rug. 'What was it? Is there some way I can help you?' She knew she sounded condescending.

'Miss Hogarth—Clare.' He paused yet again, and she began to feel sorry for the man. But at last he seemed to make up his mind. He spoke in a quick, staccato way. 'I'll give you my number. Have you got a pencil? Ever since we talked yesterday I've been wondering how I can see you again.'

It was time to cut the call, and she did not pick up the pencil and notepad her mother kept by the phone. She said coldly, 'I don't know you. I haven't the faintest idea what you're talking about. I had no conversation with anyone yesterday. I couldn't have—I was stuck on the M6 almost all day. How you know that I don't quite know. But please get off this line. It's a private number, my mother's, and I don't want her bothered.' She drew breath before he could answer. 'Please go away, or I'll call the police and complain.' She thought she heard him wince, but she replaced the receiver without waiting for an answer. Then she looked at her mother.

'He's out of his mind! Do I know a Frank Bernard, Mum? Someone I had a long chat with yesterday, or a Jill Peterson? There was another name, as well, but I can't remember it.'

Her mother huffed, ' 'Spect you know lots of people I don't 'ear about. Fruit and nut case, was 'e?'

'London people've gone as crazy as Boston people—like the madman who used to phone Aunt Rita and pester her. Unless he was just confusing me with some other woman called Hogarth—' She stopped, recalling more of his words. 'It's a bit creepy, though. He knew I've got that Fiat. Knew the colour of it. Seemed to know I was stuck in a traffic jam yesterday, as well.' She shivered.

'Never mind, dear. Your tea'll get cold. Cold already, I bet.' And her mother looked up with shrewd, bright eyes that were full of questions.

7

'Oh!' Nina Cottham's mouth formed an O of surprise as Clare came into the staff writers' office.

Clare dumped her papers on the desk. 'What's up?'

'Nothing. We just didn't expect you. Everyone heard about the tailbacks on the motorway yesterday. We all thought you'd be sleeping it off.'

Clare laughed, throwing a quick glance around the room at her other colleagues. Heads were bent, and the room was quiet except for the shuffle of papers and the occasional phone-call. 'I wished I could. I certainly thought about not coming in.' She looked at her watch and grimaced—10.45. 'But I had a deadline, and I'm late for that as it is.'

Nina's expression had gone from mild surprise to amazement. 'Wait a minute, Clare. Someone just telephoned about you.'

Clare wondered vaguely if Nina herself had been up late as well. She opened a drawer and sat down with her back to Nina. 'Oh, was there a message for me?'

'No, *about* you, I said.' Nina's voice was louder and sharper than usual. Clare swung round in her chair. 'What, then?'

'It's why we thought you weren't coming in. Only about ten minutes ago it was. A woman called, reception said, and left word that you were taking the day off.' She stopped, twisting the ring she always wore on her little finger round and round, her face puzzled. 'I thought it seemed a bit strange, especially as Sue told me the caller sounded Cockney. But when you came in—well, after the first little surprise it seemed like any other day. I'd forgotten the message already.'

Clare frowned. After the late return to her flat in Ealing,

the cups of coffee made and poured to keep her going as she wrote up her story, and two or three fitful hours in bed before taking a later-than-usual tube to work—her mind was still clouded. 'We–ell,' she said slowly, 'it must have been some-one playing a joke. Here I am, as you can plainly see.'

Nina shrugged, and her face cleared. 'Yes. I'm glad. I was starting to make a list of people who want to see you next week anyway.'

Clare shook her head. 'I'm pretty dead. I won't try to get ahead today, simply because Andy and Dave didn't expect me. I think I'll just turn this thing in and go back to the flat. There's no way it could have been on time. Glad the boss knew that, and I don't suppose we'll miss the presses just because of me.'

Turning over magazine clippings, Nina murmured in agreement. 'No. Some of the other stories are late as well. OK, so will you tell me all your news next week?'

Clare swung round again. 'Yes, I will. But I'll tell you some of it now, if you want to hear a Friday morning yarn—after I get back from Dave's office.'

The telephone on Nina's desk cut off her answer, and when Clare came back from the feature editor's office, two cups of fresh coffee stood waiting. Nina abandoned the story she was working on and smiled. 'This had better be good, Miss Hogarth. You can see how overworked we are when the senior writer is away for a while, then skives off the first day she's back. Go on, I'm all ears.'

Clare sipped the coffee and looked affectionately at Nina. If either of them were ever moved to another department, they would miss each other, she knew. She had long ago learned to appreciate Nina's gentle art of listening. At first the four-year gap between them had seemed much more—Nina had been so shy when she first arrived—but now it was closing. Nina wasn't just a junior writer; she had become her closest friend among all the journalists cramped and crowded into their hot office.

Clare took a deep breath. She knew that Nina would read

the brightness in her face. 'I met someone very interesting,' she began.

'Ah, this sounds promising.' Nina leaned back with folded arms.

'A policeman of some kind. His name's Frank.'

Nina's mouth began to twitch. 'Where on earth did you manage this momentous meeting, if you were tied up all the time doing that story? A policeman, Clare?'

'Yup—not a Martian, Nina. Why? Does it begin to sound as improbable as half the stories in the magazine?' She waited, but Nina didn't answer, so she went on. 'It will sound far worse before I'm through. He was following me on the motorway for so long that I felt I almost knew him. He was making faces at me just before I got out of the jam—it was on the M6, did you hear?—on to the M5. Then, when I saw him a few miles later at a service station where I stopped— where he stopped—we found ourselves talking to each other as if we'd already been in the middle of a conversation from some other time. A talk that had been interrupted.'

'Clare! You're making up every word of this.' Nina's face glowed with amusement and disbelief. 'But go on, we might have to print it.'

She laughed. 'Nina, the funny thing is that—somehow—I just couldn't walk past him as if I'd never met him.' She thought for a moment. 'And you know what? I have a hunch he couldn't have ignored me, either—no matter what.' She launched into her tale, then, trying to listen to it with Nina's ears. 'I was going on about Jungian psychology before I knew it, and the poor guy was looking utterly blank, except that he had a special way of looking at me—oh, Nina.' She stopped, and her cheeks felt warm suddenly. She turned away. 'I can't explain. It's all nonsense. Far too long on the road, that's all.' She turned over the morning's letters, not fully seeing them.

Nina said gently, 'It does sound strange.'

'But *he* wasn't strange at all.'

'How long were you talking to each other, then?'

'Oh, it wasn't long. But I almost met him again later on.'

Nina's face crinkled in bewilderment. 'You *do* need some sleep.'

'Yes, I know I do, but I didn't dream what happened later. The car gave up the ghost just outside Bristol. I knew he was somewhere nearby, and two of his colleagues came and waited with me until the men from the garage came. I couldn't resist the temptation to send him some sort of a throwaway message. I hadn't told him who I was or where I live—nothing. But he said he'd love to talk philosophy to me some time.' She was shaking her head again. 'I know it sounds silly, but I said the first thing I could think of. I asked his colleagues if they'd tell him they'd met the M5 philosopher. And they knew my name, by then, of course.'

'You're mad today! Love to talk philosophy—yes, I bet he would!' 'Mad today—and yesterday.' Clare left her coffee cup on the end of her desk and swung her bag over her shoulder. 'Look, I'll never see him again, so I'll grow up and put him out of my head. But you may have a few lunacies to put up with for a while, Nina.'

Her friend nodded. 'That's OK.' Her smile was soft. 'And I promise I won't tell Danny.'

Clare laughed. Nina had never met Danny anyway. At the door, she turned for a last look at her, and beyond her through the tinted glass to St Paul's and the NatWest Tower on the other side of the Thames. A bumble bee had somehow found its way into the room and was blundering from file to wall and back to the window above the other writers' desks: lost to the free air outside.

Suzanne, one of the other women, began to swat at it with a copy of the latest issue.

'Oh, poor thing,' Clare said, darting forward.

Nina stood up beside her. 'Are you a dab hand at bee-catching?'

'Not really, but I'll have a go, since I'm on my way out and that bee probably feels a lot worse than I do right now.'

'Softie,' Nina said. 'A delicate operation, that.'

Clare took her empty cup, shook the last drops of coffee

into a plant pot and upended it over the bee while it crawled dispiritedly up the glass.

'Now what?' Nina laughed.

'You're crazy,' Suzanne laughed.

'Paper, please, nurse.' She slid the paper under the lip of the mug and turned the cup over, pressing the paper down on the rim. The bee buzzed furiously. 'Rubber band, please, nurse.'

She smiled at Nina, disregarded the funny looks she got from the deputy subeditor in the lift, and went down into the sweltering heat outside. When she slid the paper away from the mug, the bee somersaulted around for a moment, then lifted off and disappeared.

8

I didn't sleep well that Thursday night. I lay still in the cool half-light of Friday morning and listened to the first birds outside, then to the early traffic building on the Clevedon Road. I'd hoped to sleep till the alarm went, but instead I'd woken far too soon. I knew I was overtired, but sleep wouldn't return. Clare Hogarth's face appeared in my mind. I pushed it gently away, but she came back again, looking with a tiny frown at the Italian baby in the restaurant; looking with concentration at that cotton wool cafeteria menu (unless, I thought, she was staring through it thinking of something else altogether); and looking me straight in the eyes on that motorway bridge. And then I remembered I was going to try to ring her as soon as I got to work. After I remembered that, sleep was impossible.

I dragged myself into the bathroom and hung over the wash basin. Sally was right: I did look awful. I stuck my tongue out at the drained face in the mirror, locked the bathroom door, and took the longest shower I'd had time for since I left for Birmingham at the beginning of the week. It was only half-five when I finished, so I knew Tim and Richard would still be sleeping. I could eat breakfast alone for a change.

It was still too early for Radio 4 news; they'd have nothing better to talk about anyway than yesterday's tailbacks. *I might as well go straight to the station,* I decided—and went.

Nigel Sands and Jill Peterson should have left by the time I got in, but they were still discussing a case at Nigel's desk when I arrived at six-thirty. At least, I suppose it was a case. You could never tell with those two. The earlies were in, going through yesterday's working sheets, and the phone-calls had already begun, but Sally had gone. She must have cleared up a bit, because the obligatory stacks of dirty cups, chip papers, and empty and part-empty bottles had all gone. The table was wiped clean: cups, spoons, teabags, coffee, milk and sugar all in place. Angel Avalon still beamed at the world. Not feeling much like beaming, I stuck my tongue out at her, too.

In CID we don't shut our doors often unless the governor has called someone in to haul him over the coals. But I didn't want to talk to anyone yet, and the incident room could wait. When the partition door was shut, my little box of an office was mercifully quiet. No one would ring yet; and I could reread all my notes from Birmingham.

For several weeks we had been working closely with West Midlands and a couple of other constabularies on a pattern of child abduction cases along the M5/M6 corridor. I'd spent a long time on the telephone with my counterparts in West Midlands, Warwickshire, and West Mercia, and hours in briefings and discussions and database interrogations with the other incident room staff. The guys in the front office were so used to seeing me come down and access the PNC that they had put up a big misspelled sign on the terminals saying 'Keep Off. TRESSPASSERS PERSECUTED. Exclusive use of DI Frank Bernard.' I'd noticed, however, the night before, that the sign was gone. The honeymoon poster on my door was hardly an improvement.

We wanted to find those children. Five had been taken under eerily similar circumstances: one in Coventry, two in Birmingham, one in Cheltenham, and another in Bristol. Of all the men on the case, I was the only one not married with kids; so I'd been surprised, when at last it began to look as if we were making some progress on the case, that the governor had appointed me as investigating officer and sent me to do the liaison work. The other men (apart from the WDCs who were spending time with the families) all cracked jokes as usual about the vagaries of the investigations and were cynical about their counterparts at either end of the country. But we all knew how desperately we wanted to find those kids. All of us.

Maybe the boss had worked out (though I can't imagine

how) that I was a soft-touch with kids—probably because we'd lost my young brother Damian when he was only fifteen. Except for the personnel department, no one in the station knew about Damian, I thought, and I wouldn't have told them. But the boss would have had access to papers I had filled in about my family when I first joined the police. Whatever his reason for sending me to help find those children, he was keeping mum about it.

I didn't get too far with my reading. The detective sergeant who'd been doing our admin. on the Bristol case put his head round the door a little before eight, just when I would normally have been coming up the stairs.

'Frank, hi. I'm just going down to the front office. I'll be with you in a moment.'

I was glad to see him. Charlie Hotchkiss was like a huge hunting dog, always nosing into something but getting at the heart of a case quicker than anyone else in the place. 'Great. I'll tell you all about yesterday. See you in a minute.'

I could hear him banging down the stairs as I went out for coffee and an ashtray for him. Then he came back with the latest sheets, and we sat down facing each other beside my desk.

'Tell me about Birmingham,' he said.

I'd been on the phone to him every day that week, so he knew most of the story. We discussed the good news that a child missing from home in Coventry had been restored safely to her parents. The case seemed, after all, uncon- nected with the others we were working on. Then I told him about some supposed sightings of one of the children in Solihull—the only real news from Thursday morning. West Midlands CID was now doing intensive house-to-house enquiries in Birmingham, but there were conflicting accounts of how one child had been taken, and I knew they had a long way to go yet.

'Now tell me the real story, Frank,' he said at last, blowing smoke at the ceiling. He had been watching me closely as we talked.

I pushed some papers back and forth over the desk. 'I've

just told you.'

'No, the Frank Bernard story. Come on, cough it all up to your father confessor.'

Funny thing, Charlie's about five years my junior, but he takes it upon himself to keep an eye on me. I tried to stare him out. It didn't work.

'You fell in love with the ravishing girl on the West Midlands end of the case, right?' He heaved his weight to the back of the chair and folded his arms, waiting.

I pictured WDI Bertram's untidy hair and pear-shaped bulk, almost as wide as Charlie's. 'Wrong, Charlie. You're slipping.'

He scratched his chin. 'Your dog died while you were eyeing up the hounds those Birmingham doghandlers had— from sheer jealousy and pique.'

'Don't have a dog.'

'Well, then, your grandmother died.'

'Don't have one of them any more, either.'

'You got back to the house and found it had burned down while you were away, and you lost your happy home with Tim What's-his-name and Richard Who-done-it.'

'No such luck.'

'You couldn't sleep.'

'Getting warmer. Maybe they'll promote you to DI if you keep this up, Charlie.'

'Aha! Well, there must be a lady in the case somewhere, if you're not sleeping. You can't tell me those tailbacks yesterday account for all your problems, or you wouldn't have been in here last night.'

'Warmer still. How did you know?'

'Oh, I have my sources. Come on, spill the beans, Frank.'

I pulled the pile of papers across in front of me again. 'You know what your problem is?' I said. 'You think because you're one of the few men I know who's still really in love with his wife after an everlasting marriage of—what, eight years, is it?—that love makes the world go round. Well, maybe it does, but I haven't found out yet. So let's get on.'

By 9.25 we'd finished the incident room briefing: earlier than I expected. I knew I would spend most of that day with the systems supervisor in front of the database, but first I allowed myself a few minutes' peace back in my own little box. I sat quiet, thinking about Clare for a long quarter of an hour—my door shut again—before I picked up the phone. The clock on the wall said exactly 9.40 when someone lifted the phone at the other end.

I felt ridiculously breathless and uptight.

Nothing seemed to go as I'd hoped. It was her voice, all right, once the Cockney woman had handed over the receiver. She didn't register when I mentioned Sands and Peterson. Then she said something that made no sense to me at all. 'I must have told you, surely? Women today. You remember.' By then, her voice was sharper, and I wondered again if she were mentally unbalanced, or if the other woman was listening, so that she felt she couldn't speak freely.

She mentioned her mother, not the woman who had taken the call for her, I concluded; and her voice got sharper still as she said they were going out. Something didn't ring true in her tone, and I knew I wasn't keeping cool enough to reassure her, either. She was sliding sideways away from me, and I only made matters worse by trying in my detective inspector voice to make sure she had my phone number. Not that I needed to—she knows where I am; I'd shown her my warrant card, after all. I was bungling the whole thing.

In the end, I heard the kind of fear in her voice that I hear when Charlie and I are closing in on someone in an interview, when all the evidence is pointing one way. 'The police,' she said. 'I'll call the police and complain.' The telephone clicked, and I got a dial tone before I could take another breath.

The police! Oh, God help me! That's rich.

The clock on the wall said 9.43. The entire call had lasted only three minutes, but it felt like thirty.

9

'I rather fancy one of them kwiches tonight, when we get back, Clare,' Edith Hogarth was saying. 'Like the one when I was over at your flat last year.'

Clare gritted her teeth. She also felt a stab of guilt at the realization that it was nearly nine months since she'd invited her mother to Ealing and made her a quiche. 'Kwiches' indeed—perhaps it wasn't surprising that she hadn't invited her since. *Snob,* she told herself half-heartedly.

Predictably, her mother went on, 'Right treat, that would be.'

They were in the kitchen, on their third cup of tea, and Clare had resigned herself to a day of lazy simplicity, no demands on her, especially now that her mother had phoned the magazine and left a message with the receptionist. She was off the hook until Monday.

Her mother wanted them to go to the zoo in Regent's Park. *Just what I need,* she thought, *to watch a troupe of chimpanzees clowning around in their cages and apes combing each other for fleas. Not a whole lot different from the way some of my colleagues carry on at the magazine.* That made her laugh, and she looked across the enamel-topped table at her mother with fresh affection.

'You want me to make you a quiche?' She said the word correctly, trying not to make her mother feel put out, but unable to bring herself to say it the way her mother did.

'Nice. Yes, please.'

'If you've got the ingredients I could. But don't you want a bite now?'

'Oh, p'r'aps some toast. That's all.' Her mother pulled at her dressing-gown and stood to push open the back door. The kitchen was as stale and hot as Clare's room had been, but now the faint smell of summer grass from the five foot by five foot patch outside drifted in. It was undimmed even by the other smells of Barking: diesel and dustbins.

Clare stooped in front of the fridge and found a cut loaf of what she called plastic bread. While it was toasting, she searched for eggs, bacon and milk to make the quiche.

'Do you have any mushrooms? Or onions? A tomato?'

Her mother sniffed. 'Fresh, you mean? Ain't got nothing like that. Tinned mushrooms, maybe. You should know, love.'

Clare let out a sigh. 'Look, why don't you let me take you to a small restaurant somewhere up by the zoo instead? Or we could—' She hesitated, stopping short of suggesting that her mother might go home with her today. She could have made a quick quiche in her own flat, stopping at the market on the way for the vegetables. *Quick quiches. A good name for a restaurant or weird cookbook.*

Her mother planted her feet apart, hands on hips. 'Ta, love, no. Well, if we haven't got the bits for a kwich, we could do a nice fry-up instead with them eggs and bacon, and go round the corner for chips if you don't fancy peeling spuds.' Clare's empty stomach rebelled. Every Friday night when she was a child, her mother had served the same heavy food and thought it was a 'treat'. They would compromise. 'No, I'd rather not, thanks. How would it be if we stopped on the way back, for the "bits" as you call them, and I'll do you a quiche after all—before I go back to the flat?'

Later, when they went out into the hot sunshine, her mother was overdressed in a crimplene dress with nylon frills round the neck. The dress didn't fit properly over her hips, and Clare wondered with amusement whether her mother wouldn't be much more comfortable shuffling down to the tube in her dressing-gown, slippers and curlers. She herself was wearing the one pair of jeans she had packed for Liverpool, so she knew they looked an odd pair meandering slowly round the paths of London Zoo.

The phone was ringing when they returned, late in the afternoon. Thinking of the morning's unwanted male caller,

Clare looked questioningly at her mother as she went to set down the vegetables in the kitchen.

'No, I'll answer,' was all her mother said.

Clare passed her, opened the back door, and began making pastry while her mother talked on the phone. Someone next door was playing the Pet Shop Boys so loudly that the cupboards were vibrating, and she could hear nothing of her mother's voice from the front room. She danced a little as she moved across the room between fridge, shopping-bag, and worktop. *I'm glad,* she thought suddenly, *that I didn't go in today, after all. Mum's good for me, even if I can't stand her for more than a few hours. She probably couldn't stand me much longer, either!*

She was slicing thin strips of green pepper and rings of onion when her mother finally came and stood behind her. 'Clare.' The voice was strangled, barely audible under the blast from next door. 'Clare.'

She turned quickly. Her mother looked ashen, blotchy, and her face was streaked with tears. 'Mum—oh, whatever's the matter?'

Her mother's face disintegrated, and a noise of animal pain came from her twisted mouth. She broke into sobs, completely unable to speak. She leaned over the table, her head bowed, her hands whitening from the pressure of her own weight. Clare stood paralyzed. Only once before had she seen her mother like this: when her father had died. Laying down the knife, she went without speaking to put her arms round her mother's shoulders. The music next door jittered and rocked the room, but Clare knew her mother couldn't even hear it.

'Sit down, Mum, for a moment. Please sit down.' She pulled out one of the two chairs and eased her into it. Her mother's eyes were blank now, no more tears, staring straight ahead. Clare felt a rush of fear. *Shock. What do I do for shock?* Then, from somewhere among the recesses of seemingly irrelevant memories, came the picture of herself at Cambridge.

Another student, drunk and filled with unexpected hatred, had pushed her hard from behind, pushed her off a punt into the Cam: someone who knew she couldn't swim. She had hit her head on the way down, and someone else had dragged her, dripping and limp but not senseless, onto the bank. Her friends had brought her brandy, then hot tea. Forced them down her until the shivering stopped and the world came back into focus again.

'Don't move,' she said to her mother, running her hands over the broad back in a useless movement of comfort. 'Don't move.' She knew she wouldn't and couldn't but was terrified by the fixed, wordless stare her mother gave her. 'I'll be right back.' Trembling with haste, she stumbled to the foot of the stairs, ran up and yanked the eiderdown off her mother's bed. There was no brandy in the house, she knew; no alcohol at all.

Back in the kitchen, she wrapped her mother in the eiderdown and rubbed her back again.

'Can you tell me?' she asked carefully.

No answer. She lit the gas and began to heat a kettle. The Pet Shop Boys had been replaced by Radio 1 news. She fled out of the back door, through the hole in the fence, and pounded on the open kitchen door of the next house.

A girl in a tie-dye T-shirt, skimpy shorts and bare feet padded to the door. 'Sorry. Is this radio bothering you?'

'No—no.' She hesitated.

The girl's head went slightly to one side. 'You from next door? You look a bit sick. What—?'

'Sorry. Have you any brandy—oh, anything like that? My mother's had a shock.' She felt uneasy, her cultured voice an odd contrast to the thick East-End accent that came back to her. She should at least have said 'mum'. The girl would think she was from Windsor Castle.

'Yeah, come on. What's wrong?' She led the way into the front room, which was stacked with drawings and empty glasses. Clare noticed all the details of the room as if in a dream, as the girl held out a bottle to her. 'Look, you don't 'ave to say anythink if you don't want. Just bring back the bottle if there's anythink left. If not . . .'

'There will be. Thanks.'

She left the girl staring after her and went back in through her mother's door. The noise of the radio ceased altogether, and on the cooker the kettle was steaming. Her mother was sitting up now, looking around. Making her own movements as deliberate and controlled as possible, she poured a small brandy, put it to her mother's lips, and bent over her, speaking softly. 'Mum, I know you won't like this much, but whatever's happened, you need to take it.'

Her mother looked up at her with a face so washed clear of emotion that she might have been a newborn child. The nakedness of her gaze wrenched Clare's insides, and her mother took the brandy as a toddler would take a mug of warm milk. She did not even register surprise at the strength of it, but sipped quietly until the tumbler was empty.

Clare sat down opposite her and waited as long as she could, her eyes never leaving her mother's face. All the time, her mind turned over and rejected one theory after another about what the phone-call might have meant. At last she couldn't contain herself any more. 'Can you tell me?' she asked again.

Her mother heaved a deep sigh, and her eyes filled again, the tears spilling onto those absurd frills. 'Oh, Clare, it was your uncle. Your aunt, I mean. Your aunt who was ringing, I mean.'

'Yes?' She waited.

'Your uncle—they was trying to reach us all day. 'Eart attack. 'E's gone, Clare.'

She knew her mother must clearly have in mind a picture of the uncle who had died. It wouldn't be one of her father's brothers—they would never have occasioned such grief. Then it must be Uncle Bert Williams, her mother's only brother. Father of her cousins in Boston. She had never got to know him as well as she had her cousins, even though he was her mother's closest relative and the original occasion of her visits to Boston.

Something told her that her mother needed to speak her uncle's name before she did, that she should be patient and play no guessing games. She murmured, 'Who's been trying to reach us, Mum?'

There was a long pause, so long that Clare wasn't sure her mother had heard, so she made a pot of tea for her and waited again.

'Your cousins,' she said at last. 'They was ringing all day.' Her face curled up for a moment, then steadied. 'From Boston. It was Auntie Rita got through in the end.'

'Yes?' She poured the tea. Her own hand was shaking now.

'Your Uncle Bert's dead. Died in the night. In 'is sleep.'

'Ah. Oh, Mum. Oh—' She did not know what to say; felt utterly inadequate.

Her mother disregarded the mug of tea Clare proffered. 'No warning—nothink. They want me to go to Boston!' The tears halted. 'Me! Go to Boston! I can't, Clare. I'll never see 'im again. I can't stand it.'

She began to sob again, huge, broken sobs that reminded Clare stupidly of the donkeys they had passed in the children's zoo that afternoon. She was annoyed with herself for the crude comparison and mentally checked herself. She moved her chair closer to her mother's, put her arm round her again, and gently turned the distorted face towards her own. They were only inches apart now, and Clare whispered, 'You *could* go, you know.'

'*No*. All that way in an aeroplane for a funeral? No.' Her mother wouldn't meet her eyes: there was anger as well as grief in them.

'But you could, if you really wanted to. Flying's OK, really it is.' She sighed, knowing it was pointless. Her mother had never flown: she had preferred years of following Clare's father round the world by boat from one port to another. There would be no sailings to Boston for them now, she knew. Certainly not in time for a funeral.

She knew she wasn't responding adequately to the news. Instead of talking about flying, she should be saying something about Uncle Bert. But she didn't yet know how to. Eventually, she said, 'I'll stay here tonight, Mum, and for the rest of the weekend. Would that help?'

Her mother wiped her eyes and suddenly fixed her with a glare. 'Of course it would help!'

Clare saw some of the usual fire return for a moment.

'And you'll go to Boston, girl, for me, won't you? The funeral's on Tuesday. Your auntie'll be glad to see you. You was wanting to go again one day, and now you'll have to.'

10

Clare found it hard to concentrate on routine Saturday tasks like unpacking, shopping in Ealing for the week's groceries, and tidying the flat. She thought of escaping altogether and going to a film or a concert in the park, but she was too hot to raise the energy. Somehow the thought of ringing Danny didn't appeal, either.

Even after only a short day in the office on the Friday, she found herself still limp and lethargic from the effort of the long drive south and the late-night wait for the car to be repaired in a Bristol garage. And since Sandy, her flatmate, was away for the weekend, she had no one to have a talk to.

She felt empty and hollow, longing for company but unwilling—for some reason she couldn't explain even to herself—to pick up the phone and ring her mother, or friends from the office. It was unusual for the phone to be silent all weekend: usually there were calls for her, or for Sandy. Today, though, it sat as mute as a sleeping cat.

Giving up on a rather desultory attempt to clear up the muddle of magazines, papers, and empty glasses in the sitting-room they shared, she poured herself a tall glass of orange juice and stood drinking it at the window. She stood on one leg, the other crooked on the arm of her favourite armchair. Below her, children chased each other on the grass in the drenching sunshine or skipped with ropes on the flagstones around the edge of the flats. For just a moment—it was never more—she longed to be among them, back in the relative simplicity and ease of childish life. But then she remembered as always the anguish of childhood: the uncertainties about where she belonged, the feeling of strangeness in Barking, the mixture of embarrassment and laughter her mother always occasioned in her . . .

No—her life at *Women Today*, and the other friends she had made in this part of London, fulfilled her. This was just a case of the Saturday blues; she would get over them as soon as she'd caught up on sleep and seen her friends at church the next day.

So far so good. But why is this man I talked to for only a few minutes on Thursday, in an impossibly artificial situation, occupying so many of my thoughts?

That evening, with all the flat's windows open as wide as possible, she sat by the same window she had stood by early in the afternoon. She wanted to make sense of the meeting with Frank Bernard.

The light curtains beside her lifted in a faint draught, as the first rain in ten days pattered outside and brought with it the hot dustiness of London in summer, then the relief of the green grass smell below. The sky over the rooftops was smudged grey with rain and shadowed darkly by the onset of night. For a while she let her mind drift on the rainy tide of late twilight, allowing herself to think only of breathing lungfuls of the freshening air. Then, quite without planning to, without consciously deciding what she would do, she began to replay the scene on the bridge over the motorway. It was a film she had watched several times already, but she wanted this time to see it from a different angle. The man could easily have passed her on the motorway without noticing her at all; and he could certainly have ignored her in the service station.

For that matter, she could have ignored him herself. What woman in her right mind, she asked herself now, would talk as she had done with a complete stranger? That was the question Nina had asked by implication, too. And Frank Bernard might have regarded her in the same surprised way, possibly even with dismay—perhaps branding her the kind of woman who propositioned unsuspecting travellers. Was that why he had shown her the ID—to warn her off? To make the point that she shouldn't be talking to anyone in that way; that she was flirting not only with him but with the law? She cringed when she remembered his warrant card, covering her face with her hand and groaning softly to herself even now.

She watched the film again. No, that wasn't what had happened at all. He would never have suggested, not even as a joke, that she make contact with him, if he had misread her in that way.

But why did we speak to each other that way? Why? She thought again of his direct, kind eyes. There was nothing discourteous or critical—or demeaning either—in the way he had looked at her when he first spoke to her, or in the way he had smiled at her: a small smile from behind the dark beard. But it was almost, she thought, a conversation that hadn't properly happened. They could so easily have gone on talking about traffic accidents, women drivers, and other things of no real consequence.

Was it he or I who started the part of the conversation that mattered? She tried to remember more clearly, but once his face was focused like a still frame on the internal film, her ability to think rationally seemed to forsake her. Emotion took over, and something in her rushed out to meet something in him. *What if it's love at first sight?* she asked herself. *No, it isn't. There's no such thing. I don't believe in it.* She had, as usual, come full circle. Back came the first question, *OK, so why is he occupying so many of my thoughts?*

A gust of cold air—the first she had felt in ten days—suddenly lifted the curtains right off the metal window-frames and threw them back into the room around her face. For a second she was lost in their folds, and she found herself asking, *Dear God, what does this all mean? Does meeting him mean anything at all? Or is it going to be no more important in the scheme of my life than the tidying up I've done today and the games I played in the street at home twenty years ago?* She couldn't recall asking questions like these before, or spending much time thinking about men she had met—not unless she was actually with them. Certainly she never daydreamed of Danny!

She listened to the rain outside, the streaking drops lit by the streetlights below like millions of gold needles. *Of course,* she said aloud, *the personalities you give us don't end inside our skin. You hold them in your hand as well. And in the loving things we do with you, for you, we stretch ourselves to understand others' personalities—to stand where they stand and sympathize. In giving ourselves as you gave yourself for us, we don't diminish but add to ourselves. What a mysterious and wonderful thing compassion is!*

Some gentle inner voice responded with dry amusement that sympathy and compassion weren't exactly what she had in mind when she talked with Frank Bernard about her old 'what if?' game of living a life parallel to her own. But there was *some* connection there, she decided now. If, as she believed, God was the giver of boundless and miraculous possibilities, he offered her many choices, and many different routes to travel. She could look back at the twenty-seven years she had already lived and see patterns of lostness—now unravelled—as well as patterns of following the road straight forward. But what about the future?

She shut her eyes and blotted out the rain, the streetlights, and the silhouetted buildings and trees of London.

You take yourself far too seriously, Clare Hogarth, the voice whispered to her.

She smiled, not opening her eyes. *Do I, Lord?*

I just said so, didn't I? Trust me. You think you're trying to follow me. All the time, I'm following you. Don't you see?

I don't see anything at all! she thought, and laughed out loud. Her eyes opened, and she realized that while she had been sitting beside the window the flat had become completely dark.

She stumbled over the coffee table, barking one shin on the corner of it but hardly feeling the pain as she reached to turn on a light. Everything in the room looked utterly ordinary and still. She was glad, after all, that she hadn't gone out to the cinema. She would never have heard the quiet prompting of that voice. *I'm following you. Don't you see?*

God was guarding her from behind as well as before:

71

forgiving her past, protecting her present, leading and following her into the future. There was no more to be afraid of in that than there had been in Frank Bernard's having followed her for those miles on the motorway two days before. Had she known that unconsciously, when he spoke to her? She shook her head, still puzzling, and went into the kitchen. Sandy had left strawberries in the fridge, and she washed a bowlful, then collapsed in the armchair again to eat them.

Strawberries. They reminded her for a moment of her Williams cousins in America: of her last visit, when her uncle and aunt had taken them all to an endless field of strawberries on a farm north of Boston. Ed, only sixteen at the time, had picked more than the rest but had eaten most of them as they worked out on the field. His T-shirt and shorts had been covered with red stains, his mouth as red as lipstick, his eyes bright in the tanned face she recalled so well. Remembering, she glanced up at a family photograph on the shelf above her work table. There was Uncle Bert: thickset and jolly, a little like her mother, his big hands tucked in the beltloops of his jeans and Superman tattoos visible on his forearms; Aunt Rita, prematurely wrinkled from years of guiding pleasure boats through north shore waters in hot suns and frigid breezes; Jack, as blonde and apparently at ease with the world as a member of the Kennedy clan, wearing a pristine T-shirt the same colour as his brother's; Ed, strawberry juice everywhere and a big grin above it all; and little Marie, black-haired and starry-eyed. *Only six years ago.* She sighed. *It seems longer.* And there *she* was, too, her red hair waving onto her shoulders exactly as it still did, but her face younger and more carefree.

She tasted the strawberries now with her eyes shut, missing her American family. *Strawberry fields for ever.*

Then Frank came to mind again. Swallowing the last mouthful of fruit, she took the cover off her old typewriter and rolled some paper into the carriage. She would write him a letter, would send it to Bristol and tell him about the journey she had been on for as long as she could remember—a much longer journey than the one she had made from Barking to Boston six years ago, or from Liverpool to Bristol and London on Thursday: the journey with God. She would write it for herself, at least; maybe she'd never send it to him. But it would not matter because if, like God, he was following her, he would, like God, also find her.

PART TWO

Way leads on to way

11

We were swimming lengths in the club pool. Sands, almost blind without his glasses, wore ordinary goggles to protect his eyes from the chlorine and could hardly see where he was going. As I'd done a few times before, I was trying to keep pace with him in the water so that he wouldn't blunder into the other swimmers; but it was a strain to keep up. After only ten lengths, the water felt heavy and resistant. While I thrashed along beside him, my lungs and arms burning more and more, he seemed to slice through the blue ripples without effort.

'You're out of shape,' Sands called on one of his turns, surfacing just for a moment to grin at me.

I didn't answer him until the next turn, or I would have been a few too many yards behind, still trying to regain my breath. 'Have a heart! I don't swim like this often enough.'

He laughed. 'Swim? This is just paddling, mate. Come on.' And he went steaming away.

For a moment, I hated him. *Show off!* I thought. *Just because Jill's up there holding your gear while you fly up and down and flex your biceps for her benefit!*

Then, catching him up more quickly than I expected—he could probably just about see a swimmer ploughing towards us and was slowing up to avoid a collision—I added to myself, *Just jealous, Frank.* But I wasn't—not of him and Jill, at least.

After another ten lengths I gave up and floated in the shallow end. Only the diehards and the lonely frequented the pool on Saturday nights: no kids (all in bed or out on the streets); no teenagers (all out at the pictures, I suppose). Only a few obsessed length-swimmers like Sands, and their mad girlfriends (some in, some out, of the water)—like Jill. I was there occasionally, too, when no parties were on offer. My last girlfriend had parted from me months before with tantrums about what she called 'lack of commitment' (meaning 'police overwork'), and 'procrastination' (meaning 'I-want-to-be-engaged-now-quickly-or-never'). So tonight I thought I might as well annoy Nigel and Jill.

I think Jill quite liked me. She was a chatterbox, and I didn't mind listening to her anecdotes and laughing at her hopeless jokes. Sands talked too much himself to let her get many words in edgeways, so perhaps I was a relief. Nigel and Jill had been close friends for a couple of years or more. They worked together whenever they could and, as far as I could see, spent all their free time together. They had never made any effort to hide this fact from me, perhaps because I was one of the few unmarried men in our force. Or maybe it was because they knew I wouldn't make an issue of their relationship. There was never any talk of wedding bells. Sands always clammed up in the station whenever anyone called his bluff, and Jill seemed more or less content to cruise along without any commitment from him. I felt a little sorry for her. Perhaps she sensed that, too. Anyway, whatever their reason, they didn't seem to mind me joining them sometimes on a Saturday night.

I floated for a few more minutes, watching Jill out of the corner of my eye. She was looking back and forth, from Sands to me. Sands had eased up and was now swimming steadily along one side of the pool, using the side as his marker—now he didn't have me any more. He would go on like that for another thirty lengths, until he'd put in his regulation mile or more.

I caught Jill smiling in my direction, waded to the side and vaulted out of the water just below the stands.

'You were quick,' she shouted. 'I thought you were going to do more.'

I stood wiping water off my arms and feeling already the relative chill of the air after the delicious coolness of the pool. 'Not tonight, no,' I called back. 'Fancy a drink while he's finishing?' I knew Nigel wouldn't notice if we disappeared together and that he trusted me well enough to know I wasn't after his girlfriend.

Wrapped in a towel dressing-gown and by then feeling much better, I met Jill round the back at the bar. All day my head had been full of the five abducted children—as well as Clare Hogarth. But I would sleep well now. My brain had been chasing its tail all day, round and round in endless circles. The swim had burned all that away, and I felt new made.

We dropped into lounge chairs and looked at each other. Jill had finally surrendered Nigel's kit to the end of her chair (I never worked out why he always dumped it on her, rather than using a locker, like most normal people) and sat almost primly, sipping her G & T, quiet for a change.

'Why don't you ever go in?' I said.

'Oh, I do, once in a while.'

'Once is right. Once that I've ever seen you, Jill.'

'Well, you're not here that often yourself, and I just like to keep Nigel company.' Her eyes softened and wandered away to the bar doorway, but there was no sign of him yet.

'Lucky bloke.'

She looked at me quickly but saw nothing more than friendly interest. She wasn't one to blush or flutter her eyelashes, anyway. If Sands wanted her as his wife, I knew she'd never look anywhere else. She smiled, and dimples appeared: 'Ah, you're just wet behind the ears, sir ... with respect, it's time you sorted yourself out a nice girlfriend.'

'I've been working on it for a long time.'

She snorted. 'Not that I can see. You come in early, and you leave late. What chance do the lovely ladies of Bristol have—bar Sally and me, that is—to get to know you?'

I shifted to get comfortable. 'Not much, it's true. I used to like the party scene. These days it seems boring.'

'You must be searching further afield.'

She was fishing, I presumed. But I wanted to set up my own fishing trip, preferably without getting caught on *her* hook. Before Nigel came out of the pool, I intended to find out all I could about their encounter with the enigmatic Miss Hogarth. I tilted my glass so that she couldn't read my eyes. 'Further afield? Yeah. Must be.'

If I asked now about 'the M5 philosopher', that would give the game away immediately. I hesitated, but her mind had been following the same path as my own, and she came slyly to the point. 'Somewhere round the M5/M4 junction, perhaps?'

'Don't talk to me in crossword puzzle clues, Jill!'

She laughed. 'Hey, I thought obscure clues were right up your street. Let's get a *Telegraph* and work on the quickie together, OK?'

I leered at her. 'I can think of better ways to spend a Saturday night, thanks.'

'Then why *don't* you, mmm?'

I wasn't going to let her take all the initiative in this interview; I decided to turn the tables a little. Pretending that I was slightly injured, I muttered, 'Anyway, what sort of a woman would hang around the junction picking up CID blokes . . . er, like Nigel Sands, d'you suppose? Lucky you were there to protect him from her.'

She didn't answer me for a moment. I saw pity in her eyes and the curve of her mouth, and perhaps what little romanticism was left in her soul reminded her of something earlier in her relationship with Sands. I couldn't tell what she was thinking, of course, but she finally said, 'If she was the one, Frank, she's lovely.'

I could have thrown all discretion to the wind and told her everything (what little there was), but somehow I didn't think there were too many secrets between her and Nigel; and if he knew it would be all round the nick in five minutes. Crude *Sun* style posters on my door and in the front office would make the more recent ones look like something out of *The Times*. No, I had to listen and let Jill run on. She probably would anyway.

She did. 'She must be pretty bright, as well as beautiful,' she began.

I didn't look at her. 'Tell me about it!'

'That magazine seems to keep her on the run. Even behind that cover-girl fair skin and red hair she looked washed out—as bad as you, in fact.'

'Well, thanks for the insult,' I growled. *What magazine?*

'To her, or to you?'

'To me, you wally.' I rubbed the side of my face wearily; my beard needed a good trim. 'You're right. I know I look awful. Sally told me so as well.'

'Sickening for something.'

'I doubt it.'

'You were having trouble keeping up with Nigel, I noticed.'

'When didn't I? That man's got a heart like an ox's. He won't be the slightest bit winded when he gets out.'

She smiled. 'Probably not.'

I wanted to steer things back to Clare Hogarth. Time was running out, and I didn't like the way my fishing lines were being ignored. I debated casting farther, and did. 'She had a long drive on Thursday,' I said carefully.

'Yes, so she said. London . . . from the M6 . . . via Bristol?' She raised her eyebrows curiously. 'There must have been someone she wanted to see in Bristol pretty badly to go all that distance out of her way.' She clicked her tongue. 'Never heard of such a journey!'

'Hmm, yes. But the M6 south was choked with tailbacks, you know. Some of the worst I've ever seen.'

Jill looked at me, her mouth twisting slightly. Her eyes sparkled. 'That's your story, anyway. And hers as well. At least you've both got your alibis lined up.'

I stupidly rose to the bait. 'You know damn well—'

'Yes, yes. Good. The old hammer on the knee trick worked for a change. You don't usually react so fast—um, sir.'

I was annoyed with myself for jumping into her net, and I still hadn't found out what she meant about the magazine.

She was all sweetness now, watching me speculatively. 'You never used to be, but you're a quiet one these days.'

Maybe that's because, worse luck, there's nothing good to tell, I thought, not answering her.

'She was telling me a bit about the magazine while we were waiting with her. Nigel couldn't see what the problem was, and once the recovery vehicle had arrived, we didn't hang around to chat any more. She was doing some work in Birmingham, she said. For *Women Today*—is that right?'

A few of the clues slotted into place. *Women Today*. So that was what she had meant on the phone yesterday. *A magazine! So much for the great intelligence skills and detective work of F. T. Bernard!*

Jill was still observing me, but this time I don't think she saw that I had just leapt out of the net. Her mind had moved on, and she murmured. 'That's the first time I've ever met anyone who works for a magazine. It sounded interesting—in some ways not terribly different from what we're doing. And *Women Today*—well, have you ever read it?'

I was so relieved at this turn of conversation that I felt like whooping for joy. 'Sure, Jill. I read women's magazines every week.'

She grimaced. 'Girlie mags, more likely.'

'Hey, I didn't ask for that! When'd you ever see any of those soft porn pics old lover-boy Nigel has on his wall in *my* office, huh?'

She registered surprise, then went serious. 'That's true. You're different.' She sighed.

Around us a few other swimmers and their friends straggled into the bar. Sands would soon be among them. There was still one more thing I would like to find out if I could. But how was I going to ask Jill if Clare had mentioned where in London she was going? Or if she'd mentioned Barking?

Too late. Nigel strolled dripping into the bar and took his towel from Jill. He was pleased with himself, well disposed to everyone. I got up and bought him a drink, and he stood next to me at the bar while they drew it, chaffing me about my lacklustre performance in the pool.

'I'd rather go dancing,' I told him.

'Oh, would you indeed?' he looked at me sideways. 'From all accounts, you were doing the tango up in Birmingham, my lad.'

'Oh, don't you start!'

'Sally was saying—'

'Come off it, Nigel.' Suddenly I didn't feel like any more banter. 'Here's your drink.'

'Thanks mate. Cheers. Let's drink to the M5 philosopher, the radiant Cara, or whatever her name is, and to the lovely ladies of London, shall we?'

Jill heard the last crack and sat up indignantly. 'Don't forget us Bristol girls,' she called. 'Bone of your bones, and flesh of your flesh, and all that.'

Again I felt sorry for her. I doubted Sands would ever grow up enough to give her a proper home and the love she deserved. Obviously, I wasn't going to find out from these two tonight whether Clare was from Barking or Blackpool. Sands had already forgotten her name, thank goodness.

Then I woke up. *Of course she's from Barking, idiot,* I told myself. *She told you she was going to London, and she told you yesterday about the magazine, even if you were too thick to pick up on what she said. You're fired, DI Bernard.*

Then why did she deny on the phone having met me? Why did she sound so vague about the car? And why did she drag 'the police' into it when I talked to her?

Beside me, Sands bent to give Jill a quick kiss. *My turn next,* I decided, not thinking of Jill at all.

·12·

On Saturday, for the second night in a row, Clare did not sleep well. For part of the time she again sat downstairs with her mother, who was still alternately weeping and staring dully at the wall. For the second night she was making tea, listening, offering what she knew was scant comfort. And for the rest of the night she tried—fitfully because of the sobs from below—to sleep in her own bed upstairs.

I'm not cut out for this, she thought, and wished she had gone straight back to Ealing instead of coming to her mother's. Then she felt guilty for the frustration and irritation that seemed to be mounting as surely as the clockhands on the mantelpiece were turning to mark the night hours.

Part of her wanted to care deeply about her mother. *But*, she mentally excused herself, *I'm an only child. How can I hope to understand the death of a brother?* She tried to project her mother's tearfulness onto herself, to feel with her the pinch of sorrow, the unsoftened finality of death; but she could not. Even trying to resurrect her own feelings at her father's death did not help. Instead, she felt numb. She tried to imagine how she would react to the unexpected death of one of her American cousins—probably the closest she would ever come to understanding what it was like to have a brother. But it was six years since she'd seen the Williams cousins, and she couldn't remember them clearly enough to feel at all moved at the unlikely prospect of their sudden demise. Then, again, she hated her own indifference, made yet more tea, and prayed she would grow more sympathetic as the night wore on, or that her mother would eventually subside into sleep herself.

The weeping frightened her. Normally it was her mother who was down to earth and practical—but now she had to be.

The broken sobs came and went—assaulting and jangling all her senses as they had done throughout the previous night and for most of the day. Several times in the night she told herself that she should telephone the doctor and get a sedative for them both, but when she suggested it, her mother flared up indignantly, 'I won't have anythink of the sort!'

She recalled features and articles she herself had written or commissioned for the magazine about the importance of grieving and the stages of grief. She even thought about the Wailing Wall in Jerusalem, of black-clad men and women with their heads bowed to the rough stone and their voices raised in tears, but none of these branching, disconnected thoughts assuaged her simple impatience to escape to Ealing.

As the dark hours passed and the clutter of used teacups and pile of wet handkerchiefs mounted, and as the invisible mountain of grief grew higher, Clare was weighed down with a weariness that seemed nearly to break her. During the moments when her mother was weeping most incoherently, she reviewed all she had done on Saturday.

Boston! Under other circumstances, she would be wild with excitement about flying across the Atlantic on Sunday, especially at such short notice. There was always so much to see and do there. Her cousins lavished presents on her, and journeys to exotic, expensive places that made her feel especially loved. Not this time, however. Her journey would be grey with grief, and despite the pleasant heat of late June in Massachusetts there would be no partying on the beach or trips to Symphony Hall to listen to the Boston Pops. The flight seemed a waste of the airfare she had exhausted her credit card limit to pay for.

She sighed; then once again she condemned her own selfishness. How could she begin to think wistfully of a sun-shiny holiday when not only her mother but her aunt and cousins too were grieving. Then a great wave of exhaustion rolled over her, and she let her head drop onto her hand. She knew she wasn't thinking clearly; if she could just get a few hours' uninterrupted sleep she would be able to cope better.

Early on Saturday she had telephoned the travel agent on London Road to ask about seats to Boston. 'To New York, yes,' they had said, 'or Washington. One to Philadelphia, if you don't mind changing in Atlanta.' But those flights would be no use. The funeral was on Tuesday, and a Sunday evening flight would not arrive until very late Boston time on Sunday, or possibly early on the Monday. To be safe, she needed to find an airline that could get her there direct.

Abandoning hope of getting intelligent help from an agent, and feeling the press of time, she decided to call the airlines one by one herself. She flipped the Yellow Pages back and forth, dialled one number after another, and endured with gritted teeth the inane music and recorded messages as the answerphones put her on hold. At last she had given up. *I'll have to go standby*.

After the round of phonecalls she had begun to think of other practical things she would need to do. She packed up all the notes she had made for the magazine after her trip to Liverpool—how long ago that seemed!—and left them in her bedroom with a note that her mother should post them to *Women Today* after she'd gone; she'd think later about her many other responsibilities at work. Grumbling inwardly about the obsolete machine, she emptied her mother's laundry basket and filled the old twin-tub to wash all her own and her mother's clothes. In Boston she would need some of what she had taken to Liverpool, as well as other things from the flat. She sighed and started a short list of things she would need to pick up from Ealing on her way to the airport (if she got that flight after all, please God). In the middle of Saturday night, as they sat in the kitchen or living-room, she remembered other things, important things, that she had to get or do. *Passport!* she suddenly thought with alarm at about 4 a.m. *I must get that, even if I forget everything else*. She added it to her list.

A worse thought set her heart pounding and the adrenalin pumping all round her body—worse because she knew there was absolutely nothing she could do until morning. To her mind came a half-formed picture of her passport's inside leaf, the letters and numbers boldly stamped in purple block capitals near the foot of the page. There was an expiry date there—some time this year—but she could not remember when. Was the passport out of date? She couldn't picture it at all.

She wanted to clear her mind, to give all her worries to God, but she could not. Then, from outside the curtains, grey light at last began to filter uncertainly into the room. Her mind was splintering with the turmoil of anxieties, but the pale wash of light brought faint hope, too. Rubbing her eyes, she remembered how the rushed plans seemed finally to fall into place. Just as she had given up hope of a flight to Boston with any airline, the travel agent she had first called rang to tell her about a cancelled booking. Would she accept a seat on the early Sunday afternoon flight to Logan Airport in Boston?

Would she! Yes, the 2.20 flight would be a rush, but it would also lift her away more quickly from the responsibility of caring for her mother, from the anguish of listening to that crying—harder, she thought, than attending Uncle Bert's funeral.

The clock drew towards 6 a.m., and already the sky was alight with midsummer brilliance. As soon as she felt the warmth of the sun seeping in, she opened the back door again, heaved a sigh of relief, and felt she could after all face whatever the day brought. Sunlight and the ordinary chirps of sparrows on the roof outside restored her. Both she and her mother would cope.

When she went out to the Fiat at half-past eight, suitcase in hand, her mother clung to her and wept all the more. With the renewed patience borne of the end of her vigil, she gently kissed and held her close. 'I will ring you, Mum. Every day. And I'll write, as well. Get busy, now. Uncle Bert would hate to see you like this. Go on, now.'

And then she drove away. She found, however, that she couldn't bear to look back. And when she turned the first corner she burst into tears.

Halfway round the North Circular, the Fiat hesitated as she was pulling away from some traffic lights. She stamped on the accelerator, and for a moment it surged forward again. Then, at the next roundabout, the engine cut out. The car cruised to a stop right in the middle of the exit.

Still weeping, red-faced from effort and exhaustion, Clare got out and stood in a daze by the door of the car. She searched for a tissue, defeat glowering at her, and wiped her face. *No, she thought, I'm not giving in to this.* Then a white Ford Escort pulled up beside her, and a man leaned out.

His voice was abrupt, and she saw on his face a reluctance to help. All the same, he switched off the engine and unfolded himself from the front seat. He was waving a police warrant card at her, and her tired mind registered his uniform a split second later. But it didn't much matter who he was as long as he stopped.

'Oh, thank you!'

He helped her push the car to one side. 'What a day!' he observed irritably, dusting off his hands and wiping beads of sweat off his forehead. 'Murphy's Law in operation, is it?'

His tone was unsympathetic, but she found herself pouring out her story anyway. 'There's no way I can wait with the car,' she ended, lamely, crying openly now and no longer caring whether he noticed or not. 'I absolutely have to get to Ealing—now—and then to the airport.' She knew how hysterical she sounded, but she was beyond everything in the place of chaos. She suddenly understood better how her mother had felt, with the whole fabric of life seeming to crumble. A quiet voice told her again that all she needed was a long sleep, that her head and heart were too full after the roller-coaster of the last week to make sense of anything. But she argued against these soft sounds of common sense, and before she was aware of it she was shouting unreasonably at the policeman, 'I don't even care what happens to the car. I don't care if I never see it again.'

He let her crying hiccough to a stop. Phlegmatically he took down her mother's address and said he would see to the car for her. 'Look, I know a bit how you feel, and it's worse when someone's died a long way off. Your luck hasn't quite run out yet. I'm just going off duty, but I can at least radio for help.' He sounded resigned now to making himself useful. 'If you're happy for me to do this, I can make sure it's repaired and have it delivered with an invoice to your mother's house. I'll see you don't get ripped off. And next time you see *me* broken down on a roundabout, you can do likewise, OK?' There was a hint of sarcasm in his voice. 'Go on. Get yourself a cab and get home quick.'

She searched his face uncertainly but then handed over the key. She hailed a taxi, and that was that.

When the driver had left her outside the smeared glass front door of the flats, she felt only a small measure of relief. *Home,* she thought dully . . . but it was already 10.45. She had lost time because of the Fiat. Her shoulders tightened, and, feeling her body crying for a respite, she knew she should push everything from her mind except what would help her get to Heathrow on time. There was nothing she could do now about the car, anyway. As she took the creaking lift to the third floor, she was overcome with a sense of strangeness at being home mid-morning on a Sunday. *Church!* she thought, *I've missed church*. But the realization slipped away again as she remembered with a jolt, once more, her passport and visa. *Lord, I need every bit of concentration I can muster*.

She pictured Sandy and hoped she would be out, trying vaguely to recall: *Didn't she say she'd be away for the weekend?* She didn't want to speak to her this morning, not when there was so much to think about. On the other hand, she told herself with a wry smile, perhaps Sandy would have provided some light relief.

The flat was empty but smelled fresh. A note had been pushed under the door, and she picked it up automatically, though with the feeling that she probably shouldn't distract herself by reading it. All the same, curiosity got the better of her, and she put down the suitcase and unfolded it.

Clare, I tried to ring, but the line sounds funny and I couldn't get through. I suppose you're out this morning, so I'll come round tonight. Let's go to a film—I've missed you. See you soon. Danny.

She knew she should feel pleased that he had been thinking about her, but she was too numb to be glad. She hadn't had time to give him a thought herself. She would be somewhere over the Atlantic when he rang the doorbell. Too tired to care, she dropped the note where she had found it, behind the door.

Two things surprised her. Sandy had left the front window open, and the flat was unexpectedly tidy. Usually, after a few days away, she came back to relics of Sandy's meals and guests all around the flat. And in her own room the bed was made and all the clothes she had not taken away neatly hung in the cupboard. Funny, she didn't recall having cleared up in the rush of leaving so early the Monday before. Perhaps Sandy had had a fit of conscience and done all the cleaning for a change.

The order and familiar smell of the flat filled her with a peace she had not known for a whole week. Ignoring the clock, she quietly chose the coolest clothes in her cupboard—many of them unworn since her last summer trip to Boston—and repacked her suitcase. She even took time to put away all the things she would not need—the clothes she had washed in Barking the day before. Then she went to the bureau drawer where she kept her passport, and held her breath.

The passport would not expire until late November this year. Muttering with relief, she fumbled to turn a few more pages. *THE UNITED STATES OF AMERICA NON-IMMIGRANT VISA, ISSUED AT LONDON ... APPLICATIONS FOR ENTRY UNTIL ... INDEFIN-ITELY.* Trembling, and thanking God out loud, she fell into the soft chair by the window. She would be back in London long before the passport expired.

She took a last glance around the flat in case she had forgotten anything. The telephone arrested her, and her mother's blotched face appeared before her. She hesitated, quickly rehearsing what she should say as parting comfort. But when she picked up the receiver, the line was dead.

'Ah—of course. Danny told me it was.' There was nothing for it but to leave for Heathrow and try to telephone from there. She walked past Danny's note and straight into the lift. Waiting outside on the main road, suitcase beside her, she felt small, exhausted, and disoriented all over again. Then a taxi came and carried her away—for a time—from all her burdens. When she woke, the driver called to her that they were at the airport. She had fallen asleep, her neck stiff from an awkward position. She looked with dazed bewilderment at the mêlée of porters and passengers outside the terminal. She remembered her uncle's death, her mother's grief . . . and the failed car. Then, quite unexpectedly, she also remembered the telephone call from that strange man. Surely one of the crazy things he had said was to do with the Fiat? Still foggy with exhaustion, she tried to recall his exact words. *'The red Fiat on four wheels . . . you've had it repaired, have you?'* Her skin prickled with alarm. *How had he known?*

She shook herself awake. *Of course he didn't know anything. He was just some crazy nuisance caller wanting to frighten people. It hadn't broken down until today—he couldn't possibly have known.*

'Miss? Are you all right?' The cab driver's curious looks brought her fully to herself now, as she pushed open the door and searched her handbag for the fare.

Without a reply she simply passed it to him.

He caught her eye. 'Going far?' he asked as he took it.

Somehow, the question sounded familiar. 'A long way, I hope,' she answered.

13

'Didn't you get my note?' Danny asked, when Clare opened the door. He stooped down and found a small piece of paper behind the door.

She was dazed with sleep; he had woken her. 'No—oh—come in. I must have fallen asleep. I was reading...' She looked over at the chair by the window. *The Daily Telegraph* had fallen to the floor, and a cushion lay at an odd angle on one arm.

'That's OK.' He shrugged, easy-going as ever, and pocketed the note. 'Well, what d'you think about a film?' He leaned towards her for a kiss. 'Mmm, I've missed you this week.'

Still surfacing from the warm waters of her dreams, she hardly let him brush her lips. 'Yes, let's go. But can you give me a few moments to get myself sorted out? I think there's some mineral water in the fridge if you like, or lager.'

'That's OK. I'll wait until we're out. Here—' He dropped into her chair. 'I hate to say this, but you look done in, Clare.'

She wondered if she should apologize. 'Yes—I'm sure I do,' she murmured, then gratefully shut the door of the bathroom. Alone again, she stared at herself in the glass. Her eyes were clear, but her skin looked pale, and her red-gold hair was a tangle. She splashed cold water onto her cheeks, made herself grin at the reflection in the glass, and touched her mouth with lipstick.

Something she saw in her own face reminded her of Frank Bernard and, when she remembered him, and the feverish letter she had written to him late the night before, she suddenly lost all desire to leave the bathroom and face Danny. She hadn't seen any note from him, but she had tried to phone and forestall him. The phone however seemed

91

to be out of order... no wonder it had been so quiet all weekend. There was nothing she could do about it before Monday. In her mind she replayed her brief conversation with Danny and decided she had been curt. Why he persisted in coming to take her out almost every Sunday evening she scarcely understood. She had always hoped for a friend like Danny: considerate, relaxed, undemanding; but as she pictured his open face and dark eyes, his look of enthusiasm whenever he saw her, she knew she shouldn't be spending much more time with him. She hadn't thought of him more than once or twice in the last week, her mind fully occupied instead with someone in Bristol.

How silly, she said to herself. But that didn't change her perspective one bit.

When they reached the cinema, the film they wanted to see was sold out. 'It's a long way to the Granada, and there mightn't be any spaces left there, either,' Danny said. 'I would have booked if I could have reached you by phone to make sure you'd be free.' He pushed his hands into his jeans pockets, and his face was unhappy. 'It doesn't matter,' she said.

They turned down the steps and walked back along the High Street. 'Well, I haven't had a meal yet,' he told her, 'and you haven't either, I presume?'

'No—as I fell asleep I was thinking of making a sandwich or something. We could go back and make supper at the flat, if you like.' He stopped beside her, and she felt uneasy about the look of hope on his face. Quickly, she added, 'But why don't we eat somewhere else, instead, for a change? We haven't done that for ages.'

He grinned, but she couldn't tell by his cheerful 'OK' what he really thought of the second idea. He was willing, though, to go along with it, and they found an Indian restaurant a few minutes later.

'This do you?' he put his arm around her shoulders as they stood reading the menu, and they went in. For a while, because she liked tandoori, her misgivings melted away.

From the moment they were seated across from each other, however—the earliest customers of the evening—Clare wished she were alone and away from him. The red flock wallpaper and the claustrophobic warmth of the place made her feel trapped, a sense only underlined by Danny's insistent gaze and possessive grip on her hand. She could not understand why any of this irked her; normally they were completely at ease with each other, but this time her week away seemed to have clarified something for him. She was afraid he was going to voice it before she had time to think how she would answer him.

Perhaps the week away had clarified something for her, too. Round and round in her mind went the image of Frank Bernard. She tried to give her attention to Danny—he was the real one, after all, sitting opposite her with his bright eyes watching: no figment of her fantasies like Frank Bernard. No, Frank was a man she did not and would never know, so why should she think of him?

But she did.

When the steaming bowls of rice and the platters of spiced meat and vegetables were brought to them, Danny at last dropped his eyes, loosed her hand, and began to act like the Danny she was used to: cheerfully piling his plate high and talking between big mouthfuls about the patients at the hospital where he worked, and the latest news from home.

For a while, she relaxed, too, but then everything seemed to go wrong at once. She bit into a forkful of food and shot out of the chair, her mouth burning and her breath coming in gasps.

Danny leapt up as well. 'What is it, Clare?'

She knew what had happened, but for a moment she couldn't tell him. She had overlooked a whole black pepper, and her throat and tongue were on fire. All she could do was bend over her plate and ignominiously spit the food out. The waiter came running, and she stared at the mess on the plate. *No black pepper*. She had swallowed it almost whole!

'Oh, Danny!' Then she caught the angry stare of the

waiter, and whether from embarrassment or the heat of the food she felt her face turn deep red. 'I'm so sorry—sorry. It was a pepper or something very hot. I couldn't—' She stopped. At the back of her mind was the thought that if anyone should be apologizing it was the waiter, for serving food dangerous to human health. She loved Indian food, after all, but this . . .! The waiter recovered his amiability as soon as he understood her frantic gestures. After an embarrassing pause while the table was cleared and rearranged—*Thank goodness there's no one else in here yet,* she thought—they resumed their meal in relative calm. She would eat no more of the main dish, however, and Danny called for cool bowls of mangoes.

The peace lasted another ten minutes, until the waiter brought coffee. He came so quietly that Danny did not hear him. He was waving his arm as he talked and his hand caught the coffee, knocking both cups flying. Coffee from one splattered and dripped down his own clean shirt, and the contents of the other splattered all over the waiter's clothes.

'Too much!' the waiter cried, his face trembling with rage. 'You, you go out, and now, quick.'

Clare turned to gather her handbag, but Danny was on his feet, his eyes blazing. 'An accident,' he said sharply. 'It was an accident—just like your hot pepper.' She noticed he wouldn't apologize, and her dismay deepened.

'Please,' she said, 'I think we should go, Danny.' She fumbled in her handbag for some money but knew even as she did so that Danny and the waiter were going to make an issue of what had happened: Danny because he did not want to lose face in front of her, and the waiter because he was afraid—even as he shouted at Danny—of losing customers. She thought all these things in a flash, faster than she could have said them aloud, and came to a quick decision.

She laid two ten-pound notes on the table and raised her voice above the argument. 'I'm going—come on, Dan.' She should never have agreed to go out with him.

But the two men went on shouting, the blood vessels in

their necks bulging in anger. They had forgotten her; probably they had even forgotten why they were shouting in the first place.

Feeling utterly miserable, she slipped out and ran all the way to the flats without stopping. When she reached the front door, her side ached, her mouth still burned, and she was almost weeping with disappointment. She did not want to see Danny again.

In the stuffy warmth of the flat she turned to pick up the two sheets of paper that lay by the typewriter. Gradually regaining her breath as the tears dried, she reread them slowly.

When she had finished, she leaned her face on her hands and shook her head. The letter to Frank was rambling and incoherent: the worst thing she had ever written. If he had doubted her sanity on the motorway, when she'd begun to talk about personality boundaries, what would he think now, receiving a letter written with all the distortions of late-night illogic? She had wanted him to know about her love for God—had held hours of conversation with Frank about him in her head, but that letter would not serve the purpose.

She tore it up and dropped the pieces into the basket by her bureau.

14

Tim and Richard were away all weekend climbing some northern hills for amusement. Sunday night was unusually quiet. There was too much time to think, and at the moment no girlfriend to distract me.

After I'd eaten the first decent meal of the day, I sat brooding by the telephone. I felt exactly as I had on Friday morning, before I picked up the office phone to dial the Barking number: *scared*. Did that sharp voice really belong to the same woman who had watched the Italian baby in the restaurant and stood beside me so companionably on the bridge, watching the traffic? Was this the same woman who had darkened the evening sunshine by her own dazzling smile—*The radiant Cara*, as Nigel had ignorantly called her?

I sat back and stared at the wall. *This is getting ridiculous,* I told myself. *Not counting the time on the motorway when I was driving behind her, I spent no more than fifteen minutes with her that day!* No one, I told myself with amused annoyance—no one had ever got under my skin as Clare Hogarth had.

Briefly, I thought again about what Dad would say.

'About time you got serious about a nice girl. Get on with it, lad. You've wasted enough time already on young girls I'd not pass the time of day with myself.'

Then I forgot about Dad for a while and went back to phone watching.

Was I being brave or stupid to try telephoning her again? The phone beckoned, and I watched it. When it rang, I jumped—as if she would be on the other end of the line!

She wasn't, naturally.

It was the duty inspector. 'Frank, sorry—I know it's Sunday. But there's been another abduction that looks very like the others. Can you get in early tomorrow to update

96

yourself? The DSs are on the job now.'

I groaned. 'When I went up to Birmingham, I thought we might be making headway. Then things seemed to go dead at the end of the week—now this.'

'That's what we all thought. But I've been in here all day since the news came, and things are hotting up again.'

I thought of the senior investigating officer's wife, widowed yet again on a Sunday. 'Poor Denise. Poor Bill. Why didn't you call me before?'

'Because we didn't need you. We're still waiting for all the details. And there's not much point in anyone else losing sleep tonight, anyhow. No, you might as well stay put for now. But if you can come—'

I finished the sentence for him, a little impatient to find out more. 'Early—yes, I will—of course.' *And*, I added mentally, *it's not as if I'll get much sleep as it is.*

'OK, then—I guess we're on child number six, now.' He exhaled heavily, in exasperation. 'Lord, but it makes you sick.'

I could tell he was about to hang up. 'Wait a minute. At least tell me where this child went missing.'

'Another from Coventry. A little girl. Very like what happened in Birmingham with one child . . . but, listen, I'd rather save this for the morning, Frank, if you don't mind.'

'Aren't there *any* witnesses? No more clues at all? Nothing?'

'Not a thing. Little girl on her way to the library on Saturday. Never got there. The parents got scared and started hunting for her, but no one blew the whistle until *this morning*, if you credit it!'

I felt like grinding my teeth. 'Perhaps someone knew them and counted on that,' I said. I could hear some of my incident room colleagues shouting in the background, and I knew he wanted to get off the line. 'Well,' I sighed, 'I'll get in early, of course.'

'Get yourself a good night's sleep and come in fresh, OK?'

I laughed and hung up. There seemed little prospect of

that. Too much was going around my head this Sunday evening: six missing children *and* Clare Hogarth.

For a while, I renewed my stake-out on the telephone, trying to pluck up the courage to ring her. Finally, lifting the receiver, I pressed the numbers—no need to look them up again.

The line rang and rang. At last a muffled voice answered. The speaker sounded as if she had a severe cold, and at first I did not recognize her voice.

'Yes? What is it?' The woman coughed.

'I'm looking for a Miss Clare Hogarth.' I tried to sound both authoritative and at ease.

'Well, 'oo is it?'

The dropped 'h' gave her away. I was speaking to the same Cockney woman who had picked up the phone on Friday. But now she sounded ill, and I hesitated.

'Forgive me. I'm Frank Bernard. I've been trying to reach—'

She cut me short. 'She's gone. I 'eard 'er tell you with me own ears not to bother me any more.' She made an odd sound, half hiccough, half sob, and I knew something was wrong. The skin on my back felt suddenly cold. Her voice rose. 'She's gone, d'you 'ear? Leave me alone, can't you?'

I heard panic, grief and terror in her voice—all at once. I shouldn't have called. 'I'm sorry. I won't call again. If when you see her again you'll tell her I tried again—that's all—I won't ring any more unless she gets in touch with me.' I wanted to add that she need not be afraid of me, though clearly something had so deeply upset her that nothing I said would make an impression. I doubted she would pass on any message to Clare. The story was ending before it had begun, I told myself as I put down the phone. I stared at the wall again and suddenly reached what, for me, was a startling decision. I wanted to write it all down. Writing things down offered a kind of release and maybe a way of understanding—as often happened in my work.

I took out a notebook and pen and got started. The more I

thought about Clare Hogarth as I wrote, however, the more I wondered why I was wasting my time. I couldn't even account for my feelings. I had met her once—for only a few moments—and I knew nothing about her. But I wasn't going to give up too easily! I wrote furiously.

It was a new kind of writing for me. 'Facts. All we want is facts—full facts,' the governor at the training school had said when he took apart our first attempts at written reports. *Little room for fantasy there*, I thought grimly, writing down facts that read more like fantasy every minute.

Tim and Richard thumped their rucksacks and heavy hiking boots through the front door at about 9.45. They were tousled and smelled of sweat.

'Working, you poor so-and-so,' Tim sympathized, seeing the crumpled papers and scrawled notes that signified my first efforts at writing a sort of diary.

'Oh, will you look at this,' Richard laughed, picking up one sheet. 'Frank's writing a love story. He's really lost his marbles now!'

'Give that back, you clown,' I protested, laughing anyway. Richard grabbed Tim and waltzed him around the kitchen singing in a falsetto voice, 'Love is a many-splendoured thing'. Then the two of them collapsed beside me and we all had a drink.

Later, though, when the house was quiet again because the others had gone to bed, I prowled around the kitchen, still trying to write my diary. Then it struck me: *She works for a journal! I wonder* . . .

I knew nothing about *Women Today*, and I knew still less about writing stories, but perhaps I should send in my account of meeting Clare, I thought.

I would address the story to Clare herself, and see what happened. What was there to lose?

15

After the rush to get to Heathrow, she need not have hurried. A bomb threat had held up the plane for four hours already, and there was no sign from the boarding staff that departure was imminent. Even so, for security reasons no one was allowed back into the main terminal. Clare had bought a couple of magazines—including Friday's *Women Today*—but already she had read them from front to back, and now that everyone had gone through passport control to the boarding gate, there was nowhere to buy anything else to read. No facilities: just a drinking fountain, toilets, telephones, and miles of carpet and plastic chairs. Sterile, empty (even if full of people) and lonely.

Outside the thick glass, planes taxied into neighbouring bays and mechanics with their ears in thick mufflers shot around the tarmac on buggies. She knew the evening sun was still blazing outside on the runways, but inside the departure lounge the atmosphere was chilled by air-conditioning. Tiredness was catching up with her again, and the cold only accentuated her discomfort. She grew listless and thirsty.

Then she remembered the long wait on the motorway only three days before. *Why*, she asked herself, *is making long journeys always so difficult, so full of obstacles and unexpected turns in the way?* Of course there was no answer, and she laid down her magazine with a sigh. She certainly ought to be used to the vagaries of travel—unlike her mother!

How would she have coped, she wondered, if, after all, her mother had decided to make the journey with her? The long delay would have been even more excruciating. Her mother—normally quite placid—would still have been lamenting Uncle Bert, loudly careless now of what anyone thought. And the fear of flying, prolonged and exaggerated by the waiting, would have made matters even worse.

The telephones caught her eye. She had already rung her mother from the main lounge. Perhaps she should telephone again, while she had the chance. She picked up her hand luggage, went to one of the booths, and dialled the Barking number. A steady bleeping answered her—the line was engaged.

Puzzled, she waited for as long as her impatience would let her, then dialled again. This time, the phone rang properly. And rang, and rang.

She stood absolutely still, her eyes fixed on the sound-proofed plywood at the back of the booth but not really taking in any of what she saw. She noticed only that the knuckles of her free hand were turning white as she clenched it in anxiety. The telephone went on and on ringing.

Mum must be there, she thought uneasily. *Why else would the line have been engaged just now?* She wondered then, feeling her heart quicken, whether she had dialled the right number. She tried again, and once again let the line ring for several minutes. At last she heard her mother's voice—strained and broken with crying, barely recognizable in the one word she seemed able to get out—'Yes?' There was a fearfulness in her tone that didn't match the grief.

Clare answered very quickly. 'Mum—Mum! It's Clare.'

'Clare? Clare? Is this a joke? I told you—'

'Mum, of course it's me. Hey, please take a deep breath a minute. I'll wait for you. I thought you'd be glad if I called again . . .'

She heard the sharp intake of breath at the other end of the line and knew that she had managed to reach through the anguish and make her listen properly. But the breath turned into a sob, and it was several minutes while the money ticked away on the electronic counter before the crying stopped. Clare felt as if she was dealing with a child, and that feeling frightened her, as the crying of the last two nights had done—because it was so much out of her control, so much out of even her mother's control. Somehow they were changing places.

For once she was the parent, and she didn't like that role.

'Yes,' her mother said at last, 'Yeah, love, of course I'm glad you're ringing. But what's going on? You was on the way, I thought. Why ain't you in Boston? Where are you? I don't understand.'

As Clare listened she had the odd sensation that although her mother was now able to get the words out she was actually thinking about something else altogether: something that worried and frightened her. She decided, however, that she would wait as long as her small change allowed her to find out what was going on in Barking. She would deal first with the questions and answers her mother could deal with too.

'Oh, Mum, no, I'm still in London—still at the airport. There was a—' How could she mention the words 'bomb scare' now? That would send her mother straight off the edge. '—a long delay in the flight. So I'm still here.' Her mother didn't answer immediately. 'Oh, that's all. That's good.' But then the anxiety returned, this time swinging in another direction. 'But what about your Auntie Rita? She'll be waiting for you, and you won't be there.'

Clare was reminded afresh of how little her mother knew of what she regarded as fairly ordinary travelling problems. 'It's OK,' she said patiently, as to a child, 'they won't drive to the airport without checking the arrival time first. Don't you worry, Mum.'

Again there was a pause, and again Clare watched the digital numbers on the counter descending rapidly. She wanted to tell her that she would soon have no more money left to talk, but her mother saved her the words.

'Clare—I didn't want to answer the phone.'

'But you must!' she burst out. 'I said I'd call you every day.'

Her mother seemed not to hear. 'It was that man again, the one 'oo rang up the other day when you was in the bath. The one you told to go away. 'E was asking for you again, Clare. Give me the creeps, 'e did.'

'Just now, you mean? He called just now?'

'Yes. Gave me 'is name again as well. But I don't like it,

Clare. There was somethink about 'im . . .'

She watched the numbers drop from ten to eight, then six. *Only six pence left.* 'Mum—please just ring the police if he calls you even one more time. And don't leave the phone ringing, OK?' She tried to sound reassuring. 'It might be me, remember?'

Four . . . two The counter dropped mercilessly.

'Okay, goodbye, love—oh—'

The line went dead before she could answer, and Clare went back towards her seat. There was just too much to face—the journey, the funeral, her mother, the unfinished work she was leaving behind at *Women Today*, the sleeplessness—and now this nuisance caller. *Please, no more!*

She shut her eyes and told herself that she had to stop worrying. Then she opened them and resolved to find something or someone to distract herself.

She noticed the woman first—perhaps about her own age or a little older. While others were slumped forward resting their eyes, or smoking, or trying to calm crying children, this woman was bolt upright in her seat, her eyes bright and watchful in a round, tanned face framed with black hair. An interesting, alive face. She caught Clare's eyes and smiled. Clare smiled back, but they were too far away from each other to begin a conversation.

Next to this woman sat a big man with a loose-fitting suit and a relaxed face. He was leaning back into the uncomfortable seat, smoking and staring out of the window, his mind miles away. She tried to work out whether they were travelling together or had just happened to sit down together, and whether they were British or American. There were no obvious clues in either case, because neither was speaking, and both seemed self-contained. She looked at the woman's hands and was surprised to see that her fingers were entirely bare of rings. Then she began her old game. *What if I were travelling with one of them—on holiday or for the job? What if she was my sister, or he my brother?*

She shrugged and smiled slightly to herself. She was so

tired now that the game wouldn't work. All she could think of was falling asleep on the plane. She shut her eyes and drifted, half-hearing the dull roar of all airports, and the crying of children. Then—it might have been a moment or quarter of an hour later—there was a stir as the ramp door was opened and the first-class passengers were called to the gate. Outside the windows, the shadows had lengthened and the sky was paling from a humid blue-grey to white. She looked at her watch. Almost seven. She would be in Boston by about eight o'clock Boston time. The sky would look the same there as here, but for her it would feel like 1 a.m. She could hardly bear the thought of another long night like the last two.

She lost sight of the couple she had been observing in the departure lounge; they had gone some way ahead of her up the ramp and had turned right into the plane before she could see whether they were yet speaking to each other. Then, when she found her seat—a window seat in a set of three seats in the economy class—she discovered them sitting in the two outer seats. They would be travelling together, as in her 'what if?' game. Tired or not, she was glad.

The woman's face lit up as soon as Clare reached to put a few things into the compartment overhead. 'Oh,' she said, 'that's good. It's you. I saw you out there in the lounge.' Her voice was bubbly, the intonation exactly as she remembered that of her Bostonian cousins.

Somewhat taken aback by the directness, she could only murmur, 'Yes. I saw you too.' And then she was struck by the clipped, almost curt sound of her own voice, and added, 'Well, we've got a long way to go yet.'

'You're English!' the other woman exclaimed. 'Great.' She jumped out of her aisle seat and touched the man's shoulder. 'Pete, we'll have a good trip, I think. Hadn't you better move so that the lady can take her seat by the window?' The man focused on her for the first time, and his eyebrows rose. Without hesitation or any word of acknowledgement to his travelling companion, he stood to let Clare pass, his head bent awkwardly under the luggage holders above. As she scrambled across to sit down, she felt his eyes running over her body and undressing her. She prickled with resentment and flushed indignantly. *A good trip, is it?* she thought. *I wonder!* She wished she were sitting next to the woman instead of the man.

If she had wanted to ignore him, it became impossible. Apparently recovering his good manners, he turned on the charm and began the usual passenger-to-passenger questions about destinations and reasons for travel, expressing the proper amount of sympathy when she explained about her uncle, then—later—asking her if she'd excuse him while he went to the back of the plane for a smoke.

With the middle seat temporarily vacant and the plane already at cruising height, Clare began to relax. Again, however, she found she couldn't sleep. The woman started to talk immediately.

'When we were too late for the business class, he wanted seats in the smoking section,' she confided, 'but I said I'd prefer these, and the plane was so full anyway. We had to take what we could get . . . I'm Bobbie, by the way.'

Clare stared. 'Bobby!'

The woman twinkled at her. 'No, not Bobby. Bobbie— B-O-B-B-I-E. You know? Bobbie-Ann Rizzo. We Americans seem to go in for weird names compared to you Brits, I guess.'

Clare laughed. The woman's simple gaiety was infectious. 'And I'm Clare. Clare Hogarth.'

'Oh, that's beautiful. I don't know anyone called Clare— except some Italian saint who features in the calendar some time in August. Not that I know anything about her, really.'

'Me neither,' Clare answered. 'And I'm no saint, for certain.'

Bobbie looked at her speculatively. 'But you've got that gorgeous English skin everyone in America dreams of having—so clear. And you remind me—' She stopped.

Clare thought of her cousins again. Were Americans always like this? So quick to engage in personal conversation—about the sorts of things she had only begun to discuss with Nina after months of working in the same office. She had no idea how to reply.

Bobbie ran on, apparently not noticing her discomfort, almost thinking aloud. 'I'm trying to catch hold of who you remind me of. Someone . . . wait, I know.'

Clare smiled. 'Poor woman, whoever she is.'

'Oh, not at all. Not a woman, anyway. A painting. Pete and I took some time off in your galleries between meetings in London—we've been doing some interviews and picture sessions, you see, but also some scouting—I'll tell you all about that in a minute . . .'

Yes, Clare thought wearily, though unable to dislike the woman at all, *yes, I'm sure you will.*

'A painting. I'm not sure who by, but it was one of those late nineteenth-century artists . . . can't think of the name of the school.'

To her own surprise, Clare's tired mind supplied the name. 'You mean the pre-Raphaelites?' She felt herself blushing again and regretted this 'gorgeous English skin' Bobbie had so envied; she blushed far too easily.

'Yes, that's it,' Bobbie was saying. 'Your blue eyes and that beautiful auburn hair.' She lifted one hand, and for an uneasy moment Clare thought she would touch her hair, and drew slightly away. 'Yes, you look like one of the pre-Raphaelite women.'

Clare wanted to make light of the conversation and divert it altogether if she could. 'Wow—thanks!' *Already*, she thought, *I'm beginning to sound like Bobbie*. She grinned. 'Look out Holman Hunt and John Millais, here I come!' Then she added, resigned to sleeplessness, 'So, tell me, what do you mean by "scouting"?'

Before Bobbie could answer, the man loomed over them, and Bobbie twisted sideways to let him into his seat. He dropped into it heavily, his left arm bumping Clare's right arm hard enough to make her start away. Really, he was full of contradictions: boorish one moment and charming the next, then boorish again.

'Pete—this is Pete by the way, and Pete, this is Clare, OK? Pete, why don't you tell Clare what we've been doing this last week?' Bobbie's happy little face was full of devotion.

'Oh,' he drawled, 'I'm sure she wouldn't be interested in the least, Bobbie. And anyway—' He turned away from Clare, who thought he was probably winking at Bobbie, '—not all we've been doing this week is news fit to print, exactly, is it?'

It was Bobbie's turn to blush, but Clare saw the light in her eyes dim slightly. The man had embarrassed—perhaps even humiliated—her. Clare jumped in quickly, wanting to save the situation. 'Seriously, I did ask her what you were "scouting" for. It's my job to be nosy... but you can tell me to mind my own business if you like, and I'll go back to this.' She twitched at another magazine she had found tucked in the seat pocket, but she knew she sounded unconvincing.

Pete's eyebrows went up again, this time in enquiry. 'Your job to be nosy? Now you really do fascinate me.'

His face came closer to Clare's, and she felt the same sense of danger and annoyance she had felt when he had first appraised her. Even so, she stared him out, not caring now if she were equally rude. 'No, I'll tell you about my job later, if you like. But Bobbie promised me your tale first. Go on.'

He seemed surprised and was just about to open his mouth when Bobbie burst in, 'We work for magazine publishers in Boston. Pete's one of the senior editors.' She paused and sent him a quiet smile. 'I'm just one of the photographers. I can't tell you how excited I was when he asked me to come along... we've been friends for years... but this is my first overseas trip for the magazine, isn't it Pete?'

Magazine? Clare's throat went dry. *What an amazing coincidence! But I don't believe in coincidences*... Was there, she wondered, some important reason why she had met these people?

Bobbie was rushing on without confirmation from Pete. 'And I just loved London! Everyone we met was so gentle and kind to us. We had a lot of fun, and did all the big sights—you know, Big Ben, Westminster Abbey—' (she said the word

'Westminister', as Clare's cousins always did), 'Trafalgar Square, Oxford Street—oh, you know—all that stuff. Oh, so much to see! History everywhere! I do hope we come again. And in between all that, we were half hoping—or, Pete was, I think—' she threw him another look, 'to meet someone in particular.'

'Ahah,' Clare at last intervened, 'now we get to the hook in the story!'

Pete looked sidelong at her, with a slight frown. Was he guessing that her own work was similar to theirs? Had she given the game away, saying that it was her job to be nosy?

Bobbie had not noticed her particular choice of the word 'hook' and gushed on, 'Yes, we—I mean, Pete—had to be over in the UK anyway for some—er, well perhaps I'd better not say too much. Anyway, he lined up a list of interviews, and we flew out about ten days ago. But I guess it's no secret he had a hunch we might find someone for a special job while we were there. Oh, it's been such a good time.'

Clare saw Bobbie's eyes soften, but Pete's face was grim. Clare wondered if she had said more than he wanted her to. In a level voice, he said, 'Well, Bobbie, no, I'm not sure I agree.'

Bobbie looked as if someone had taken away a present just given to her. Completely deflated, she sank back in her seat so that Clare could no longer see her face behind Pete's wide shoulders.

Pete took up the story himself. 'As far as I'm concerned, Clare—' he used her name for the first time, and his eyes rested insolently on her mouth, so that she began to hate him. 'As far as I'm concerned, the trip has been an utter waste of time and cash. We got our interviews and pics OK—no problem—but my other agenda called for . . . well, we didn't find the person we needed, even if we did see a whole lot of London.' He grimaced. 'I guess I'd seen most of it before, anyway.'

Quite involuntarily, Clare drew a sudden breath. His insensitivity to Bobbie's enthusiasm was almost cruel. She decided to be as cool as she knew how to be. 'Too bad, Mr—er—'

'McEnroe. Peter McEnroe, but you can call me Pete.' He did not offer his hand, and she wouldn't have taken it if he had. Instead he gave her another insolent look that made her want to slap him. She deliberately adjusted her position and turned her back on him to look out of the window. When she turned around later—longing to sleep herself—both Pete and Bobbie were asleep. Their heads were bent together, his fair hair mingling with her dark curls. In sleep he had lost the Casanova look and seemed strangely vulnerable.

She turned again and sank into a shallow sleep. When she woke, Bobbie and Pete were having a perfectly ordinary conversation over two trays of airline dinner. Before making it clear that she was awake, she lay still and listened. Their voices were soft, like those of familiar husbands and wives, or colleagues long used to talking together and working out differences. She was surprised.

'I think she is,' Pete was saying.

'You could be right,' Bobbie acknowledged, 'but I don't think so. At least, if she is, she wasn't giving it away at all. She could have said something when we mentioned *Citizen*, couldn't she?'

Clare heard laughter in Pete's tone as he answered, 'Yes, if she could have got a word in edgeways, sweetheart!'

'Oh—Pete—' Bobbie sighed. 'I wish I'd heard what you told me she said about her uncle dying and all. I probably wouldn't have chattered on as much as I did.'

'No?' His soft answer was dry but affectionate.

'Poor woman. She's lovely,' Bobbie said, 'but she sure looks shattered.'

Clare sat up, and they stopped abruptly.

'You're awake,' Bobbie said brightly. 'How about a meal? We just got ours, and the stewardess said to buzz her when you woke, if you wanted any.'

When her meal came, any previous tension between them seemed to melt away. Rather than waiting for questions they might now feel unable to ask, Clare volunteered her own tale.

'I work for a magazine as well,' she said, carefully watching their expressions. 'I'm a journalist. I've had a contract with *Women Today* for almost six years now. That's not why I'm flying out now, as I told you. But it's a big part of my life. That's what I meant when I said it was my job to be nosy.'

When she stopped, she caught some sort of a signal flashing between Pete and Bobbie. A warning? A question? She could not be certain, and she waited. Bobbie's face was transformed with frank delight, while Pete's had lost its mobile, intent expression and had assumed some sort of mask. She could not guess why.

'That's good news, Clare,' he said. His eyes were serious and direct, but she wasn't sure she trusted him. 'The fact is that . . .' He hesitated, and she could see him holding some kind of internal debate with himself before he went on. 'I needed to find a new society columnist pretty badly. We went to London, like she said, on the pretext of some interviews that our features editor couldn't handle because she's going on maternity leave any time. But we didn't manage to set up a columnist for the magazine, as I'd hoped.' He shrugged.

She couldn't cope with the hints in his words and deflected him swiftly. 'Which places did you try?'

Quickly he named a network of agencies and magazines she knew—groups where he should not have been 'headhunting' but should surely have found the talent and skills he sought. Or *evidently* sought—if indeed she could believe the story at all. No editor she knew would be so open about headhunting among other magazines—especially not overseas. His story didn't quite ring true.

'And still no joy?'

'No.'

She took a mouthful and spent as long as possible chewing it. She did not want to hear any more. She was going for a funeral, not a job interview.

In the end, Pete broke the silence by pulling out a business card. 'Listen, that's where I am. If you're ever interested, I'd like to talk with you about the column. Just give me a call.'

She hesitated, looking across at Bobbie, who was closely

watching her face for signs of interest. 'I—er—thank you.' She took the card. 'Thanks, but I don't think so. I would be a pretty long shot for you.'

Pete nodded at Bobbie in some kind of cue, and Bobbie smiled winningly at her. 'Just think about it, okay?'

Clare could make no sense of anything. In response to Pete's rudeness, she had been equally rude in return. They wouldn't want her around, surely? And she was tied to *Women Today*, to her cousins, and to Aunt Rita. Writing a column for a Boston magazine was a ridiculous idea.

'Just think about it, anyhow,' Bobbie repeated. Pete nudged her again, this time harder, and she added, 'Clare, listen, we can talk about this some more later if you want, but how about you give us your card, too?'

Again she hesitated. Pete was playing a clever game, using Bobbie to get what he wanted: apparently already aware of her own wariness towards him. And if Bobbie had been alone, she knew she wouldn't have held back; there was still something in Pete's now smooth face that unnerved and unsettled her—though nothing she could give a name to.

'No,' she said at last, her voice measured, 'no, I can't see that you need my card. Thanks, though. I'm flattered. But I'll only be here a short while. There are things to get back for, and my relatives in Boston will need me all the time I'm over there.'

Even as she said this, she knew she wasn't speaking the whole truth. Rita would far rather have had her mother there, and in the Blackfriars office the other writers could cope quite well for weeks on end without her. She had often wished she could work for a while in America. So why was she turning from such a chance now?

She slid the card into a pocket of her handbag. Trapped by the window, she could not escape her seat, but she wasn't going to be pushed by Pete McEnroe. Especially when she saw the relief on Bobbie's face as she refused to discuss the job. Bobbie, she saw clearly, wanted Pete to herself.

16

The late June heat continued unabated into July. In their office, Clare, Nina and the others sweltered and grumbled, but during lunch-times when they were able to slip outside and lie in the park—just a few hundred yards from the revolving doors of the office—they were glad of the bright weather.

Clare wondered laughingly during the second week in July whether the shimmering heat was somehow making the freelance journalists who worked away from the office even more prolific than usual. Copy rolled like a landslide across the desk of Dave, the features editor. The weekly conferences she had with Dave and Andy, the editor, lasted longer than usual.

'Am I imagining it,' she asked Nina early one afternoon, 'or is there more work than ever?'

Nina groaned. 'More, I'm sure.'

'We'll never get through all this.'

'You're too conscientious, Clare, that's the trouble. Most of the other writers in this place leave so much to the subs.'

'Rubbish!' someone else shouted from the other side of the room.

'Rubbish, anyone? Here you are!' Clare wadded a piece of paper into a ball and threw it with a laugh at the protester. 'Oh, Nina! You're just as bad as I am. You do at least half the researchers' work as well as your own.'

'Yes. You never know when you might turn up some little gem of a story amid the dross of these cuttings.'

'Yuk. You need a break. Clichés already, and it's only half-past two.'

Nina rustled some wrappings into the overflowing bin and studied a thin sheaf of white, A4 papers. She was quiet for a moment, and Clare stopped to watch her.

'Something good?'

'Hmm—I don't know yet. It's come down from Coventry—that story we asked for about the woman whose child was abducted, then brought back safe after all.'

Clare went back to her own press cuttings: telephoning, thinking, making notes as she worked, and wishing as usual that the magazine had more of a budget for secretarial help. Then she heard a murmur from Nina and turned. 'What?'

'Clare, the rewrite's come out really well.' She passed Clare the papers.

Child abuse was always in the news these days, Clare reminded herself as she began to read. It sickened her, but this abduction story was a little different—so moving that she knew instantly Dave would want it for the magazine. 'Yes,' she said, when she'd finished reading it, 'there's still some work to be done, on the psychological angle. It *is* good, though.' She thought for a moment. 'But the mother will find it a real strain seeing everything in full colour in a women's magazine—and we don't want to exploit her.'

'You wouldn't, Clare.'

'I hope not. But the magazine might, now that there's been a criminal charge.'

Nina was still watching her. Clare turned the story over in her mind again. 'You're frowning,' Nina laughed. 'That looks promising. Such concentration!'

Clare was trying to recall two newspaper reports she had read some weeks before. Details eluded her, but she knew they were to do with other abduction cases that sounded similar. The masthead of the paper came suddenly into sharp focus in her mind. '*The Daily Telegraph*!' She exclaimed. 'Nina, that was it. But it was two weeks ago, I think.'

Nina shook her head. 'Sorry, I'm about five steps behind. What was?'

'A couple of articles about another abduction, something like this. Just after I came back from Liverpool, I think it was; I didn't have time to look properly at the press while I was up there, but I remember there was an issue of *The Telegraph* some time that first week back in London.' She reached for the telephone. 'I'll get Valerie to bring down the cuttings.'

Dave suddenly appeared between her desk and Nina's, and Clare replaced the phone without having made the call. 'Clare, can you drop everything and come over to my office for a moment? There was something in the last conference—'

He gave Nina an inscrutable look and was out of the room again before Clare could answer. She followed him reluctantly, making faces at one of the other writers by the door and muttering, 'No wonder we never get finished before seven!'

'Still alive?' Nina asked when Clare returned.

'Yes—it was just a note someone had made on the third issue in August—he couldn't work it out himself . . . well, where were we?'

'The abduction story.'

Clare pushed her hand through her hair. 'Oh yes.' There was something important she'd been about to do to follow up that story, but whatever it was now escaped her. She frowned, and Nina smiled encouragingly. 'Oh—yes, Nina, I think you'd better sort out another interview with the mother on the psychological angle. I'm not sure the story so far has quite enough of that, but it's almost there. I like it, as I said.'

Nina's face turned pink with pleasure. 'Yes—are you sure you don't want to do that yourself?'

'No, this one's yours.' She smiled. 'Oh, this could be excellent! But we'll have to talk more with Dave, of course. Soon . . . and can you get some trannies done as well?'

'If the story attracts a lot of attention,' Nina suddenly interposed, her face thoughtful, 'we might even help some other families get their children back.'

Clare sighed. She had had dreams of that kind in her early days at the magazine—dreams that even some of the mundane work she did might one day benefit someone beyond the concrete and glass of King's Reach Tower. 'Oh, Nina, that would be wonderful. Let's hope you're right.'

She turned back to her cuttings and heard Nina making

notes in preparation for her call to the freelance journalist in Coventry. She decided to leave her alone while she placed the call. 'Listen, I'll go round to Sarah's desk for a bit with this pile. I don't suppose she's back from lunch yet. That'll leave you in peace.' Nina looked up in surprise. 'All right, then. We'll put any calls through.'

'I'm not expecting any, but thanks.'

As if on cue, the telephone rang twice as soon as she had sat down in the next office. It was cooler, less crowded than her own corner, and once she had dealt with the calls she settled down more easily to the latest story.

Then the telephone rang for the third time. 'For you again,' the secretary told her. 'Sorry, should I block the calls?'

Clare sighed. 'No, better not. Who is it?'

'A Mr Bernard. Frank Bernard.'

Clare felt her face turn scarlet, even in the coolness. She tried to take in what the secretary was saying about the call, to pick up what was left of her scattered wits and listen. Frank was waiting for her, somewhere on the line.

'He wouldn't tell me whatever it is he has to say. Insisted on speaking with you. Says he's sent a piece in—marked to you personally for some reason. And he's worried you might not have got it.' Clare groaned helplessly. 'Oh, dear, has anyone binned any unsolicited stuff lately? Oh—and did he say what it looked like?'

'Clare? Whatever's the matter? This happens all the time. Wouldn't you rather I told him to get lost?'

'No!' She said it too fast. 'No—put him through, please.'

She sat utterly still and unable to see anything around her, so intent was she on this one moment. She gave up trying to make sense of the secretary's message. *A manuscript from Frank Bernard for* Women Today? *But how, what—?*

It was his voice speaking to her. The voice she had tried to recall for more than two weeks. Her breathing shortened until she felt as if she were running in a race. A race she was losing to a pursuer. A race she did not mind losing.

'Miss Hogarth?'

She heard doubt and hesitation in his voice. 'Yes,' she answered, the same doubt in her own voice. Her body was full of lightning, and she had to shut her eyes and grip the telephone hard, or she felt she would have disappeared into white light. Her voice sounded completely unreal to her.

'I've tried to talk to you before.' He began to gather momentum, and she was happy to let him talk. 'I don't know if you remember, but we met just over two weeks ago. Had a conversation on our way south . . . at a motorway service station.'

'*I don't know if you remember,*' she thought, wanting to laugh with delight as she listened to the slight roll of Somerset 'r's in his voice. 'Yes,' she managed, trying to get control of herself, 'I do remember.'

His voice changed. 'You're the motorway philosopher.'

She laughed aloud, and some of her nervousness dissolved. 'And you're the detective inspector.'

For some unaccountable reason, he laughed, too. 'Yes, and I want to talk to you.'

She had found her wits. 'Oh, am I wanted in connection with a heinous motorway crime, is that it? You should have arrested me then, surely, while the evidence was hot.'

'Hmm. Theft, I think. That's what I'll do you for.'

He sounded altogether too serious, and she swallowed hard. 'Theft?' Her voice rose to a squeak.

'Yes, I'll explain all about it later. But there's a little matter of an article I sent in. A story, really. Sorry I was a little slow, but it took me a while to track you down. Then I realized what you meant about "women today", and I decided it was time to launch my investigations into the literary world.'

Clare twisted the phone cord around her fingers, smiling and smiling. 'Oh, just like that? But I didn't think I mentioned *Women Today* to you. And we don't get many submissions from men, let alone men we haven't commissioned . . .'

'Well, and have you read what I sent you?'

She burst into laughter, strung so tight that it was hard to stop. Finally, she said, 'Oh, if only you could see the work we've got now you'd know why I haven't read your story yet. But I will. If I ever find it.'

'Great! Such efficiency sounds commendable.'

She knew she needed to calm down, and she decided suddenly to pour cold water on everything, as much for her own sake as for his. 'And if I do find it,' she improvised, 'I may have to give it to one of my colleagues to read, I'm afraid. As I said, we don't take unsolicited stories.'

'Even so, giving it to a colleague might not be such a good idea.' He was laughing.

She did not know how to answer, and waited for him.

'I marked it for you. I was hoping—as I tried to tell you on the phone before . . .'

Tell me on the phone before? She frowned, rubbing the side of her face. *When?* Surely he had never phoned her before!

'I was hoping we could meet and chat again. About the story, this time . . . of course. Is that quite out of the question? Listen, here's my number, if you've got a pen there—'

Clare stopped chewing her biro and wrote down the number. She could not believe what she was hearing.

This time, he was waiting for her, so she said, 'I'm glad you rang me. I'll find your manuscript. And I will read it. And if you like—' She broke off, breathless, and annoyed with her obvious excitement. Then she realized with a catch in her breath that she had not actually answered the question about meeting him, but she did not know how to bring the talk back to that loose end. An important loose end.

He too seemed hesitant. After a moment, he said, 'You— you do live in London, don't you?'

She wanted to give him her own phone number, but something stopped her. After all, she told herself, she'd met him only once, under completely artificial circumstances. *I've got to stop thinking of him so much.* Even so, a slow warmth was spreading through her as they talked.

'In Barking, isn't it?' he pursued.

She was caught off balance. 'What? Oh, no. I left home

years ago.' *How does he know . . .?* 'No, I live in Ealing.' An internal alarm sounded, and for a moment she stopped doodling on the paper next to his phone number. *He's been doing his detective bit and finding out all about me.* She felt suddenly very unsure that she should pursue the conversation any further, and the inner warmth vanished into a careful neutrality which she knew would come across in her voice. She added, 'It's a long way from Bristol to London, you know.'

'Are you sure?' She found she could not answer him and felt torn two ways.

'Look, I'm not often in London, but I'd like to see you again when I do get up there. What do you say?'

She took a deep breath and did not allow herself to think about the answer or about how she would feel afterwards. 'I—er—thank you. Thanks, but I don't think so. Bristol to London would be a long shot for both of us.'

As she replaced the receiver, her hand closed on the notepad beside her where she had written his telephone number. What had she done now?

17

I must have been mad, I told myself after I sent off the story, to think I could write anything more complicated than a report for the governor. I'm no writer, and Clare surely isn't the kind of person who would help publish anything just for personal preference—if indeed she feels any. She didn't give much away when I called her at the office. But perhaps she was too surprised. And she said, didn't she, that she hadn't found time to read the story yet?

I'd kept a copy of it, and I kept looking at it and finding things I would have changed or rewritten. 'Never mind the story,' I confided to my new diary that night, 'The story is just an excuse. I'll ring her at home one day . . . when I have the nerve and the time.'

In fact, there was too little time altogether to think much about Clare. Detective Superintendent Bill Longley and I had some house-to-house enquiries going on in Bristol.

'I feel pretty uptight about this abduction case,' I told Charlie one evening after work when we'd gone out for a drink together.

'I'm not surprised,' he said. 'We all do. It's cross-border, as well.'

I stared into my beer. 'Yes, and we've both got more responsibility than usual.'

'That worries you?'

'Of course it does. I seem to spend most of my time thinking about the children.'

'Me too. Let's pray abduction doesn't turn into murder—or worse.' Charlie looked grim.

I shuddered. 'Right. It's the usual agony, isn't it? We may be missing something so obvious it's already staring us in the face.'

Charlie shrugged, a movement barely perceptible in such a big frame. 'Who knows?'

'And another thing—I'd love to know for sure if what's been happening in Warwicks and West Midlands and down here is all connected.' I found I was frowning. 'I'm haunted by the thought that whatever we do we won't be acting at the right speed.'

'Yeah. If we go too slowly,' Charlie agreed with a nod, 'the families will be complaining of negligence and indifference—and rightly. But, if we go too fast, we always run the risk of chasing off in false directions.'

'And perhaps missing further abductions behind our backs, or wasting time running surveillance in the wrong places.'

We fell into a meditative silence, sipping our drinks. I began to see a parallel between the conundrum Charlie and I faced at work, and the puzzle I had with Clare.

'Penny for them?' Charlie prompted me.

I didn't meet his eye. 'Ah, I was just thinking of someone.'

'Missing her?'

'Who says "her"?'

'Your face, mate.'

I laughed. 'Well, you've been trying to weasel my story out of me ever since I was in Birmingham. I'm so fed up with going in circles over those children I'm almost tempted to tell you.'

He gave me his broadest smile. 'Go on, then.'

'I was thinking I've got the same problem twice over,' I began. 'If I go too slowly, she won't know I like her. If I go too fast, I'll drive her away—if I haven't already.' Unhappily I remembered her cool words, 'Bristol to London would be a long shot for both of us.'

'Sounds very original, Frank.'

'I never claimed it was an original problem, did I?'

'Aren't you going to tell me all the details? Where you met her, what she looks like. Come on, I haven't got all night.' He was teasing, grinning at me. 'It's a sacrifice, you know, spending part of an evening in the pub with you when I could be off home with my wife.'

'Listen, then,' I said—and told him all about Clare.

He reacted the way I'd guessed he would. 'Frank, you make me laugh.'

I took a long swallow of beer. 'Why?'

'All these days of mystery since you came back from Birmingham. What's the big deal, huh? You're only telling me about a *girl*.'

I gave him a mock scowl. 'Hasn't anyone—your wife especially—ever told you about the word "girl", Charlie?'

He glowered back and grunted irritably.

'And anyway,' I went on, 'You of all people have spent years joshing me about not making up my mind about my choice of a *woman*. Now I begin to think I have, you shrug and say "only a woman".'

'Then what's the big deal, Frank?'

I cast about in my mind. For all our banter, I'd known and worked with Charlie too long to want to play games with him, and I knew he'd have some kind of encouragement. 'I don't know if it's a big deal, really, but there's something I'd like to work out, if I could.'

He was giving me his full attention. 'Try me, then.'

I wanted to look him straight in the eye but found I couldn't. 'Pride, I suppose. I've procrastinated so long I hardly know how to go ahead when I meet someone I *do* like and want to know better.' I turned my glass round and round so that it made a pattern of wet circles on the beer mat. 'But it's more complicated than that.'

'Always is.'

'No, I don't mean like that. I mean that I've prided myself on being cool and objective, not quick to make snap decisions.'

Charlie threw back his head in a big laugh that shook his belly. 'Oh, you're a riot, you are! That doesn't sound like you at all! You're making snap decisions now—every day—in front of the database. Some of them are bound to lead us somewhere, right? And the prisons would be three-quarters empty if CID blokes didn't at least start with snap decisions. You know how it is—if I don't like the way someone got his hair cut, or the shape of his face; if my gut tells me all's not well—' I opened my mouth to argue, but he held up his hand. 'No, you know I'm right. OK, so when we get those gut feelings we all probe deeper, even if—maybe especially if—things look fine on the outside. But isn't that what it's all about? To start with, I mean? Snap decisions, like the one you made about this woman the first time you spoke to her?'

Listening to Charlie, I wanted to be convinced. I found I was far more frustrated about not being able to get through to Clare than I'd allowed myself to realize.

'And this time,' he pursued, 'all that's happening is that instead of a bad gut feeling about someone you have a positive feeling about this gir—woman. That's all.'

'I did, anyway, until she gave me the brush-off when I called the magazine.'

'Hey, cheer up, will you? Any truth in the rumour that you're the real Problem Petronella for *Women Today*?'

'What!'

'When will we see you on the problem page, Auntie Frances?'

I gave him a shove, but his big body was as immovable as ever on the stool where he sat.

'Maybe she doesn't like phones. You said she was abrupt when you phoned her in Barking, didn't you?'

There was some comfort in that thought. 'Yes, you could be right, though I doubt if someone working on a magazine would get far without a good phone manner. Anyway, where do I go from here?'

'Maybe you should write her another letter. Maybe she's the Problem Petronella herself.'

I laughed. 'I doubt it. And she's got my letter anyhow—all two thousand words of the story spelling out my heartache.' I clutched my left side, so Charlie would know I wasn't taking the whole thing as seriously as it sounded—or as seriously as I *was* taking it.

'Or you could take out a subscription for the magazine in the name of the nick.'

'Nick Who?' I said lamely.

'Feeble, Frank! You've really got a bad case, haven't you?'

I threw up my hands. 'Looks like it, Charlie. I'm tired of watching you and Nigel having all the good times in life and being a spectator.'

Charlie scoffed. 'You! The Bristol disco copper himself! Hah! You're Barking mad, you are! What you need is a nice trip to London to find her and make her listen to sense. She can keep you miles away when you're just a voice on the phone, but wait till she sees your smiling face, Sunshine. The irresistible DI Bernard himself—in the flesh.'

'I should be so lucky!'

'Well, what are you waiting for? Where did you say that story was now?'

'With her, as far as I know.'

'Well, then. Why not go and fetch it back, if she's turned it down?'

'Go to London for a day in the middle of this case? Don't be daft! Anyway, the story's probably already coming back to me in the post, if she hasn't tossed in the bin by now. I'd make an utter fool of myself.'

Charlie just grinned back. 'Did you say "*make*" an utter fool of yourself?'

I drank some more beer and considered the implications. 'Maybe I will go,' I said slowly.

18

'We won't keep you waiting long, Ms Hogarth,' the receptionist told her brightly. 'Mr McEnroe should be finished with his meeting any time now.'

Clare nodded and tucked her handbag under her arm. Even in the air-conditioned coolness of the Boston high-rise, her linen suit made her feel overdressed. She knew her cheeks were bright pink.

'Do take a seat, Ms Hogarth.' The words were more of an instruction than an invitation, and Clare felt like a schoolgirl going to her first job interview. Did Peter McEnroe have this effect on everyone he spoke to about a job? She clutched a well-thumbed back issue of *Women Today* to herself; she had brought it to illustrate the kind of writing she did best.

'You'd like a cup of coffee?' the receptionist was saying, her eyebrows arched in amused enquiry.

'Mmm? Yes—well, no. A drink of water would be better. Thanks.'

Hiding her hot face behind a conical paper cup full of iced water, and sitting now behind a bank of philodendra in the reception area, Clare frowned to herself. *What on earth am I doing here?* She stared unseeingly at the thick crimson carpet and lost herself in visions of the last two weeks.

Was it Rita Williams, her aunt, who had tipped the balance of persuasion that had begun to swing away from London two weeks before? Rita had been so pleased to see her in time for the funeral. At once Clare had been taken into the family as if she had never been away. All the largesse of the last few visits was renewed. No stinting because the household was grieving; no stinting because her mother could not, would not come for the funeral; no stinting because she was a niece rather than a daughter. Rita instead went on giving as much love and welcome to her as if Uncle Bert were still alive to join her in that welcome, and for the first few days she felt as if she had fallen into a warm bath. Rita wanted her to stay longer, and already she had twice put off the return home. 'You've got an open return flight, I thought you said,' Rita had reminded her. 'Why not stay a while longer?'

Or was it her cousins, Jack, Ed, and Marie, who had most influenced her? Two evenings after Uncle Bert's funeral, they had driven her up to the North Shore.

'Mom needs to be by herself sometimes, you know,' Jack had said.

'We'll build a fire at the top of the beach and barbecue some steaks,' Marie agreed. 'Then you can tell us all about England and Aunt Edie.'

'And we'll talk you into staying longer, just see if we don't,' Ed added, grinning in that shy little-boy way that melted her heart but didn't fool her for one moment. Did they always speak so fast, in alternating lines like the chorus of a Greek comedy? she wondered. No, she decided, the novelty of her presence in the house, of her English accent and English mannerisms, would soon wear off. Rita would return to her work in the family's marina office and out in the harbour; Jack would drive back to his job in Springfield; Marie would go back to spending time with her teenage friends, and Ed would pull out his fishing tackle and renew his annual summer break from college by going bass fishing farther up the coast. If she stayed, she would be alone, at a loss, and once again a tourist rather than part of a family. Then there was her job in England. *What about that?*

But for the first two weeks after the funeral, at least, her cousins still wanted her as part of the family.

'Listen,' Ed argued, 'we couldn't even show you a good time on July Fourth this year—not with the funeral and all— so for goshsakes let's do a barbecue one night. C'mon, fair Clare. "Yes" is such an easy little word to say.'

'Oh, you're full of it! You're awful. Those poor undergrad girls don't stand a chance.'

'We call them "co-eds"—co-*ED*'s,' Marie laughed. 'Ed the girl-chaser. Look out Clare, your own cousin as well.'

'Too young,' Clare laughed. 'Don't worry, Ed, you're safe.'

Jack, more serious than the other two, insisted, 'Never mind all the sweet talk, Clare. We want you to stay a while. We can make plans on the beach.'

And so they did. It was the summer treat she had longed for but not expected in the family now so uncharacteristically subdued by her uncle's death. It was a night she would remember for a long time to come. In the end, with phosphorescent creatures glowing just below the tide line in the wet sand (Marie had called them 'diamond dust' as a little girl), and with the first cold stars echoing them in the utter darkness of the ocean's eastern sky, she found herself telling her cousins about her flight: about Peter McEnroe and Bobbie.

They listened in complete silence. At last, Ed said, 'I've never heard of a magazine called *Citizen*, though that's not surprising since I never read magazines.'

'But the name of McEnroe is one to conjure with—if he's any relation,' Jack said. 'I've read *Citizen* for a long time—it's a sort of hard-hitting review magazine—social and political stuff. But I never thought about the McEnroe connection.'

Clare sat forward in the sand, pulled her jacket more closely round her shoulders, and linked her hands around her knees. 'Any relation to whom? Tell me about him.'

'You mean Senator McEnroe?' Marie turned her face towards her brother's, and Clare saw in the faint moonlight how pretty her cousin was.

'The very one,' Jack answered.

'Wait a minute, Jack.' Ed put a hand on his sleeve. 'There must be a hundred McEnroes in the phone-book.'

'Probably are.' Jack shrugged.

'But one of them's special?' Clare asked.

'Yes. Senator McEnroe. He's a Democrat. Much loved by some people, and feared by quite a few. He's a prosecution lawyer, and he doesn't lose too many cases. He was up for district court judge, but they passed over him for a Republican. Still, people in Massachusetts think highly of him. He's done a lot of work for the inner city over the last twenty years or so.'

'Yeah, Jack's right—cleaning up the dope peddlers and setting up rehab clinics for addicts. He's a prime candidate for a knife in the back from some quarters, but he's got so many friends that it may never come to that. And he's old now—very old.'

Clare smiled. 'How old is "very old", Ed? You probably think I'm "old", don't you? ... On second thoughts, don't answer that.'

They sat still for a moment, listening to the wash of waves fifty feet below them on the harder, ridged sand. Then Jack said, 'There was a story, maybe fifteen or twenty years ago, about Julius McEnroe. Maybe this Pete of yours—or not of yours, Clare—is his son. I was just a little kid, but I heard the grown-ups talk about it. The senator had a daughter—a son, maybe, I'm not sure. She—or he—was found dead in mysterious circumstances. But I've no idea if the story's true. Too many "maybes".' He spread his hands. 'Well, it doesn't matter. Probably no connection at all. But if this Pete of yours is a relation, watch him. If he's anything like the old senator, he's a man worth watching.'

Yes, Clare thought wryly. *Definitely worth watching.* But then, as a cloud shadow fell over the moon, she thought of her mother, and her smile faded. 'It's a tempting prospect—working at *Citizen*, I mean.'

Jack's eyes glinted. 'But—? You're going to say "but".'

'But there's Mum ... by herself.'

'She's been by herself for a long time, though, hasn't she?' Ed suggested mildly. 'I thought you said Ealing was miles from Barking and you hardly saw her?'

Clare nodded. 'Ye-es. Yes, but I'd just been thinking, especially now your father's dead, that I should do much more for her than I do. Be with her more ...'

'Would she want that?' Ed asked sharply. 'Really?'

'I'm not sure.'

Marie giggled. 'I'm sure Aunt Edie's sweet, and all, but wouldn't Mr McEnroe be much more fun for a while?'

'The man worth watching,' Jack chipped in again.

A man worth watching, Clare repeated to herself, remembering. *Yes, worth watching, and watching out for.*

She could not forget the way Pete's eyes had raked over her on the plane. Nor could she put out of her mind the unexpected welcome in the secretary's voice when she had finally been persuaded by her cousins to telephone Pete's office and ask for an appointment. 'The job will be gone, or it'll be one I can't possibly do,' Clare told them. 'Try anyway,' Marie had urged her. And then the secretary had sounded so encouraging that she felt Pete must have alerted her to the possibility that she would call. Half of her was warmed by his optimism, but half of her feared it was cold calculation.

And now here she was, sitting in the reception area outside his offices. *What am I doing here?*

Women Today seemed many more than three thousand miles away; her friendship with Nina and the weekly grind of scouring papers, checking and following up stories seemed to belong to someone in another life. Not even the daily phone-calls to her mother brought London any nearer, especially now that some of the sharpness of her mother's grief was abating, and even her mother had joined her aunt and cousins in encouraging her to stay longer.

Did she want to enter similar work here, instead? She knew the routines, after all, and perhaps the novelty of different people, a different city, and different projects would sustain her for a few months while she discovered what it was really like to work in America. The change would be good, and she'd have more (she reasoned) to offer *Women Today* on her return (assuming, of course, that her job would still be open).

Suddenly, a long pair of expensively tailored trouser-legs obscured her out-of-focus vision of the carpet. She looked up sharply, then jumped up.

'Nice to see you, Ms Hogarth.' The mask was in place, Pete's manner polished and urbane. He held out his hand.

She shook it—a grip as firm as she would have expected, but far cooler than her own hot hand. His eyes burned blue into hers, and in a rush she remembered the magnetism and the sense of danger she had felt on the plane.

'I'm glad you changed your mind and gave us a call.' He pointed the way through a set of fire doors to a long corridor that somehow reminded Clare of the standard hotel. 'Please come this way,' he said, 'and we'll have a nice long talk about how we might help each other.'

Bobbie came out of swing doors that were marked 'art department' to their right, saw her, waved, hesitated, then crossed to another set of doors. Clare thought her smile looked forced and had no trouble guessing why.

She followed Pete down the hushed corridor with a heavy sense of inevitability.

19

Clare had put Frank's story in her top drawer—saw it every morning as she opened her desk to start work—but did nothing about it. Frank had searched so diligently for her—that frightened her a little. She half wished that she had never spoken to him; the burst of joy she had felt in the first moments after she'd met him had vanished completely, replaced by unhappy misgivings, long rehearsals of their telephone conversation the week before, and more than one sleepless night.

After a week of trying to ignore the envelope, thinking but not deciding what she wanted to do about it, she finally took out the story first thing the following Tuesday and turned to Nina. So far no one else had arrived in the office, so she felt safe in the relative privacy and peace of early morning.

'You read this, Nina,' she said. 'This is one I don't want.'

Nina reached out for the A4 envelope. 'Why? Just too many at once?'

Quite deliberately Clare began to sift the cuttings for the first story she would be working on that morning. 'No, it's not that,' she said slowly. 'It's because I've met the person who sent it in, and I don't think I want to handle it—that's all.'

Nina looked blank. 'You've read it, then? It's worth sending over for Dave to see?'

'I don't know, and I haven't read it.' Clare knew she sounded unreasonable, almost petulant. 'No, I'd rather you read that one, if you don't mind.'

'Sure—I'll be glad to.'

Clare could not bring herself to turn around again and show her face to Nina. With a sense of doom she waited for the exclamation of recognition from Nina's desk.

Sure enough, before she'd read more than two pages of the

paper in front of her, Nina had swung round in her chair and was giggling. 'Clare? Clare! What *are* you up to?'

She flushed and reluctantly half-turned in her chair. 'Nothing at all.'

'But this is from that man you met, isn't it? Frank Bernard—that was his name, wasn't it? And didn't he ring you last week, as well?'

'Yes.' She shrugged, her face burning. 'I don't want to talk about it.' She turned back to her desk but couldn't read one word of the page in front of her.

For fifteen minutes their corner of the room was quiet. Even the telephones had not begun; the only sound came from the intermittent rustling of paper as page after page of Frank's story was turned over on Nina's desk.

When eventually Nina cleared her throat and sat back, Clare discovered she had been so distracted that she had doodled an elaborate leaf design on the side of the article she was supposed to be reading. She groaned.

'Clare?'

'What?' She didn't move.

'You do know what this is, do you?'

Something in her snapped. 'Yes, of course!' she said sharply. 'It's a story from a man I met once in—'

'And haven't stopped thinking about.'

'So?'

Nina's eyes assessed her face calmly, a gleam in them. 'It isn't just any story, you know. Oh, Clare, he must be a most romantic and gorgeous man. It's a story of how he met you! You didn't tell me he's a writer. I thought you said he was a policeman.'

For a second, she could not take in what Nina said. Then she leaned forward and snatched the pages from her. She should have read Frank's story after all! 'Sorry. Oh, but this is crazy . . . And he *isn't* a writer.'

Her eyes jumped from one sentence to the next. Phrases she recognized and had repeated to herself many times since—phrases he had used to her when they met on the

131

bridge—leapt at her from the paper. Her face was radiating, and she did not know whether to laugh or lose her temper.

In the end she handed the story back to Nina and covered her face. 'I can't finish it. I more or less told him last week not to expect anything from me. So if the story's worth anything at all, I'll have to leave it all to you. I don't want anything to do with it. He isn't one of our writers—Dave didn't commission it, of course. So wouldn't it be better if we told him to send it to another magazine? As a piece of writing, it's not up to much, is it? But, Nina, if you really think—'

'Clare, I don't know. By the second page I knew something was familiar. Then I looked back at the name on the top . . . and I suddenly put two and two—'

'No more clichés, please!'

'Sorry. Oh . . . all right. I'll try to reread it as if I knew nothing about anything. He sounds so nice. Trust you to meet the man, not me! But if I had . . .'

Clare laughed. 'Oh, Nina! You're so sweet. If *you* had, love, you would have walked straight past him without listening to a word—as I should have done. You wouldn't have got yourself into such a scrape in the first place. And you certainly wouldn't have sent him a message afterwards, just to complicate matters even further.'

Nina sighed. 'No, I s'pose not. Ah well. You can let me inherit your cast-offs any time, Clare. I know you've got good taste.'

Frank's face swam up behind Clare's eyes, and something in her bristled. *What, jealousy?* she thought, and wondered. *Don't be daft, Clare!* 'Maybe, maybe not, Nina. Perhaps I should introduce you to Danny, though. He's much more your type.'

'Too late!' Nina crowed. 'He's all mine now, you said. Frank Bernard, love of my life, here I come. This is a fantastic tale, Clare. Or it will be when I've finished with it. No one will ever know it's about you. I'm sure I'll be taking it across to Dave.'

Clare felt as if she had been caught in her own net. She had rejected Frank, and she had delegated his story—and therefore the relationship, if the piece were ever published—to Nina. There was nothing she could do now. The story was—by default—Nina's to do whatever she liked with.

She stared back at the papers on her desk and heard Nina behind her leafing through Frank's story again. She felt foolish, disappointed, and confused.

Nina's phone rang, and she was so unable to concentrate now on her own work that she listened instead to everything Nina said.

'Yes . . . put the call through, please. Good morning! Yes, we did. Yes, we're so pleased with the story . . .' Nina's voice was bright and welcoming.

Was she speaking to Frank? The warm sound of his voice came back to Clare from the previous week. *What have I done?*

Nina went on, 'It's an excellent story. You went to a lot of trouble. David says we'll be printing it in a few weeks' time . . . we may get a—I'm sorry? Yes, of course we'll send her all the letters we get in response.'

Clare had been so absurdly convinced that Nina was speaking to Frank that she hardly heard Nina's precise words. But then the phrase 'we'll be printing it in a few weeks' impressed itself, and she realized that someone other than Frank must now be talking to Nina.

'I'll confirm all this in a letter to you . . .' Nina was saying. 'Today, if I can . . . Oh, have they? Well, thank you again—and I do hope we can help the family by printing the story.'

Hearing the words 'the family', Clare relaxed and waited for her to put down the phone. 'That was the freelance in Coventry about the little girl who was abducted. She was so pleased we're doing the story. She said the mother is still traumatized, even since they got the child back.'

Clare murmured in sympathy. Her own struggles were petty by comparison, and she felt ashamed of her lack of commitment to her work and to more important concerns than an idiotic interest in a man she didn't even know and had rebuffed anyway.

She dragged her mind back to what Nina had said and suddenly focused. 'Remember I was going to follow up some articles I thought I'd read in *The Telegraph*?' she asked. 'The ones about some other abductions?'

'Yes—I think so.'

'I got diverted that day, I'm afraid. But now I think I do want to know what's going on. If there are other cases in Coventry, someone somewhere would know. We might be able to run more than one story. Nina—I know this particular story is yours, but would you mind if I got in on the side of it and did some investigative digging for a while?'

Nina shook her head. 'Good idea. Do you have time?'

'No, but I'll find it somehow. And we'll keep it all under wraps, except for telling Andy, of course.'

Staring out of the window above her desk at the tops of the trees drooping in the heat along the river's edge, Clare decided that such a project would take her mind off Frank Bernard once and for all.

Especially if, at the end of it, at least one child were restored to her parents.

20

For the first weekend in several, I wasn't on call. The incident room would have to get on without me.

Staring out of the train at banks of nameless tall weeds on the edge of the tracks, I wondered about Nina Cottham. Would she look like Clare? And now that Clare wasn't looking after my story (so Nina had told me), did I really care whether the story was published in *Women Today*—or in any women's magazine, for that matter? After all, what was the story worth if it didn't melt her heart?

I began to hum an old BeeGees number: 'It's only words, and words are all I have to take your heart away,' but the two passengers facing me gave me funny looks, so I stopped and went back to the papers I'd set in front of me on the Pullman table.

My concentration didn't last long. In CID it's easy enough to concentrate—everything and everyone to do with the case is right to hand. But on the train . . .

We whooshed past a field of grey horses. They lifted their heads as we passed, spikes of grass hanging in mid-munch from between their teeth, their eyes alert and unafraid. Then the train curved round a bend, and they were gone.

Nina had sounded nice on the telephone. Younger and shyer than Clare, I thought: her voice bright and with the kind of unplaceable home counties accent Clare had as well—and shouldn't have, if she was from Barking. But was she? I still didn't know with absolute certainty.

When Nina first called my home number, Tim took the message, so I had to call her back. I was hoping—without knowing anything about the set-up in their office—that Clare herself might answer when I rang back, but the call was relayed by an anonymous secretary, and no voice in the background reminded me at all of Clare's. It seemed strange that Nina wanted to meet me so soon after I'd sent the story. I'd supposed, after all Clare had said, that the process was much longer and that I'd be lucky if I heard in months—if ever. A long shot, as Clare had said.

As it was, Nina was taken aback that I couldn't get to London during the weekdays or spare her any time if she came to Bristol, and I got the impression anyway that she was not senior enough to be gallivanting all around the country-side like Clare Hogarth or Frank Bernard. So we agreed on the last Saturday in July. And there I was—in a train packed with early holidaymakers already returning from the West Country—on my way to Paddington to see her. She would meet me in just over an hour for what she'd called an 'editorial meeting'.

'How will I know you among all the thousands on Padd-ington Station?' I'd asked her. She had paused. 'Well—'

'Go on,' I told her. 'If you're a journalist and can't even describe yourself to me, who would want to read anything you've written?'

She laughed, then, a light, bell-like laugh that made me smile in return. 'I'm short. I wear glasses—'

'Come on!' I interrupted. 'You'll have to do better than that for the police line-up, you know. I suppose you have three warts on your nose and teeth like a rabbit's. Your hair's a thick black thatch tinted with vermilion highlights. Oh—and I almost forgot—you've got five earrings in each ear. Or maybe in just one.'

She laughed again, only this time she sounded embar-rassed. 'No. I'm blonde.'

Not like Clare, then. I sighed.

'But don't get excited—' (She must have misunderstood my sigh. Not a pavlovian response to the word 'blonde'; only a wish that she would be tall with waving red hair.) '—I'm the sort of person you wouldn't notice unless you fell over me on a staircase.'

I was just wondering how I should interpret that, and

136

whether she was really as unsure of herself as she sounded, when she brought me down to earth. 'I'll wait for you just outside the station entrance of the Great Western,' she said quietly. 'At noon—when your train gets in. Is that all right?'

I admit I couldn't resist launching into more banter. 'And with a red rose between your teeth and a rolled copy of *The Times* under your arm, yes?'

'Only if you like *The Times*,' she said, more quickly than I expected. 'Can't you buy it in sleepy old Bristol, then?'

Not so unsure, after all, I decided. 'Touché,' I answered. Then I added lamely, as an afterthought directed more at Clare than the woman on the other end of the line, 'I'll provide the red roses anyway.'

She rang off with more embarrassed laughter.

Now I nibbled the end of my pen and wondered if Clare would come to the station with Nina to meet me. Perhaps they shared a flat as well as an office. Somehow, I would find Clare—and not one but at least a dozen roses to lay at her feet.

I'd given myself the best part of two days to find her and had arranged to stay overnight with a friend. After I'd finished with Nina, I guessed I'd have most of Saturday evening and all of Sunday to see if I could find Clare at home. Would Nina help me? Was it even fair to ask her?

Avon went flashing past the window, then the edge of the Cotswolds. The soil changed from rich red-brown to duller grey-brown the farther east we came. The train was rushing on into cloudy fields, and as we neared Chippenham, rain began to fall in slanted needles across the landscape framed by the splattered windows of the train. A typical July day in the west of England. Friesian cows under weeping willows along the edge of a canal lifted their heads and remained motionless as we passed. Then, for a moment, the view was obscured as we shot past another train going in the same direction on a parallel track. Our wakes burst against each other, and the train was a blur of windows, doors, and multi-coloured paint. I wondered vaguely where the other train was going; who was on it, and why.

Soon the train was slowing for Reading, gravel quarries dotted with windsurfers marking the perimeter of the town, and gasometers the industrial band across its centre. *Only another twenty minutes or so,* I told myself, and stretched. But then, before I knew it, we were pulling into Paddington; I had fallen asleep.

In a daze I stepped off the train, only just remembering my umbrella, and went to a flower stall in the corner of the station before going to find Nina Cottham. The red roses I bought were to be (I soon discovered) one of the few successful things about the meeting.

Clearly, in spite of my warning, she wasn't expecting flowers. I identified that petite blonde by the hotel entrance as Nina immediately, because she paled as soon as she saw me carrying them towards her. Would I always frighten women, I wondered wistfully, then laughed at myself.

I shook her hand and looked into her worried face. She was eager to please, but very nervous. At first, I couldn't think why; after all, this was her home ground; this meeting was one she had requested. If anyone should be nervous, I should. So I thrust the roses at her in case she read my mind. I had intended to offer her one or two and tell her to take the rest to Clare. But how could I?

As we turned into the hotel I became aware of how tiny she was—how I dwarfed her—and how she probably needed to be protected from men like me. I also felt guilty. *You're using her, Frank Bernard,* I said to myself when we'd been facing each other in the hotel coffee lounge for a few moments. *Using her to help you get closer to Clare. Pathetic!*

She laid the roses reverently on the dark green carpet beside her small feet. I thought suddenly about Clare's size six-and-a-half feet. This was absurd!

We stumbled into a discussion about changes her boss wanted her to make to the story of my encounter with Clare. All the time she was talking to me, I was longing to ask her if Clare was OK, or if she was angry with me (and perhaps with Nina) for the story. Nina was still nervous, twisting a ring on her little finger and meeting my eyes with quick glances followed by pained withdrawal. Once we'd finished our discussion, I wanted nothing more than to escape as soon as I could. Nina looked troubled, anxious to smooth over the criticisms she'd made, to make light of everything, but too tongue-tied to get out the words I saw lurking in her shy eyes.

The reason for her nervousness suddenly occurred to me. She was meeting me on her own initiative; surely the magazine would never have sent her to meet me—an uncommissioned author (as Clare had so pointedly told me) on a Saturday. Especially when only one story was at issue. It suddenly occurred to me too that I was likely to hurt her if I expressed anything warmer than simple good manners.

'Listen,' I said finally, and picked up the roses again. 'These are for you, not Clare, OK? Just in case you were wondering.' I tried to summon all the sincerity I could into the smile I gave her next. 'You're obviously good at your job. I'm sure the story will be fine when you've polished it up for me. I'm delighted the magazine is printing it—and well—' What more could I say? If I had tried to use her help to find Clare that weekend—even if they did share a flat—I would have been more insensitive than I cared to be.

Her face cleared. I had convinced her, even if not myself. 'Thanks,' she said, her voice constricted. She stood to go and offered me her hand. The hand was to be shaken, but the hopeful eyes said more.

I felt terrible when she walked away: a sweet girl with a romantic heart. But she wasn't Clare Hogarth. If I was to meet Clare again, I resolved, it would not be by any contrived means that cost others pain. I would wait, and I would keep my eyes open.

The rest of the weekend proved to be a waste. Having lost the opportunity to get information from Nina, I dawdled around London without any sense of purpose or direction. It was too much to hope that I would meet Clare by happy coincidence, and I didn't.

I caught an earlier train home on Sunday than I had originally intended, by then frustrated with myself for sparing Nina's feelings and in the process damning myself to ignorance about Clare. My quest for her was fruitless, barring miracles I didn't believe in. Was it something called 'hope' that would keep me going? I tried again to concentrate on my file of notes, but couldn't. The passengers around me would, I decided, be far more appealing objects of observation.

For an instant I caught the eye of a woman passenger. She was diagonally opposite me, on the other side of the aisle. Something about her made me look a second time, a little longer than I should have looked. Her hair was the same colour as mine—dark, and crinkled in tight waves like mine. Her eyes, like mine, were blue, but there the resemblance ended. While hope would warm me at least a little longer, this woman was wrapped in misery so visible that it might have been a heavy grey sweater around her shoulders.

She sat hunched in the corner seat, arms folded, head slightly bent, but she looked neither out of the window nor (except for the uneasy glance in my direction) at the other passengers. Beside her a listless child of about four dozed, fretted, or—like her mother—stared into middle distance.

Something in the dark, unhappy eyes of the child reminded me of Damian, the brother I had lost. She sat with her thumb in her mouth, her eyes unblinking and roaming all around the carriage. Her skin was dull and her arms as slack and thin as willow wands. I had to look away, as Damian's hurt face came to mind, and I stared at my papers again, determined to fit together at least one piece of the puzzle before Bristol. It was hard to concentrate. I kept thinking, *Where was God when those kids were taken . . . and when Damian died?*

Then I heard the girl whining over and over again, 'Sweets'—the long 'e' dragged out like a piece of loose elastic. 'Swee-eets!' I looked back as the woman bent and reached into a deep canvas bag lying at her feet. Producing a scarlet lollipop, she fumbled to peel off the plastic wrapping, every sticky piece catching at her fingers as the child grew more and more impatient, reaching for it and waving her hands inches away from the woman's.

'Wait, can't yer?' she said harshly.

The child didn't answer immediately, but when she did she sounded unperturbed by her mother's gruffness. 'Red's my best,' she informed the whole carriage at the top of her voice. 'My very very *very* best.'

I found that my eyes had narrowed in concentration. Her face was already streaked with the red food colouring. She leaned forward to wave the lollipop perilously near the equally red face of an old man blissfully asleep opposite her—asleep and unaware. I realized suddenly that I was looking at the mother and child the way I would observe someone during an interview.

The woman felt my gaze and returned it with an angry stare. She was debating whether to express her indignation, seemed to think better of it, and instead glanced at her watch.

I dropped my eyes and began to think carefully. Of course it was wild and ridiculous to imagine even for a moment that I had found one of the abducted children. Why would an abductor take a child on a train under public scrutiny? And why would the child not be protesting and crying for her real mother? I realized suddenly and with pleasure that my mind was back on the case.

I turned back to the papers on the table in front of me. We stopped in Swindon, where more passengers crowded on. Then, as the train gathered speed again, I could just see out of the corner of my eye that the woman was once more reaching for something in her bag, though I could not see what. I did allow myself to watch for one last time as the child wriggled, closed her eyes at last, and fell asleep with her mouth open and the remains of the lollipop glued to her dress. Then I returned to the reports written up after the Bristol house-to-house enquiries. Surely something would turn up, I thought—though not with any confidence. Chippenham ... Bristol. I did not let myself look up again until we were almost into the station. Then, beside me in the aisle, the woman was gathering her belongings and pulling a pink jacket across the little girl's shoulders. Their backs were turned to me as they prepared to leave the train, but I saw the woman stoop with a folded magazine and push it into the bag. I saw too that it was a copy of *Women Today*.

The magazine had an electrifying effect on me. I wanted to laugh at the coincidence, but I knew I was frowning with frustration. *All that way to find out about Clare, then nothing!* As I gathered my own things, I knew I had to pull myself together. *Thousands of women read that magazine every week,* I told myself.

PART THREE

*Miles to go
before I sleep*

21

The front door clicked shut after Rita and Marie, and Clare tasted the disappointment they had left behind. For the first time since her arrival in Boston, she was not going to church with her aunt and cousins on a Sunday morning. The aroma of roasting chicken floated up to where she stood at the head of the stairs watching the door they had just shut, but it did nothing to take away the pungent flavour of uneasiness they left behind. *Have I made the right choice? What if . . .?*

Because Ed always stayed at home during the weekly Sunday exodus, she could blame on him her decision not to go, but she wouldn't. She knew that if Jack had not returned to his apartment in Springfield he would have talked her into going as usual. Instead, she had excused herself by saying that she had a vital letter to write and needed utter quiet to do it. Never mind Marie's mute appeal that she change her mind and go. *No, I'm missing church whatever anyone says.* Suddenly her usual hunger for the sort of people she knew she'd meet there—the sort of people she had cared for in London—had disappeared. She wanted to be different now she was in America.

In the guestroom which had now become her own room she turned on the radio and opened the closet. Perhaps if she shut out the smell of the meal cooking below she could also shut out the memory of her aunt's pursed lips a few minutes before.

Even above the throb of the music she could hear Ed thumping about in the shower next door. Always boisterous, loud, and cheerful—teasing her, ruffling her hair every time he passed her in the house, and winking so suggestively that she never failed to turn scarlet—he was, she realized, her favourite among the three American cousins. Nevertheless, for no reason she could name, she trusted him the least.

Stepping to the door, she called to him, 'Hey, Ed, turn it down in there, will you?' She laughed, hearing the sound of her own voice. Already, after only a month, her inflections were shifting: becoming more American.

He laughed in return: a merry, infectious laugh she loved. 'Come in here and tell me that!'

'Don't be crazy,' she shouted back; but although she knew he was joking, she felt her face grow warmer. *Naughty!* she thought. *Just as Marie and I said, those poor college girls must fall for him all the time.* Thinking of that, she stood still in the middle of the room. *A crush on my own cousin, five years younger as well? No way!* And then she remembered her new job with Peter McEnroe, shivered, and turned again to the closet.

While Ed started singing tunelessly next door, she began pulling out the clothes she had brought from England and laying them on the spare bed. Two dresses followed a pair of slacks, two shirts, a skirt, a sweater, a pair of shorts, sandals and shoes. She stared, hardly recognizing some of the things: London clothes, relatively shabby and warm, for a shabby and cool place. Clothes (almost) from another life, a less sophisticated life, a life she had left behind.

She would have to find others—now, before she went to work for Pete McEnroe.

Examining each garment and piece of footwear as if she were seeing it for the first time, she worked her way through the pile and divided it into two small heaps: the things she would fold up until her return to England, and the things she could still wear. The first pile was higher than the second, and she winced at the thought of the expenses to come.

After a while the sounds of running water and singing next door ceased. She barely noticed, but then she suddenly became aware that the door of her room had opened. From the doorway, Ed was standing watching her. She turned, surprised. He had not knocked.

Something about him unnerved her. Wrapped loosely in a terry-cotton dressing-gown, he stood barefoot in the door-frame. Water glistened in his hair, and she took a quick breath as she noticed the beads of water still clinging to his tanned legs.

'Hi,' was all he said, and leaned against the jamb. He smiled, but the boyish charm was gone, replaced by something as unwelcome and unfamiliar as it was unexpected. There was hunger in his eyes.

She realized then with dull dismay that he might have misunderstood her determination to miss church. She straightened up, a skirt still hanging from one arm, and found she was now scared of this her youngest cousin. The boy had turned into a man.

Something prompted her to undercut the electricity between them—and quickly. She imitated his quirked eyebrows and spoke in a voice that suggested complete incomprehension. 'Oh, Ed, it's you. Why don't you run along and get yourself dressed?' She made her voice sarcastic. 'Or maybe you want to try on my clothes?'

It had seemed like a ridiculous enough suggestion, but Ed took her words and twisted them in a way she should have foreseen. He leaned slightly towards her. 'Come on, sweetheart,' he said, 'I'd much rather try you for size than a bunch of boring clothes.' Her heart was knocking against her ribs, but she knew that he must not see any fear. She swallowed, her eyes locked to his. She would not be the first to look away.

'Go on,' he whispered. 'I know you haven't got an American boyfriend yet. How about a kiss, huh?'

Mustering all the chill she could—even more than when that lunatic had phoned her at her mother's house—she said, 'No, Ed. Not that kind of kissing, thanks. I can't believe you're so hard-up for girlfriends yourself that you have to come chasing after me.' She made herself turn away. 'Please, go and get dressed. Get lost. I didn't invite you in, anyway.'

She could hear the smile in his voice again. 'Oh, but you've been giving me looks from under your lashes all this week. Come on, Clare baby, I know you've got the hots for me. Let's give it a whirl, yeah?'

146

She pretended to be intent on her task, but her hands were sweating as she fumbled with the clothes on the bed. She was moving them randomly from one pile to another now. *Why didn't I go with Marie and Aunt Rita? Oh, why? My own cousin!*

At last, after a silence of no more than five seconds—one that seemed much longer—she faced him again. 'Listen, Ed. I'm flattered that you like me, but it's not the way you seem to think it is. I enjoy being with you, sure.' She spread her arms. 'You're my cousin, for heaven's sake! But you've got it all wrong if you think I fancy you.' She feigned a light-heartedness she did not feel. 'You're looking at an old lady of twenty-seven, remember? Go on, I mean it, scram! I'll take you clothes shopping tomorrow if you're good. You can help me choose, OK?'

He narrowed his eyes in anger, but she saw his confidence evaporate. With a shrug he turned away from the door. 'Right, Clare.' Even his voice sounded different now—the silky persuasiveness gone—much more the voice she normally heard from his lips, if a little more tense. 'OK. But don't forget I'm around if you need a shoulder any time.'

She recovered a few shreds of self-possession and moved to shut the door behind him. 'No, I won't forget. Thanks.' *A shoulder?* Was that all he was really offering? She doubted it.

He turned at his own bedroom door, only a few yards down the landing from hers. 'Guess I was a bit pushy just now. Forget it, willya?'

Gripping the key in one hand she gave him a faint smile in return. 'I'll try to. And I really meant it about helping me tomorrow. You've got good taste, I know.'

He shrugged. 'Sure I'll help you—you've got yourself a deal.'

She locked the door behind him, fell onto the bed, and found that she was shaking. *My cousin, my own cousin!* she kept murmuring to herself. Her aunt would be mortified, full of anguish, if she knew what Ed was like. Perhaps, she thought, his father's death was affecting him in strange ways. Anyway, her own mother must never know, either.

Mum—must write to Mum.

By the time she heard the yard door slam behind Ed, about fifteen minutes later, when she realized he was cycling out as usual for the Sunday newspaper, she'd collected herself a little. She stared at the piles of clothes again but felt a leaden apathy and turned her back on them to pull writing paper from the desk in the corner. She wrote first to her mother—a shorter note than the week before, this time careful not to mention Ed at all. She debated writing to Danny as well; he would surely be puzzled by her disappearance; but then she decided she had one to write that was far more important. She began to draft yet another letter to *Women Today*. She had put off sending her news to Andy for quite long enough— several weeks now. She had written and rewritten the letter, but every copy had ended in the same place as its predecessor: in the wicker bin by her bed. Unless she sent it now . . . *Oh, dear!*

She sighed, growing more and more irritated with herself. No matter what she wrote, her reasons for staying in Boston sounded contrived and improbable. How could she mention her new job at *Citizen*? There was no assurance that she'd keep it for more than a few weeks, anyway. Bobbie had told her, with a gleam in the eye, that the last columnist had survived only a breathless six weeks. And no one she knew in London would understand her sudden impulse to try life on the other side of the Atlantic . . . yet she had to tell Andy *something*. Yes, she must resign.

The hardest piece of copy I've ever had to write, she told herself, scoring out more words on the newest draft.

Just as she was giving up the letter, promising herself she'd return to it again later, she heard Rita's Pontiac outside in the driveway; then Ed's voice hailing his sister from the other side of the yard. Everyone was coming home at once; it would be safe now for her to leave the room, abandon her tired old English clothes for a while, and join Rita for the customary cup of coffee before lunch. After facing down Ed's hunger for

her, what Rita or Marie thought about her missing commu-
nion seemed trivial by comparison.

They sat downstairs in the family room with the air-
conditioner humming softly behind them. 'Finished that
letter, did you?' her aunt asked her immediately.

Clare looked up briefly—long enough to see that the
sharpness in her aunt's voice was matched by an unfamiliar
and hard expression on her face. Then, shamed, she looked
down to stir her coffee. 'Not quite. It's a difficult one.'

Her aunt's head went to one side, and glancing up again
Clare did not miss the speculative look in her eyes. 'About
your job? Surely you're not uptight about writing to your
mother, not now she knows you're staying a while.'

'No, not to Mum. You're right. Yes—it is about the job.'
She looked out of the picture window to where one of the
neighbours was trimming bushes only a few feet away. She
shook her head. 'I've been trying almost all week to think how
to say it.'

Rita's eyes burned into hers. 'Just tell them the truth,
that's all, Clare.'

She could not meet her eyes. 'I really want to. But I don't
think the boss will understand. It's not that easy.'

And she still thought so, the following day, as she stood
with Ed in the breezy sunshine of Copley Square. On the
edge of the square, a US mail carrier had parked his truck and
was emptying the mailbox. She hesitated, clutching her
letters. All she had to do was take six steps forward and drop
the letters into the sack.

Ed nudged her. 'Go on. Get it over with. You'll feel much
better when you've mailed it.'

'Oh, I hope you're right.' She smiled at him. The episode
of the day before seemed a bad dream from which she had
awoken to the real Ed: concerned about her future, willing to
listen to her doubts about posting the letter resigning her job,
and fun to be with. She had already wondered several times
that morning whether she had imagined yesterday's scene in
her room.

149

He was pushing a bundle of envelopes into her hands. 'Here. These can go, too. Mom must have had a blitz paying off all her accounts this weekend. She asked me to mail these as well.'

Clare took all the envelopes. Her heart speeded up as she thought of the senior staff at *Women Today* reading and discussing her letter. When she went back to England, she would almost certainly be unable to win back a writing job with her old colleagues. But she could not think of that now. She would have to leave things with God, she reflected, struck with the new unfamiliarity of such a thought as she glanced at the overshadowing tower of Trinity Church.

A gust came up, just as she held out the letters to the mailman, who was grinning appreciatively at her as she approached. Her skirt ballooned over her shoulders, flapping round her ears. She beat it down, laughing, blushing, but lost all the letters in the process. They went scudding away across the flagstones, beyond a fountain that was spraying water in a fine mist around them. Ed went chasing after them.

'Red ones on today, I see,' he shouted, going past.

Her face was burning, but she was laughing anyway. 'Don't be such a pain.' Holding her skirt carefully this time, she bent forward to retrieve two of the letters she could reach herself. As Ed returned with the rest, she thanked him, her eyes on the mailman.

'Hey, lady, come on, I haven't got all day,' he was growling. 'You gonna let me have that mail, or not?'

They passed the letters to him. No time to check. Clare sighed heavily. So it was done! They then walked the half-block to Lord and Taylor's.

'You were right,' she said to Ed as they went through the glass doors. Inside, the blissful coolness of efficient air-conditioning seemed to pour calm over her. 'I feel better already. *Citizen*, here I come.'

Ed stopped beside her. 'Yes, Clare. And they're lucky to get you. Come on—we're going to get you all dolled up. No society columnist in Boston can go round all those parties and caucuses without dressing as stunning as they look. And you're stunning. You really are.'

She hardly knew what to say. The boyish enthusiasm was back, and she could cope with that far better than with the lust of the day before. 'Thanks. I don't believe a word of it, but let's go and unearth all those *stunning* clothes you've been promising me I'll find here.'

'Critic, dress designer *haute couture*—that's me. At your service.' He took hold of her hand and led her forward, and this time she did not push him away.

22

How typical! Clare thought wistfully. She turned the key in the lock of her Fiat but then did nothing about opening it. Instead, she stood still, under the birches that overhung all the cars in the church car-park, and turned her face to the sunshine that filtered through the silvery leaves. Beyond them, the sky was a hot blue. *How typical that when I have extra work to do the sun is blazing down and I can't even enjoy it.*

Getting into the car, she sighed, slammed the door, and started the engine. *No—well, that's not quite true, is it?* she admonished herself. What if she stayed at the church for the weekly lunch with some of her friends? The birch arching over the car branched right, reaching toward other branches. Or what if she chose to go to the park with some of her other friends for a picnic and forget everything else? The birch also branched left, reaching over the car-park railings.

For some reason, though, she wanted to be alone. And because Sandy was away so often at weekends, she had already made up her mind to stay in that afternoon and read through a pile of press clippings. A completely mechanical exercise: something that would take her mind off the loneliness she had felt since she gave up her weekly get-togethers with Danny. Something that would take her mind off the loneliness that had dogged her for about six weeks now, loneliness that would not be assuaged by church lunches or picnics. Strangely, she needed solitude to ease the loneliness. And the birch trunk went up straight and silver—a tree by itself, though in a row of others.

'You're not really taking all those cuttings home with you, are you?' Nina had said, late on Friday when they were packing up at the end of the week.

Clare had been standing by the door, loaded with a heap of library folders. 'Do you think I'll get away with them?'

Nina pulled a face at her. 'Not sure. It's an awfully big pile. The dragon lady's certain to see you. How are you going to get past the library with them, anyway? Didn't you sign them out?'

'Of course I did! It'd be more than my life's worth to take things out without signing for them. But I think she's gone home already.'

Nina pushed her chair back. 'I'll check for you, if you like.' Her eyes glinted, and she was giggling. 'You've got a nerve, Clare. I'd never do that, you know.'

As Nina passed her and walked around the fiction editor's desk to the cuttings library, Clare shrugged, thinking how empty the weekend would be. She hugged the heavy folders closer and told herself, *It's just that I want to get to the bottom of all those abduction stories. That's all.* But she knew—and would never admit to Nina—that if she'd had something special going on, she would probably not even have taken home this week's issue of *Women Today*.

Nina returned a moment later, shaking her head. 'Out of luck, Clare. She's still here, I'm afraid.'

Clare slumped down in her chair again. 'Then I'll just have to wait until she's gone, and come in early again on Monday. There's no way I'm going without this lot, even if I'm in trouble for it.'

She dropped the pile back on her desk and made tea for herself. Nina hovered nearby, a light jacket pulled round her shoulders, ready to go home for the weekend.

Something in Nina's manner made Clare look more closely at her. Normally her skin was pale, her eyes steady, but that evening her colour was high and even her voice had an excited edge to it. Curious, Clare asked, 'So what's going on this weekend? Anything nice?'

Nina flushed and looked away. Clare noticed that she too was taking a few folders home with her, though they were

153

tucked inconspicuously into her folio bag, and she could not see what they were.

'Yes, I hope it will be special,' Nina was saying quietly, her blue eyes resting on a point somewhere on the other side of the Thames. Her mouth curved into a wide smile.

Clare leaned back in her chair, folded her arms, and smiled too. 'Now I'm curious.'

'That's OK. It's your job to be nosy,' Nina said, her laughter louder than usual, louder than their conversation justified.

'Well, go on—I've got all evening, at least until the dragon lady's gone. Tell all.'

Nina shook her head again. 'I can't. I'll tell you in a couple of days.'

Clare squinted up at her and put her head on one side. 'All right, Nina. I'll let you off this time. Have a good weekend.'

And there the loneliness had begun. Even though she knew that it was only temporary, it had pursued her all weekend.

When she let herself back into the flat after the short drive home from church, she was faced again by the papers she had left scattered around her the night before: extracts from colour supplements, sheet after sheet of newspaper clippings, all dated meticulously by the magazine librarian—all of them to do with missing children. Ignoring them, she flung open the windows and went into the kitchen to make a sandwich.

The papers were still on the table when she came back into the room. The night before, she had read all the cuttings from *The Telegraph* and *The Mail* about the first girl taken from Coventry. She knew Nina was still looking after that story for the magazine, but she wanted to refresh her memory; and the editor was already suggesting some sort of sequel. A man had been charged for that abduction, but because the clippings also dealt with other missing children in the Midlands, she wanted to satisfy herself that there were no other parallels with the one case that had been solved.

She wondered, as she lost herself in reading once again,

whether she should ring the Birmingham police for more information. She hesitated, looking up at the clock. *Two-thirty on a Sunday afternoon*. No, that was a hopeless time to call! But then . . .

The Mail mentioned that the West Midlands police were (and she smiled as she read the customary constabulese) 'appealing for anyone with information to come forward' by telephoning an emergency number set up in Birmingham for the purpose.

She stood up, stretched, and crossed to the window that overlooked the grass rectangle below, where children always played. For once the grass was deserted except for a few pieces of paper eddying about in the air-currents around the base of the building. She watched them idly, still debating. *Since I don't have any information to give*, she thought, *What good can I do? I'll ring them tomorrow, perhaps*.

She flipped back the papers until she found the article that mentioned the incident room telephone number, wrote it on her pad, and went on reading. At last her eyes strayed to the photograph of her American relatives. Uncle Bert's eyes seemed to arrest hers, and she looked back at him affectionately.

It suddenly occurred to her how unfaithful she was as a member of her own family. Frowning slightly, she told herself that if anything she should have given more attention, not less, to her mother since her father's death. But it was longer than she could remember since she'd picked up the telephone to ring her; months since she'd invited her mother to the flat for a meal; weeks since she'd been to see her.

She stared at the phone. Should she ring her? She thought of that Cockney garrulousness at the other end: the invariably cheerful voice full of the gossip of Barking and sometimes of the relatives in Boston. *No, not today. I can't face it*. She winced, not knowing when she ever would. She didn't belong in her mother's world any more.

She sighed yet again, aware suddenly of how erratic was her concentration. She should have gone picnicking, after all.

A knock on the door of the flat brought her to her feet. *Danny!* she thought immediately. On a Sunday afternoon, even though they hadn't seen each other for weeks, there was no one else it could be.

But it was Nina who stood on the threshold, her face bright with the afternoon sunshine. In one hand she held a thinly rolled newspaper. 'It's me!' she said.

'Hello! Come in! You're a stranger here—on a Sunday as well.' Clare smiled back at her, stepped aside and held the door wide. 'Thanks.' Nina passed her, then turned back as Clare followed her into the middle of the room. 'Oh, Clare,' she murmured, 'it looks as if you've been working this whole weekend. You make me feel guilty!'

'Don't be daft!' Clare sat down at the table again and offered Nina the overstuffed chair by the window. 'Yes, do sit there. It's a bit cooler. And don't feel guilty. This was my choice.' She looked down. 'In fact I've hardly been able to concentrate.'

'I know the feeling. I couldn't sleep last night, either.'

Clare looked quickly at Nina but saw no tell-tale shadows under her eyes. 'But you look bright as a hundred candles, Nina. What's going on?'

Nina jumped up again. 'Listen, can we talk a bit? Could you bear to be parted from these cuttings for a few hours?'

Clare laughed and clapped her hands together. 'Bear to be parted . . .? Were you reading my mind? Yes, I'll take a break, and gladly.' She stood and faced Nina. 'How about . . . hmm . . . a walk in Windsor Forest? Or somewhere else cool, and out of London a bit?'

Half an hour later, fortified with a plastic bag full of French bread, cheese, tomatoes, and cans of cola, they pulled out of the tight parking space behind the building and onto the main road west. As she drove past the church, Clare noticed again the birch trees that lined the car-park and reconsidered the parley she'd held with herself about how she should spend the day. She glanced at Nina, then back at the traffic ahead.

'I'm glad you came round. This is what I should have done

before. I was feeling so blue. You're a tonic.'

Nina was quiet. 'I'm not sure you'll think so,' she said softly, 'when you hear what I did yesterday.' She took a breath, waving around the same rolled paper she'd been clutching since she arrived at the flat. 'But I'm going to tell you anyway. And—'

'I'll wait. Mmm—let's just enjoy the drive. It gets better and better the farther out we go. It's good to get out of London for a while.'

Nina seemed not to hear her. 'Clare, I was just trying to tell you that I've got something for you, as well.'

For a few seconds Clare let her eyes leave the road. 'Well, I hope it's something nice. But I'm determined not to think about anything more important than speed limits and zebra crossings until we get across the other side of the M25.'

They drove on through the relatively leisurely flocks of Sunday afternoon motorists, at last emerging from the greys and browns of industrial parks, housing estates, and leggy suburbs onto a tree-lined Roman road near Windsor Great Park. With the car windows open fully, the scent of pines burst in on them.

By the time they had crunched and bounced their way over an uneven gravel path to a public car-park near the forest, it was already after four. The stifling air, however, was scarcely cooler than it had been two hours before. Crickets sang invisible from the grass verge of the woods, and in the heavy heat Clare felt a warning of thunder.

She was lifting out the food when Nina stopped her, with a hand on her arm.

'Wait. I should have given this to you before we left the flat.' She held out the roll of newspaper.

Clare took it uncertainly. 'What's this? An article the dragon lady missed? Or something sensational for a story next week?'

Nina's face was pained. 'No, but it's for you. Go on. See what's inside. I'm afraid they'll die.'

Clare eased the paper away and found a dozen red roses

157

swathed in a damp piece of kitchen towel. She wrinkled her brows and looked up. 'What—?'

'He said they were for me. But I know they were for you. He would far rather have seen you.' Nina's words came out in a rush, then she caught her bottom lip in her teeth, and Clare saw that her eyes were swimming.

'Nina, I don't—*Who* said these were for you—or for me? What d'you mean?' She spoke gently; Nina now looked as tired as she'd said she was.

'I did something I shouldn't have done, Clare.' Nina sounded sad. 'Yesterday—you know I told you the other day I was doing something special?'

'Yes—go on.' Clare stood quite still. Had Nina somehow met Danny? And were these roses a kind of peace-offering from him?

Nina looked directly at her but for a moment seemed unable to say more. After a moment, she gabbled, 'I'd arranged a meeting ... with Frank Bernard. I should never have done that. He was yours to start with, not mine, even though you gave me the story to look at. It was completely unprofessional.' She took a quick breath and looked away into the trees. 'I didn't need to see him. He's not one of our regulars—I hardly have to tell you that. He can't write well. No one commissioned him ... It was just that I was so moved by his account of meeting you ... I wanted to see for myself what this man was like.'

At the mention of Frank's name, Clare had felt her face begin to glow, but now she felt something inside go cold. She waited, wanting to laugh off what Nina was saying. How Nina spent her weekends was up to her, surely. And if she wanted to meet with a freelance writer (if that's what he was, as well as a policeman), she had every right to do so. *But Frank Bernard!* She began to ache, and all the loneliness of the past few weeks came rushing in on her with renewed intensity. She was missing—she had been missing—a man she did not even know.

With lips compressed because she had no idea what to say,

she stared at Nina, shaking her head. Then she laughed, a giddy, unnatural laugh that was lost immediately in the close air.

A large drop of rain fell between them onto the dusty gravel at their feet. They looked up simultaneously, and more large drops followed, splattering and plashing all around them. The gravel began to darken, and the smell of wet soil and sweet wet leaves came to Clare's nostrils.

Somewhere in the distance above the branching trees of the great forest, thunder rolled. They ducked back into the Fiat, wiping rain from their faces and bare arms.

'Only a summer storm,' Clare murmured at last. 'It'll pass.' She looked into the tight petals of the roses and found that her own eyes, too, were wet.

23

Charlie came running over to where I sat in front of the database. *I might as well be married to that machine,* I'd told myself a few minutes before. I was tied to it for life; and we were getting nowhere.

Charlie was waving a message form in his hand, his face cherubic. 'We may have a lead.' He was speaking so loudly that half a dozen heads went up. 'Look what just landed in my tray.'

I stood up and steered him away from the audience. 'Hold on a minute. Something big, is it?'

'Could be.'

'Let's see if we can find the guv'nor, in that case.'

We walked around to the SIO's office but couldn't see him. Charlie grinned. 'Probably popped out a moment. Fancy a break from the madhouse for a minute or two? I'm going out for a smoke. This place gives me claustrophobia after a while.'

When Charlie said he was 'going out for a smoke', he usually meant he wanted to talk without being overheard. He'd got me really curious now, so we strolled out of the incident room together and left them all speculating behind us.

'Canteen all right?' I asked. 'We'd better be quick.'

'No. Let's enjoy some real peace before the tempest. Outside, if you don't mind.'

We clattered down the back stairs, walked to the end of the car-park, and sat on the wall under the shade of the only tree anywhere near the building: a scraggy birch. Someone sentimental had carved two pairs of initials in the flaking bark. 'D'you know PC McGavran at all?' Charlie began.

'New lad, isn't he?'

'Yup, that's the one.' He waved the message form at me again. 'Seems he got called out on a fool's errand to look at a

160

car blocking a lay-by. A woman phoned in yesterday and complained because her husband couldn't turn his car around there as usual. Tight space, apparently. The front office ignored the first complaint, but the second time she rang, someone thought the new bobby on the block should look into it. The car's been there two days.'

I knew it was no use hurrying Charlie. No matter what I said he would tell me the story at his own pace.

He lit a cigarette. 'It was an old Morris Marina—M registration. McGavran was just going to list it as apparently abandoned—it's a rusty old crate, and the tyres are pretty worn, he says. But he noticed a school lunchbox and a rag doll on the back seat. Just one of those hunches we were talking about, you see?'

I didn't see at all—yet. 'How do you mean?'

'Well, there's nothing odd about a lunchbox and a rag doll on the back seat of a car, is there?'

'Not really.'

'But McGavran says here that something didn't "feel" right about it. Something about the age of the car, and the fact that all the seats inside were covered in blankets—the way old people often cover them.' I visualized McGavran's fresh face: the youngest PC in the station. 'Smart lad. But I'm sure I wouldn't have given the car a second look myself. What's he getting at?' I began to feel slightly irritated with Charlie for dragging me outside just to rabbit on about an old car parked in the wrong place.

'Ah, but you're not a car buff the way McGavran is. And he says that it struck him as weird that someone regularly responsible for children or grandchildren wouldn't have any signs of safety straps in the back. I know a lot of parents aren't bothering yet if they've got old cars, but nothing adds up quite right anyway. The woman who phoned about the car in the first place told him that the driver is an old man. *And* there's the fact that although the car's been there two days, no one's ever come to get the lunchbox out.'

I took the message form from Charlie and read it twice.

The car had been left in one of the most isolated parts of Bristol's outlying villages: near Blagdon, about ten miles out of the town. 'So the lady who phoned in to complain knew the car and the owners of the car?' I said. 'That's strange—why didn't she go and complain herself, then, directly, instead of wasting our time?'

Charlie scratched his head and waved away the smoke he was blowing around us. 'Complain directly? Who knows? You know the kind of thing—neighbourhood grudges. Anyway, this probably wasn't a wasted trip after all. McGavran's certainly all hopped up about it.'

'Well . . .' I was sceptical. 'It's a very long shot. You know that as well as I do, barely worth a try. I don't suppose we need to talk to the boss yet. We could get a couple of the lads out to see why an old man in a secluded place like that has kids' things in the back of the car.' I sighed. 'Probably a complete waste of time, and no doubt an embarrassment at the end of it all. Some poor innocent grandpa giving the parents a break for a few days . . . still—' I scuffed at a piece of gravel with the sole of my shoe.

Charlie grinned at me. 'Come on, Frank! Where's your usual buoyant optimism?' I thought of Nina Cottham and of how I had made her unhappy last weekend—just because she wasn't Clare Hogarth. It was all so silly and out of proportion. 'Left it somewhere on Paddington Station last week, I think. Left luggage office, I expect.'

He guffawed. 'You get madder every day.'

I stood up. 'No use hanging around here like a couple of loiterers. Time to get cracking, crazy as it may seem.' While Charlie ground his cigarette into the tarmac, I squared my shoulders. 'I want someone down on the PNC right away to find out more about the registered owner of the Marina. Then we'll have a look on the box to see if it's shown up anywhere else in suspicious circumstances along this "corridor" of ours. And let's find out if one of the families has lost a rag doll as well as a child.' I grimaced at Charlie. 'All a bit unlikely, let's face it. McGavran is being a little over-zealous, that's all. Bill won't want us rushing into surveillance without a lot more info first.'

'Yeah. You're probably right. From a distance, it all sounds pretty asinine now. I'm clutching at straws.' Charlie followed me back into the station, but his steps on the stairs were heavier and slower than usual.

'You're dragging, aren't you?' I teased him. 'Better give up that foul weed tobacco, chum.'

'Yeah—must be tired. This case is barely moving, and it's getting me down.'

'Come on,' I chaffed him. 'Where's your buoyant optimism, hmm?'

Back in the incident room I sent one of the PCs down to the computer and arranged immediately for two others to keep observations on the car in case the owner returned. Then I sent a message downstairs for McGavran to come up right away. I also wanted to bring the Drurys—parents of our locally abducted child—into the picture as soon as possible, but I knew I'd have to talk to the boss first . . . if this 'lead' of MacGavran's was worth anything whatsoever.

As soon as I'd seen McGavran and got the details from downstairs about the Marina, I sat down again at my old post in front of the H.O.L.M.E.S. database. The car's keeper was listed as a Mr Harold Lomax, and for a moment I remembered looking up Clare's Fiat a few weeks before—in another life. *But it's no use thinking of her at the moment*, I told myself.

I sent someone else scurrying down to the criminal records officer to see if we knew anything about Mr Lomax. We didn't, I was told, but for the first time in days I began to feel mildly happy about the case. It was very likely we were following a wrong trail, but we might just have stumbled on something that would lead us to the Drury child. At least we were following *something*. The incident room was buzzing for a change.

The systems supervisor hunted through the database for mentions of the Marina. I sat beside him, though I still felt sceptical. At last he crowed, 'There you are. See? Sighted in

Coventry a couple of weeks ago, once near the home of one abducted child. Parked so long that neighbours noticed. Where would we be without the curtain-twitchers' brigade?'

Everyone heard him, and cheers broke out.

I slapped my thigh and called over to Charlie, who was now deep in some other message sheets only a few feet away. 'The plot doth thicken into pea soup,' I laughed. 'Eye of newt and toe of frog, Wool of bat and tongue of dog . . . Double, double, toil and trouble—'

'Shakespeare now?' he interrupted, just as I was getting warmed up. 'Got your quotations a bit twisted up, though, haven't you? Plot or pot? Anyway, it was a cauldron, surely.' Then he added, 'Pea soup, my foot! What use is that when you can't see through the damn stuff.'

I was meditating a suitably pompous reply and a recitation of the whole speech from *Macbeth* (the only one I know), when I became aware that the detective superintendent was standing at my elbow.

'Jesting on the job?' he barked. 'Well, what's the story, Frank? On to something, are we?'

Charlie and I filled him in. Bill sat hunched in his usual pose, elbows on knees, and didn't miss a word. I was glad as we talked that a man like this—whom I knew well and respected—had been appointed as 'head honcho' for our cross-border cases. It was good to be able to work closely with someone I trusted, even if he sometimes pretended that we were all incompetent.

His eyes went flicking back and forth between me and Charlie all the time we talked. Finally, he said, 'Good for young McGavran! I presume you've called him in here?'

'Yes, sir, and then I sent him over to the car with those other lads,' I told him.

He winked. 'I want a full description of the rag doll, and any other info we can get from the families about a missing doll. Get the allocator to sort you out all the DCs and DSs you need. And I do want the car under surveillance. Starting now—and overnight. Then we'll do a reassessment in the morning—the full treatment. Not a stone unturned if anyone comes back to it. Hope you lads aren't too late already.'

Charlie and I exchanged glances. 'Yeah—I know what you're thinking,' the boss murmured. 'It may all be for nothing. But these are missing *children*. We can't sit on our backsides any more. This is the only "lead"—if it is a lead—we've had for a long time. All the rest has been a useless paper chase or electronic game. Utterly fruitless! I want that Drury kid found fast. We all know the chaps up north are breaking their backs on their end of things. They probably think all we do is sleep. McGavran may have done us all a big favour. And Frank, you really ought to send someone to talk to the woman who first complained about the car—find out all you can about the registered owner—if she knows any more than we do. Then we'll watch his house.'

For a moment I felt somewhat like a child in front of a headmaster. What did he think we'd been planning and doing for the past few hours? But I tried to keep my voice even. 'Right. We'll get over there straight away.'

He put his hand on my shoulder, his grip like a vice. 'And don't be surprised if you're on the road again next week. That Marina being sighted in Coventry could be what we've been waiting for. I may want you up there again for a few days. If we have any grounds to nick anyone down here, who knows, maybe the whole case will crack open for us.'

I met his eyes. 'Yes. If the owner is as old as everyone seems to think, and if the car's as clapped out as McGavran says, it'd be interesting to find out for starters why he's making the trip up there at all.'

'It may just be utter coincidence, God knows.' He stopped, wiping his forehead with the back of his hand. He was trying not to let on that he was a little excited. 'But I hope not.' He stood up, then turned to the office manager, who had been hovering nearby throughout. 'I'll see you all at the briefing, and I want all this on the database quickly, so Warwickshire and West Midlands can get their lads plugged in. OK?'

Again Charlie and I looked at each other. Charlie was

smiling. 'Score one for buoyant optimism,' he said.

When the boss had gone, I said, 'Yup, a faint hope at last. But you heard what he said—I may be up north again—any time, by the sound of it.'

'Is that such a terrible prospect? What about the ravishing Miss Bertram?'

'Very funny! Anyway, she's in Birmingham, not Coventry.'

'Hah! The guv'nor's sent you to Coventry!'

'Pitiful, Charlie. That joke's so old—if it's a joke at all—it's got moss growing on the north side.'

'Like the rest of Coventry, I suppose,' Charlie answered. 'Except the new cathedral, of course.'

24

Clare's new office formed part of a corner suite that looked north from the fifteenth floor of the high-rise that *Citizen* occupied. On the first morning, hazy sunlight slanting into the east side window welcomed her to a new life. She was glad to have an office to herself for a change, glad to have exchanged the stuffy air and hot rooms of King's Reach Tower for the spacious coolness and plant-decked greenness of *Citizen*'s offices.

Appropriately enough—she thought with a smile as she first sat down at her desk—she could see the gold dome of the State House from her chair; and if she stood close to the window and looked towards the western skyline, the Charles River and Longfellow Bridge were plainly visible, too.

For the first half hour in her new surroundings, she simply gazed around her and revelled in it all. She opened drawers and cupboards and made a list of supplies that had not been left by her predecessor; then, thinking uncomfortably of that woman's short tenure, she determined she'd have something to show for her first day's work.

She stood up and stared down at the dome of the State House. So far that morning she had not yet seen her new boss, but the conversation with her cousins on the beach about other members of the McEnroe family had aroused her interest, and she thought the family would at least be a starting-place for an intro to the social and political life of the city. *I wonder what I can find out about this Senator McEnroe. I wonder if Pete's any relative, or . . .*

As she would in London, she reached for the telephone, but then replaced the receiver. She'd rather find her own way through the office systems, would rather meet as many as possible of the rest of the staff, before the work became so

167

heavy that she would have no time to get to know them. It was one thing to have an office to herself—a luxury—but quite another to work without reference to others and start off with the cold impersonality of a telephone call to someone who had never set eyes on her. The library would be her first port of call.

Kathy, her secretary—a cheerful, intelligent woman who had just graduated from college—showed her to the cuttings library, introduced her to the assistant on the desk, and left her there.

'I want everything you've got on Senator McEnroe,' she told the assistant. 'Everything.'

The other woman blinked, then twisted her mouth wryly. 'You've talked to Mr McEnroe about that, have you?'

Clare hesitated. She did not want to start her job conveying the impression that she was too dependent on Pete McEnroe for all she did and wrote. He had hired her, he'd said at the interview, because he liked her flair—the way she wrote, the way she reached decisions, and the fact that she could work alone. 'Your instincts for a good story will be the making of that role. You'll transform it into what it should be—recreate it in your own image,' he had said. 'I read all the *Women Today* stories you showed me. So don't let anyone tell you you'll have to earn the right to write about this city's VIPs—or people who think they're hot-shots. I told you—I did want an outsider. Half the people in this place are so caught up in the narcissistic roller-coaster of social life here that they don't even know what's going on. But you—you'll bring a fresh angle to all of it. A little mockery won't hurt at all, either.'

'I said,' the assistant repeated harshly, 'you've checked with Mr McEnroe about the cuttings we've got on file for Senator McEnroe?'

Gathering herself, Clare looked at her coolly. 'I don't think that'll be necessary.' She raised her chin. 'I'm here to learn some background. I won't be writing anything right away, of course.'

The assistant barred her way with arms folded. 'The

McEnroe cuttings are special,' she said.

The battle was on, and Clare's irritation mounted. 'Confidential? I'd be surprised if they were.'

'Of course they aren't,' a half-familiar man's voice shouted from behind a filing cabinet. Peter McEnroe himself appeared beside them. He was wearing glasses, and his fair hair fell untidily over his forehead. Under his left arm was tucked a thick and closely written notepad. She had not seen him since the interview, and his debonair good looks were a fresh shock to her. She could not trust him.

Moving a silver pen into his left hand, he held out his right and gave her what seemed a genuine smile of welcome. She had forgotten the blue magnetism of his eyes, and as soon as he looked at her she found her guard dropping—just as it had done in the interview, and again on the telephone at Rita's house when he had called to offer her the job. He was warm and attractive, and she couldn't think now why she had disliked him so much on the plane.

'Miss Hogarth—Clare. I see you're making yourself at home.'

She knew she was blushing, and the assistant stared at her with undisguised dislike. She murmured, 'Thank you . . . I'm just finding my way around.' But then, not willing to seem passive, she took the initiative; if she couldn't be direct with him on the first day, she would never be able to be direct. She met his eyes. 'I thought I'd start by reading about some of the city's important families. And I gather—'

'Yes.' He gave her an inscrutable smile. 'And why not? The McEnroe clan makes an interesting study.' Pete shot a sharp look at the library assistant. 'But I have to warn you that you'll be reading for weeks and weeks without producing a single column if you start trying to read about Julius McEnroe. No moss grows under that man at all—nor under his wife. You'll find that out the next time he drops in here to see me.' He wanted her to be impressed. 'The files must be bulging.'

'That's just what I was going to say, Mr McEnroe,' the assistant interrupted. Her face had brightened, and Clare felt with a pang that she had already made an enemy. 'I was just going to tell—er—Ms Hogarth that myself.'

Pete's eyes narrowed. 'Quite right. But there's no need to give the impression that there's anything in the McEnroe history to hide. No need to protect Senator McEnroe, Ms Enright, you know. He's big enough to stick up for himself, I imagine.' He turned away, calling over his shoulder to Clare. 'Come and see me in my office when you get your bearings, would you? Before lunch, please.'

Clare took a deep breath. Had Nina been facing her, she would have broken into giggles at the sheer discomfort of the last few moments' conversation, but here in Boston she knew nothing about the protocol and could only stare at the assistant with a blank face. She felt no desire to give a 'told-you-so' smile of victory in the first round of skirmishes with this woman. There would be more, she was sure.

'I'll show you the files,' the assistant said grudgingly.

'Thank you. And I'd like to know how everything is stored—in general. I'll be spending a lot of time digging around in here, and I don't want . . . I wouldn't want to upset your system at all.'

The assistant gauged her sincerity and, apparently half-placated, led the way to the back of the library.

'Cuttings for political figures in Massachusetts are all here—alphabetically by last name.'

Clare ran her eye over the hanging files and shelves that held them, noting how much more efficiently arranged they were than their counterparts at *Women Today*, but still feeling the sting of the encounter with the assistant too sharply to want to compliment her yet. The name 'Kennedy' appeared most prominently, and she pulled out some sample folders and browsed through them with a smile.

'A lot of material is on microfiche as well,' the assistant told her. She assessed Clare. 'I presume you're not used to microfiche?' Plainly, she expected the answer 'no'.

'I've used a microfiche in the UK,' Clare said steadily, deciding that a little honey might sweeten the woman.

'Perhaps it's the same here. But I'll rely on your expertise, if not.'

The librarian thawed slightly, and soon Clare was back at her desk with a six-inch pile of cuttings from the 1980s. Tomorrow, she decided, she would read about Julius McEnroe's life in the 1970s, and earlier. At the very least she would like to discover Pete's relationship to the man.

'I'm his nephew,' Pete told her flatly, when she met him later. She had left the cuttings at 11.30 and found his office door wide open. Shutting it behind her, he offered her a seat and rang for coffee. 'That was an interesting little inter-change I overheard this morning. I like a journalist who's got a nose for a story.' He smiled at her, his teeth very white. 'I knew the first time we talked on the plane that you had that sort of mind: inquisitive. I like it. We need you here. Don't let anyone stand in your way when you want information.'

Across the corner of Clare's memory came the voice of the editor at *Women Today*. He spoke the same language as Pete, she realized. '*All that matters is to get the magazine to bed. Even if you have to climb over each other to get stories.*' She looked again at Pete and saw that he would be even more purposeful than Andy and her other London colleagues. Here was a man who would stop at very little to get what he wanted. Not for the first time, as she thought this way, she shivered. Then she hauled her mind back to what he was saying.

'That particular assistant—Virginia Enright—is the she-bear protector sort. Know what I mean? More concerned to have the files in place than actually help anyone.'

'Good, though, when you want to find info in a hurry. It's a well-organized library,' Clare said cautiously.

'Well . . . yes, I guess it is.' He turned the silver pen round and round in his hand, and she found herself watching the play of light on his skin and over the sinews and flesh on the backs of his hands. He looked away from the pen and out of the window. 'Yes, Julius McEnroe is my uncle, if that's what you want to know.'

She blushed furiously and blurted out something about

her cousins' comments to her on the beach.

He smiled indulgently, and she felt foolish and as naive and ignorant as she had felt in her first conference with the features editor in London.

'My father, Anthony McEnroe, was his younger brother—quite a lot younger.'

'Was?'

He looked at her sharply. 'Geez—you *are* on the ball, aren't you? Yes, was. Died a while ago. Cardiac arrest. Total surprise, especially as my uncle always used to be in much worse shape—heavy, I mean. But you'd never know it now. Julius McEnroe is as lean and elegant as I'd like to be when I'm that age.'

She picked up her pad and wrote 'Anthony McEnroe & Sen. Julius McEnroe—brothers' on the top line. 'And how old is Senator McEnroe? I hear he's pretty popular in the city.'

Pete let the air through his nose in a short laugh, but his eyes didn't smile. 'Among some, he is popular, yes. You'll find out as you read. Organized crime wouldn't mind catching him with his back to the door of some restaurant, but he's a cunning old fox. He's going on for seventy now—but he looks like fifty-five and has a mind sharp enough to cut diamonds.' The corners of Pete's mouth turned up slightly. 'Someone in the family once told me that he has a soft spot for younger women, but if he does, there's certainly never been a scandal, and my aunt is so dynamic and on the move that I doubt if he gets too bored with her around. Go down to the art department if you don't believe me, and have a look at some of the pics down there of Marianne. She's still a stunner. They both are.' He leaned back in his seat and stretched out his legs towards her feet. His eyes were steady and fixed directly on her new shoes. 'No, on the whole I don't think you'll find much on my family to titillate your readers. News, yes, but not scandal. And I'll tell you straight, at the outset, that I didn't get this job because I'm a McEnroe. Nor will I let my last name dictate what we do and don't print in this magazine. It would be good if you remembered that.' He looked up, at last.

Clare nodded, feeling slightly dazed. She had tried to watch his face as he talked, but the way he sprawled in his chair distracted her completely. Still, she knew him well enough already, she thought, to have worked out that he was economical with words unless he was trying to charm someone. Clearly, now that she was on his staff, that was not the case; he had wooed and won her already. But what if he was trying to hide something with this barrage of words? It seemed unlikely, especially after what he had said to the librarian only two hours before. *Nothing to hide*. All the same, why had he switched so quickly from speaking about the senator to speaking of his wife?

She would start by learning about the McEnroe family—as much as she could. He wanted her first column in two weeks, and already her appointment diary was filling with parties, concerts and exhibitions she would have to attend to gather the raw material she needed, and to give her a full orientation to Boston.

After leaving Pete's office she did not go directly back to her own but found her way, as he'd suggested, to the art department. As soon as she walked through the swing doors into the sunny, open-plan room where the layout people worked and the photographers camped in between shoots, she felt at home. The familiar astringent smell and the bins overflowing with trimmed edges greeted her here just as they would have done in London.

A few heads turned as she walked through, her eyes on the photo-library at the back of the room, and one man whistled at her. She smiled and kept walking.

'Hey there!' he called. 'Don't we even get to know who you are, since you're in our back yard?'

She stopped, her face colouring as usual. 'Clare—Clare Hogarth.' She tried to sound at ease. 'I'm the new society columnist.' She smiled around at them, and they all smiled back.

'Well, good luck to you,' another man said, pushing back a

173

long pony-tail that had fallen forward over his shoulder onto the pictures he was pasting down. 'You'll need it, from all accounts.'

Her smile froze, and she said stiffly, 'May I scout around here a little and see what you've got?'

'Sure,' one of the women said, 'be our guest. Anything in particular you want to know?'

'She's British,' one of the men whispered.

She turned. 'Yes, I am. Hope that'll suit you.' She knew she sounded acerbic, but even in the six weeks she had been in Boston, she'd grown weary of the feeling that because she was English she was some sort of 'exhibit A'. Her nationality did not define her, she wanted to tell them. Instead, she simply said, 'And, yes, there is something specific I want to see—photos of Senator McEnroe and his wife.'

The man who had whistled at her chortled into his coffee. 'Oh! She's going to have them all running, this one is.'

As his colleague handed her a fat file of pictures and showed her to a clear desk where she could look at them, Clare wondered what he meant. Was he referring to her propensity for attracting the attention of men, or was he suggesting already—as Pete had done—that she would make her mark on *Citizen* by having her ears and eyes out for a juicy story? *Well, what does it matter what he means?* she concluded. No one could know yet what would happen during her tenure at the magazine. This commentator knew her name, and that was all. She didn't know his, and didn't want to. He had no way of knowing—any more than she had—what sort of stories would flow from her mind into the magazine each week.

She turned over the pictures one by one, starting with those dating from the early 1980s. Marianne McEnroe looked about forty in the first photographs, but something about the way she used her cosmetics to conceal fine lines at the corner of the eyes, over the bridge of her nose, and something about the quality of her skin, hinted that she was much older. *She must be sixty now,* Clare calculated, flipping over the plastic-covered photographs more quickly.

She came finally to the most recent picture of all, a colour photograph of the senator and his wife coming out of church together on Memorial Day weekend: Julius McEnroe tall and silver-haired as Pete had described him, craggy white brows beetling over keen blue eyes, an open, intelligent face; Marianne McEnroe with her arm loosely through his—hatless, her platinum blonde hair neatly coiffured and her smile showing still perfect teeth. Her clothes were carefully designed to show off her petite figure and delicate bone structure. She was beautiful, Clare decided.

She found herself smiling back at the photograph as if they were smiling directly at her. She could not tell if she would like either of the McEnroes, but their faces held some of the same compelling interest that the nephew's expression demanded, too. She knew she would meet them in a few days at a garden party in Bedford—one of the first gala events to which she was invited, and she wanted to imprint their faces on her mind. She stared long and hard.

A voice behind her arrested her, and for some reason the skin on the back of her necked prickled a little. She turned.

It was Bobbie, her black curls shining and her face pink. 'They are fascinating, aren't they?' She nodded towards the heap of McEnroe portraits.

Clare felt as if she had been caught doing something illegal. She blushed again, then laughed, remembering Bobbie's comment about her 'gorgeous English skin—so clear'. 'Yes,' she murmured, 'they are, rather.' She stood and offered her hand to Bobbie, but Bobbie lifted her shoulders and took a step backwards.

'Sorry, I can't.' Her hands were full of rolls of film, a heavy 35mm camera dangling on a strap from one arm. 'But I heard you were back here and thought I'd come and say "hi". Everyone's talking about you, you know.'

'They'll soon get over it,' Clare said drily.

'Anyway, welcome, Clare.' Shyness crept into Bobbie's voice. 'You look as if you're already getting the hang of the place.'

Clare did not want to sound over-confident. 'Not quite yet,' she answered. 'But I hope I shall.' She glanced down at the desk. 'By the way, did you take any of these? There are some good ones.'

Bobbie's eyes lit up. 'Thanks—yes, quite a few. I see the McEnroes at church sometimes, and that Sunday—' she pointed at the most recent photo, 'Well, I just happened to have my camera along. I couldn't resist, and I don't think they objected at all.'

'Mrs McEnroe,' Clare ventured, 'What's she like? She's as gorgeous as a model.'

Bobbie wouldn't meet her eyes. 'Yes, isn't she? And a long time ago—' She broke off. 'But listen, I really can't talk now—sorry.' Her face was flustered. 'I'm in between shoots. Could we eat lunch together one day?'

Clare frowned, wondering at the abrupt change of subject. 'Yes, of course, but—'

Bobbie had already reached the last file and was turning away. 'It's funny,' she said, hugging the films to herself, 'but when I first saw you—when Pete and I first saw you—I had a hunch that you might end up here. And now here you are.'

Clare tried to judge how friendly Bobbie really felt towards her, and failed. The woman was smiling, but her eyes were unhappy and her voice unsteady. 'What d'you mean?' she said carefully.

'I could just just tell by the way Pete was talking to you, I guess.' Bobbie looked down at the floor. 'Er—have you seen him yet today?'

'Yes, I have. That's why I'm in here—because of a suggestion he made.'

'Oh, I see.' Bobbie smiled uncertainly. 'I haven't seen him in over a week, now. So busy.' The smile was fading.

'He seemed fine,' Clare said cheerfully.

Bobbie looked up, her eyes full of pain; tried to say something, then turned and fled.

After she had gone, Clare put away all the photographs and returned to her office. She knew she and Pete were supposed to write a letter to the US immigration office, changing her visa so that she could legally work in the country, but somehow she lacked enthusiasm for anything as mechanical as a letter about a visa. It could wait.

Instead, she remained at her desk reading cuttings until the sun had passed overhead and was slanting in at the west side window. Her life was moving on, but something about it was giving her a bitter taste.

25

'I definitely want you to do a follow-up, Clare,' Andy said. 'All the thumbs are up on the abduction story—I know it'll go well, and I'm pretty certain there's a lot more mileage yet in the whole subject.'

Dave, the features editor, was nodding. 'He's right, you know.'

Clare looked from one to the other. The press cuttings she had read the weekend before swirled around in her brain. She would have more than enough material to write several pieces for *Women Today*, but she hesitated.

'What's the matter, Clare?' Dave asked.

She shook her head and leaned over the conference table, staring at the polished grain of the wood while she collected her thoughts. At last she looked up. 'Two things. First—Andy, I'm in the middle of another story at the moment, remember?'

The editor spread out one of the flat plans with a slight look of irritation. 'Yes—childhood allergies and vitamin therapy, wasn't it?'

'Right. It's taking a bit of time. I've had to work in the library as well as here, and I really ought to interview one of the specialists from Wimpole Street. But it's more than that—there's Nina, you know.' She let her eyes wander to the window. From Andy's office she could see down to the Festival Hall, and she thought fleetingly of concerts on the Embankment with Danny, now worlds away.

She remembered telling Nina that the abduction story was all hers—as long as Nina didn't mind if she herself read further into the background for her own interest. She looked back at Andy. 'Is it fair for me to take the sequel away from Nina?' The editor threw a quick glance at Dave. 'Ah—yes.

We passed on the first abduction story to Nina, didn't we?'

Clare wasn't sure from Andy's dry tone and the use of the word 'we' whether she had said the right thing or not. Her hackles rose slightly at the hint that he was patronizing both her and Nina.

He was toying with his glasses, looking up at the ceiling as though for inspiration. 'Nina did a creditable job getting that story in and polished up. She's coming along very well now, but I've heard on the grapevine that you've been taking a particular interest in the abduction story yourself, anyway.'

Dave leaned forward. 'Is that true?'

Her eyebrows rose in surprise. 'Got your spies in Ealing, have you?' she laughed.

'No,' said Andy, 'but I know you've been furiously reading everything on the cases up north and in the West Country. You think there's some connection, do you?'

'Not with the abduction of the first little girl in Coventry,' she answered quickly, now fully absorbed. 'They've got their man in that case, as you know. But if you mean—is there a connection between the other abductions in Coventry, Birmingham and Cheltenham—well, I don't know.'

'There was one in Bristol, as well, wasn't there?' Dave asked.

Clare was surprised that both men had found time—amid the myriad of stories and features that commanded their attention every week—to read up on the abductions so amply covered in the daily press. At the mention of Bristol, however, she felt the colour rise into her face. 'Bristol—yes, there was. And the most recent was a second case in Coventry—at the end of June.' She wanted to divert them from mentioning Bristol further, did not want to think about that city or about Frank. His red roses—wilting even before she'd got them into water the previous Sunday night—had now dropped their petals on her bureau. Nina meanwhile seemed hardly able to talk to her.

But while her mind was following one path—travelling west—the two men in conference with her seemed to be

179

travelling in an altogether different direction.

'I want a sequel to the first story,' Andy said, 'as I indicated. And I want you on it, not Nina.' He stopped, sending Dave a slightly apologetic look which made no sense to Clare, then continued, 'I know I've teased you sometimes about your beliefs, but this is where someone like you— someone with some real compassion—will do the best job. These children have been missing so long that I can't believe we'll be the first magazine to cover the story. But I certainly don't want to be the last.'

She knew she was frowning at them, even though this was just the encouragment she had hoped for. 'We-ell . . .' She drew the word out on a long breath. 'I'd love to do it. But what's the angle? I'm sure everything's moving too fast for us to do anything now on these later cases.'

'Yes, of course it is.' Dave was smiling at her. 'But what the readers will want to know is how the parents are feeling *now*— and how they'll feel later, assuming the children are brought back. So there are two stories here, and neither will be invalid just because the world moves on and the abductors are caught.'

'If they are,' Clare put in.

Andy set his glasses on the table. 'Bound to be,' he said. 'So, will you do it? You'll have to go to Birmingham and Coventry. And soon, if you're going to get the new story—I mean, about how the parents are feeling now.'

Clare breathed out and leaned back, still glowing from Andy's praise, if a little suspicious that she was being manipulated. 'I'd love to do it.'

'That's settled, then. You finish that allergies piece, will you, and we'll have you up in Coventry first thing next week. How does that sound?'

'Fine. Oh—' She suddenly remembered another story she had expected to work on the following week. 'Just a minute. Dave, you asked me to interview Angel Avalon next week, remember? I had it all set for Tuesday, at the studios. The photographer's already lined up to do the shots for us.' She looked across at the editor. 'Andy, she's coming over to record first thing next week—a special album for the UK. And she won't be in London very long, as far as I know.'

Andy winked at Dave. 'There you are, Dave! The chance you've been waiting for. Just tell me all your staff writers are tied up, and off you go and do the interview yourself—for a delectable change.'

Clare pushed back her chair and laughed. 'Oh, you two! So that's what this is all about, is it? Never mind the poor mothers and fathers of the missing children. The real issue here is whether Dave can get to meet the adorable Angel Avalon, while she's over here from the States.'

'Got it in one, Clare.' Dave's face was split into a grin as wide as an opened melon.

'Oh, you make me sick!' she said, but still couldn't help laughing.

'Don't be daft, Clare,' Andy advised. 'Who knows, while Dave's discoing down here in London with the lovely AA, you might meet the man of your dreams in Coventry.'

She snorted with laughter and left them to the rest of the conference.

26

It didn't take long for me to get settled in the Coventry incident room and meet all my colleagues there. One incident room is pretty much the same as another—as it should be—though the atmosphere depends a lot on the SIO and the DIs who run the show. I found right away that I liked and trusted the Coventry people—much as I had felt in Birmingham a few weeks before. We were pulled together by that same driving concern: to find those children. In my mind, at least, there was no doubt now that the six cases were linked.

I was on the phone to Charlie quite a bit, dead curious as usual to know what was going on in our own patch—especially since the discovery of that old Marina.

'The house-to-house enquiries are in full swing,' he told me, but his voice was flat, and I wondered why he wasn't his usual cheerful self. 'The owner of the Marina's a lively old fellow—we've got two of the DCs following him all around Bristol and back again.'

'Anything unusual?'

'Oh—lots of excitement, Frank, I can tell you. He's out doing a bit of shopping every day, or picking up his pension from the post office, or some cigarettes and a paper. All the scintillating things old men of his vintage do in cars of that vintage.' Charlie sounded sour and disappointed. Our hopeful lead of the week before was turning into a dead end.

I had scouted around outside the old man's house just before I left. The thick screen of oaks around it would make our surveillance difficult, I thought, but Charlie said the lads were getting on with the job anyway. 'The old chap is keeping his car nearer the house, these days—must have got the message that the lay-by was out of bounds, or else got nervous about it for some reason. But McGavran says he feels like a peeping tom watching a dirty old man. Voyeurs, come one and all! This is all young McGavran's fault, you know. I think we're wasting our time.'

'So there's nothing of interest at all so far?' I heard myself sigh.

'Only that he's pretty profligate with the electrics—leaves lights on all round the house, all the time. But maybe he can afford it, and maybe no one's told him this is one of the hottest, sunniest summers in years. Oh—and, there's just one more thing.'

I waited. He would tell me, whether I answered or not.

'We did find out that the old boy's married—one of the older neighbours gave us that little gem of news. Had a daughter, only child, years ago. But no one's seen the daughter in ages, and the wife seems to be invisible at the moment, too.' What Charlie didn't need to tell me—because the bad news had come as soon as I sent the men to watch the Marina—was that the rag doll and lunchbox had been removed after all, even before we could bring anyone to identify them. A setback, that, especially as none of the parents could recall a missing rag doll, but I knew that if he had anything at all to go on, the detective superintendent would first bide his time, making sure of his ground, before he swooped. We still did not have enough evidence to convict the old man of anything more serious than a minor parking violation.

Late on the first morning I was with them, Joe Cafferty, one of the Coventry DIs, took me to both the council estates where children had been abducted. At each home I met the women detectives involved in the case—each detailed to stay with the family as much as possible. Even after all those weeks the mothers hadn't lost hope that we'd find their children for them, but the strain was beginning to tell. I saw pinched faces and eyes dark-ringed with lack of sleep. I felt when I left both the houses as if I had left wakes—and the grieving had only just begun. *Please God, let it end soon for them.*

Children on the street where a boy had gone missing stared open-mouthed at us as we walked away. They watched us from the safety of padlocked gates or curtained windows. *What a way to spend a hot summer like this one!* I thought, seeing their funny mixture of nosiness and fear.

'You've interviewed all these other neighbouring families, I presume?' I asked Joe. 'How are they taking it?'

He smiled. 'Fair to middling. These are practical, stoical people, Frank. Strong as the Irish, sure they are. Not like you softie southerners.' He winked. 'Yeah, they'll keep their children well guarded now, but they won't lose sleep the way the two families still are. And it's been weeks since a child went missing, so things'll maybe die down now for everyone except the two families.'

I watched four little girls playing in a parking area. They were skipping and singing in time with the beat of the rope on the pavement. 'The farmer wants a wife. The farmer wants a wife. E-I, E-I, the farmer wants a wife!'

Then a boy rushed at the rope and stopped it. 'Ugh! 'Oo'd want a *wife*, then?' He pulled grotesque faces and blew a raspberry.

'Shut yer face,' one of the potential 'wives' snapped. 'You ain't the farmer. Get lost, Billy!' Joe and I exchanged smiles. Summer holiday life went on for these kids, even when their friends disappeared. I smiled to myself. *Some things never change*, I thought.

Joe and I turned back to his Sierra. That must have been when I noticed a woman, her back turned to us, walking out of a broken gateway about twenty yards ahead. Tall, dressed simply in a pink and grey patterned blouse and skirt, she somehow looked out of place in that housing estate. She carried a folio brief-case and walked quickly, though not without moving her head to look around as she walked. Perhaps that's what drew my eyes to her—I'm not sure: the waving red hair bouncing on her shoulders as her head turned. She was as slender and upright as the kind of pedigree racehorse my Irish grandmother would have spent all her money on, given half a chance.

But how could it be Clare?

184

My colleague was looking at me sidelong. 'Whatever's the matter with you, Bernard? You look like you've seen one of the little people.'

We kept walking, but I felt as if all the breath had just been knocked out of my body. The woman kept walking, too, but crossed the road. As she looked left and right for traffic, seemingly without anxiety, she looked straight through Joe and me: two men in grey raincoats, nothing to distinguish us. But I saw her profile, and there was no mistaking her.

Joe nudged me. 'Hey, who's herself, Frank? Not so little, at all. Nice legs, eh?'

I caught my breath, irritated with him. 'Shh!'

He stopped. 'What, is there a description on the database of someone like her? Is that it? Could never do her justice, if there is.'

'How do I know!' I snapped. I wished Charlie were with me—or someone, anyone I knew well—to give some clue to my clueless mind of what on earth I would do next. My mouth had gone dry. *Why is Clare Hogarth in Coventry?*

She was walking so fast; it was clear that if she turned a corner we would lose her.

'Listen, Joe,' I said. 'This woman has nothing whatever to do with these cases—that I know of. But she's someone I need to see anyway.' I stopped in the middle of the pavement but did not take my eyes off her retreating back. 'You don't need to come with me. Write me off as a madman if you like—you wouldn't be the first. And I'll find my own way back, thanks.'

He looked at me in speechless amazement.

'What, don't you trust me?'

'Trust you?' he echoed, gaping. 'Aye, to the ends of the earth. The question is—' he eyed me beadily and glanced after Clare, '—can Somerset men run fast enough?'

'Avon men, you mean,' I called back over my shoulder, already several yards down the pavement.

'Better than Avon ladies, at any rate! Ding-dong! Avon calling.'

'Oh, take your Irish blarney away.'

I left him by his car with an impish grin on his face and continued my pursuit. Had she seen me? She seemed to be walking faster than ever, heading towards the main road that bordered the housing estate.

I followed her at a distance of about thirty yards, all the time thinking what I would say or do if she looked back. She had seen me once or twice already without apparently recognizing me. Would she rush away now? And how would I appear to her, a CID bloke on duty, my face hot with anxiety and bright with hope.

We passed a small garden billowing with blue delphiniums and wide-open peace roses. I saw her hesitate for a moment by the low wall that enclosed them. She was not aware of me, I decided, or she wouldn't have stopped even briefly. For a moment, because she bent over the wall as if to smell the roses, I thought she might turn around. Then she went on, almost running now.

I was now only twenty yards behind. I smelt the roses' soft perfume as I passed them. They were nothing like the bouquet of tight red buds I had handed to Nina Cottham on Paddington Station. My mind was working overtime, rehearsing the words I would say to her, but every piece of conversation I invented ended in a cul-de-sac.

I played back to myself the last conversation I'd had with her—about four weeks ago, now, on the telephone. She had taken my phone number, all right, so she might have called me. But I guessed that she wouldn't. She wasn't to know that I'd given up hope she wanted to hear from me. We had laughed together on the phone that day... until I mentioned Barking. Then she seemed to go cold on me. I'd lost her.

I had lost her! Suddenly, she wasn't walking ahead of me after all. Instead, a taxi was pulling away from the corner—from where the estate opened out onto the main road. Running after it, sick with disappointment, I saw her face through the grit on the windows. She was winding down the back window for air, but I don't think she saw me. I stood helplessly at the side of the road and watched the taxi pull away into the traffic.

A white car cruised past me, stopped, and reversed until it was parallel with where I stood. Joe leaned out of the window. I was in such a daze that I hardly recognized him. 'Frank—you'd better get in, man. You look as destroyed as an Irishman in a dry town. Get in.' He leaned over and released the catch so that the front passenger door opened.

I sank into the seat. 'Thanks. Didn't anyone ever tell you that kerb-crawling's illegal?'

He drove through the first set of green lights without comment, then asked, 'Do you want to talk? Are all you Bristol boys so intense and preoccupied?'

I stared at the passing pedestrians, dogs, shop awnings lifting in the slight breeze, and road signs to places I'd never heard of. I had to pull myself together. There was a job to be done. I had imagined the whole thing. How could Clare Hogarth be in Coventry?

'I'll be OK in a while,' I muttered. 'A cup of tea would do wonders.' I thought of the drawn face of the father at the last home we had visited. How could I get worked up over a woman when people were suffering like that?

'Tay. Right you are,' Joe answered. He glanced at his watch. 'We'd better step on it anyway. There's a journalist coming to interview the SIO and the press officer this afternoon. I have a feeling we might be wanted. Or I might, at least.'

'Journalist? What paper?' I asked, not really interested. Anything to keep from thinking about that woman in the disappearing taxi.

Joe stopped the car for a blind woman and her dog. The dog looked straight ahead as they crossed, and I marvelled as I always did at the woman's trust, allowing another to lead her where she could not see.

'What paper?' Joe repeated vaguely. 'Don't ask me. Some rag in London, I think. This must be some pretty high-powered fella—the guv'nor usually does all he can to keep the

187

press out.'

When we returned to the incident room, the journalist was sitting outside the SIO's office. It was Clare Hogarth.

Joe glanced at Clare, then at my face, laughed, and said he'd find us all a cup of tea. I stood there and just smiled. The smoky incident room was flooded with light. I had no idea if anyone else was there or not.

Clare Hogarth didn't smile at all. Her skin turned pink, then pale, then pink again.

Something inside me was somersaulting like a skylark. I could only smile at first; there were no words to say.

As it was in the beginning, when I first saw her on that motorway bridge, I was the first to recover my cool. I said, 'Aren't you the one I was following just now, in that housing estate?' *Something familiar about those words,* I thought. Then I took a slow breath and looked at the way she was sitting, one leg crossed neatly over the other, her skirt falling to mid calf over those long legs Joe had noticed. I didn't care, this time, whether she knew what I was thinking. She would know, anyway, having read my story.

'And aren't you,' I went on, 'the motorway philosopher turned magazine writer turned journalist?' I looked at her sandals and saw the pink toenails lined up like so many small pink shells on a beach. 'Size six-and-a-half, I believe. The magazine writer who never travels alone, or so she told me once. Five-foot-nine, or so, and drives a red Fiat.' This time I was careful not to mention Barking. 'The lady who's convinced there's more to her than meets the eye, standing on a motorway bridge or sitting at the other end of a telephone. The lady with "another me" lurking somewhere out of sight.'

She was smiling now, her grey eyes full of laughter. 'Oh,' I continued, warming to my theme now and pretending to myself that I was building a case in an interview, just before I pounced. 'And how am I supposed to know which Clare Hogarth is sitting before me here?'

She stood up and came towards me, abandoning her brief-case on the seat behind her. She gave me her right hand, and I shook it, but I did not let it go.

'There's only one of me, I assure you,' she said. 'You misunderstood what I said that day.'

I made as if I was squinting at her, turning my face sideways and narrowing my eyes at her. 'I remember telling you even one of you would suit me fine.'

She blushed even more, and out of pity I let her hand go. A foolish move, because she turned her back on me and retreated to the safety of her brief-case, and no doubt her filofax, and her executive identity. I couldn't presume anything.

When she faced me again, she had recovered her poise. 'You did offer me a cup of coffee that day.'

'Yes. Though I didn't know I was offering it to a lady who'd turn me down.'

'You, or the story?' She fairly twinkled at me, and I knew I'd given away far too much in that story I'd written.

'We won't get into that now,' I told her. 'Look, here comes some tea, at least.'

The SIO's door opened; I could see the Coventry press officer hovering inside, and I knew my time with Clare was over. The detective superintendent stood framed in the doorway, raising his eyebrows and surveying the scene with bland amusement. Then Joe came down the narrow aisle between the desks, bearing a tray laden with four steaming mugs. Clare's face had changed. Where she held the brief-case, her knuckles had whitened. Her pupils were dilated, her eyes wide open like the peace roses we had both passed half an hour before. *Anxiety*—that's what I saw on her face. I hazarded an optimistic guess, hoping I was right and that she was wondering whether I'd still be around when she came out of her meeting.

'It's OK,' I told her. 'I guess you're here on a work assignment, and so am I. Coventry constabulary coffee tastes pretty bad. Joe and I recommend tea instead. And I promise I'll wait until you've finished.' I sat down on the seat where she had been waiting before. 'The trail stops here.'

'Ho! No service for you, my lad, if that's how you feel. I made coffee after all.' Joe was grinning, and the SIO looked from one to the other of us with candid amazement.

For Joe's benefit as much as my own, I added, 'We'll get some real coffee later, OK?'

She smiled at me, and once again all the light and warmth in the world centred on this beautiful woman. I was in love.

27

'I want you over here right now, Clare,' Pete's voice said in her ear, louder than usual.

She moved the receiver away from her head slightly and felt her hand go damp. It was late on the Tuesday afternoon of her second week in the *Citizen* offices, and she had worked so late the night before on her first column that her eyes ached and her brain clamoured for rest. 'I'll be right over,' she said, and replaced the phone.

She did not, however, leave her desk immediately. She was piqued by the way he had summoned her so peremptorily, and wasn't inclined to hurry. Instead she sat with her head in her hands, rubbing her scalp and trying to think clearly. *Why am I so exhausted?*

The excitement had begun at the end of her first week at work. It was Rita, her aunt, who had unwittingly given her the idea.

'So you're going to a garden party at the McEnroes' home next week, dear, are you? Oh—you'll have a great time, I'm sure. But you know something? There are parties every bit as interesting almost every night these days—down at the yacht club next to the marina. Our marina, I mean.'

Clare's attention was fully focused for the first time in the long, lazy summer evening. 'Yacht club? I didn't know there was a yacht club next to the marina.'

'You'd know all about it,' Ed put in, 'if you'd come out in the boat with me some time and see for yourself.'

Rita frowned at Ed, who was lounging beside them by the open window. The air outside was at last cooling with the onset of night, and they had switched off the air conditioning. Fresh air and birdsong came to them through the twilight, and in the distance Clare heard the faint sound of someone's lawnmower.

'Thanks, Ed, I will one day.'

Rita looked from one to the other of them and smiled a tight smile. 'Ed,' she murmured, 'don't bug your cousin all the time.'

'Oh, he's not,' Clare said, '—at least, no more than usual. But tell me about the yacht club parties.'

Rita settled back in her chair and swirled iced tea round in the glass she was holding. 'I began to notice it in the late afternoons,' she said. 'People and cars. Then there was that night when I had an evening trip scheduled. I brought the tourists back, oh, it must have been around nine. Quite late enough for me these days, without Bert to meet me off the boat when I come in.' She stopped, but Clare heard no self-pity in her voice. She was too strong a woman for that, she thought.

'So what happened?' Ed asked eagerly, leaning forward.

'A lot of shouting. Lights on everywhere. And big cars in the lot when I pulled out—cars I've never seen there before.'

Ed pursed his lips and glanced at Clare. 'Nothing too special about all that, surely?'

Rita shrugged. 'Maybe not. But I—no, it couldn't have been.' She shook her head.

'Go on,' Clare urged.

Her aunt looked at her quizzically. 'Have you ever heard of an American actress called—er—Angel Avalon?'

Ed sat bolt upright. 'Yes indeed-y! Why? But she's a rock star, Mother, not an actress.'

'Oh, well. And you, Clare—does the name mean anything to you? I'd never heard of her, until that night.'

Clare exchanged a quick glance with Ed. 'Yes, she's popular in England as well, Rita. In fact I think she's on tour over there soon.'

'She is,' Ed confirmed. 'I saw it all in the media.'

'*Women Today* would love to get an interview with her, I know,' Clare said. 'I bet they're falling over themselves to arrange it.' She pictured Andy and Dave and chuckled to herself. 'Slavering at the mouth, I expect. Worse than you, Ed.'

Ed grinned at her. 'Well,' he said. 'And what about her?'

Rita's eyes wandered out over the patio to the street light that had just flickered on and now bathed the lawn in a faint orange glow. 'I was with a party of youngsters—all from some company in Cambridge celebrating a promotion or something. We were out, as I said, about as late as I care to be these days. Then, after I'd moored the boat and we were walking beside the fence at the edge of the yacht compound, one of the kids in my party stopped.'

'Then what?'

Clare saw that Ed was even more intrigued than she was. She touched his arm and felt the warm, smooth skin under her palm. 'You'd be a good investigative journalist,' she murmured, then withdrew her hand. He leered at her, and she looked away, reminding herself not to touch him again for any reason at all.

Rita seemed not to have noticed the tension between them. 'He was just a young kid—not much older than you, Ed. He was peeking through a knot-hole in the wood. The compound's lit up at night like the Fourth of July, to keep down larceny, I guess—there was a spate of boat thefts for a while, last summer. Anyhow, the rest of us were walking on, when this kid suddenly straightened up and came running, shouting about Angel Avalon. Said he could see her plainly. She was with a big crowd of people, apparently. All my kids went wild to look through the fence.'

Clare watched her aunt's face. 'That must have made you a bit nervous.'

'Yeah—I was tired anyway. And I had no idea who this woman was or what all the fuss was about. They told me later, when we were driving away. But I didn't want to get the marina in trouble with the yacht club for prying and peeking through the fence at their parties. And I doubt if someone as big as they told me Angel Avalon is would be down in our little old harbour, anyway.'

Ed whistled through his teeth. 'Some party, if Angel

Avalon was along. But I believe you—the harbour's had plenty of big names around over the years.'

'It wasn't just then,' Rita said. 'There have been more and more crazy parties since. Not every night, of course. Some are obviously out on the water—I hear those people pulling in and out of the harbour and anyone can see the lights shining back across the water. But I just have a hunch . . .'

'You think I should wangle my way in some time, do you? Write a piece for *Citizen* about these parties?'

'Just a thought.' Rita shrugged again.

'Wow! What a thought, though,' Ed had said, meeting her eyes.

Now, as she recalled their talk that night, she knew quite well why she was so tired. First there had been the anxiety about gate-crashing a party whose host she did not even know. Though Ed had reassured her confidently that they could brazen their way in, she knew she would stick out like the proverbial sore thumb with her English voice, her ignorance about protocol, and her red hair. Only Ed's wide-eyed but close-mouthed presence beside her—impeccable in white tuxedo and garish bow tie—kept her firm in her resolve to see the party to its conclusion.

With mounting tension, she had watched cocaine being passed among some of the guests—quite openly. She'd watched one after another of Boston's public figures drink too much. All the time Ed whispered the names in her ear for future reference. He was her ally again. Something had told her to run while she still could, before the customs or DEA men came snooping and swooping. But something else prompted her to stay, to watch, and then to write her first column—not naming the club. The copy had gone onto Pete's desk early this morning.

Was that why he wanted to see her?

She made herself stand up, seized a notepad, and left her office. Outside Pete's door, his secretary looked up from her screen and smiled vaguely. Clare saw that his door was shut. *Peter McEnroe, Editor*, the door announced.

'Is he tied up, after all?' she asked.

'He was expecting you, I know, a few minutes ago,' the secretary told her. 'But someone showed up unexpectedly.' She waved at a single red rose lying on her desk, wrapped in tissue paper. 'Senator McEnroe! His *uncle*,' she confided, colouring. 'He brought me that, would you believe?' She rolled her eyes. 'He does this once in a while.'

Clare dropped into a low seat opposite her desk. 'Would he mind if I waited?'

The girl looked at her watch. 'No, I guess not. But we never know when the senator's coming, and sometimes he's here for three hours.'

The thought of falling asleep outside Pete's office seemed more than appealing. Her eyes were heavy, and she knew she'd get no more work done this afternoon. 'I'll take a chance on it,' she said. 'I'd like to get to know Senator McEnroe, anyway.'

'Wouldn't we all! He may be seventy, but he's gorgeous. Like a movie star with all that silver hair.'

The secretary went back to her typing, and Clare watched the door as if at any moment it would open and reveal the old man whose photographs she had studied in many different cuttings throughout her first week. He was one host she would not mistake at that garden party on Friday!

When the door did open, it made her jump. Pete stood in the doorway, his height almost filling it, and was turning to say something over his shoulder to his uncle. Then, when he caught sight of her, he said, 'Ah. Here she is.'

Clare looked past him to see the senator. Not as tall as his nephew, he nevertheless drew her attention. She noticed his eyes first—piercingly blue under the shaggy grey brows— and the generous mouth. An intelligent, warm face. A man she felt somehow that she could trust.

She stood up, feeling as awkward as if she had been eavesdropping. Just as she was wondering what she was supposed to say, the secretary intervened.

'Ms Hogarth came to see you just after the Senator arrived,

195

Mr McEnroe.' He smiled, and again she noticed how very white his teeth were. 'Come in, will you, Clare. My uncle should hear what I was going to say to you.'

She stepped past the two men and Pete shut the door behind her. When she turned, both men were smiling at her.

Pete made the introductions, then, 'Please sit down. Clare, I want to congratulate you. I've been speaking to Senator McEnroe—'

'Pete, for heaven's sakes, Julius will do.' The old man winked at her.

'No one calls him Julius, except my aunt,' Pete said. 'Nearly everyone calls him "McEnroe".'

Clare nodded, dazed. *Congratulate me for what?* She found herself slightly awed by the senator, and surprised that she felt that way. 'I'm very happy to meet you. Everyone I've met speaks well of you.' As soon as she'd spoken, she regretted the words. They sounded tinny and insincere.

Perhaps McEnroe thought so, too, for his face quirked into an amused, dry smile. 'Nice of you to say so, my dear.'

She saw his eyes flick to her hair. Everyone gave a second look at her hair, but his expression was slightly different, as if something—a memory—was stirring beneath the lines of his face.

'Pete's just shown me your first piece for *Citizen*. He thinks it's outstanding. Well done! I try to keep my nose outta what's going on in here, but when he suddenly hires an *English* journalist, I can't help being intrigued. So you're going to write about us all, are you?' He put his head to one side and seemed to scrutinize her face closely. 'A view from the outside, right?'

Pete's tone was smooth. 'Not outside for long, I suspect. She's got the eye of a hawk, this woman.' He turned to her. 'That piece you wrote's sensational! I'll have a lawyer cast his eye over it, of course—' He flashed a smile at his uncle. 'Just in case anyone comes after us for defamation. And we'll dream up an alias for you, to protect you. You know what? This must be the first time since I sat in this office that I haven't had to shred the first piece of copy a new writer did for me.'

Clare flushed with pleasure, but she could feel the senator's eyes still riveted on her in a way that made her squirm inside. Someone—she remembered vaguely—had warned her that the senator had 'an eye for a pretty face'. Yet she felt there was more to his obvious interest than that.

She lifted her chin and smiled at Pete. 'Thank you. I hope I can keep it up.'

Pete spread his hands. 'I'm sure you can. And if you do,' he said, 'you'll turn that column into something juicy and fun to chew on, for a change. Like a good piece of prime steak.'

'Interesting comparison,' McEnroe said wryly, catching Clare's eye again. 'I always thought—' He cleared his throat. '—that the old column was more like a timid little peashooter. Now it looks like you're turning it into a sophisticated modern rifle. Fit to blast the head off anyone who stands in the wrong place.'

Amused at the mixture of metaphors—prime steak and guns—Clare nevertheless listened carefully, trying to gauge whether the old man was serious or sarcastic. His craggy eyebrows were low, and the blue eyes sparked at them both.

There was a slight pause, then Pete said with a laugh, 'Coming from you, that gun talk's pretty funny! You Democrats cant on about reducing the weapons in the nation's arsenal, but you sure don't mind rifling a few metaphors along the way.' He winced, glancing at Clare and enjoying his own pun. 'It's fine, isn't it, just so long as you're not in the firing line. Right, McEnroe?'

The senator shrugged. 'Oh, I'm sure this lovely lady would have nothing but good to write about me.' He smiled, but Clare saw that the smile was cooler now, that it did not reach his eyes. Was she being warned off? 'Anyhow,' McEnroe continued, 'You've fingered some of the drug peddlers in this first column of yours. Indirectly, of course—clever gal.' He unfolded his long body out of the chair. 'That's good. We're on the same side in that battle, I think. I knew nothing about those parties you've described.

197

It's something we'll definitely be looking into.'

Clare wondered why he didn't ask her how she got her story. Perhaps he thought she had made up the whole thing. And was Pete wise to show him an unpublished column that no doubt named some of his own colleagues in government and on the bar? She sighed. *Well,* she thought, *I've really started something now.*

Aloud, she said, 'If you do find out more about those parties, Mr McEnroe, I'd be interested to know. And if there's another story to be told somewhere, please tell Peter.'

The senator held out his hand to her. 'Or you, my dear,' he said. 'Any excuse to call a lovely young lady like you.'

The words sounded as tinny as her own, and as the senator said goodbye to Pete and left the office Clare was puzzled by him. Thinking the interview was over, she moved to the door to return to her own office, but Pete put a restraining hand on her arm and closed the door again. 'You really knocked his socks off,' he said. 'I'm very pleased to have you on the team. It'll be good to see what you produce next week.'

Although his eyes were alight with enthusiasm, there was a hardness in the way they assessed her now, a scrutiny different from his uncle's and uncomfortably like that of her cousin Ed. As he looked at her, there was that same taste of bitterness again, and she glanced away. His hand remained on her arm. She wanted to shake it off, though his hold was slack, but she did not want to make the wrong move so early in their professional relationship.

Without looking at him again, she said, 'Oh dear! You make me feel like that princess in the fairy story who had to keep spinning more and more gold from straw every day—or Rumpelstiltskin would never be satisfied.'

He laughed shortly, but his hand left her arm as quickly as if he had been burned. 'Good grief, I hope not!' he exploded. 'You don't really feel that way, do you? That's crazy—you're at the top here, Clare. You can't afford to think like that.'

A sudden yearning for the relative simplicity of her relationships at *Women Today* passed through her. It was true, her colleagues there jostled and pushed to achieve deadlines and build the readership, but here she sensed an even more aggressive world—harder, more competitive. She had wanted to belong to it, but now she was welcomed with such apparent ease that she did not trust it. No one rose to the top unless someone else was pushed to the bottom of the ladder. Her success would be at someone else's expense. *Can I live with that?*

She met Pete's eyes again, realizing he must be puzzled by her silent reflections and seeming diffidence. 'Perhaps I'm exaggerating,' she said. 'But I'm not like a lot of the other women here who'll push all they can for what they want.'

He frowned. 'What—you mean "hard-nosed" women like *Bobbie*?' he jeered.

'They don't all seem in the least like Bobbie,' Clare answered evenly. 'Bobbie's unusual. She's gentle and sweet and lively.' She bit her lip and stopped. Why was she selling Bobbie to Pete? He must know quite well what sort of a woman she was.

'And you can't be like "a lot of the other women"?' he said, ignoring everything she had said about Bobbie and adding ironic emphasis to her own words.

'Sometimes I can. It depends what's at stake.'

'But you're very motivated, self-directed. And confident, too, I thought.'

She threw out her hands, not wanting this analysis to continue, wanting only to return to her own office, to leave for the day. Tiredness pressed down on her again with increased weight. She laughed uneasily. 'Right now,' she said, 'I'd like to direct myself straight home. Listen, I'm sorry, but I didn't sleep much last night. I think I need a long bath, an early night and a few extra hours' sleep.'

Pete's expression changed. The tenderness she had heard in his voice on the plane, when he was speaking softly to Bobbie, now came into his voice again. 'I'm so sorry, Clare! I guess I got carried away. Yes, you do look a bit washed up.' He turned away from her, leaned over the desk and spoke into the telephone to his secretary. 'There's nothing else in my diary today, is there?' He looked up again. 'I'll take you home, if you like.'

She wanted to say 'no', but the softness in his expression was so unfamiliar and welcome that she felt her resistance crumbling.

'I do like,' she said. She pushed back a wave of her hair that had fallen across one eye. 'That would help. Thanks—if you're sure.'

He was waiting for her outside the elevator when she returned from her office. Taking her brief-case, he shepherded her into the elevator. She let him take charge.

They were standing at the front desk to sign out, his name a bold scrawl immediately above hers, when Bobbie came through the revolving doors. In one hand she had a black holdall, a 35mm camera was slung jauntily over her shoulder, and her other arm was crooked around a tangle of flash equipment. She was walking fast, her face bright, as if she had just come from a successful session on the other side of the city. She headed for the desk to sign in, and Clare saw her eyes jump straight to Pete, then swerve to herself. She wanted to say, 'It's OK—not how you think it is', but couldn't find the words.

'Hi, you guys!' Bobbie's smile froze. 'Cutting out early, are you?'

Pete frowned and looked at his watch. 'Not really, Bobbie,' he said crisply. 'This lady's had it. I'm taking her home—that's all.'

They went down into the underground car-park. Clare felt hurt by the pained expression on Bobbie's face and dismayed by the dismissive way Pete had spoken to her.

'You didn't need to be quite so sharp with Bobbie, did you?' she said. The words were out before she could stop herself. For the second time, she was surprised by the sound of her own voice. Not tinny and insincere, this time, but critical, even aggressive. *Not like a lot of the other women here?* she quizzed herself. *Are you sure?*

Pete looked almost as surprised as she was. He held the car door open for her. 'Oh, you do have claws, after all, Ms Perfection. That's a relief.'

'I must have,' she said shortly.

Dropping into the seat beside her, he slammed his own door and faced her. In the dead air of the closed car, his voice sounded as if it was inside her head, almost pressing on her. 'Better and better! A woman of spirit after all—as well as a damn good writer.'

She felt indignant, felt the rush of blood to her face. 'Well,' she said, 'you'd have to be blind not to see how Bobbie feels about you.'

He turned the key in the ignition, and the car surged to life. 'I know perfectly well how she feels about me. She's a lovesick kid—calf love. But I don't feel the same at all. Now you—you intrigue me. You interest me.'

Something in her went numb. She heard again the predatory voice of her cousin as he'd stood in her bedroom doorway. She could not reply but stared straight ahead as the car shot forward, up the ramp and out into the traffic.

'I don't want to talk about Bobbie,' he was saying. 'Let's talk about you, instead. Yeah, I know you're tired, but maybe what you need is a bit of fun. How about if—'

She did not wait for him to finish. 'No,' she said quickly. 'Just no, Pete.' She tried to remind herself that she was speaking to her boss, not someone like Danny she'd known for years, but it didn't work. *He shouldn't be taking advantage of me, and if he stops treating me like an employee and starts treating me like his latest prey, I'll have to fight back.*

His voice was like silk. 'Ah—you don't like me.'

She shut her eyes briefly and saw behind her eyelids the compelling blue of his eyes, the shock of fair hair, the expensive cut of his clothes and the powerful width of his shoulders. Her mouth went dry. However foolish it would be now to tell the truth, she couldn't help but tell it. 'Yes, no, I do,' she said breathlessly. She felt gauche and naive, and the words almost choked her. She roused herself and added feebly, 'But you're my boss.'

'Off-limits for you, huh?'

She thought of Andy and Dave in London. 'Usually, yes.'

'Don't like mixing business and pleasure?'

'Oh, yes, I do,' she answered, before she thought further. 'If the business isn't a pleasure, why bother at all?'

'Exactly my sentiments, Ms Hogarth. So why not drop the coy English lady routine and get your glad rags on and come out with me tonight? How about it?'

She thought of Bobbie, of the hurt look on her face as they had left the lobby. 'Thanks, but I meant no,' she said.

'Another time, then?' He braked for red lights and looked across at her. His eyebrows were raised in enquiry, and his eyes were very blue.

She hesitated. Heat rose again into her face and ran through her body in a fire. 'Maybe,' she said in a non-committal voice.

28

When she came out of the detective superintendent's office, Frank was not waiting for her after all. She stood quite still and looked around the room at the heads bowed over screens, papers and telephones. *No Frank.*

She suppressed a sigh. What had she expected? A white knight with a huge bouquet of roses—red roses, pale roses, any roses? (But not shedding their petals everywhere like those she had left in London.) It had seemed too good to be true when she had seen him on that housing estate. Had she dreamed that rush of panic and excitement when she turned from the roses and saw him following her, heard his footsteps coming after her? He was a detective with a job to do—a job apparently not limited to Bristol. And (as the senior investigating officer had been pleased to remind her), he was working on a set of cases that had affected hundreds of lives for two months now.

So what had she expected? To find him waiting for her—a lowly member of the press?

In spite of their apparent willingness to sketch in some of the information about the missing Coventry children, Clare realized she had probably learned less from the superintendent and the press officer than from her random house-calls that day to some of the neighbours of one missing child. In contrast to their obvious delight in being interviewed, the SIO had almost abruptly put her in her place. Even if *Women Today* had run one good story about the child now found, she was only a writer (he implied), after all, not a senior woman inspector with the right to ask the really hard questions. The press officer, too, had made it plain that her conjectures about the children still missing were insignificant. How could she have expected hard-nosed CID men to talk much about the feelings of the families involved? She would need to go back early the next day to both housing estates and talk directly with the two families. She half smiled as she decided she would do that, even though he had made it clear that he would prefer her not to.

Slowly she began to walk away from the SIO's office, along an aisle that separated the desks. A few men looked up with enquiring faces. Screens were turned away and papers abruptly covered. She felt out of place, unwanted, a person who could make no real contribution to the finding of the missing children. And now Frank Bernard had vanished, as well.

'Would you be looking for Mr Bernard?' a voice asked her suddenly from behind.

She swung round, in the process knocking down a pile of papers balanced on the edge of one desk. Flustered, she stooped to retrieve them; but the man who had spoken to her snatched them up first. It was the same man, she noticed, who had brought coffee to her before her interview with the detective superintendent and the press officer.

'Is it Frank Bernard you'd be after finding, pet?' he asked her again.

'Well—yes.'

'I'll dig him out for you. I was just having a wee chat with him. He's over there on our database right now. I won't be a minute.' He winked and disappeared, genie-like, into the cloud of smoke that hung across the entire room.

She stood where he'd left her and stared around again. The big room might have been a games room at other times, she thought, perhaps for snooker or table tennis. She knew she was privileged to have found her way into the heart of the Coventry abduction investigations. The guardedness, she decided, was natural. And at least they had not fobbed her off after her long journey with an insultingly short press release.

She wasn't sure exactly what she had expected in an incident room—but probably not the untidy yet quiet atmosphere; certainly not the intensity, in spite of the tragic reason for its operations. The serious atmosphere was broken only by an incongruous poster of Angel Avalon on the back of a desk. Over her microphone, Angel pouted and glowered at the world. Glad that she was not in London as planned, interviewing the rock star for the magazine, Clare glowered back; and, as she did so, Frank rounded the corner between two desks to her right, appearing out of the pall of smoke as if she had conjured him out of her imagination.

'I saw that!' he laughed. 'Jealous, are you?'

'Of course,' she shot back. 'A voice like a piece of tearing silk—who wouldn't be?'

His eyebrows lifted in surprise, and he laughed uncertainly. 'You do have a way with words.' He stretched out his hand towards her brief-case. 'May I take that for you? We're going this way. There's a mad Irishman who wants to meet you properly.'

She surrendered the brief-case. 'All right. Mind you don't go off with secrets meant for women today.' She went ahead of him along a corridor he indicated, glancing back over her right shoulder. 'What mad Irishman, anyway?' She felt at ease with him already, as if she had known him for a long time.

'Joe—the one who brought us that brown stuff masquerading as coffee. The one who just told me you were finished in there.' He waved his free hand back the way they had come. 'Sorry I wasn't standing to attention when you came out, but we just got some news, and I had to ring down to my boss. Now Joe says he wants a proper meeting with the only journalist who's ever made it into the inner sanctum in the middle of a major investigation. He wants to know your secret.'

Standing by a bubbling hot-water urn, Joe was nursing another cup of coffee when Frank showed her into what must—she thought—be the tea-room. Windowless, with pock-marked walls and scuffed floor, it was a bleak place. She took it all in at a glance. 'We meet again,' Joe said cheerfully. 'I'm Joe Cafferty.'

Clare smiled at him. Was he one of Frank's friends? She searched her mind for something to say but was so attuned to

Frank that her head was empty of all but him.

She offered Joe her hand and tried to remember that the true reason she had come to Coventry was for the magazine, not to find a man she had never expected to see again. 'Clare Hogarth. From *Women Today*,' she said mechanically.

'The wife reads your magazine,' Joe said. 'Good, is it?'

Clare laughed. 'Your wife must think so. Why don't you read it?'

He ignored the question. 'So how'd you weasel your way in to see the guv'nor? It's unheard of, you know.'

Clare remembered the phone-calls placed by her colleagues in advance of her journey north on the train the day before. Andy and Dave had spent a good part of the day phoning first the police press officer and then the neighbours of the families whose children had been abducted. 'My boss set it all up,' she said, shrugging. 'I'm not sure exactly how, but it may be because we ran the story of the family up here whose child was taken earlier in the year and then restored.' She saw the two men exchange glances, but went on, 'I didn't organize that story myself, but I got very interested in it.'

Joe smiled encouragingly. 'Well done, *Women Today*.'

She smiled back, hearing another comment he had not made, except with his eyes: '*And you got very interested in Frank Bernard, too, by the look of things, didn't you?*' She would dodge even the unspoken comments, she decided. 'Your wife will be reading the story we did—oh, any day now. One of our freelance people here wrote it with the child's mother.'

'And you're hoping to do the same sort of thing with the families who are still going through that heartache?' Frank asked her. 'Is that it?'

His tone was neutral, but she tried all the same to gauge whether he would be critical of what Andy wanted her to do. 'Yes,' she said steadily. 'But we don't want—I especially don't want—to exploit anyone who's going through that kind of grief.' She caught another look between the two men but could make no sense of it. 'I got as far as interviewing some of the families today who are neighbours of one of the missing children.' She felt her mouth curving up as she remembered the street, remembered him following her soon after she had made her last house-call. Frank's eyes caught hers. 'That's when—' She stopped. *How can I say that I met him again this afternoon? I didn't. I ran away in a fright when I saw him.* She tried again, 'That's when . . .'

Joe came to her rescue. 'Oh, I get the picture now,' he said. 'Frank explained to me, er—' He broke off in a cough, and bent to rub his shin. Clare wanted to laugh. Had Frank kicked him to stop him saying any more? If he had, the attempt had failed. Joe went on blithely, 'So he bumped into you in June—not far from here, I believe. He's your ticket in here, is he?'

She would dodge that one, too. 'What's this? Cross-questioning?' She threw another quick look at Frank. His eyes rested on her, warm, full of light. She felt the same warmth she saw in them spreading like sunshine through two bright windows into her whole body.

'Yes,' Frank said lazily, 'I did say I'd do you for theft, I think. But, Joe, if I'd known that Clare—'

'Stolen heart.' Joe nodded sagely. 'Nice to know not all the romantics are on the other side of the Irish Sea or north of the Watford Gap.'

Clare knew she was blushing again but blundered on, 'Well, I certainly had no idea, either, that I'd meet Mr Bernard. No, as I said, it was my boss who organized this trip. I'm hoping I might be able to help you—now, or later—in what you're doing. And that you might be able to help us, that's all.'

Joe snorted. 'Oh, sure but you must have kissed the blarneystone, Miss Hogarth. Well, never mind. It's past time when we should be letting your friend go for the night.'

Frank cupped his hand round her elbow and steered her towards the door. 'Exit cue, I think,' he said.

Joe grew serious. 'You'll be here in the morning before you go, will you, Frank?'

Frank nodded. 'Have to be. Let's hope there's some good news for the briefing.'

Clare watched the way they spoke to each other, all business now. She was forgotten.

'Yeah, let's hope so. You've come a long way for nothing, if not.'

'A long way for a long-shot! Well, you people've got enough on your hands without West Country coppers and London journalists poking their noses in.' He threw a cheeky look at Clare. '*And* this poor woman has waited a long time for me to buy her a cup of real coffee. So we're going.'

After collecting his own papers, he led her down through the public entrance at the front of the station. Her mind was hurtling forwards. In her imagination over the past weeks she had travelled many journeys with him, but now that they were actually together, she found herself swinging between bubbling exhilaration and abject terror. What on earth was she going to say to him?

They stopped outside the front door of the police head-quarters and turned to each other. The evening rush-hour traffic coming off the Ringway hurtled past them, the heat of exhaust fumes and of pavements baked for a day in remorseless sunlight rose and swirled around them in a palpable wave. She looked into Frank's face and felt lost. At the same time, a ripple of happiness running through her told her that she was found, too.

'You're staying here overnight, are you?' she managed at last, then realized she was holding her breath as she waited for the answer.

'Yes,' he said. 'Just a two-night stand this time—this is the second night. And you?' His voice was polite, distant, and she was puzzled by the apparent change in him.

'I'm in a bed-and-breakfast near the cathedral.' She wanted to ask him where he was staying but felt it was too soon. Then she heard again in her head the last few words he had said, and decided to tease him. 'Two-night stand! That sounds interesting.'

Immediately she felt embarrassed by the way she had picked up his words, for his expression became utterly serious. 'Come on,' he said. 'I promised you coffee, but it's dinner time, and we have a lot to talk about, you and I.'

'No coffee, then?' She tried to restore the lost light-heartedness.

'Oh, yes, but later.' He moved a step or two away from her, but seemed as unsure as she was how to cross the unfamiliar territory of Coventry—or the uncharted space of their unexpected meeting.

Saying little, they walked aimlessly until they found a small restaurant on Fairfax Street—not yet open.

'Hmm. Opens at seven. How much time have you got?' he asked.

She looked at her watch, then let her left arm fall to her side. 'All evening if you like.'

'I do like,' he laughed. 'Listen, I'm not that hungry yet—are you? No? Well—shall we see the sights of Coventry?'

'I'd love to, but let me carry that brief-case of mine—you've got two, now.'

He grinned. 'I'll swap you one brief-case for your free hand in mine.'

'Who needs to make bargains about that sort of thing?' she laughed, and gave him her hand. His fingers closed around hers: warm, dry, chafing her skin. They strolled on. Clare felt dizzy and incredulous, joy more real than the evening's heat washing over her.

'That charge of theft I was levying against you,' he said suddenly. 'I don't think I'll bother booking you after all.'

She looked at him sideways, saw the corner to his mouth turning upwards into his beard. Like herself, she saw, he had recovered his wits. 'Why not?' she asked.

'Well, now that you're here—I'm here, we're here—I've got back what you stole.'

'What did I steal, then?'

'A lot of sleep. A lot of time spent wondering about you and writing up a story you didn't like—' He pulled a face at her, and she laughed. '—And my heart, of course. But, now, look, it's safely back on my sleeve.' He raised his elbow to nudge her. 'You can see it there, surely? All sewn on like a sergeant's stripes.'

'Yes, there it is,' she said, not seeing anything but the criss-crossed white threads of his shirt, 'quite as visible as the Emperor's new clothes.'

'Thanks a lot! So this is how magazine writers spend their lives, is it—jetting up and down the country just chatting to people?'

She wanted to talk about their work, but now was not the time. 'And being chatted up.'

'You don't mind, do you?' He squeezed her hand.

'Not one bit.' She wanted to say, *No one better. No one I'd rather spend my time with. Oh, I don't believe this!* But she didn't.

'That's good.'

'By the way,' she murmured. 'Where are we going? Do you know?'

'A long way, I hope.'

She thought of their meeting on the bridge over the motorway and his account of it in the story he had sent to the magazine. She blushed. 'No, that's my line, not yours. Now who's stealing?'

'And tell me—who *was* the person with you the first time I saw you.'

'Or I saw you—which way was it?'

'Does it matter? So tell me—who was it?'

She hesitated. Would he understand? She looked into his eyes: blue and as wide open as the roses of the afternoon. 'I'm not sure what you'll make of this,' she said.

'Try me.'

Clare looked ahead of them, across the stones, to where the ruins of the old cathedral stood next to the new. Westerly sunlight streamed onto their faces and fell too on both buildings, illuminating every niche and nub of the stonework in the ruins; every plane and edge of the pink sandstone slabs that made up the new cathedral. 'All right,' she said slowly, 'I'll try... For a start, I never feel alone when I see a place—two places—like this.'

'The dream the master builders had, you mean?'

'Yes, their vision, and the hope and worship of all the people who've been here since. Ordinary people, like us. The people who built here first, years ago. Then the people who stood and wept after the bombs fell. Then the people who knelt in the ruins and had a vision of a new cathedral. And now all the thousands of people who come from all over the world to see one cathedral risen out of the ruins of another.'

He was frowning slightly, looking back and forth from her face to the two cathedrals. 'You mean you have a sense of—' He dropped her hand, waving both his hands in the air so that the brief-case flapped and bumped against his side. He put it down. 'I can't think what I'm trying to say. A sense of the saints here before us?'

She began to smile more and more. 'Saints, yes. But sinners, too.'

'Is there a difference?

She put down her own brief-case and shrugged. 'Oh, hard questions, Mr Bernard!'

'Well, and is there?'

'I doubt it. We're all sinners, for sure. But saints, too, if we let our lives belong to God, if we allow ourselves to be reconciled—I mean—' She stopped, frowning, wondering how to explain, '—if we ever find peace with God.'

Frank was shaking his head. 'Ah—my parents would love to talk to you, Clare. They speak your language.' His face was soft. 'I just don't know if I do, though.'

'Yet,' she said.

'Yet,' he agreed. 'Anyway, I'm no saint. I enjoy life too much.'

She watched him, not fully believing him, wanting him to understand what she was getting at. 'Who says life isn't to be enjoyed? And heaven isn't a boring, grey, comfortless place, either. I'm sure it's full of partygoers. I'm sure it's the biggest party in the universe. We're only standing in the doorway here.'

211

He threw back his head and laughed so loudly that his voice echoed back to them even in the humid air. 'Hmm, I wonder what my parents would think of that. I'll have to ask them. But you still haven't answered my question, you know, about who was with you.'

He stooped for the brief-cases, bundled them both awkwardly under one arm, and took her hand again. They walked on into the ruins and stood together, facing the altar of the old cathedral, silent for a few moments. Above them stood two charred roof timbers shaped into a cross, the words 'Father forgive' inscribed behind it. In front of it was another smaller cross made of old nails.

'Those words,' she said at last. 'It's God—he's the one who is always with me. And not just me, Frank. The same One who was with the people of Coventry—Dresden, too, for that matter—when the bombs were raining fire down everywhere.'

'Yes,' he answered thoughtfully, 'other friends have said the same. I can't talk about God the way you do, but even a chap like me—here I mean—can feel there's something special about this cathedral. A presence, if you like.'

'I do like.'

He put his free arm around her shoulders and drew her to his side. 'There you go again, Miss Hogarth. Petty theft! One of my lines, this time.'

She was torn between wanting to stop just where they were, abandon all her doubts and fall into his arms, and wanting him to hear fully what she was trying to say to him. 'Never mind that,' she said. Her voice was choked, but she went on, 'And yes, there *is* a presence here.' She pointed to the broken stones that made up the new altar. 'See what the builders did?' she asked. 'Took rejected bits of rubble and made something new and beautiful to praise God.' Then she added, 'The God of second chances, and third, and fourth . . .'

'Ah, if so, that's a God I could learn to love. Look at this second chance we've got now—you and I.'

Tears came suddenly to her eyes, catching her by surprise.

212

The intensity of the moment made her want to dance and weep simultaneously. 'I hope so,' she murmured. 'But that's not what I meant.' She bit her lip. If she shut the door on the path he wanted their conversation to take, would there be a way to open it again? She had no idea how long they had together—now, or in the future. But then, *the God of seventy-times-seven chances*, she told herself. *Don't fret*.

She turned to him. 'What I mean is—well, look at that gorgeous new cathedral, will you? Stark as anything, a sign of suffering. But a sign of hope, and forgiveness, and friendship between two peoples who were enemies once. That's what I meant . . . the God of second chances. The God who wants us to be at peace with him.'

'Oh, Clare, you darling woman.' Frank dropped the brief-cases again and gathered her to him.

She went into his arms gladly. He kissed her first on her hair, then her ear. She turned her face slightly and lifted it to his, feeling the rough edges of his beard brush her cheek lightly. Then his smiling mouth found hers, and she was breathing quickly, her heart running faster than a rabbit across a field with a hound following. She did not want the kiss to end, felt all the boundaries of her being stretching and bending out towards his, felt the rush of a passion she had never known kissing Danny—or anyone else—before.

'You're lovely,' he said at last, holding her face close to his own. His eyes were blue as the sky she had seen behind the birch trees a couple of weeks before. As blue. As deep. 'I don't want to let you go, you know.'

She did not know how to answer him, though she knew they would have to walk on eventually. But nothing was the same as it had been a few minutes before.

After a while they left the ruins of the old St Michael's and mounted the steps into the new. Pale light slanted in uncertainly on the left, and Clare listened to the sound of their joint steps echoing in the vast spaces. *Together,* she thought, still not able to believe.

'I like this place,' Frank said softly when they came to the little chapel of Gethsemane. Inside it, beyond the ring of iron thorns, a woman knelt in prayer with a child close beside her. They stayed quite still, their heads bent under the picture of Christ lifting the bright cup of suffering. Tears came again to Clare's eyes. Not just a God of second and seventy-times-seven chances, but a God who understood sorrow.

When they turned under the great tapestry at the north end, Clare gasped. From the entrance, the cathedral had looked shadowed, but from where they stood now, light seemed to pour upon them. It gilded the wings of the carved birds flying in a flock at the side of the cathedral and lit up the warm wood of the choir seats.

It was almost seven-thirty and pigeons were whirring up over their heads as they came back out into the late sunshine. The air outside smelt cooler and fresher than when they had gone in, a contrast to the echoing stillness of the huge building behind them, and they walked hand-in-hand down to Fairfax Street again.

'Here's where I can get you that coffee I promised you,' Frank said, stopping by the menu board of the restaurant they had peered into before. 'Sorry, but I don't think I can eat anything much at all.' He winked at her.

'You won't sleep, either, if you don't,' she said.

'Probably not. But I'll feast on your eyes, instead, sitting opposite you while you eat to your heart's content.'

'Oh, nonsense. You think *I'm* hungry?' She screwed up her face. 'At the moment, I don't care if I never see another fry-up again. But I'll eat a little, all the same, unless you—'

'Come on, then. No Coventry fry-ups in here, I'm sure. This looks far more digestible.' And he steered her through the door.

A waiter showed them to a table at the back of the restaurant. The place was crowded now, almost as close and hot as the incident room, but Clare hardly noticed. In the small space, there was no room for them to sit across from one another, but as soon as they had sat down next to each other on the squashy, vinyl-padded seat, Frank turned

214

slightly so that their knees were bumping under the table. He smiled at her, and she smiled back. 'I'm glad we went up to the cathedral,' she said.

'Me too. But I'm afraid this evening will make tomorrow seem like a bad dream.' He grimaced. 'I'm going south again, of course. But you—I haven't even asked how long you're here for, yourself.' He pushed back his hair.

She wanted to run her hands through the dark waves of that hair and kiss him again, but she already felt breathless from the time they had spent together. *Plenty of time,* she told herself, meeting his eyes. 'I'll be here until tomorrow, as well. That's all. I'm hoping to see the two families in the morning, then—'

His eyes gleamed. 'Then I suppose your slave-driver of a boss—editor, whatever—wants you tied back in her slave-ship by the end of tomorrow afternoon?'

'*His* slaveship—yes, something like that.'

'But you're here for the same sort of reason as I am, I thought. Does she, sorry, he, really expect you to interview all those people in depth within twenty-four or thirty-six hours?'

She broke into a smile. 'Well, I suppose I could be out pounding the pavements now, if I hadn't met you again.'

His face was deadpan. 'Go on, then. Who's stopping you?'

'No . . . I think I'll interview you, instead.'

'Good! Shall we have half a bottle of something to wash all the words down with?' He signalled to the waiter, and they ordered. 'Fire away. This is one time in my life when I don't mind being on the wrong side of the interviewing table. If all interrogators were as—'

She frowned. 'Hush! Let's be serious for a minute, at least.'

'Oh, sorry.' He made his face solemn. 'That do you?'

'For now, anyway.'

'Right. I'm ready now. But don't forget, anything you say could be taken down and used as evidence.' He rubbed her knees with his own, grinning. 'In the next story I write about you, I mean.'

She giggled. 'Oh, that's how it works, is it?'

'Yes. I'm a dangerous person to be with. One of those artistic types, you know. A would-be *writer*—watch out, or I might put you in one of my books one day.'

'Listen, who's the real writer here anyway, I'd like to know? You're just a policeman.' She gave him an Angel Avalon pout, then laughed.

'A novice with a novel in my head. But maybe a future Dickens, you never know. Which the light, which the shadow?'

'More M5 philosophy?'

'No—that's Plato, I thought.'

She shook her head. 'You've lost me, sorry.'

'OK, then back to business. Where were we?'

She leaned away from him and pulled a notepad and pen out of her handbag.

'Oh, time to sharpen the quill, I see.'

'That's right,' she said, 'but you don't need yours this time . . . For a start, would you tell me how much I can legitimately ask you? Your boss up here—and his press officer—made it clear that he wouldn't fill me in any more than he had to, and that I was lucky to get in to see him at all. I felt a bit like a peasant supplicating a lord of the manor. He wasn't sour, exactly, or hostile. Just very dour and guarded. I'd hate to disillusion your colleague Joe Cafferty, but my session with those men wasn't very helpful in the end.'

He winced. 'I'm sorry! Well, I can't speak for the guv'nor here—he's not my boss in any sense, even if he happens to be my superior when I'm working up here. But, Clare—' and his face was genuinely serious now, 'you can ask anything you want to. Anything at all. If there's something I can't answer for reasons of confidentiality and security, or something I don't know how to answer, then I'll say so.' He reached for her hand. 'As you were saying to Joe a while ago, it would be good if we could help each other. The police and the press aren't always at loggerheads, you know, and there are children out there somewhere who need all the help they can get.'

As the meal was brought to them, and as darkness fell outside the restaurant, Clare learned not only what was happening in the Midlands and West Country investigations, but also about Damian, Frank's dead brother. She began to understand why it might be hard for him to believe in a God of love and mercy.

'He's why I'm on these cases, I think,' Frank concluded. 'Yes, I know it's different—he died of leukemia, not child abuse or ill-treatment after abduction—or murder. But I know a little of what the families are feeling. Grief is deep and painful, no matter what the cause.'

She had watched his face soften as he'd told her about Damian. 'No apologies, Frank, for feeling as you do about these cases.' She thought of their conversation in the ruins. 'The way you're thinking about these children is the way God does—with so much love and care.' She watched his face as she said this, not wanting to alienate him, but seeing that he did not know himself how close he was to God.

He looked away but gave her hand a squeeze. 'Is it? Well, you can think that if you like.'

'I do like.'

'We're getting repetitive, you know.' Then his face changed. He released her hand and straightened his back. 'I've just had an idea! It's not particularly kosher, but since you'll be helping us in our investigations—as the saying goes—I could probably get away with it.'

'What?'

'I'll finish my work here around the same time you finish yours, I imagine. If you could telephone the magazine and clear it, why don't you come back to Bristol with me and talk to some of my colleagues there for a day, or to the family there who've lost a child?—instead of going back to London.' He rushed on, 'You could stay with Jill Peterson, if you like.'

She caught her breath. 'What a thought!' *Another day with Frank. And maybe far more of a story to go home with. But can I spare the time, and am I going with him for the right motives? And what if there are strings attached?*

He must have seen the play of delight and doubt on her face. He took a sip from his glass and said, 'Think about it, at least. And see how your chats with those families go tomorrow.'

Leaving both the restaurant and the cathedral behind them, they walked together back to the police headquarters' car-park. Frank paused before he opened the car door for her. 'I'll take you over to the B & B,' he said, 'unless you've got that Fiat of yours?'

'No. I didn't trust it after the last time. I came on the train.' But she saw that he was still hesitating. 'What is it? Did you want to go into to the incident room for anything?'

In the ugly orange light shed by a street lamp a few feet away, she saw his eyes widen in surprise. 'Oh, you don't miss much, Clare Hogarth, do you? To be honest, yes, I would probably have put my head round the door again to see what's going on—if I hadn't met you.'

'Go on, then. Who's stopping you?'

With one hand he unlocked the Sierra passenger door, and with the other he hugged her to his side. He broke into an impression of Joe's accent, laughing. 'You're a terrible woman, Clare.'

She settled in her seat and watched him walk around the front of the car. She liked the way he held his head up as he moved, his back straight, his eyes lively even in the orange darkness.

They got lost among the unfamiliar streets of Coventry, somehow finding themselves too far away from the cathedral to use it as a marker.

'How on earth did we manage to get all the way down here?' Frank said. His voice was on the edge of laughter. 'Surely we had only to find our way back to near where we had supper?'

Clare leaned forward and peered outside the car for any sign of a familiar landmark. 'Hmm. That sign says "Mile Lane". But you must have a map. If you want to know the way,' she teased, 'ask a policeman.'

'We were talking so much,' he accused. 'What did you

expect? I wasn't paying attention when I turned left out of that car-park.'

'Driving without due care and attention,' she laughed.

'Watch it, or I'll turn you out and you can get a taxi.' He pulled the car into a lay-by, switched on the inside light, and found a map. 'It's your fault. You distracted me. Ah, I see. Look, we're right near where I'm staying. How about that?'

She glowered at him. 'You drove down here on purpose.'

'I didn't, but what a nice idea.' Then he rushed on, 'Wait— at least put your head around the hotel door so you can come and find me in the morning. It's only small, but I'll treat you to breakfast here, if you like.'

This time, she didn't say, 'I do like' (though she did like). 'Maybe. But I'm in a bed-and-breakfast, remember. The best English breakfasts anywhere. Perhaps you should . . .'

'No. Breakfast here, or nothing. I've never had breakfast in a hotel with a gorgeous journalist before.'

'Some of Joe Cafferty's own blarney's rubbed off on you, I think,' she said. 'All right, I'll come and find you in the morning.' She felt relaxed and happy, glad to be alive. Glad to be with him.

He stopped the car outside the hotel reception. 'Just so you know my intentions are honourable,' he said, 'I'll leave the car here, where it'll block the entrance for five minutes. But come and see what luxury the Avon and Somerset Constabulary affords its employees, will you? Then I'll take you back, I promise.'

Inside the front door of the hotel Clare stepped on to deep red carpets and looked around at the flock wallpaper and dimmed lights.

'It's a family hotel,' he told her.

'Are you sure we haven't stepped back into the fifties?' she asked.

'Why are you whispering?' he whispered.

'Because you're obviously almost beyond the hotel curfew. What a funny little place! Look, there's no one around at all.'

'Yes there is,' a voice said sharply, and a tiny, red-faced old man appeared from behind the reception desk. He had been bending down behind it, invisible when they came in.

Clare jumped.

The little man's eyes looked narrowly at them. Frank coughed. 'I'm staying here,' he said.

'I know you are. Saw you going out first thing this morning,' the man returned crossly. 'Room number?' He reached up to the board of keys, waiting for Frank's answer and eyeing Clare as if she were a prostitute. 'And you, Miss?'

She backed away, colouring with embarrassment.

'No,' said Frank, 'It's room twenty-eight, but I don't need the key yet, thanks. And Clare's not staying. I was just—'

Again the little man's eyes glittered at them. 'I see.' He frowned—then suddenly seemed to register. 'Oh, you're Inspector Bernard. Sorry.' His manner became deferential. 'Er—will you be much later, then, sir?'

'No. I wanted this lady to see where she'd be meeting me for breakfast, that's all. I'll be back easily within half an hour.'

Clare suddenly felt desperately tired, wrung out from the day's interviews, even from the excitement of seeing Frank again. He took her arm, and she saw over his shoulder the inquisitive eyes of the hotelier fixed on them both.

'I'll take you right back, as I said . . . You've had it, haven't you?' Outside in the car, he added, 'That man would make a brilliant watchdog, don't you think? About as friendly as a Rottweiler.'

'Rather you than me in that hotel,' she laughed.

'Thanks,' he growled. 'I think I should have booked in at your B & B instead.'

She smiled into the darkness and watched the lights of the city flicker over his profile. She wanted to say, 'I wish you *had*,' but it was pointless. She was too tired even to pursue the 'what if?' of their staying in the same guest house. *Life's complicated enough as it is*, she decided, checking that line of thought.

He caught her eye, lifting one hand off the wheel. 'I said—'

'I know,' she told him quietly.

He tousled her hair. 'You're great.'

This time, he had no trouble finding the guest house. She gave him a pale smile when he pulled into the kerb and turned off the engine.

'I'll see you tomorrow morning,' he said.

She tried to work out from the tone of his voice whether the time they'd had together so unexpectedly meant as much to him as it had to her. She didn't want to rush anything. 'Yes,' she answered quietly.

Perhaps he understood her hesitation. 'Listen, I once gave you my phone number. Have you still got it?'

'Yes.' She nodded.

'I'll give you the CID numbers as well—here and in Bristol. Just in case something changes our plans at the last moment and you can't come to Bristol with me after all. When you've talked to those families tomorrow, if you think there's something—*anything*—we might not know, just tell me.' He leaned across and brushed her mouth with his own, and she realized he would not see her out of the car this time. He tilted her chin, so that they were looking directly into each other's eyes. 'And call me anyway, will you?'

She watched him scribble down two numbers and tear off the top sheet of a small pad attached to his dashboard. He handed them to her. She tried to smile again, but her face was lop-sided now with exhaustion. 'Yes, I will. And here's my number, as well.' She tore the sheet in half, wrote her Ealing number on the empty half, and gave it to him.

'Go on,' he said. 'You'll be up early with those families. Go and get some sleep.'

She stepped out into the cooling air and smelt Indian food cooking somewhere.

'Good night, Clare,' he called, over the hum of the engine. He waved and drove away.

Not far away, the new cathedral loomed over the houses, shops and pubs, its shadows extending like grey wings over the city. She looked up but saw no stars.

29

On the Wednesday night, after I'd left Clare at Jill's flat, I couldn't sleep. *Euphoria*. But it wasn't only the happiness of replaying in my mind the journey south with Clare that kept me awake. I had a terrible case of the shivers.

In the middle of the night I got up to see what time it was and to shut the windows. The weather must have changed, I realized; the house felt chill and damp. I could hear Tim breathing quietly in the next room, his door open slightly. I remember thinking how cold he must be, as I shut his door softly, and then went round the house shutting everything else.

Still I couldn't get warm. I padded into the kitchen, lit the gas, and put on a kettle. The clock said three-thirty, and the thermometer by the window said seventy-two degrees. I stared at it, rubbing my eyes. The heat of Wednesday must have broken it. I'd heard of thermometers sticking if the temperature plummeted suddenly, and that's obviously what had happened. The temperature in the kitchen, even with the kettle steaming for my tea, could surely not have been more than forty-five.

Huddled over a hot mug, I picked up, then discarded, Wednesday's paper. Instead of reading, I went back to thinking of Clare. What was it she'd said in Coventry, trying to convince me? The charred wooden cross with its words 'Father forgive' came to mind, and, immediately, I remembered. *'It's God—he's the One who is always with me . . . the God of second chances . . .'* Statements, not questions. She was completely certain.

Once I had been certain about God, too. My parents still were, even after what had happened to Damian. But how could a loving God let an innocent boy like Damian die so

222

horribly and so young? Damian. *It isn't fair!* I used to rage at God. *What had Damian ever done to hurt you? Or my parents?* They had never, to my mind at least, adequately answered that question.

In Coventry, Clare had come closer to it. I pulled my dressing-gown more closely around me and thought about what she had said in the restaurant only a day ago. *Or is it two days ago?* I wasn't sure which day was which, for a moment. But we had ended up talking about Damian again. She probably thought I was obsessed with the death of my brother, and I suppose I was.

'Don't you think,' she had said simply, 'that he's safe in God's keeping, and well again? Don't you think he's found peace now, and real joy?' There it was again, that confidence in a God who *loves* rather than condemns the people he's made. Foolishly, I kept looking over her shoulder, as if I'd see him myself at any moment. Francis Thomas Bernard. *Doubting Thomas.* My parents had named me accurately enough. But even Thomas was convinced in the end, falling on his knees and shouting 'My Lord and my God'. Would that, could that be me one day?

Clare must have thought so, for she persisted in talking about him. I'd listened to people talking about God before—street evangelists, for a start, and some of my parents' friends in the church—but I always used to tune out. This time, though, I was listening. More importantly, she was making sense.

'And don't you think that God's with those six children? And their parents? Frank, that's what he promised. Jesus—God with us—Emmanuel. That's what the name means, you know.'

Something irreverent in me made me want to push her theories to their limit. 'And with the abductors?' I asked.

She only smiled, and on anyone else the smile would have been infuriating. 'Yes, with the abductors, too. D'you think he doesn't love all his children? If you can mourn all this time for Damian; if that care for children and for the helpless is what's driven you on in this case, how much more do you think God can care for us—all of us—and long for us?'

I had no answer, of course, for all this. 'Motorway philosopher' was what I'd first dubbed her—and rightly. Instead, as I should have guessed, she had to have the last word on the subject. 'I care about you, Frank.' She was smiling. 'And God cares far more than I do.'

I wanted to believe her. That was a start, I thought—to want to want to want something. She had said as much to me in Coventry that night, her face almost as incandescent as the candle that lit our table.

Did she, I wondered, want me—or at least want to want me? I wasn't used to women like Clare who were thoughtful and gentle, and I was nervous of going too fast for her. We'd had the journey back to Bristol together to exchange more stories and get used to each other, and today we'd spent every moment together when the governor and the electronic pager weren't pushing me around, and when she wasn't out interviewing people about the abductions.

'I'll take you swimming,' I'd offered, 'before you go back.'

'*Swimming*?' she echoed unhappily. 'But I can't.'

'Can't what?' I teased.

'Can't swim at all.'

Something about her voice was quite unfamiliar and unexpected. 'You're afraid?'

She grinned suddenly. 'It's one of those things I want to want to like,' she said.

'Then I'm taking you Thursday—before you get your train.'

'No costume.'

'Lame excuses! Borrow one from Jill.'

Now, at three forty-five in the morning, the thought of swimming wasn't welcome at all, though I knew I'd go through with it anyway if my 'beeper' didn't summon me first. With that miserable possibility seeming far more real than the prospect of working, then swimming, in a few hours, I crawled back to bed.

When I woke again, my tongue was furred and the room

seemed like a furnace. I staggered out of bed and into the bathroom for the daily dose of reality in the mirror. Within the curves of my beard, my cheeks were as pink as if I'd sunbathed all the previous day. Except on my feet and hands, all the skin on my body radiated heat. I groaned. *I must have a temperature*. I flung open the window.

Tim heard me moving around and shouted outside the door, 'Frank, why on earth is everything closed up like this?'

His loud voice reverberated painfully between my ears. 'I was cold,' I said stupidly, wincing. I opened the cupboard above the sink and took out two paracetamol. The bottle was almost empty. How long had I had this headache anyway?

'You must be mad. It's eighty in the kitchen already!' he shouted.

I couldn't summon the energy to justify myself or even crack a joke. 'Sorry. I'll be out in a moment.'

My arms felt leaden as I dressed. Even knowing that Clare would be waiting for me at Jill's flat didn't help me hurry. By the time I was hunched beside Tim at the kitchen table, however, I felt almost normal again. The wonders of love and modern medicine.

'Where are you off to, with that smile pasted on?' Tim wanted to know. He had been out of bed longer than I had but was still in his blinding red boxer shorts, his hair standing straight up as it always did first thing in the day.

'You're a sight,' I told him.

'Thought I'd go surfing,' he growled sarcastically.

'Well, I'm off to work.'

'How original.' He took a mouthful of cornflakes and looked at me reflectively over the spoon. 'But I thought Clare—the invisible Clare . . . Where is she anyway?'

'She's real enough,' I said. 'At Jill's flat. But you won't meet her. That's a promise, chum.'

'Spoilsport!'

'And after work you won't see us, either. If the SIO is still feeling merciful, I intend to take her swimming, then out for a slap-up supper before I put her on the late train.' It all sounded wonderful, but I thought suddenly, too, how exhausting it would be unless I could shake off this headache properly.

'Good thing too,' Tim said. 'Nothing in the fridge this week but a bottle of ketchup, a pint of milk, and some leftover potatoes growing rather exotic flora. Great housekeepers we are!'

I ignored him. 'This morning she's going to meet one of the families involved in that case I've been on.'

His spoon stopped midway between bowl and mouth, and his eyebrows went up. 'You won't be very popular, will you?'

I grinned. 'Popular with who?'

'The girl, of course. Not to mention the guv'nor. Frank, you're really losing your marbles. First you tell me you're going *swimming* the first evening you've ever had with this girl—'

'Woman,' I corrected. 'Next you'll be calling her a "bird".'

He scowled. 'And then you say you're taking her out for a *real* treat—to meet someone on the case. Of all things, Frank Bernard! You're mad.'

'So I've been told.'

'She must be mad as well, to put up with you.'

'Well, you and Richard seem to put up with me most of the time, don't you?'

'Only because we hardly see you in here.'

'Tell me all about it,' I said, and left him to his breakfast.

When I parked the car outside Jill's flat, Clare was standing with her luggage in the sunshine outside the door, looking as relaxed as if that were where she spent every day of her life. Her smile was as warm as the summer sun on my back when I went up the steps to meet her, and I forgot my headache for a while.

30

Outside on the patio and across the smooth lawn, the McEnroes' guests stood with drinks in hand and talked. Some moved from group to group, laughing and waving their hands as they spoke, while others, like Clare, were more watchful. A buzz of chatter floated through the french windows to where she stood, and the softness of the twilight was almost spoiled by winking red and green lights that someone had arranged along the edge of a swimming-pool.

Clare had just been admitted through high double doors into a wide lobby at the front of the house. For a moment she had wondered whether she had stumbled into the wrong house altogether, for no other guests were in evidence, and—late as she was—she could not possibly be the only guest. An aproned woman who might have been a housekeeper served her a glass of wine, and she stared round, glad she had a moment alone to survey the home of the family that had most interested her since her arrival in Boston.

The housekeeper indicated her way across the lobby and through what must be a family room to the party outside, but, after hesitating, she had remained in the family room by herself. There would be time enough to move outside and join the others. Feeling the depth of the faded oriental carpets under her sandals, she stared around her at the muted pastels and greys of the room's wall decorations. Then a series of small glass shelves opposite the fireplace caught her eye. Arrayed on them were dozens of framed photographs.

Forgetting the party, forgetting her drink, she stepped closer and examined them. *I wonder how many people I'll be able to recognize,* she thought, recalling file after file of press cuttings. She bent towards the lowest shelf and picked up one frame; McEnroe himself looked out at her, his silver hair blowing back in a breeze no camera could catch; his lips curved in a half-smile.

She replaced the first photograph and picked up another. Marianne McEnroe this time, but one taken many years ago, she guessed. Beside her stood another woman whom Clare had never seen among any of the press cuttings. A young woman with a cloud of red hair—darker than her own, and thicker. As tall as herself, she noted. Both the woman wore such short skirts that the picture could only have been taken twenty years before. The women looked directly at the camera, not at each other, both smiling. And although there was no physical contact between them, no arm around a shoulder, not even eye contact—Clare sensed a close relationship between the two. Except for the age difference, she might have guessed that they were sisters.

Another, larger photograph in a clear plastic frame drew her eyes next. Someone had arranged a formal family portrait, though the background of the photo—a farm barn—was by no means formal. In the centre of the photo stood a tall man with thick black hair that was streaked with silver. Beside him, one arm linked with his, was a short, round-faced woman with untidy brown hair and happy eyes. The two stood close to each other, relaxed in each other's company, with three young people—one on one side and two on the other—grouped around them.

Something about the older boy made her look more intently. His hair was fairer and curlier than the others', more the colour of Marianne's—*or Pete's*. Were these Pete's cousins, then? She frowned. The father was tall like Pete, but his jaw was deeper and the expression on his face more open. Were they cousins, or was this man Pete's brother? She tried to remember what Pete had said about his father, Anthony McEnroe, then realized that there would probably be a wide difference in age between Pete and his cousins if the two McEnroe brothers had been born years apart. Cousins, or brothers? *Well, it doesn't matter* . . . she thought.

She turned the picture over and found some of the answers. In a tight, meticulous hand, someone had written: 'Summer 1988, Arcade, NY: Don and Maggie with Rachel (15), Joel (14) and Billie (12).' Then underneath, in an untidier but nevertheless quite readable script, someone else had written, 'Love to GraMar, Christmas '88'.

She looked again at the front of the photo. Either the man or the woman—and she couldn't think that this tiny woman could be a McEnroe—was Pete's cousin.

She went back to the photo of the two women and searched for identification, but none was visible. That older photograph was enclosed in a brown frame that obscured the back of the photo, and she could hardly pull it apart to look for names.

She bent down again to replace the photo on the lowest shelf, then felt something splatter onto the bare skin of her feet; her wine was brimming over onto the carpet. A dark blue stain spread out on the pile deepened the rich blues and crimsons of what must once have been a lavish rug.

She started back in alarm.

'Caught in the act!' a man said.

She straightened, turned with her heart in her mouth, and found Pete McEnroe near her. 'What a pretty behind you have, my dear,' he said, and leered at her.

'Oh, you!' She tried to laugh it off. He had been avoiding her—or perhaps it was that she had deliberately avoided him—since he had taken her home three days before. She wanted to keep everything between them to a light patter or on a strictly professional basis. He was far too dangerous, and no doubt Bobbie would appear at any moment, and her face would fall when she saw them. But Clare could think of nothing funny to say and instead ended up staring at him rather longer than she meant to.

'And what bright eyes you have, my dear,' he said.

'All the better to see you with,' she answered nastily.

'Ah, but you didn't see me, did you, Clare?'

'Obviously not.' She mentally shook herself awake from

the hypnosis of those blue eyes, still blue even in the dim light. 'And anyway, why are you talking like the big bad wolf if you want to convince me what a nice boss I've got?' She forced a smile. 'Excuse me. I have to find a cloth. I've just—' She waved her empty glass at the carpet.

'So I see,' he said drily. 'Allow me.' He reached into his pocket and found a spotless white handkerchief.

'Sure you haven't any rabbits in that?' she asked caustically. 'Why not flourish it about a bit and see if you have?'

She did not thank him for mopping at the carpet but instead went straight past him and out of the french windows. As her sandalled feet touched the coolness of the flagstones outside, she felt her face flooding with colour at the thought of her rudeness to the man. *But really,* she justified herself, *he invites it.* She pictured Andy and Dave at *Women Today* and knew she would never have spoken to either of them in the same way. But boss or no boss, she decided, he shouldn't provoke her, either.

Deliberately she went as far as she could down the lawn and lost herself among the laughing people. A group of women she might normally have avoided because of their cliquiness admitted her to their fellowship, and she felt suddenly safer. As soon as she opened her mouth, they oohed and cooed over her English accent, and for once she was glad to engage their attention as long as possible—anything to forestall more advances from Pete.

The burble of Boston social conversation washed over her, but she hardly heard it and wondered how she would ever write a column from the scant gleanings of the night. Gradually working her way through the crowd, where the mixture of perfumes and the scent of the cedar trees were heavy in the humidity, she eventually stopped in the shadows of the widest cedar. Women whose faces she half recognized from press cuttings, but could not place, surrounded her. All the time, she kept her eyes on the big house, certain that Pete would not leave her alone now that he had caught her at a disadvantage.

For a while, Marianne McEnroe joined them, and she

forgot about Pete in her study of McEnroe's wife. The reserve of the older woman surprised her—it seemed somehow out of character with the bubbling tinted curls and clear eyes. Was this really the same woman someone had addressed as 'GraMar' on the back of a photograph?

At last, plucking up her courage, she bent towards Marianne. 'Mrs McEnroe,' she said, 'forgive me if I'm being nosy.'

Marianne looked at her with faint but quickly disguised alarm. 'You're a journalist, you said. That's your job, isn't it?' Her lips formed into a curve. 'Fire away, if you've got a question.'

'Thank you,' Clare murmured, but she knew that there was no smile behind those lips, only slight irritation—or perhaps nervousness. She moderated her tone and stepped back a little so that she would not threaten the woman in any way. 'I noticed a nice picture of you by the french windows.'

Marianne's face tightened slightly. 'Oh, yes?'

'A photo taken some time ago, I think. A picture of you and another woman—younger.' She tried to sound gentle and reassuring but was again struck uncomfortably by her own insincerity. 'Her hair is red—but not like mine. Darker, and thicker. In curls. You know the picture I mean?' She watched Marianne stiffen.

'Yes.'

'I was wondering—'

'One of our relatives.' Marianne looked away. 'She died a long time ago.' She put her hand up to her hair as if to push away a stray strand, but every curl was in perfect order. 'Please excuse me.'

Clare took a sip of her drink and tried to get her bearings. What was there about this family that fascinated everyone, and who was this girl who had died?

The women around her were gazing at her with something approaching awe. 'Hey, you're some sleuth, you are!' one of them said, rolling her eyes. 'I've never seen Mrs McEnroe act like that. She really blew her cool.'

'You've never seen Mrs McEnroe act like anything,' another answered sourly. 'You've never seen her at all until tonight, let's face it.'

Clare wandered away. A breeze came up, blowing the scent of the cedars around her again, and for a moment the huge branches seethed like a dark ocean over the heads of the partygoers.

Ed had tried hard to persuade her to let him be her escort again. 'After all,' he said, 'you'll hardly know a tenth of the names. How're you gonna write your piece this week without me, huh?' 'I'll have to get used to it,' she'd told him. 'You'll be back to college in a couple of weeks, anyway. You just want to suss out the McEnroes' house, that's all, isn't it?'

He had grinned and shrugged. 'We-ell, maybe you're right. But why not?'

Why not? Why not indeed! Now she wished Ed were with her.

Bobbie suddenly materialized, camera in hand, from among a knot of men at the top of the steps on to the patio. 'Clare!' she called. 'It *is* you! I thought I caught sight of you a half-hour ago, but I was stuck up here. Great to see you!' This time the smile was genuine.

Clare smiled back. 'Oh—and you. Have you been snapping away all evening with that thing? Get any good ones?'

'Yes, I think so. Nothing to put up anyone's back, though. No long soulful conversations between men and women married to other people, if that's what you're wondering.' She laughed. 'I saw your first column. Wow! You pack quite a punch with those words.'

'And you do too with that black box of yours,' Clare said. 'So why don't we see if we can stir something up between us?'

'Stir what up?'

It was Pete again, and Clare gritted her teeth. While Bobbie glowed beside her, she looked up angrily and said, 'Really, you have the most appalling talent for appearing out of nowhere and making people jump.'

232

He sized her up, and the whiteness of his tuxedo reflected up onto his face and gold hair so that she had again the impression of someone who compelled alertness. Even in the darkness, he was bright.

He only laughed. 'Glad I can still make my staff snap to attention. Hi Bobbie!'

'Good to see you, Pete.' Bobbie sounded in control of her feelings, Clare thought, not giving anything away this time.

'Can I get you both another drink, or some canapés?' he asked smoothly.

Clare realized then how hungry she was, and when he returned with a silver platter of finger sandwiches and three filled glasses, she ate gladly, almost grateful after all that he was there. She noticed, too, that Pete no longer ogled her but instead paid court to Bobbie, his hand sometimes touching her arm, his eyes resting on her face. The tenderness was back, and she marvelled again at how mercurial he was. In turn, Bobbie glowed, her eyes never leaving his face, laughing at all his jokes about the people who walked past, amenable to all his suggestions of those he wanted photographed for the magazine.

For a moment she felt a stab of jealousy. He did know, then, how sweet and natural and good Bobbie was. Perhaps she had misjudged him after all. Perhaps he wasn't at all the big bad wolf he liked to appear.

Eventually she decided to leave them to their conversation. Julius McEnroe passed them, winked at her, and went down to stand by the edge of the pool. She took her glass and joined him. In the still water, floodlit by underwater globes, the lights winked, too: red and green stars blinking on and off.

She was going to say 'What a good party this is', but she could hear the sound of her own insincerity. *I must stop this,* she told herself, looking at his shrewd eyes. Instead, she said something quite undeniable and neutral. 'You certainly have a lot of people here tonight, Mr McEnroe.'

He turned towards her. 'Yes.' He sighed. 'Don't know the half of them.'

'But I thought—' She wavered on the edge of saying more, then hung back.

'Lot of them are friends of my wife's.' He threw out the hand that was not holding a glass. 'Oh, sure, lots of guys from the golf club and one or two cronies of mine from work, but mainly Marianne's people, come to think of it.' He stopped, set down his glass on a low table at the edge of the water, and lit a cigar. She watched his face as the lighter flared and showed the lines and loose folds of his old skin around the jawline and above the collar. Yes, he had once been much heavier, she thought.

He seemed to rally himself and concentrate more, suddenly, on what he was saying. 'You're here to get another column, are you?'

She flushed and looked at the lights in the water. 'Yes.'

He growled, 'Well, be nice to an old guy, willya?'

'Of course!'

'Fine, then. Now, tell me—' He cleared his throat. 'If you'll pardon the corny intro and all, what's a nice English girl like you doing in a place like this?'

She felt more able to deal with this sort of conversation. The soft underbelly of the man—his vulnerability and even loneliness which had flickered out just a minute before were far more disquieting. But banter was all right.

'Pete—I mean, your nephew—met me when I was travelling over.'

'So he said.' McEnroe breathed blue smoke across the pool and did not look at her.

'I was flying because my uncle had died.'

'And now you want to check us all out and see about staying?'

'I'd like to for a while, anyway.'

He glanced sideways at her. 'I guess Pete's got you all squared away with the immigration folk? You'll be here on the wrong visa, if not, you know.'

She did not look at him directly, either. It was easier for both of them to stand shoulder to shoulder facing the water, their backs to the partygoers on the patio, and their faces hidden from all the people on the lawn below. 'Yes, I know. We're working on it.'

'Good. And you've got a social security number as well, I hope? You don't want that nephew of mine ripping you off. He can't pay you without one. Keep an eye on him, will you?'

She did not yet have the right visa or a social security number, but Pete had paid her anyway. 'For the copy that's gonna raise the ratings through the roof,' he'd said, handing her an envelope stuffed with dollars. Her first American paypack, and she'd hardly even stopped to consider whether he was following the system or not. But perhaps he wanted to keep everything unofficial until he had tested her for a few more weeks. More straw to spin into gold. And more, and more. No, he had said he wasn't like that, and she had just seen again that gentle side of him that made her almost wish that Bobbie was out of the picture.

'I said, keep an eye on him,' McEnroe repeated. He winked again and drew on his cigar slowly. 'He fired his last columnist in nothing flat. I hope he treats you better, my dear.'

'He has so far,' she said steadily.

'You know something,' he said, looking at her at last, 'you remind me a little of someone in our family a few years back.'

Instantly the photo of Marianne and that other woman came to mind. She held her breath, wondering if he would say more. 'Yeah—she's gone now.' His voice took on a dreamlike quality. 'She was a red-head like yourself. A model—tall and slender like you. We loved her.' He shrugged. 'Ah, well, God's been good anyway, even without her. I've got three lovely grandkids and the best daughter-in-law a man could wish for.'

She thought of the family portrait. Somehow, she knew that curious questions now would be misplaced. She said nothing.

Pete came and joined them, this time without an ambush. 'Bobbie had to leave,' he told Clare. His voice was slightly slurred, and she saw McEnroe look sharply at his nephew.

235

'Go on, Pete, you'd better call it a night, hadn't you? I'll call you a cab.'

Pete put his arm round Clare's shoulders, his breath in her face a blast of gin and expensive aftershave. She flinched but felt unable, under the scrutiny of the senator, to pull away. 'Well,' he said huskily, 'I was hoping I could take this little lady home again.'

'Not you.' McEnroe looked severe. 'You're not driving an auto—not by yourself, and not with a lady, either. I'll call you a cab, I said.' And he stalked off. Over his shoulder he threw back, 'I'm surprised at you, Peter McEnroe. An upstanding *Citizen* of Boston getting destroyed in the presence of all these ladies and gentlemen.'

He was gone. Peter turned with a quick laugh towards her. 'Oh, don't mind the old guy. He's crabby like that some days.'

'But you're half seas over, aren't you?' she accused.

He stroked her arm and took another sip of the clear liquid in his glass. 'Yeah, maybe I am. I was lonesome for you.'

'Rubbish!' she laughed uneasily. 'You had Bobbie there to keep you company. She's lovely, Pete. The more I get to know her—'

'Aw, give me a break!'

She pulled away from him, but he grabbed for the soft stuff of her blouse. She stopped, so that it wouldn't tear.

'Come here,' he said thickly. 'Give me a kiss. I've waited long enough, for pete's sake.' He creased into a boozy laugh. 'Get that? For pete's shake, huh?'

I'm looking at my boss, she said to herself. *My boss*. She felt again the same sensation of that Sunday morning in her bedroom when Ed had made a pass at her. (*My own cousin*.) Yet, perversely, something deep inside her did want to kiss Pete. On her own terms, though, not because he had hold of her clothes, and not when he was drunk.

She lifted one hand to push him away. 'I don't want—'

He tightened his hold all the more, his breath hot on her face: frightening now; no longer attractive or tender in the least. His teeth were gritted, the veins in his neck standing out above his white collar. 'Damn you,' he grated.

'Leave me alone!'

She began to struggle. Two wine-glasses shattered and splattered on the flagstones at their feet and, as well as feeling the pinch on her arms, she heard the crunch of broken glass under his soles as he twisted her towards him. She went limp as a rag doll in the vice of his arms, and his mouth covered hers.

His arms relaxed so suddenly that she almost fell backwards. 'Oh, Clare. You—there's something about you,' he murmured. He was shaking his head. 'I saw it that first day on the plane. It's still there, though not so much. I want you, Clare.'

She felt the blood beat up into her face. His silky words were utterly at odds with his hard, frantic kissing. 'That's gin talking,' she told him, rubbing her bruised mouth with the back of her hand and stepping backwards. 'No, you don't want me, Pete. You don't know what you want.' She thought of Bobbie. It was Bobbie he wanted, but she would not say so now. She would say nothing to rouse him again. She must get away.

'I'm shorry,' he said, and moved back himself. In the blinking red and green lights his skin was livid and mottled. He reached out his hands for her again, though now his face was different: naked, vulnerable, like a small boy who has hurt his mother. 'Honest, I'm shorry. I didn't mean—' His arms were almost around her for the second time.

She did not think, this time, before she acted. A wave of fear and frustration overcame her, and she met him with an almighty push. He toppled backwards and teetered on the brink of the pool among the broken glass. Then, at the moment she expected to hear the splash as he hit the water, he lunged forward and dragged her after him. Her feet scraped over the glass, and water closed over her head, Pete's arms clenching her to him. In the water, the red and green lights scattered and splintered like so many small stars across her vision.

When they surfaced, gasping, his arms still around her, two thoughts came to her at once. *Pete's drunk. How will he*

*ever get out of here? I should never have pushed him. . . . I can't
swim!*

They went under again, Pete kicking against the water.
Dimly she heard voices shouting by the pool's edge, and
when they came up the second time a knot of people had
gathered. Panic took over, and she screamed like a seagull,
struggling against him. As if it were happening to someone
else, she heard him laughing, *laughing*. She drew a great
gulping breath, then Pete's weight pulled them down a third
time.

The waters broke near them, and she opened her eyes to see
another swimmer thrash towards them. In the viscid underwater light she saw the gleam of silver hair and the anxious,
lined face of an old man. *McEnroe*. A thin line of bubbles
rising from his mouth, he worked to separate them, then
pulled on their elbows.

They surfaced in a line, McEnroe in the middle, treading
water. Her panic subsided. His vigorous movements were
holding all of them above the waterline.

'Get us out, willya,' the senator shouted harshly. On his
other side, she heard Pete retching and coughing. Then she
began to cough herself. Her teeth chattered violently, and
several pairs of hands reached over the side of the pool to help
them. By the time they were all on the flagstones, the party
had stopped and they were surrounded by an amused crowd
of well-dressed people whom she felt she had never seen in
her life.

Where's Bobbie's camera now? she thought bitterly.

McEnroe was swearing at his nephew. 'What in the—what
were you playing at, for heaven's sakes?'

Pete pushed himself off the stones and crouched, water
streaming off his hair and clinging clothes. He leaned across
his uncle, ignoring the question altogether. 'Got your column
now, have you?' he said harshly. 'Go on. Write this one up,
Ms Hogarth.'

Shaking, she scrambled to her feet. Someone draped a long
shawl across her shoulders, but she scarcely felt it. She

noticed abstractedly that she had lost one of her sandals in the water. 'I hate you!' She knew her face was contorted with rage and heard the tears in her own voice. 'I hate you!'

'Well, you've certainly made a splash in Boston social life,' a man's voice nearby mocked her.

Clare looked straight through the speaker and turned away. Behind her she heard McEnroe still berating Pete, then a woman calling from the patio steps that a cab had arrived for him. Shuddering, she dragged up the steps and across the patio.

'Wait a minute, Cinderella.' Pete caught up with her. 'You've lost a cute little glass slipper.'

She tried to outrun him but hesitated long enough to debate running through the family room in her dripping clothes across those priceless carpets. It was just long enough for him to corner her by the french windows. She was breathless with shock, hardly recognizing the searing, heaving, sobbing sounds of her own throat and lungs.

He was holding out a sodden white sandal towards her. 'Don't forget this, Ms Hogarth,' he said. His voice was no longer slurred, and in the indirect light that spilled from the family room she saw again the whiteness of his perfect smile.

Marianne McEnroe suddenly appeared between them. her mouth a tight line. She opened it as if to speak sharply to Pete, but then seemed to change her mind. She held out heavy blankets to them both.

'What size shoes do you take, dear?' she asked Clare kindly. 'Maybe you can borrow something of ours and get yourself dried out.'

Shivering, dripping, Clare met her eyes. 'Six-and-a-half,' she said miserably.

Marianne's eyebrows curved up. 'Are you sure? Your feet look about seven or more.'

Then Clare remembered. She was in America, not England. The sizes were different. A curious sense of having had this conversation once before with Marianne . . . or someone else . . . overtook her.

239

PART FOUR

*But I have promises
to keep*

31

'Where to first?' Clare asked him. She looked at Frank's face and frowned; dark circles shadowed his eyes, and in the brilliant light of an early August morning the skin above his beard looked taut and dry as parchment. She guessed uncomfortably that she was only adding to the pressure of his responsibilities for the day. 'I know you need to get to the HQ as soon as you can—I don't want to hold you up.'

His face softened, and he flicked his eyes off the road to catch hers. 'It's OK, really. And the sooner we both get our work done, the sooner I can take you out.' He pulled down the visor and frowned into the glare that bounced off the car ahead of them. 'First stop, the Drury family. You'll find one of our WDCs there; we briefed her yesterday.'

Clare thought of her conversations the previous two days with the families in Coventry. It had been much easier speaking to the neighbours than to the grieving families, but she knew her best story would come direct from the parents themselves.

Clutching her notepad and with her suitcase and brief-case at her feet, she rang the doorbell of the pebble-dash council house where Frank had left her. A stout woman answered the door and beckoned her in. 'Mr Bernard rang and told us you'd be here. You're from *Women Today*—is that right?'

'Yes, and you're Mrs Drury?' Clare ran her eyes over the woman's round face, quickly assessing how she should conduct the interview. The eyes were shrewd, any misery well concealed, at least for the moment.

The woman laughed. 'Lord, no! I'm just the guardian angel around the place—for as long as they need me. Chief opener of doors, answerer of telephones, and maker of tea. Mrs Drury's out in the back, hanging up the washing. I'm sure she won't be long. Do sit down.'

The tiny front room was claustrophobic: a huge television set dominated one corner, and every shelf was crowded with framed photographs of a red-cheeked girl at various stages of growth—from babyhood to about ten. The vast overstuffed chairs were far too big for the room. By the door a drop-leaf table, perhaps generally used for family meals, had been pressed into service as a work space for the policewoman; it was littered with newspaper cuttings, files, envelopes and cards.

'The family gets a lot of letters?'

She nodded. 'Yes, right from the beginning. They're quite well known round here anyway—Mr Drury runs a corner grocery shop just down the road; popular sort of chap. The child herself was—is quite—well, you'll hear for yourself in a minute.'

Clare sank into one of the chairs and started writing. 'Only child?'

'Yes.'

At the back of the house a door slammed in the breeze and was reopened. The sound of slippered feet shuffling across the kitchen reminded Clare fleetingly of her mother. Then a big-boned woman came into the front room.

'Oh, she's here.' Mrs Drury couldn't seem to look at Clare but addressed herself to the policewoman.

Clare stood up and was about to offer her hand when she saw so much pain in the mother's face that she withdrew it and sat down again. 'I'm Clare Hogarth,' she confirmed, wondering if she should begin with some sort of apology.

'And it's our Jen she's come about, is it?'

'That's right, Mrs Drury.' The policewoman was nodding. 'No one's going to press you, though. You can talk as much as you want—or not at all, if you prefer. Clare's from a woman's magazine, not from one of the dailies. She's been talking to the families up in Coventry whose children have gone, and her magazine's going to print an account of how all the parents are coping.'

243

Clare felt that she had to speak for herself and somehow win Mrs Drury's direct attention. '*Women Today*,' she said. 'I don't know if—'

For the first time, Mrs Drury's face registered mild interest. She jerked her thumb towards the television set, and Clare saw what she hadn't noticed before: a copy of the most recent issue of the magazine lying open on the top of the set. 'Read it every week, dear. Nice magazine. I like the stories—helps keep me mind off . . .'

The policewoman jumped up. 'Tea, Mrs D? I brought along some buns from the shop on my way over. Would you like a cup, Miss Hogarth?'

Clare had already lingered too long over toast and coffee with Jill Peterson, but she guessed that the tea was a ploy. 'Yes, please.'

Mrs Drury looked Clare up and down and seemed to decide that she would talk to her after all. 'Nice of your magazine to take an interest.'

Clare wanted to say that the editor would be happy to print anything at all that might help restore the abducted children to their parents, but she stopped herself in time, deciding it would sound banal. 'Tell me about Jennifer,' she prompted gently.

The woman's eyes misted, but her strong voice didn't waver. 'Happy kid. Always skylarking about. Bit of a tomboy. Cheery as you please, and lots of friends . . . but she wouldn't never talk to strangers—not on the street, I mean. We still don't understand . . .' Her eyes wandered to the photographs. 'She knows every family on this estate. Helps her dad in the shop, half-terms and holidays. Everyone likes her.'

Clare glanced at the pile of envelopes on the table. 'Are those all the cards and letters you've had?'

'Yeah. Such kind people. They've been a help, I can tell you. They won't bring Jen back, but they make a big difference.'

Clare scribbled furiously, asking her if she would mind repeating the story of the child's abduction.

244

The shutters went down again. 'You'd better ask our police lady here for all that. I'm sorry—' She stopped, frowning fiercely with the will to hold back tears.

'That's fine. I'm sorry I asked the wrong thing. But what about now? Would you be willing for me to tell our readers about how you and your husband are managing?'

There was a long pause. Clare watched the woman's face patiently and saw the battle for control that went on at the corners of her mouth, the trembling of her big chin. At last she took a deep breath. 'We decided, Mr Drury and I, when we first talked to our police lady, that it wasn't no use crying all day, blaming the school, blaming ourselves, or even blaming our Jen. My husband's up the shop now, and that's where he's been every day after the first day. We just had to carry on. We'll get 'er back, I'm certain of it. Just when is what we don't know.'

Clare's pen paused over her notes. 'Do you see anything of her friends from the school?'

A slow smile touched Mrs Drury's mouth. 'Jen's teacher went round to some of their houses at the beginning of the summer holidays and found as many of the children as she could to do a big card for us. Some of the kids was off on their holidays, but I know most of these kids.' She reached to one of the piles on the table and pulled out a wide piece of folded grey card. On the front was a child's drawing of a little girl complete with bright red cheeks, bright pink ribbons, and scarlet shirt and shorts. Inside a dozen or more names were written in childish scrawl, the whole card adorned with crayoned hearts. 'That's little girls for you, ain't it?' With a choked laugh, Mrs Drury pointed at the smudged X marks around the words, 'Come back soon, Jen, we miss you—class 5B'.

Clare took the card, tears blurring her eyes. 'Look,' she said, 'even the little boys have sent kisses.'

Mrs Drury smiled. 'Yeah, wouldn't be seen dead as a rule writing soppy "X"s on a card to a girl, I bet. But they all felt it when she disappeared. Right near the end of term, it was, when the teacher's doing class photographs and they're finishing their projects, and the like, and they're close chums together, and full of fun as kids get when the summer starts . . . so full of naughty—' She broke down, then.

Something in the woman's grief seemed to echo another conversation for Clare, but she couldn't think what or when it had been. Another time when she had sat listening to someone weeping, when she had felt helpless, much as she wanted to help . . .

As if by magic, just at the right moment, the policewoman returned to the room with a tray loaded with cups and saucers, a steaming pot, and a mountainous plate of white-iced sticky buns. *Comfort food,* Clare thought, suddenly recalling her mother's usual strategy for dealing with exhaustion or an overdose of homework. The half-formed memory of another woman in grief niggled again at the back of her mind, but fell away as Mrs Drury diverted herself by pouring tea.

'I was hanging out my wash when you came in,' she said, just as if they had been chatting like old neighbours over the fence, about nothing that mattered. 'That's what I mean, dear—' She caught Clare's eye and gave her a cup of tea so dark that Clare wondered if it were coffee. 'That's what I mean—we got to get on with life. No use moaning all the time. The shop's got to be opened; the books have got to be done of an evening; the house has got to be cleaned, and I've got meals and ironing and all the rest of it to get on with. The garden's a great comfort, as well. Roses never so good, in spite of the drought. I've spent hours out there, digging and pruning, and fussing with them.'

'I think you're very brave,' Clare said. It was hard to take notes. *I'll remember everything she says, anyway,* she thought.

'I change the sheets on Jen's bed every week, like I do normally. Dust in there and keep it nice. Never know when she might come back. Could be any day, couldn't it?'

Clare caught the policewoman's eyes. 'I was wondering . . .'

'She wants to ask you about the day Jen went missing.' Mrs Drury unexpectedly creaked out of her chair and went to the door. 'I'll just go and see about the potatoes for lunch.'

Clare relaxed a little and wrote down the whole story as the policewoman unfolded it.

'Not a long tale,' the other woman sighed, when she had given her the details. 'But a very sad one.'

'It's beginning to sound all too familiar.'

'And they're such dear people. I feel like part of the family—they needed me especially at the beginning, but some days I wonder what it'll be like when I get back to the usual routine again and don't spend half my life in this house. They've fed me like a princess.' She patted her stomach ruefully. 'As you can tell.'

Clare replaced her cup and stood to leave. 'You've both been generous with your time. Look, here's my card. I'll be in touch when I've written the story.'

She took the card from Clare and added it to a pile of other cards and small papers on the table. 'Thanks. You're off to interview a few others in the city before you go, are you?'

Clare stooped to push her notepad into the brief-case. 'Yes. the magazine's given me most of this week to work on this story. But I'll be leaving tonight for London.' Frank's face swam up before her eyes, and her stomach seemed to drop away. As long as her interviews had lasted in Coventry and now Bristol, she had managed to put him out of her mind, but as soon as she went back to something mechanical—the repacking of her suitcase or brief-case, a walk from one house to another—he came inevitably to her thoughts.

Mrs Drury came out of the kitchen, drying her hands on an apron. In the cramped hallway, she squeezed Clare's arm. 'Thanks for coming, love. I'll tell all my friends I met you, all the way from *Women Today*. The newsagent next door sells lots of copies, you know.'

Hesitating on the front step, Clare turned. 'Oh, it'll be a few weeks before the story's out, though quicker than usual for this story, I think.'

'That's all right dear. Just get it printed as soon as you can—if it'll help.'

The two women stood waving to her as she went out into the street. *The hardest one down,* she thought, *and a few more to go before I see Frank again.*

When at last she came out of the door from her last interview at a neighbouring house, Frank was craning his neck out of the Sierra to catch a first glimpse of her. His face split into a wide grin, and she smiled back, unable to wave because of her brief-case and overnight bag.

'You've been lugging those all day? Oh, Clare—I don't know what I was thinking of this morning. I should have locked the bag in the boot for you. Sorry.' He jumped out of the car and swung her things into the boot. 'Did Jill lend you a swimming costume?'

She hesitated. 'Yes, but are you sure—?'

Then she searched his face and saw that the circles under his eyes had darkened further. Bright spots of colour stained his cheeks. He looked thirsty and exhausted, and she forgot her anxiety about swimming. 'You haven't stopped since I saw you this morning, I bet,' she accused. 'Is it always like this?'

'All work and no play? Yes, sometimes. Especially when we're in the thick of anything involving children.'

She thought back to midsummer and a stranger flashing his lights at her and laughing at her on the motorway; then to the moment in the Coventry incident room when they had met each other again. She felt they had known each other for years.

He opened the door for her. 'Can't grumble. Just tired, that's all.'

Warmth spread through her. She wanted to cuddle him and kiss away the circles, hold him until he wasn't tired any more.

He got into the car beside her and started the engine. He grinned at her. 'Maybe Bristol to London isn't such a long-shot after all.'

She blushed. 'Ah—don't quote me! I wish I'd never said that.'

'Then why did you?'

It was hard, now, to remember. 'I'm not quite sure,' she said slowly. 'Something to do with the strange way we met, perhaps. And the fact that you mentioned Barking. I have a thing about Barking. You'd obviously done your homework and found out something about me—I don't know. It made me nervous.'

'But you're not nervous now.'

'No. Not now. Especially now I've seen you in action, Detective Inspector.'

'A most interesting statement! I'll have to pursue that one with you later. In action! Hmm. I wonder which kind of . . . talking of action—' He signalled and pulled into another lane. 'I told you I'm officially still on call. That means I can be brought back in, any minute. But I think the SIO was sorry for me—so we may be OK. He said he'd see things covered later for a few hours. I can lose the pager then. And Nigel and Jill aren't on this case. Nigel's a fanatical swimmer.'

She caught her breath. 'So we really are going swimming?' She had hoped he would change his mind.

Frank braked for a red light and took her hand for a moment. 'Can you bear it? It's been so hot. I thought a swim would be marvellous.'

She thought he didn't sound as convinced as he had the day before. *Poor, tired Frank.*

Nigel and Jill were waiting for them in the club's lobby. Anxious about swimming, Clare had tried but failed to remember Nigel's face from the long midsummer's evening when her Fiat had broken down. All she could recall was Jill's now familiar talkative nature, and that Nigel had asked her about the kind of petrol she had put in the car. She wanted them both to like her.

Frank's arm went round her waist as they entered the lobby. He gave her a squeeze and said under his breath, 'Jill likes you already. Don't mind Nigel's banter.'

She thought no more about Nigel, once again more nervous about going into the pool. And yet, because she was with Frank, she felt less afraid of the water than usual. She trusted him completely; felt safe with him.

'Well done, Frank!' Nigel looked Clare up and down. 'Yup, this is the lady.'

'Hello, Clare.' Jill's smile made her feel included in what Frank had told her was a frequent threesome.

'Don't be fooled,' Nigel said as he shook her hand, looking straight into her eyes and seemingly able to read her mind. 'Your friend Mr Bernard doesn't always deign to burn his precious evenings here.' He glanced at Frank, then back at Clare. 'Only once or twice this summer, I think?'

'That's right,' said Jill.

'Off discoing downtown as a rule.' Nigel winked at Frank.

'Rubbish,' said Frank.

'Well, you certainly *used* to be,' Jill accused.

'Yeah,' drawled Nigel, his eyes still on her face, 'I think he just wants to show you off.'

She wondered what he had been saying to them about her, and she blushed. 'I won't do him credit at all, I'm afraid,' she laughed. 'I can't swim.'

'I'm going to teach her,' Frank said quickly.

Nigel scoffed. 'Frank can hardly paddle, himself. Didn't he tell you?'

'Don't listen to him, Clare,' Frank said. 'He's the show-off if ever you saw one! If he weren't, he'd have taught Jill by now, anyway.'

Jill was nodding. 'I can't swim more than a few strokes myself,' she said lamely.

'Never mind,' Frank said. 'Let's get this show-off on the road. Peacocks to the left.' He waved towards the men's changing room. 'Ladies to the right.' He released Clare and gave Nigel a nudge in the ribs. Come on, you.'

Clare walked with Jill into the women's locker rooms and, shivering slightly, started to strip off her clothes. Jill meanwhile sat on a bench and took off her shoes, but no more. 'Didn't you bring your other costume?' Clare asked.

Jill shook her head. 'I don't think Nigel would have the

patience to teach me. If I'm ever going to learn at the grand old age of twenty-nine, I'll need lessons from a professional.' She shrugged. 'It doesn't bother me, really. Swimming is his great passion, and I always keep him company. My own passion is walking—anywhere but in Bristol—and he keeps me company. We don't do too badly, I suppose.' She smiled, and Clare warmed to her.

'It sounds like an old bargain between good friends,' she said.

'It is. Oh—you look cold.'

Clare pulled her straps over her shoulders and grimaced at a mirror. 'No—it's just my skin. Always pale.'

'And,' Jill added, 'you're scared, aren't you?'

Clare flushed again. 'You people don't miss much, do you? I'm not sure if I can cope with three pairs of hawk-eyes at once.'

'Oh, don't worry about Nigel and me. Nigel'll tease you, but you'll get used to him. And Frank—well, he's absolutely—' She stopped.

Bending to leave her trainers under the bench, Clare straightened up, full of curiosity. She longed to hear the second half of Jill's last sentence, but already Jill had gone ahead of her towards the pool entrance.

'Come on,' Jill called back over her shoulder. 'Nigel's probably swum ten lengths already. He likes me to keep his holdall for him, and poor Frank's probably shivering worse than you are, waiting for you in the shallow end.'

Splashing water and the pervasive smell of chlorine greeted them as they stepped through the footbath on their way to the pool. A white spume flew up as two men swam parallel with each other towards the shallow end; otherwise, the water was deserted. One of the men wore goggles, his hair thinning slightly, his back muscular and streamlined in the water. Not Frank. The other, swimming several yards behind, turned his bearded face to breathe, saw her, smiled, and let himself drift to a stop. He came to his feet in the water, waved and called to them.

'Hello, ladies. Make sure you don't miss the show. For your benefit, you know.' He pointed at Nigel, now almost at the other end of the pool again. Then, laughing, he duck-dived under the surface and swam towards where they stood, at the shallow end.

Tentatively, Clare sat down on the edge and let her ankles and feet dip into the water. For a moment, faint panic welled up. The coldness brought back unbidden her memory of the punt on the Cam, the shock of cold water over her body as she fell forwards into it. Her teeth began to chatter.

'Hey! This won't do!' Frank surfaced beside her. His face contorted, and he sneezed hugely. Then he laughed. 'Chlorine!' he grumbled. He took hold of her feet under the water and massaged her toes. Nigel came thrashing towards them again. He turned by the wall, grinning maniacally from behind his goggles, and shot back towards the deep end. Jill, she saw, was now retreating to the safe distance of the spectators' seats along the side of the pool.

Clare forced her lips to curve up, but her jaw was clenched. Between shivers, she said, 'Sorry. Water makes me a bit uptight, that's all.'

'But your feet are getting warmer already, aren't they?'

'A little.' The chafing of his hands under the water was soothing.

'Great! But you don't have to get in at all, if you don't want to. It's a free country, you know.' He let go of her feet and began scooping water to pour over her knees. His smile was infectious, and she smiled back—a real smile this time. The drops of water gleamed on his beard and black hair, and his eyes were very bright.

Her teeth stopped chattering. She knew the quickest remedy against the cold was to plunge straight into the water, but she wasn't quite ready for that yet. Still, there was a playful gleam in Frank's eyes that told her he wouldn't let her sit dry on the edge for long—even if he forgot his intention to teach her how to swim. She suddenly leaned back and began to kick up a great spray that soaked herself and sent

Frank somersaulting backwards away from her.

'Hey! What a mean trick, Clare Hogarth!' he protested.

Before she knew what was happening he had reached up and lifted her off the wall. She felt the power of his hands and arms as they circled her waist, then the water closing round her legs and hips. For a second, she laughed helplessly, breathless with the sudden cold, but, strangely, no longer afraid. 'I may not be a swimmer,' she teased, 'but I do know how to make a splash.'

'You certainly do that, all right.' He tipped her towards him, dangling her half in, half out of the water so that her feet couldn't yet touch the bottom of the pool. She grabbed with one hand for his shoulder to steady herself, and with the other for his wet hair. Her own hair fell over his face, and she felt the warmth of his laughing breath on her neck.

'Ouch! Cheeky so-and-so,' he said. He dropped her suddenly into the water, catching her shoulders before her head went under water, and set her on her feet at last. His arms still held her, his face only a few inches from hers. 'You asked for that. If you could swim like Nigel, I'd have held you under as well. No mercy for you. Troublemaker!'

She ached to kiss his wet, laughing mouth. Perhaps he saw the look in her eyes, for he bent his lips quickly to hers, then let her go.

Nigel churned back to the wall beside them and stopped. 'None of that hanky panky here, you two. This is a respectable establishment.'

'Oh, listen to old frog-eyes. You're so blind without your specs, you just *thought* you saw me kissing Clare.'

'Who said anything about kissing?' Nigel shot back. 'Some swimming lesson *you're* having!' He dived again, surging away from them with powerful strokes.

Clare looked after the white spray of his wake. 'It's easy for him, isn't it?'

'Yes. He's strong. But that's not the secret, not really.'

'What is, then?'

Frank thought for a moment. 'Trust, I suppose. He

learned to trust the water. Throw yourself onto it, into it—and it holds you.'

'I certainly don't trust it.'

'But you'd like to?' The smile had gone. Frank was the teacher now, intent, and ready, if she wanted to learn.

She moved her shoulders slightly, remembering her thought that she could at least trust Frank. 'I've tried before. My father loved swimming—I tried hard for him.'

'Tell me later,' Frank said, 'about your father. We'll freeze if we just stand here in the water.'

'You'll have a go at teaching a terrified non-swimmer, then?'

'I'll have a go. But you don't need to be terrified.' He took her hand and walked her through the water to the steps in the corner. 'Let's stay over here—out of Nigel's way. Hey! No need to crush my fingers. I won't let you go.'

'Sorry! You promise?'

'Yes. I'll make a deal with you. At the very least, if you don't *enjoy* the water by the time we're finished this evening, you can splash me all you want, and I'll even buy you a drink afterwards.'

'Generous to a fault.'

'Glad you've noticed. Now, first lesson. See the chair behind you?'

She turned but saw only the blue-green whorls of water around her waist. 'No.'

'Yes, you can see it. I've got one, too.' Back straight, he lowered his body into the water, stretched his arms sideways, and pretended to sit in the water. 'It's a bit shallow here for this, but if I lift my feet off the bottom, like this . . . and keep my hands moving . . . like this . . . then I can sit on the invisible chair. See?'

Under the water, his legs were distorted out of all proportion. 'I'm sure you've got the fourth toe of your right foot on the tiles,' she teased.

'Then you can, too.' He grinned. 'Go on, try it. Fourth toes only allowed on the bottom.' She imitated his posture, but her back was tense, and she went under. He hauled her out, turning away only to sneeze again. 'Sorry about this. Either I'm allergic to you, or I'm getting cold. Try again.'

For fifteen minutes she played at sitting in the water. They began to laugh each time she failed. Frank popped up and down in the water beside her like a bearded jack-in-the-box, and the more he urged her on, the funnier she found it. Soon she was giggling so helplessly that she forgot all fear. She stretched out her arms, and suddenly she was floating on her back. Her feet broke the surface, and she stared with open mouth and raised eyebrows at the miracle of toes above the slapping water. Not even thinking what she was doing, she sculled with her hands and kept herself afloat.

Frank stood up beside her and clapped. From the spectators' stands twenty yards away, Jill shouted and clapped as well. Clare lay spread on the water, completely relaxed, beaming at Frank and full of triumph. 'I'm floating!'

'You like it?'

'Oh, yes.'

'You've trusted the water to carry you. It can't, unless you trust it. Now you know it can.'

Nigel doubled past them again, cheered her, and went on with his frenetic lengths. She luxuriated in the weightlessness, lay suspended and staring at the ceiling.

Frank floated beside her now, his face turned towards her. 'If you can do that,' he said, 'swimming's easy. But not now. Next time? OK?'

She hardly heard him. Instead, she heard again and again his words, *You've trusted the water to carry you. It can't, unless you trust it*. She struggled to stand up again, rolled sideways underwater, and he had to pull her out, gasping, choking—but still full of joy.

He banged her on the back. 'Hey! What happened all of a sudden?'

'I thought of something.'

'You're crazy,' he said affectionately. 'I knew it. All that philosophizing when I first met you about someone with you, someone I couldn't see. You're crazy!'

'But that's exactly the point!' She hugged him, and his wet skin felt cold against her own. 'You couldn't see him, and I couldn't see that chair of yours. Not until I sat in it. Lay in it, in fact. Now do you see?'

'Sorry!' His fingers curved over her shoulders. 'You're talking to a copper, not a whizz kid with words.'

'Ah, you admit it,' she laughed. 'So Nina made that story up all by herself after all?'

He threw water over her. 'No! Now explain what you're talking about, you wretched woman!'

She heard a slight Irish lilt in his voice and irrelevantly wondered at it. Surely he hadn't been with that Irishman in Coventry—Joe Cafferty—that long? 'Can't you see?' she said. 'You told me to sit in the invisible water chair. I couldn't see it, couldn't believe in it. Couldn't trust it.'

'Yes?'

'And you—you couldn't see who was with me that day. The one who's with us now. But until you trust him, you won't know, will you, that he's there.'

He pushed one hand through his hair and half shook his head. 'No-o,' he answered doubtfully.

'Then it's *my* turn now,' she crowed. Joy and love bubbled up in her so high that they drove away the fearful coldness she had first felt in the water. 'My turn to teach *you*, Frank Bernard.' She twisted away from him, leapt off the bottom of the pool as if she were shooting a basketball into a net, and brought her hands suddenly down onto his shoulders. With a whoop he fell backwards into the water pulling her after him.

From within the tangle of arms and legs and bodies, she yelled, 'Ever been baptized, Frank?'

He came up laughing and shaking water all over her face out of his hair. 'Baptized? Of course I was—christened as a baby.'

'Sprinkled, I bet. Well, how about a little total immersion.' And she pushed him under the water again.

He came up again, blowing water out of his mouth. 'Clare,'

he said, 'I love you. But you're a wild woman, and you're really asking for trouble.'

He pulled her towards him. She let her legs float out behind her, and he raised her until her face was level with his. She was beginning to be at home in the water now. 'Oh, you of little faith,' she said softly, 'I love you too.'

'Miss motorway philosopher,' he laughed, 'is that a proposition or a repetition, or a metaphysical statement?' She looked over her shoulder. 'Where's the motorway philosopher? When you use words of five syllables I have no idea what you're talking about.'

'Then take it on faith that I love you. Simple as that.' He hesitated. 'And I'll take it on faith that you love me. Simple as that.'

'But how do I know you love me, if I can't *see* that love?' she asked, her head tilted to one side, seeing quite clearly the light of love in his eyes.

'Precisely the point, love,' he said. 'You don't know until you try it.' His mouth found hers again, cool and tasting of chlorine, but nevertheless warm to her. 'This is no place, though, is it? I'm starting to shiver, myself.'

They waded towards the steps, and she threw him a quick, anxious glance. The tiredness had melted, but his face was slightly pinched, and he breathed hard as he wiped the drops of water off his face. To cover her desire to protect him, without sounding over-protective, she teased, 'Hey, I thought you detectives were so fit! But look at you.'

'I'm fine,' he laughed. 'Just tired. I always look like this when I'm tired. You'd know that if we could see more of each other.' Her heart leaped as he went on, 'We need more time together, lots more. What about this weekend? Or next—it'll be a bank holiday—a long weekend.'

At the steps, she rested against him, quite still. She visualized her diary for the rest of the month. 'Here?' she said. 'Shall I come down here again?' She was dizzy with happiness. 'It's only two days till the weekend, you know.'

'Yes, and I won't be on call. I'll come up to you. You'll have to believe it enough to show up at Paddington and meet me off the train. Pretty empirical things, trains, you know.'

'If empirical people don't miss them. Then they're pure theory, or speculation, or hope.'

'Faith, *hope*, and love,' Frank said. 'That's one verse of Bible I can quote you. We seem to have covered all three tonight. But the greatest of all is love.'

'Maybe not the love you're thinking of.'

'Is it so very different?' he asked.

'Maybe not,' she said.

32

'Leaving on time for a change, I see,' Charlie shouted through the door to me as I put my things together.

'Come in, if you want to,' I offered. The stairway door had been propped open for air, and the sound of my voice echoing down the stairs hurt my head. I found myself wondering again when the everlasting headache would ease. The swim with Clare the day before now seemed years ago.

Charlie filled the doorway, as beefy and smiling as the proverbial laughing policeman. 'Hi.' His smile suddenly faded. 'Lord, Frank, but you look tired.'

I straightened up and loosened my tie. It was dangerous to tell Charlie that I hadn't slept properly all week, but I had blurted it out before I thought what I was saying.

'So it seems. Girl troubles?'

I couldn't answer right away because a sudden and violent itch caught at the base of my throat. My chest squeezed and wheezed like a set of old bellows, frightening me. For a moment I was half doubled over, coughing. When I regained my breath, my face hot from the effort, I saw Charlie's anxiety and said quickly, 'Women troubles? Not really. You would assume that! Overtiredness, perhaps.' That was what I'd been telling everyone for days, at least.

Charlie looked suspicious. 'And we're nowhere near the end of this case yet, either.'

'I've had a headache, too, since—' I could no longer remember when it had started. All day I hadn't been able to concentrate; I was viewing the world through a fuzzy glass. And now this cough! I took a swallow of what was left of a cold cup of tea on the desk. Charlie frowned. 'I think you mentioned it the other day. What kind of headache?'

'Oh, you're turning medical man as well as matchmaker,

are you? We'll soon need a whole set of pegs over your desk for all the hats you wear: father confessor, CID counsellor, surgeon, matchmaker . . .' It was a feeble joke, and he didn't even crack a smile. I put my hand up to my temples. 'Well, there's a pain all down here and around my eyes. It's been an effort to do the smallest thing.' I sounded small, sorry for myself.

'Frank, dashing up to Coventry this week wasn't "the smallest thing", you know.'

I shook my head; even that slight movement hurt. 'Yes, I know that. This case is something else altogether. I think I had the headache—can't remember—but even if I did . . .' I broke off, coughing again, waiting for my wits as they went in slow, confused circles.

'Oh, you sound dreadful!'

I shrugged. 'Yeah, and I know we don't get emotional in this job, do we . . . but everything about this week's made me very emotional.'

'Seeing your friend?'

I heard my voice crack with irritation. 'Oh, lay off! Yes, I'm in love, but there's been a lot more than that going on. I just can't wait to see those kids locked in their parents' arms again. God! You'd have to have a heart of stone not to weep for all the pain there's been.' I met his eyes, suddenly feeling breathless again, afraid if I started to cough again that I might not stop. 'D'you know what I mean? It's all so much at once.'

One of Charlie's big hands suddenly reached with un-expected gentleness to my forehead. 'You're *hot*, Frank my lad.' My temperature had been almost one hundred and two before I took another dose of paracetemol that morning. 'I know,' I said drily. 'But most of the time I'm shivering.' I knew now that I should never have gone swimming.

Charlie turned suddenly and I heard him thumping back across CID, between the desks. I followed him as far as the door to see where he was going. He came back after a few minutes with Sally and the guv'nor.

Sally took one look at me, threw a glance at Charlie, and turned her eyes up to Bill's face. 'Could you send this man home with a flea in his ear?' she said.

I held up my hands. 'This looks like a posse, if ever I saw one. I'm going! I'm going, Sally.'

'He's sick and tired of being sick and tired,' Charlie put in.

'Can you get to a doctor?' Bill asked. I had never seen him look so concerned.

I lifted the jacket I had alternately pulled on and tossed off again onto the back of my chair all day. 'Don't think so, sir. I'm supposed to be going to see my family tonight.' The thought of supper at my mother's house was like an oasis in the desert of the day. I longed to get out into the air and meander through the traffic to a meal someone else had cooked for a change. Then tomorrow I'd be off to see Clare—first thing in the morning.

'Well,' the boss said, 'suit yourself, Frank. But if you look like this next time I see you, I'll more than have my doubts about letting you near this station. You look, as they say, like death warmed up. You're not fit to be in the building, in my opinion, let alone pursuing a case like this. It doesn't take much training to see you should be in bed with aspirin and a doctor.'

I wanted to make a joke, *That depends on whether or not my doctor's a nice lady*—but thought better of it. I could say that sort of thing to Charlie, but not to Bill Longley.

Charlie caught my eye, however, reading my face, and it was all I could do not to laugh.

'I've been taking paracetemol all day,' I said soberly. *And most of the week,* I added mentally.

'All the more reason to see a doctor,' Bill urged, but his heart wasn't in it. He had far better things to do than play nursemaid. He turned and started back towards the incident room. 'See you all soon, I suppose. Cheers, Frank, you're doing a good job.'

Left with Charlie and Sally, I stood against the jamb of the door. Somewhere—was it all over my body? there had been no time to think about it before—there was an ache. All day I had only been sitting in front of a screen or in a meeting, but my legs felt weak.

I was just about to make a crack about carting myself off to the local morgue when the phone rang behind me.

'D'you want me to take it for you?' Sally asked. 'You'll be here all night if you stand here much longer.'

I glanced at the clock. Six-thirty. My mother would be expecting me by seven, and I had hoped to shower and take another dose of paracetemol before I set off for Weston-super-Mare. 'Yes, thanks, Sal.'

Charlie thumped me on the back. 'Go on,' he said. 'Get out while the getting's good.'

I saluted him. 'I'm getting.'

By the time I left the station, the traffic was steadying to the usual evening pace. I pulled down both visors above the windscreen; the westerly glare of the sun over the Bristol Channel was almost as painful as the headache.

'Come in, Frank!' my father boomed when I got to the familiar front door.

My mother stood right behind him, as usual. I would have their undivided attention for a whole evening—something I relished just then; Lucy and Agnes had married long ago and came home to visit only slightly more often then I did: not often at all. And probably not often enough.

My mother folded me to her, and I smelled the scent of violets that she always wore. 'Good to see you, Mum,' I said. 'Sorry, I didn't bring flowers this time.'

She held me at arm's length and looked into my face. 'You're very hot, sweetheart. And pale, as well. Sure you're not overdoing it?'

'Now, love, don't start clucking the minute he gets through the door,' my father said—quite predictably. We had this sort of conversation every time I went home. In a moment he would swat her behind and tell her to stop playing mother hen with a grown man of thirty.

'I'm not overdoing anything,' I said, looking her straight in the eye. 'Just not on top at the moment.'

'Come you and have a nice long cold drink,' she said, and

led me like a child into the kitchen. 'Dinner's almost ready.'

Walking behind us, Dad patted Mum's bottom affectionately. 'There, now, stop playing mother hen to a grown man of thirty,' he said.

I laughed.

'That's better!' Because Dad was beginning to go deaf, he usually shouted, and this time I winced. He didn't notice, going on at the top of his voice, 'Been busy, then, have you?' He knew it was a safe question and that I could only answer him in general terms. He wouldn't want details, anyway—far more interested in dwelling lovingly and at length on his latest fishing trophies.

I took the drink my mother had poured me. 'Very busy. On the road, as well.'

'Anything interesting, Frank?' My mother didn't turn around as she spoke; she was at the hob stirring a saucepan of something unidentifiable that made my mouth water.

'Yes. Also one of the hardest and most emotionally exhausting cases I've ever worked on. Child abductions.'

'Oh,' Dad grunted, and I wasn't sure at first if he'd heard me properly.

'Did you get the poor children back safe and sound?' Mum did look over her shoulder this time.

'Not yet, I'm afraid.'

Dad said heartily, 'If anyone can do it, you will.'

I was touched by their simple confidence in me.

'But you, Frank—why *are* you looking so ill?'

I might have known Mum wouldn't give up once she had made up her mind that I needed to be fussed over. For once, she was probably right. I might even let her do it. I smiled at her. 'I haven't slept much. I've got a headache—for starters,' I said.

'Too many late nights partying, Frank?' Dad wanted to know.

I grinned. 'Ah, don't be such an old spoilsport. You were just the same—about a hundred years ago or more.'

'Cheeky! I thought you'd given up wine, women and song, anyway.' He gave me a wink.

'Whatever made you think so?' I looked into my drink and realized that it was so long since I'd seen them that they hadn't even heard of Clare. Still, I wasn't going to miss getting a bit of fun out of teasing them a little. As long as I didn't start coughing again.

'You were going to look for a wife, last time we talked,' he said.

'Is that what I said? Sounds like one of your ideas, not mine.'

Mum clicked her tongue. 'Nonsense. Come on, now, I'm serving up. We'll eat outside.'

I knew she wouldn't leave matters alone, and as soon as we'd sat down at the wooden table outside, she began again.

'You really ought to settle down, you know.' She was serious now, sighing as she talked. One of those long west of Ireland sighs she'd learned from my grandmother, I suppose, and very effective against the male of the species. I began to have second thoughts about teasing her.

'I'm giving it some thought,' I admitted grudgingly.

Dad's mouth skewed sideways doubtfully as he looked across the table at me. 'About as much thought as I'm giving to the idea of giving up fishing, I imagine.'

I laid down my fork. The chicken meal my mother had so lovingly cooked smelled wonderful, tasted good—but somehow I could hardly swallow any of it. *Losing my appetite as well. Wonderful!* I thought.

'Give him a chance to get a word in, Tom,' Mum said severely to my father.

'Who is she?' Dad pursued, pretending he hadn't heard her.

'Oh, you're worse than the guys at work. Women and sex—that's all they ever think and talk about.'

'And you don't, I suppose,' Mum said drily.

I drew a circle around my head. 'Not me, of course. Saint Francis himself, that's me.'

'Rubbish!' Dad laughed. 'Mum and I know better.'

'So you're going to give up running around and settle down at last, are you?' Mum persisted.

I was too weary to want to banter any more. Even the smell of violets and mouth-watering chicken made me feel sick, suddenly. It would be easy enough to tell them about Clare. The telling might almost make me feel she was here with me now instead of far away in London, out of my reach until the weekend.

'I'm going to have a try,' I said, '—you'll be happy to hear. I met someone in June and then spent weeks trying to track her down. I caught up with her this week.' I saw Mum glance at Dad, and Dad raise his eyebrows. 'Her name's Clare Hogarth. She lives in London and works as a journalist.'

Mum leaned forward, all her inbred Irish nosiness surfacing, and no effort made to conceal it at all. 'Name, address, and occupation, Frank! Is that the best you can give us, now? You have to write better descriptions than that at work, do you not?'

I laughed. My father went on cramming chicken and salad into his mouth, losing interest for a while. He would tune out when he wanted to think about fishing, and I could almost see him standing in the rising tide, choosing the size of the sand-eel bait, arching back with his fibre-glass rod to cast line, weight, and bait into the sea—dreaming of the fourteen-pounder that would swim to gobble the bait. *Charms them to him, so he does,* my mother always said.

'Is it you're going deaf as well?' Mum said sharply to me, giving Dad a soft little smile. 'Thinking of this woman you haven't described for me yet, are you?'

'Believe it or not, Mum, I was thinking about fishing,' I said.

'Not you as well.'

'No, not really. Clare? Ah—' I leaned against the cushioned back of the garden chair and closed my eyes briefly. 'She's beautiful.'

'Of course she's beautiful if you like her. Going blind, too, are you? Come on, let me *see* this girl of yours.'

'Red wavy hair.'

'Irish or English?'

Dad tuned in again, winking at me. 'Give him a chance to get a word in, dear.'

'Might have known you'd ask that,' I said to Mum. 'English, of course. One Irishwoman in this family's enough already.'

'Go on, then,' she said impatiently, but smiling, thriving on the insult. 'And eat up your dinner as well, would you.'

'She's tall. Fair skin. Grey eyes.' Then, unable to resist the jibe, I added, 'She's religious, as well, so you'd be bound to like her.' I picked up my knife and fork but did nothing with them.

'Herself religious!' Mum scoffed. 'And what d'you mean by that, if you please?'

'She talks about God as if he's a friend of hers,' I said.

Dad sniffed. 'She might be good for you, at that, then. A journalist, you said? What sort of journalist? Not a fishing magazine, is it?'

'Ever hopeful!' Mum laughed. 'Don't be so daft, man.'

'Women's magazine,' I told them. 'It's—' I stopped, feeling again the desperate urge to cough. I tried to hold it back, but my chest suddenly convulsed, and once again I was bending over in a spasm, my face close to my plate, feeling my lungs trying to blow themselves inside out through my throat.

Mum must have thought I was choking on a piece of food. She started banging my back with her hand, but that only seemed to make the cough worse.

When it was over, my face was still burning. Neither of my parents said a word: just stared at me. I thought I would go on as if nothing had happened, and I took a sip of water. When I spoke again, my voice sounded congested, foreign to me. 'I was saying—it's a magazine called *Women Today*. She writes features and articles for them.' I knew that the sketchy details I had given them weren't enough, but how was I supposed to describe the woman I'd been pursuing for weeks, the woman I was in love with?

'Just look at him smile,' my father said after a while.

+ 'Never mind the smile,' my mother parried. 'It's the cough I'm worried about. You never said a word about a

266

cough, Frank Thomas. And now I'm looking at you properly, you surely have a temperature.'

The energy I'd been driving myself with; the will and effort I'd been forcing for the last week—suddenly gave way. All my reserves crumbled. I had nothing left to give; could do no more. I opened my mouth to speak, feeling like a child. My teeth began to chatter, and Mum jumped up, her face full of dismay. 'Go you in this minute, sweetheart,' she said. 'And your dad'll go with you. Into bed with you, and not a word. I'm after ringing the doctor.'

Shivering in spite of the warm evening, and only then finally admitting to myself that I was ill, I went ahead of them into the house. My head no longer felt as if it belonged to my body. I was ready to give up, lie down, and let someone else do the running.

The last clear impression I had, once I was wrapped up in my old duvet, looking at the pictures of Elton John I had hung on my wall years ago, in another life, was of a young doctor I'd never seen before jabbing at my mouth with a thermometer. 'A hundred and four,' I heard him pronounce to my mother—perhaps one minute later, perhaps one hour later. All time seemed twisted, and the ceiling above the bed was doing an odd trick of rolling sideways down the wall without crashing on me.

I think I fell asleep then, though I don't remember sleeping. Dad woke me when it was dark and made me swallow a pill as big as a tomato. I dreamed that I was Damian and that Clare was searching for me in Coventry's old cathedral. I hid, cross-legged and peeping out from behind a pile of broken masonry, watching her through growing darkness as she hunted and called, 'Damian! Damian!' In the gloom, her red hair was a blaze of light.

Then in the dream her voice changed, and it was my mother's, laughing in Irish Gaelic that I only half understood, 'Well, he'll be all right, Tom, for sure.'

My mother's voice, too, faded; and another began in its place: sweet and somehow familiar, though the words were bitter in my ears. 'London to Bristol's a long shot.' The voice echoed around the ruins and took flight like a flock of iron birds overhead, clanging and ringing until my head was fit to crack.

The dream changed again. Now Clare was not looking for me; I was searching for her. One minute she was near me in the gathering evening sunshine of Coventry Cathedral, both of us facing the words, 'Father forgive'; and the next minute she was bounding away from me like a rabbit in a field of sunshine. I was Damian no longer, but a hound calling after her and chasing, bounding over buttercups and daisies, the walls of the cathedral never closing us in as the fields of heaven stretched out to eternity under the light that poured like honey in and through me. Under the light that itself pursued me like a running river—though not a river that I feared any more.

I woke, panting, coughing, with the sweat in rivulets down my face.

'Look, Peggy Bernard,' my father was saying, 'he's pulling through.'

I opened my eyes. The light had not been a dream. It was daylight again, and my mother and father were standing near the foot of the bed.

'What is this?' I said when I got my breath. 'You look as if you're fit to ring the priest for the last rites—the way you're standing there like that.' I tried, and failed, to smile.

'Oh, Frank!' Mum fell on her knees at the side of the bed and wrapped her violety arms around my neck. 'We thought we'd lose you. We've been here for hours. I was praying for you, and Dad was reading to you, so he was.'

My father's voice had an edge of unusual irritation in it. 'Don't you go weeping all over him, Peg. He's mending all right.' Then to me, 'You've gone and got yourself pneumonia. We thought we might have to put you in the hospital in the night, but at least for now you're fighting it back.'

'The doctor's given you the strongest antibiotic he can prescribe. Says you've been walking around ill for days,'

Mum interrupted. She laid a cool hand on my wet hair. 'You foolish man.'

I remembered Clare running across the everlasting field in the ruins of St Michael's, Coventry. 'What were you reading to me?' I asked. Since meeting Clare, I thought I might view everything differently now.

My mother gave me a small smile. 'Some words from Isaiah,' she answered. ' "Do not be afraid, for I have redeemed you; I have called you by your name, you are mine." '

I moved my eyes from my mother's face to that of my father. In both I saw the half-formed fear—something they wouldn't even dare express to each other in bed late at night—that I might follow Damian and die on them.

I grinned at them. 'Don't you worry,' I said. 'God must have heard you. I'll be fine in a day or two.'

They exchanged glances, then my father looked down at me sternly. 'You're a sick man, and you're not through the worst of it yet, according to the doctor.' He sat down in the chair by the bed, where I guessed he must have been sitting earlier. 'We're not talking days, Frank, but longer,' he said.

'I'll be all right,' I told them wearily.

My mother bent and lifted me against a stack of pillows. 'You need to be sitting up as much as possible,' she said.

Yet again I felt like a child, resenting even their kindness and concern, but then I began to cough again, struggling for every breath between bouts.

One of them gave me water to drink: I can't remember which. The wall began its odd sliding dance again, and I shut my eyes to block it out. It occurred to me for a second that I should ask them to telephone Clare and tell her I was ill. But when I opened my eyes again to tell them, the room was empty, and I had forgotten whatever it was I wanted them to know. Was it something to do with Clare . . .?

Clare, poor Clare. There was some problem, I was sure. Memories slipped and slithered around my clouded brain. *Yesterday? The day before? What day is it, anyway?* I couldn't concentrate on anything at all.

33

The security locks slid shut behind her, and she stood quite still in the twilight of the unlit reception area to get her bearings. Empty of her colleagues, with word processors, printers and telephones silent, the place was eerie and unfamiliar. Sweat prickled on her upper lip and around the collar of her shirt.

It's Saturday! she reminded herself. *I must be crazy!*

She turned on the first set of lights. Other journalists, she knew, sometimes came to work at the weekend, so it had not been difficult to discover in advance from someone else the procedures for gaining access without setting off all the burglar alarms. All the same, she had half-expected to find secretaries at work as usual; to smell the sharp odour in the corridor outside the art department, the tang of smoke outside the rest rooms; or to see Bobbie or Pete passing the door of her office. But no, the offices were completely deserted.

The air conditioning was humming quietly as usual, but in the absence of the other staff the journalists' suite seemed abnormally dry and cold, more so because of the pall of humidity she had just left. She shuddered, not liking to be alone, and threw a quick glance over her shoulder as if at any moment someone might come in and find her unlocking the door to the offices where she worked Monday to Friday. She laughed softly. *How silly! Why shouldn't I?*

Outside the windows of her own room, a low haze hung over the city. It softened the edges of the highrises and turned the Charles River into what might have been just another turnpike—a winding grey ribbon like the others. A few minutes before, she had been walking in the milky early morning sunshine under that haze, fifteen floors below, where Saturday drivers and weekend shoppers were already nudging and trudging their way round the city. Ed would be jostling among them, shopping for the fall semester of his last year at college; they had driven downtown together, and he would be waiting for her later.

She sighed. Cambridge in England seemed a million miles from Cambridge, Massachusetts. She didn't miss England, but she knew she would never understand American men like Pete McEnroe. Tender and courteous one moment, drunk and boorish the next.

For a moment, as she took her pen and a block of paper out of her desk drawer, she relived the scene at the McEnroes' garden party. She shut her eyes as the fine hair on her arms and legs rose again in shock at the cold suddenness of the red-and-green-starred water—a faint echo, too, of the time someone had pushed her into the water off a Cambridge punt. Behind her eyelids she saw again the faint luminosity of the underwater globe lights and relived the surge of terror and claustrophobia. *I can't swim*. Then McEnroe was ploughing through the water towards her, his hair silver in the dimness, pulling her and Pete to the surface again.

She opened her eyes and gasped. She had been holding her breath as she relived it, and the grip of fear made her angry all over again. There was little room for forgiveness, she decided. Pete was a dangerous and confused—perhaps even a cruel—man.

And that's why I'm here, she told herself. *To stop him before he does some other crazy thing*.

Switching on lights as she went, she made her way to the cuttings library and returned to the McEnroe collection that she had frequented during her first week at *Citizen*. This time by-passing J for Julius McEnroe and M for Marianne McEnroe, she went straight to the file marked 'P McEnroe'.

It was thinner than she expected, and as she opened it on a table next to the hanging files she saw immediately that the press clippings contained within were all eight or more years old. Her mouth twisted. Somehow, the man had contrived to

271

stay out of the limelight at least as long as he had been an executive editor of the magazine. All the articles, she found as she began to read with almost breathless concentration, in fact predated his employment in the world of journalism. Here she met a Pete McEnroe she did not know: the blue-eyed Notre Dame basketball star.

She frowned. How was she to write an article on Pete the playboy, Pete the big bad wolf of the Boston social and editorial world—if there was no evidence to back her case? Of course he would never print it—an absurd notion. She chuckled to herself. But at least she would have warned him away from her—and perhaps have warned Bobbie away from him as well. *Pete McEnroe—all is revealed by his own magazine. Exclusive coverage—read about Boston's most eligible bachelor*. She could see the fantasy headlines now!

She consoled herself, as she began to jot down her ideas, that even if there was nothing reprehensible in Pete's past she could at the very least write a damning piece about the McEnroes' party. *Nothing sensational,* she told herself. *Just the facts.*

Tucking the file under her arm, though not expecting to use it again, she returned to her office and finished her notes. Then, her screen turned on, she began to type furiously. Her second column would not have the same eyebrow-raising appeal to Massachusetts criminal investigators as the first, perhaps, but it would certainly make an impact on her boss. *But what if I lose my job?* she wondered fleetingly. *Well, fine, who needs to work for a man like Pete anyway?* For the first time in her life as a journalist, she was going to write without fear of censure. She was tired of kow-towing meekly, as she had done for so many years in London to Andy.

Mentally shrugging Pete away, she wrote about the poolside scene as if someone else—not Clare Hogarth—had known the wave of panic as she hit the water. *I want to sound objective,* she thought, and a few words of instruction and encouragement from her tutor at Cambridge floated in her head as she wrote. *Eyewitness accounts aren't as easy as they ought to be, Clare. You can't step outside them enough. But you have to. And I need to write this, anyway, to get that night out of my mind.*

When she'd printed off a draft copy of the column, she left it unread on her desk. She would come back to it after a break and polish it for submission. Something prompted her to cross into the art department and search once again in the McEnroe family photograph holdings. She had never thought of looking up Pete's earlier pictures, but she wanted to see them now.

It made her smile to see him portrayed as a star on the basketball court. Yet, now that she thought about it, there was no reason why a man studying journalism and English for a double major should not excel equally on the sprung boards of a gymnasium floor; that he had to stoop under most doorways should have given her a clue. But was the laughing college athlete with the shock of gold hair and his arm round two Notre Dame cheerleaders truly the same man who had pulled her down with him into the pool the night before? She shivered, remembering the way his face had changed from puzzled tenderness to savage desire; remembering the strength in his arms as he pinned her against his chest. For a moment, when she pushed him, she had felt in her heart the red fury of murder. Although he could not have known she was no swimmer, he had perhaps been drunk and desperate enough to want to hurt her, too.

OK, so she'd agreed to work for him—though it might not last much longer—but she wasn't going to belong to him.

One press photograph detached itself from the others and slid sideways out of her hands and across the table, face down. She flipped it over. It was one she had not noticed before— taken after a college all-star game in Chicago, as the first line of the caption informed her. Not one but two familiar faces filled the picture.

She heard her own quick in-drawn breath and spoke out loud, 'Bobbie!' Both faces were wreathed in smiles. Neither looked out at the camera, but at each other. She frowned and read the rest of the caption: 'All-star favorite Pete McEnroe hugs college sweetheart Bobbie-Ann Rizzo in celebration after his stunning performance Saturday night.'

She left the photo file on a table and ran—stumbling over chairs and cannoning into swing doors in her haste—back to the cuttings on her desk. With trembling fingers she riffled through the pile until she matched the date on the photo with a date on an article about the same game. It was unlikely, very unlikely, that Bobbie would be mentioned . . . but she was— in a final paragraph she had overlooked.

> 'Notre Dame cheerleader Bobbie-Ann Rizzo told our staff reporter that it was the first basketball game she had attended without her pom-poms. "Strictly audience this time!" she enthused. Pete McEnroe's female fans will doubtless bewail the news that Pete and Bobbie-Ann have just announced their engagement. Both journalism majors, they will graduate this spring and already have jobs awaiting them in Boston.'

Engagement. Clare reread and reread that paragraph. So they had been engaged! No wonder Bobbie watched Pete's every move around the office.

Her eyes strayed to the clean print of the column she had just written. Bobbie might see this column—even if it were as she expected excised long before publication. No matter how badly Pete had behaved, what about *Bobbie's* feelings? Could she forgive herself for bringing Bobbie into the ugly scene by that swimming-pool in Bedford? Her column would do more than hurt Pete; it would douse what little light was left in Bobbie's eyes. Bobbie who had begun work at *Citizen* with Pete but had watched him claw his way to one of the most senior positions in the magazine while she remained relatively junior and adored him—now from afar. Bobbie who had befriended her on the flight to Boston and who had tried to overcome natural animosity towards her once Pete began his pursuit.

274

No, she could not let anyone see that column. She tore it up and pressed the onscreen delete button. Her Saturday morning's work was as if it had never been.

She stared at the blank screen. Her anger against Pete was melting, but in its place came a stab of envy so unexpected and keen that she winced aloud. In spite of all that had happened the night before, the image of those two faces close to each other hurt her. She wanted to believe that she was warm with indignation against Pete for the way he must have betrayed Bobbie, years before; but instead she felt once again a perverse, insidious warmth running through her blood for the man himself.

She shook herself, angry with the beguiling fantasies: Pete appearing beside her now and taking her away for a long weekend by the ocean. Pete calling her for their regular weekly meeting and looking at her with the same laughing eyes and young, hopeful expression that he had turned on Bobbie in the picture. Pete holding her to him in love, not fury; longing, not savagery. *I'm jealous,* she realized with dull surprise. Hoping to push the daydreams away, she stood abruptly and gathered all the press cuttings into her arms. Making herself think deliberately about every movement, she refiled them and then went back to the photo-library. There too she removed all traces of her work and pulled the doors shut after her. Then she stopped, took a deep breath, and doubled back to the cuttings files. She would start again, this time following a different track.

The bulky size of 'J McEnroe' arrested her once more, but she searched slowly for other files labelled 'McEnroe'. Remembering the family photograph and the names 'Don' and 'Maggie', she looked under 'M' again (Marianne's file was still in place, but none for 'Maggie' or even 'Margaret'), then 'D'. No file there, either.

She sighed, sat down on the black-topped stool left by the librarian for short writers and tall shelves, and rested her elbows on her knees. *No 'D'; no 'M' except Marianne,* she thought. *How strange!* She went back to 'D' and was just giving up when a thin file which had been wedged farther back than the others attracted her attention. 'E McEnroe.'

The folder was grimy and bent at the corners, and when she opened it she saw that, like Pete's, here was the press file of someone who had been out of the public eye for years. In this case, many years. The last clipping showed a date of December 1971. *Years ago!*

Her curiosity leapt, but she would not allow herself to read the most recent first, instead turning to the back of the file for the very oldest articles. 'Julius McEnroe's daughter wows PC'—an article about a girl named Eleanor McEnroe who had been voted homecoming queen in her freshman year at Providence College. She skimmed it and set it aside. She flipped through several more without bothering to read them; at least she knew now that McEnroe had a daughter. 'Lawmaker's daughter stars in controversial production'; 'Ellie McEnroe sensation'; 'Ellie McEnroe dismissed by dean'; 'Gerard's favorite new girl'; 'Woodstock: Senator's daughter shock'. The headlines careered forward, each one showing somebody more out of control than the one before.

At last she reached the most recent cutting, at the front of the file. Eleanor McEnroe had been found dead by hotel staff in Miami, the report stated blandly. *Aged 24*. As she read those words, she felt her face grow hot.

Two memories rushed in on Clare: her cousin Jack talking under the stars on the beach a few weeks before about a young member of the McEnroe family who had died 'under mysterious circumstances'; and the photograph she had seen only hours before—of a bubbly, red-headed girl standing beside Marianne McEnroe. Everything seemed to fall into place: the pain on Marianne's face; the way Julius McEnroe had looked at her own red hair that first day in Pete's office. Perhaps even Pete's interest in her . . .? Though, no, his interest in her couldn't possibly be accounted for in that way; Ellie McEnroe had been dead for eighteen years. She calculated quickly: Pete would only have been about twelve when she died.

She read the article about the discovery of Eleanor's body. Cold sentences such as 'The Dade County coroner is suspending judgment pending autopsy results' and 'Police report alleged evidence of illegal substances in the room of the deceased' chilled her. A woman of twenty-four had died alone in a hotel room a thousand miles from home. That was the end of a life, and that (or so it seemed) was also the end of anyone's desire to chronicle her life in the press cuttings folder. There was nothing more to give her a clue of the eventual findings of the coroner about Eleanor McEnroe.

She slumped forward over the file and let her eyes run blankly over the files in front of her. Julius McEnroe's face came swimming towards her, a trail of bubbles behind him and the impassioned, angry look of a parent wanting to save a child from disaster. Wanting to save her from the water— even though he could not have known she would drown if he didn't.

So was this why McEnroe had given most of his latter years to prosecuting cases against drug traffickers? Another part of the puzzle resolved itself, but she convinced herself that there had been some sort of a cover-up—about Ellie McEnroe's death. Why else were all the cuttings after her death missing?

With both the 'J' and the 'E' files in hand, she chased out of the cuttings library and back to her office. There she hesitated a long time before typing a new column. *Julius McEnroe saved my life,* she reminded herself several times. But the reminders dwindled to silence. She tried to tell herself that here was a lawyer and senator of integrity who had saved many other lives in addition to her own, but the more she thought and wrote about the old man, the more certain she became that he had built almost twenty years of his career on a false foundation. What drove him was an obsessive desire to cover up for his daughter's criminal behaviour by crusading against the very world she had lost herself in. *That fits. It really fits,* she reassured herself, gathering conviction.

She steeled herself to be more like the other journalists at

277

Citizen—more 'hard-nosed' than she had been in England. *It's about time, perhaps.* She put out of her mind the silver hair and lined face she had first trusted and warmed to, and saw instead the press pictures of a politician on the hustings, stumping his way around the state, condemning drugs . . . but never fully acknowledging his own daughter's involvement.

Well, hadn't Pete McEnroe said that any person in the public eye in the city was fair game? And if after her first exposé McEnroe could inveigh about the need for DEA investigations into drug parties at the yacht club, why shouldn't she also expose his family and hurt Pete—indirectly, of course—after all? This way Bobbie would not be hurt too. *Why not?*

She smiled to herself and went on typing.

34

'Where are you off to?' Sandy asked.

Clare was standing in front of the mirror by her bedroom door. All the windows and doors of the flat were open, but the becalmed air hung heavy and still; and even though she had just taken a cool shower, sweat ran in tickling rivulets between her shoulder-blades as she wielded the drier and tugged at her hair with a brush.

Looking into the mirror, she grinned at her flatmate and tried to keep her mind off the stifling heat. 'You know perfectly well where I'm going,' she said, shouting to be heard over the drier.

'To meet your new boyfriend. But where? Anywhere nice?' Sandy sat on the arm of a chair a few feet away and swung one leg. 'You didn't tell me.'

'Well, I could ask you the same thing,' Clare said pertly. 'You're quite dressed up, yourself.'

Sandy laughed. 'Never you mind where I'm going. I've got to stay here, anyway, to keep you in order this weekend.'

'Thanks!'

'So where are you meeting him?'

Clare switched off the hair-drier and turned round. 'Paddington Station,' she said. 'How about that for the most romantic venue of the year?'

'You won't even notice the din of the place or the trains going in and out—except his, of course.'

'Probably not,' she said dreamily. She bent forward and twisted her hair into a knot; it would be cooler off her shoulders.

'Go on, then, or you'll miss him.'

Clare looked at her watch. 'Plenty of time yet, but I think I'll go now anyway.'

She hurried across the small green and over the bridge towards Ealing station. She passed the familiar landmarks automatically, her mind inevitably on Frank. She sighed. It was strange that he had not telephoned her since Thursday night, but that didn't matter now . . . she was on her way to meet him.

Music from a small French café bounced out onto the pavement as she passed. From somewhere within, a radio DJ announced the 'golden oldies' show, and the first bars of an old BeeGees song floated through the windows with the smell of chicken and fresh bread. Farther along the street, the fatty smell of frying fish and chips fell out of another shopfront. *The local chippie,* she murmured to herself, thinking with a shudder of her mother and the Friday night fish-and-chip binges that had marked the end of the week as she was growing up. *And I ought to ring Mum!* she rebuked herself. *It's been so long . . . but not today.*

Ealing station platform was deserted except for a young couple oblivious to everything except each other, arms wrapped around necks and shadowed faces close together. Clare threw them a quick glance. *In an hour or so, she thought, that could be me.* She looked away and watched two pigeons quarrelling over a curl of bacon rind.

A westbound Picadilly Line train rattled over the rails without stopping. Fleetingly, the two others on the platform separated and turned their heads. They had not seen her, but she immediately stiffened and pulled back behind a hoarding. *Danny!* Yes, there he was—with someone else. She felt a wave of surprise, then relief flooded her. *I don't have to think about him any more at all.* Her mouth curved up. *One less burden to carry around.*

At last a District Line train crawled sluggishly down the line with its brakes squealing. She waited until Danny and the girl had stepped into a carriage about twenty yards away, then shot into an open door near the front of the train. It was unlikely she would see them again.

When she reached Paddington, there was still half an

hour before Frank's train arrived. In the noisy impersonality of the huge station, she wandered from one concession to another, staring blindly at flowers, sandwiches, croissants, and racks of tabloid newspapers. On one stand *Women Today* was prominently displayed in front. She gave it a smile of pleased recognition; Frank's story had come out on Friday.

At the barrier she waited, hot with impatience, for the first sight of the train's engine through the gate. At last, the hiss of releasing brakes and the slam of heavy doors. She stood on tiptoe in the crowd of waiting people, craning forward, her heart beating fast and her mouth dry with excitement. Weekend travellers rushed past the gates, faces tense, hands thrusting forward tickets for inspection. *One of these has sat with him,* she thought dizzily, then laughed at her own sentimentality.

Eager children were followed by suitcase-laden grandparents visiting their families for the weekend. Boxes of Lego and beady-eyed dolls peeped out of Bristol and Reading shopping-bags. She returned their empty stares with an equally glazed expression. *Where is he?*

Cold disappointment slowed her heart and made her hate the passengers and the welcoming crowd around the gate who shouted and fell into each other's arms. *Where is he?* she wondered again.

The crowd dispersed, and the ticket collector gave her a pitying look. 'You lost someone, miss?'

'Yes,' she said.

'The train ran out a fraction early.'

'Early? British Rail?' Disappointment sharpened her voice into rudeness.

The man grinned back amiably. 'A person might have missed it, coming from Reading, perhaps.'

'He was coming from Bristol.'

'Ah, well. You'd best wait for the next one.'

'When will that be?' She sounded bitter, but checked herself. Frank would never have chosen to be late, and he would be tired—probably more tired than he had been last week in Bristol after the shattering pursuit of those six children. She steeled herself.

The official consulted a timetable pasted to the box's glass panel. 'Sorry about this. Not my usual post on a Saturday. Let's see ... yes, two-thirty, it'll be.' He turned away to answer a phone that had begun to ring behind him, and Clare meandered towards the station buffet to sit out the time until the next West Country Intercity.

She drank her coffee, watching abstractedly as the buffet workers washed the floor and others like herself stared expressionlessly out of the streaked windows. The station was temporarily quieter, and she would have felt desolate if she hadn't been sure of Frank's eventual arrival. She decided to telephone Sandy in the flat, in case there had been a message.

If Sandy's still there, she thought morosely. *Hardly likely.* Sure enough, the phone rang and rang. She could hear in her head the insistent sound of it, not only as it rang in her ear at Paddington but also as it rang in the deserted flat in Ealing. *Sandy did go out, after all,* she thought as she hung up. *And why not?*

Still standing abstractedly in the booth, she wondered if she should ring Frank's house in Bristol. A sense of icy doubt spread through her. The 'what if?' game wasn't a happy one this time. *What if he's decided not to come after all?* She dropped her head into her hand and shut her eyes, smelling the stale smell of the station. *Is that why he didn't ring?* She pushed the doubts away and made herself turn back to the main concourse of the station.

As two-thirty approached she waited by the same barrier again, this time without the delirious anticipation. The passengers who walked past her when the train came in had none of the same magic and light as the last herd she had watched pouring through the gate. Nor was Frank among them.

'How long until the next Bristol train comes in?' she asked

the same ticket collector after the last straggler had passed them. 'Four,' he said mechanically. 'That's when I go home.' He peered doubtfully at her. 'You by yourself?'

She remembered another man, weeks ago, asking her more or less the same question the first time she had met him. 'No,' she said faintly. 'There's someone with me. It's all right, thanks.'

Someone I haven't even spoken to this afternoon, she reminded herself. *Please God, wherever Frank is, look after him. And me, too.*

Back in the buffet the waitress who was sponging down tables and emptying ashtrays smiled vaguely at her when she sat down for the second time with a cup of coffee.

She returned to the phone booth at three o'clock and dialled Frank's Bristol number. *His housemates will answer it, at least,* she consoled herself.

The line rang interminably, the sound even more desolate in her ear than the bell of her Ealing phone an hour and a half before. And now tiredness was creeping up on her. She wasn't even sure that she could smile when Frank stepped off the train at four. She redialled, praying that she had dialled the wrong number the first time. *No one there.* Dully she replaced the handset, hope evaporating. Would he let her down? On Thursday night the thought would never have entered her head. *Well, but would he?*

She groaned, feeling as if she were pressed against a blank stone wall. A wall of puzzlement and perhaps even rejection. Danny and his new girlfriend came into her mind, but she shoved the taunting pictures away. No arms around her, not now at least.

I'll go home, she decided. *If he's on the next train, he'll ring me.*

When the tube train left the underground she sat with her face pressed against the window, watching lightning play over the shops and houses. Then, as she stepped onto the Ealing platform for the second time that day, the skies opened. The rain brought relief and was strangely soothing; the air smelled cooler than it had for weeks, the hot stink of melting tarmac and diesel fumes for once abated.

She splashed back to the flat with her hair plastered to her head, feeling hollow and a little sorry for herself.

That feeling persisted, hanging over her like the grey humidity left by the storm, for two more days. It pursued her on Monday morning as she went back to Blackfriars to fill the void of the bank holiday with overtime work. Still not knowing why Frank hadn't come, she listened absently as the wheels of the almost empty train sang out the familiar District Line stops.

Ealing Common, Acton Town, Stamford Brook . . . she sat with one arm draped across the folio-case on her knees, and the other resting on the empty seat beside her. Running first under breathless sunshine, then into the airless darkness of the tunnel, the train hurtled her eastwards. If she stayed on it long enough, she remembered, she would find herself in Barking. The thought came again, *Should I go and see Mum?* She shifted uncomfortably. *No—not now.* She would let this train carry her only as far as Blackfriars. Far enough!

At Hammersmith the train was still almost empty: just two men with drawn early-morning faces, one yawning, the other glazed, both staring as stupidly as she did at the parallel lines of pipes running along the dark wall of the tube, both swaying rhythmically to the dance of the carriage on the rails. The train was close and hot, despite the holiday.

Barons Court, West Ken, Earl's Court, South Ken . . . For a moment, forgetting where she was, she relived her conversation with Mrs Drury in Bristol only the week before. *Poor woman. And poor child, wherever Jennifer is.* Her own troubles were paltry by comparison, she reflected. Still, sleep had been slow in coming to her for the last two nights . . .

She had tried to pray for the lost children and for Frank, but the hurt and puzzlement about why he hadn't come sliced into prayers and dreams alike. Because she had met him again, because they had talked so freely in the cathedral and at the little restaurant on Fairfax Street, then on the way to

Bristol on Wednesday, about things that mattered to her more than anything else, the weekend had seemed empty and incomplete without him.

She wanted him to be beside her: where she could ask him more about his family and tell him about her own—about her father's life in the merchant navy, about Barking (something told her he would be interested, not scornful); about her cousins in America; about what it was like to be a journalist (a non-swimmer) in a family of Cockneys (all sea-lovers). She sighed heavily, slightly ashamed of fantasizing so much about Frank when life had to go on and work had to be done—his and hers. She was no longer sitting in his car bound for Bristol, but on a tube bound for Blackfriars. It was not Wednesday afternoon, but Monday morning. A Monday that might have been a holiday with him.

Victoria, St James's Park, Westminster, Embankment, Temple . . . the train was still empty. She shifted in her seat and stretched her legs. One more stop.

In the *Women Today* reception, she glanced at the vacant reception desk and headed straight for the lift. The staff writers' offices were empty, too. Without unlocking her desk or raising the venetian blinds, she collapsed into her chair and fumbled immediately for the special issue that contained Frank's (or was it Nina's?) story. She read the pages slowly, relishing every word and feeling her cheeks grow hot. Never again would ordinary black-and-white print on the pages of this familiar magazine have quite the same effect on her. When she'd finished she discovered that Nina must have written her a note late on Friday. It was taped inside her diary for the next day:

> Guess what! I forgot to tell you. While you were away this week Andy came in and said he'd get Frank to do another story. He wants me to work with him again. What do you think of that? See you soon.
>
> Love, Nina

Several things ran through Clare's mind simultaneously as she stared at the note. One was that under ordinary circumstances—had the story been written by anyone but Frank—she would have been glad about Nina's news; it was only fair, now that she herself was taken up with several stories about the abductions, that Nina should have something other than the usual run-of-the-mill writing tasks. At the same time, it bothered her that she hadn't confided in Nina about meeting Frank again. Nina's face on Friday had told her plainly that she was still infatuated with Frank, still hopeful that something would come of her professional contact with him. Suddenly Clare was struck with self-doubt, struck with the impossibility of a close relationship between Frank Bernard in Bristol and Clare Hogarth in London. She thought, *Well, what claim do I have on Frank? How do I know what's going to happen? He didn't even show up this weekend.*

She raised her eyes to the blankness of the blinds. The same sense of empty incompleteness that had niggled at her on the train this morning returned with renewed intensity. What on earth was she to say to Nina tomorrow? 'Good for you. The story reads very well—honestly.' She shrugged and felt the colour rising to her face as she imagined herself saying it. 'Of course I'm bound to be completely biased. Frank Bernard—er, you—did a brilliant job with an uneven bit of copy.'

It was no use. She simply could not look at Nina and say this. She got up and went to the window to open one of the blinds. She fumbled with the cord, and the blind stuck halfway up the window, skewed at forty-five degrees.

The dome of St Paul's came partly into view, and she sent up a quick prayer. *Lord, what shall I tell her? There may be nothing to tell.*

Grateful for something mindless to do, she worked patiently at a knot in the cord until the blind fell to the sill and she could raise it again, this time straight. The temperature in the office seemed immediately to soar as the north-eastern light spilled across the room.

Rather than sitting down again she stood dreaming by the window for a few moments. Outside the plate glass, the Thames wound away east and west under the thin veil of a heat haze, the clean lines and clear blue-greens of the foreground smudging to greys in the distance. Something about that wide expanse of the city soothed her, the way the view from her favourite armchair in the flat soothed her. It reminded her that beyond the narrow walls of office, flat and underground carriage there were longer journeys to be made. She sighed. *So long since I went overseas!* Sydney Harbour Bridge and the Golden Gate Bridge of San Francisco—even the less dramatic Longfellow Bridge in Boston—were almost as clear in her memory from trips over the past ten years as the bridges she could count spanning the river here. She lost herself in speculation and memory.

35

My father told me it was the bank holiday, but I wasn't sure I believed him. Where had the three days gone? In clear moments I had sat propped by a mountain of pillows at an angle that allowed me to see out of the window. I realized I had never before watched the Bristol Channel tide going in and out; never found time to. The long sands were dotted with holiday makers, children on donkeys, the occasional crowd gathered around a Punch and Judy show, and fishermen like my father digging for lugworm in the early mornings. I lay there, when I wasn't asleep or unhinged by fever, watching the shadows on the beach melt, the tide rise and fall inexorably, and the sun edge round until it blazed straight into my eyes and finally dipped for the night into the sea. Those leisured moments were the good ones.

My mother told me it was the hottest bank holiday in August for years, but I wasn't sure I believed her, either. In the bad moments I could think of nothing but how to stay warm. For some reason she kept opening the windows, but every time she left the room I tottered out of bed on legs like thin, aching sticks and shut them. I asked them to keep the door shut, too, when the smell of food from the kitchen downstairs sickened me.

It wasn't just my sense of smell that was distorted. Everything seemed louder, brighter, stronger than usual. Quiet noises thunderclapped in my ears; soft lights flashed fork lightning across my eyes; sudden movements made the room swirl and slide. And in the midst of the nightmare, I had to concentrate simply on catching my next breath. If this was pneumonia, I knew I never wanted to get it again.

The doctor came several times, and my mother was never long out of the room. 'You've been run off your feet, haven't you?' she accused, once she'd established that at least for the moment I was *compos mentis*.

My rambling mind wondered vaguely where a simple answer to an apparently straightforward question would lead me. She had a way of turning ordinary conversations into something extraordinary. *Maybe that's why my father loves her,* I remembered thinking, years before. *Because Mum's the only one who'll give credit to the long, tall tales about fish the size of church pews.* To Mum, all the world was a miracle, and it was no trouble for her to believe in the smaller ones.

She was eyeing me suspiciously through the habitual wisps of hair. 'But you'll be all right, surely?'

'You know I'm rudely healthy,' I told her, choking back a coughing fit.

She raised her voice as loud as my father's. 'Sure you haven't gone deaf like your daddy?'

I winced and covered my ears with my hands. 'One of us'll have murder to confess if you shout like that,' I whispered.

She laughed, this time softly. 'Sorry. I asked if you've been rushed off your feet.'

'That's putting it mildly.'

'So you think you're indispensable, I suppose?'

The question sounded ominous. I was about to get a rebuke for pride. 'I—no—in fact, Charlie—' I didn't get any further. An uncontrollable cough had me bouncing up and down on the pillows for two minutes and sent my mother scurrying downstairs for a fresh glass of grape juice; it was one of the few things I could tolerate.

While I was fighting back my lungs' involuntary intention to quit my body, I remembered again that no one except the family and the doctor knew where I was. There were important phone-calls to make. I opened my mouth to say so, when at last I swallowed the final cough, but Mum cut me off before I could say anything. 'Has it occurred to you, Frank—'

I lay back meekly and shut my eyes. *Here we go,* I thought.

'—that there might be a reason for your being ill like this just now?' Her warm hand covered mine on the quilt, and I gripped it hard. My own was cold, but sweating.

I hesitated before answering. What sort of a question was that to ask a man with a temperature of a hundred and something? 'Not really,' I said, opening my eyes again in the hope that she would merely hand me the juice and thus spare me the sermon I could see massing on her brows like a storm over the Channel.

'Don't you think that God allows illness for good reason?'

I groaned. 'Oh, Mum, don't you ever let up? For goodness sake—I'm not up to that today. I'm sick.'

Her smile was knowing. 'I can see that quite well, son,' she said drily, 'but I'm thinking now that God never lets us go through the smallest illness or problem without a good reason.'

'Your experience—' I sighed and pushed her hand away. 'Not mine.'

She thought she had caught me, but she had fallen into the trap herself. She should have known better than to push the conversation that way. Damian had belonged to us all, and now he was gone. For a moment the image of the Christ of Coventry Cathedral lifting the cup of suffering came into my mind; but I rejected it. Clare wasn't with me now to offer consolation. *Clare . . . I must remember to tell them . . . and to tell her . . .*

Another cough brought me out of the reverie. 'Life's pain is dreadful. My illness is trivial, but what about Damian's? I can't see any reason for his death. Why should I believe in a God who *allows* that—or any illness at all?'

My mother sighed and frowned in dismay.

'You're still angry about that?'

I gave her what I hoped was a reproachful look. 'Of course I am.'

'That's what I've been driving at, partly.' She was leaning forward now, smiling and wanting to carry me with her.

I groaned again; I didn't want a lot of cant right then about

290

reasons for suffering. Theology would only give me a worse headache.

She pursued, 'Perhaps you need time to take stock of everything. You haven't had a holiday for far too long. How can you go on like that, Frank? You need time to think. About Damian, yes, and about yourself.' She was warming to her theme. '*All of us* need time to take stock, reflect, understand what's going on in our lives. Otherwise we just journey on along the surface of life, skimming along like larvae on a dirty pond, never looking for sweeter waters.'

If I had been feeling more energetic, I would have regaled her with arguments about the madness of taking time to take stock of anything in the middle of a case like the one with those children. *A time for action. That's in the Bible, isn't it?* Instead, I decided to tune her out, so I shut my eyes again. I liked the phrase 'sweeter waters', and I followed it across the desert of my tight breathing. It reminded me of Clare's laughter in the pool, of the waters closing around my ears as she shouted about baptism. It reminded me of the balm of those words from her sweet mouth as we stood in the ruins a hundred miles away. *The God of second chances.* I screwed my eyes shut again. Here after all was Clare's wisdom.

I heard my father tiptoe through the door. 'I think he's falling asleep on us, Peggy,' he whispered. 'I'm afraid all the talk has been a bit much.'

Mum's tongue clicked. 'Whisht. Never you mind. I'll just see if he'll take this drink. Look at the sweat standing on him, will you? It's a wonder there's much of him left at all.' Her hand came under my neck, and I smelled violets close to me. She wiped my face with a cool cloth. 'Can you sip at this, love?'

I obliged both myself and my mother and emptied the glass in cautious, sometimes spluttering gulps, annoyed at my own helplessness. Then I fixed her with what I hoped was a chief constable's stare and said, 'I want to sleep now, if you don't mind.'

She hovered anxiously. I wanted to kiss the frown off her

face, but the lines were too deep for that. 'Yes, you sleep,' she said.

I wrestled with my slippery memory. 'Tell Dad to phone the station, could you?'

She scoffed, 'Sure and don't you think he did that two days ago?'

'Oh, I suppose he would have. Thanks.' *Isn't there something else I meant to ask her, or tell her?*

In the quiet, my parents' concerned faces slid away again. My body was full of fire, and I lost track of something I had been chasing in my mind. My dreams were all of running: myself running, Clare running, and another figure running—a man whose face I could not see but whose hands and heart (in the jumbled logic of such dreams) were both translucent and red with blood. I dreamed, too, that I was frowning with the effort to understand my dream. Moaning and frowning, then kissing away my mother's long-etched frowning marks; kissing away the small lines of puzzlement that often furrowed Clare's forehead, too. Nothing made sense until I opened my eyes to twilight and found that Nigel and Jill had come into the room. Automatically my eyes strayed to the window. The tide had been full as my mother had tried to talk to me; now it was half ebbed. I felt at half ebb myself.

Jill coughed nervously as if in sympathy, and Nigel scowled and pushed a bunch of chrysanthemums towards me. My head was clear then, though I still had no idea whether it was Monday or Wednesday, dawn or dusk. But I could think straight enough to know I was glad to see them, glad they had made time to see me.

'How are you?' I asked them.

'We should be asking you that, old man.' Nigel looked uneasy. He had never called me 'old man' before—all sorts of rude names, but never a term of affection like that. (Well, the warmth would wear off soon enough when I was back on the job.)

'You look dreadful,' Jill said, sitting down near me. 'Nigel, leave the flowers on the end of the bed, and I'll ask Mrs Bernard about a vase before we go.'

I looked at Jill's face more closely. There was something new in her voice; I couldn't decide what it was.

'Sorry we couldn't get here sooner,' Nigel said.

'Please find a chair,' I begged. 'You're making me dizzy, dancing about there as if you've got ants in your pants.'

He shot a surprised look at Jill. 'Dancing? But I'm standing stock still!'

'Not to me, you aren't. I've been hallucinating. Any minute you'll turn into Robocop. Just sit down, would you?'

He sat, grumbling under his breath and uncomfortable with the role of sick room visitor. 'Least you haven't lost your insane sense of humour.'

'But your face is so *thin*,' Jill said in an agonized voice.

'Don't you start! I've got my mother clucking and flapping enough as it is.'

'How can you complain?' Nigel grumbled. 'Got the good life here, you have. Waited on hand and foot. Sleep the days away.'

'Tell me all about it! Preferably,' I added in my most pathetic voice, 'when I'm not dying of tuberculosis.'

Jill made more noises of sympathy that got me laughing, then coughing again. When I recovered, I asked them what had been going on in Bristol.

'Charlie's working his tail off,' Jill said. 'But your mother said not to talk shop at all, or she'd throw us out.'

'Oh, don't pay any attention to her Irish shrewishness.'

'We will though, old man. We want you fit again.'

Jill smiled in my direction. 'Is Clare coming to see you?'

Everything came back to me then with agonizing clarity. I screwed up my eyes, thought of several choice words, but bit them back. 'Oh, no!'

'What?' Jill was looking back and forth from my face to Nigel's.

'I knew there was something. I've been trying to think of it for days. I wanted someone to phone her.'

293

'We can do that for you,' Jill said gently.

'With great pleasure,' Nigel added, smacking his lips and winning a mock scowl from Jill.

Jill took a pen out of her handbag. 'Her number. I'll need—'

'I think it's in my pocket. But I don't know where they put my trousers. I was going to London this weekend.'

'*This* weekend?' Nigel echoed. 'You told me you were going Saturday.'

'So where on earth are we? Is it Monday or Friday?' I threw out my hands bitterly. 'Here's Lazarus, half back from the dead, but no one to hold a party for me.'

'Ah,' they said simultaneously, exchanging laughing glances, 'let's hold a pity party for Frank!'

'Good friends, you are.'

'Yes, aren't we?' Nigel said in injured tones. 'Came all the way down here on a holiday night, when I can think of many better things to do than sit in a stuffy bedroom listening to Frank N. Stein himself moaning on and on about his pneumonia.'

I couldn't answer that.

'Ouch,' said Jill. 'We did come to cheer you up. We've got some—'

Nigel leaned over the bed and covered Jill's mouth with his hand. 'Don't tell him yet. He'll die of apoplexy if the pneumonia doesn't kill him first.'

'Don't tell me what?' I protested. 'Go on, Jill, I had a feeling you had something up your sleeve.'

Predictably, she pushed back the thin dress material that covered her upper arm. 'I have,' she said, straight-faced. 'My arm, silly.'

I saw something glinting in the fading light, something like starlight twinkling from her hand. I caught at it and dragged it right under my nose for a proper examination. 'What's this? What's *this*? All jewellery on the counter for inspection, Miss Peterson. This is your custody sergeant speaking. Hop to it, now.'

Shaking her head, but wreathed in smiles, she spread the

fingers of her left hand for closer examination. A tiny diamond surrounded by even tinier red stones that I couldn't identify glittered from her fourth finger. 'Nigel, you rogue. You did it at last!'

He was grinning. 'Blame Jill. She got stroppy and said "Now or never, slowcoach, or I'm catching the next bus".'

'I never said anything of the sort!' Jill was blushing furiously.

'Get the champagne,' I shouted, and began to cough again. 'I don't believe it. About time.'

'You can talk!'

'No I can't,' I spat out between spasms. 'Seriously, let's drink to this marriage of yours.'

Jill groaned. 'It's been parties all weekend, Frank. CID's gone down the tubes. Sally made ruder-than-ever posters and hung them all around Nigel's office. The guv'nor thinks we're all mad ... He'll probably transfer me to some place in the sticks like *Weston*—' She wrinkled her nose in distaste, but then beamed again.

I looked at Nigel, whose grin was equally manic. 'So you finally popped the question, did you?'

'No, she proposed to me.' The westerly light gleamed on his glasses, but his smile was far brighter.

'I did not!'

'I can tell I'll never win that argument,' Nigel laughed.

'You'll get no sympathy from this quarter,' I told him severely. 'As I said, it's about time. When's the wedding?' I expected Nigel to prevaricate and murmur vaguely that they'd set a date later.

Instead he looked me right in the eye. 'End of next month. And save your breath for breathing, old man. We'll be geriatric if we don't get on with it after all these years. Nothing fancy, mind you. Only about half the force and their families, that's all. The best day for local lags in years, it'll be. And before you say anything else, listen to this.' He wagged his finger at me. 'You've got to get well, and quickly. I need a best man, and Charlie's too fat to fit any of the morning suits in the shops, so I suppose we'll have to scrape the barrel and ask you to do the job.'

'Am I meant to be grateful for this huge demonstration of undying friendship and trust?'

'Of course you are. And you're meant to get well.'

'Yes,' Jill interrupted. 'No more malingering here in the land of counterpane. Your county needs you.' She stood up and retrieved the flowers. 'I'll put these in water myself, I think.'

'Give us a kiss, then.' I put on my pathetic little boy voice again.

'Don't fall for it,' Nigel instructed her.

'Keep your kisses for Clare,' Jill said. 'I'm off to have a chat with your mother downstairs.'

We waited until Jill's footfalls reached the front hall. 'She's great. Well done, Nigel.'

'Well, I thought—'

'Don't look so demure, you fool. You did the right thing. I'd love to be your best man.'

He stood awkwardly. I had rarely seen him look so pleased with himself and at the same time never heard him so free of the usual barbed wit. 'I think I understand better than I did,' he began stiffly, as if he was going to deliver a chief constable sort of speech, 'why you kept quiet at first about meeting Clare. It knocks you back a bit, loving someone like that. I don't know how it took me so long to see what I'd got in Jill.'

'She didn't propose, I bet.'

'Not a bit of it!'

'Good. Now do me a favour and let me have some sleep, OK?'

'Yes. And I'll see if we can phone Clare for you.'

I shut my eyes, suddenly exhausted again. 'Mmm . . . yes. That's important. I don't want someone else running off with her, and she won't know where I am. The number—'

'I know, is in your trouser pocket. We'll find it.'

'Probably minced up somewhere on the wrong side of my mother's washing machine,' I told him, starting to drift away like the tide. 'Or maybe stuffed into one of my father's hideous fish by now, for all I know.'

'Shut up and get well,' Nigel said bossily. 'That's an order.'

'Yessir,' I muttered. Then sleep claimed me again.

· 36 ·

'Hi, Clare!' her secretary sang as she dragged in through the heavy doors. 'How are you this bright and lovely August morning? It's Monday, you know.'

'I had noticed.'

The girl leaned forward and glanced over Clare's shoulder at the clock. 'Well, and did you have a great weekend?'

Usually Kathy's cheerfulness made Clare laugh, but the Monday after she had written the column about Julius McEnroe found her enervated and preoccupied. She was late—she knew that herself, without turning to look at the clock—and after the party on Friday and the extra day's work on Saturday, Kathy's high spirits grated on her. 'Not really,' she answered dully.

She opened her door and came back to the secretary's desk with the text she had composed two days before. She would not let herself read it. 'Here,' she said shortly. 'I doubt if Mr McEnroe's in yet, even though I'm late myself this morning. Would you see that this is waiting for him when he arrives?'

Kathy pursed her mouth, took the sheets, and offered no comment. Clare shut her door and slumped down at her desk. Where to start now? In a few hours she might be back at Rita's house without a job. At the moment she no longer cared what happened. She wanted nothing more to do with any of the McEnroe clan except strictly in business meetings; nothing more to do with the subject of drug abuse in Boston society. Nothing more to do with features on Angel Avalon—she'd had enough of her in England, already. Her next column would turn to other matters altogether, she decided. Something more light-hearted next time, for sure—if there was a next time.

Warm sunlight pooled on the floor by her desk and

brushed her left arm and shoulder. It was comforting, and after a while she lost herself in the day's Massachusetts press releases and news briefs. She noted several ideas for her next few columns, but nothing struck her forcibly enough to make her excited about what she was doing. Some of the exhilaration she had felt in her first week in the office had already dissipated. She glanced at her phone. It would ring at any moment, and Pete would summon her again.

The door opened suddenly, and Pete himself came through it without knocking and without invitation. He walked past the seat that faced her desk and dropped into a second chair, right beside her. For a moment he said nothing, his face expressionless.

She turned uneasily, without any clear idea of how—or whether—to greet him. She wished he were at least four feet farther away from her, preferably on the opposite side of a desk.

He bent forward unexpectedly and pointed at her feet. 'Two glass slippers, today, I see. That's a relief.'

She felt the colour leave her face and tightened her lips to bite back the sharp retort that came to mind. All the anger flooded in again, as overwhelming as the cold waters over her head on Friday night. 'No thanks to you,' she said tersely.

'Oh, don't be like that.' He was smiling. 'You're far too beautiful and far too good a writer to waste all your energy getting cranky over a little kiss and a frolic in the pool.'

She caught her breath. *He doesn't know I can't swim. He doesn't know.* She gritted her teeth and looked away from his tanned face and shiny smile. She didn't—somehow couldn't—tell him.

'Clare, I haven't come to talk about the party, anyhow,' he said.

No, I bet you haven't. She tried to stare him out, not answering.

'I just read your second column.'

Again, there was no need to answer him. Of course he had just read it. She had been anticipating his reaction for several hours. 'And?' she said grudgingly.

'It's interesting—though I don't know if I can publish it.' He pretended to be examining his fingernails, but she knew he was thinking hard and that the column she'd written had somehow reached him in a way that her hopeless screaming 'I hate you!' had failed to do.

He sighed. 'Rather a hit below the belt for my uncle. An old wound exposed again. And it's very speculative. When you write about someone's motives for going into certain types of public office, you're on tenuous ground anyway. And there's also a nasty tone about it that I can't quite associate with the woman who said she "isn't like a lot of the other women here". I don't much like the piece, and I'm not sure where you're coming from, or why.' He fixed her with a shrewd, hard look that made her quake. 'I've got my theories, however. But the satire is funny, and you might get away with it. Plus, I guess I asked for it last week when I said I don't let my last name dictate what we do and don't print in this magazine. Anyway, you're a damn good journalist.'

She absorbed all the contradictions, trying for a frantic few seconds to remember exactly what she had written two days before. But she couldn't; nor was she going to be swayed by provocation or flattery to answer the question about why she had written so harshly. She leaned back, still closer to him than she wanted to be. 'So you'll run with it?'

He met her eyes steadily. 'Maybe, maybe not. I'm going to talk to a good lawyer first. I would do that anyway, but there's more at stake here than what's legal, or what's libellous.'

'You mean I—'

'I mean exactly what I say. Whatever you, Ms Hogarth, feel about the McEnroes in general—on the basis of a very short acquaintance—' He leaned on the word 'very', and she felt her cheeks flaming. '—I am not totally devoid of scruples, and I retain a great respect for my uncle.'

She lifted her chin. 'Run it past him, then. You said he was interested in my work—well, let him see this piece before we print it.'

'You assume we'll print it.'

'Not necessarily. I assume that if you don't, I'm out on my ear.'

He stood up. 'I hadn't thought of that,' he said sarcastically. 'You could be right.' His hand was on the door.

She felt the same sense of powerlessness against him that she had felt before. He was like a tiger: fierce, bright, unrelenting, his eyes burning into her. This time there were no arms around her, only an overbearing will and a terrible animosity.

All the desire to fight him suddenly left her. She looked down at her hands on the desk, her pale fingers spread on the polished oak. They trembled slightly, and she felt weak and exhausted. Ashamed too of the way she had used the column to attack a family (yes, he was right) that she did not yet know.

'Look,' she said at last. 'I was angry when I wrote that.' *I'm apologizing! Shouldn't he, too?* 'I can do another piece if you like.' She sighed. 'I don't want to hit the senator below the belt. He's a good man, I'm sure.'

Pete's head inclined to one side, and his eyebrows rose. He moved away from the door again and sat down where she had hoped he would sit in the first place. 'Yes, he is. A better man than I am. Left to myself I'd follow our usual controversial style—publish and be damned. I'd like the stir the article would cause. It would bring a lot of other letters out of the readers' mailbag—out of the woodwork, if you like. But—'

'I was angry, I said,' she interrupted, hardly hearing him. 'I wanted to get at you.' Now that he was sitting down, she was no longer afraid of him.

Again he registered surprise. 'Yeah, well—'

'I can't swim, Pete. You made me furious! Even so, I shouldn't have pushed you.' She could not credit what her voice was saying, seemingly of its own volition. 'And you don't need to print this—I can easily write another column for you.'

'No—don't. Not yet, anyhow.' He put out his hand to her, but he was now too far away to reach her, and he let it drop. 'Wait a minute—did you say you *can't swim*?'

She nodded. 'That's right. So I owe your uncle a big

favour anyway. Please—I'll tone down the column—if you do run with it anyway.' She hated the way she was backing down, but she knew she couldn't go on with the fight any more. It wasn't in her nature to be vengeful.

'No,' he said. 'As I said, not yet. I'll think about it first. But I guess the column's irrelevant compared with what you just said—that you can't swim . . . I'm afraid you must think I'm some kind of a madman. I had no idea. I am sorry.' He threw out his hands, his mouth turning down. 'I don't know anyone who can't swim. It would never have crossed my mind. I'd had too much to drink, as well. And—'

She cut in, 'And Bobbie had gone.' It was the third time she had supported Bobbie's cause to him, and she expected the same sharp reply.

This time, however, he didn't jeer or snap back. 'Yes. Bobbie had gone.' He turned his head and looked out of the west window.

She took a deep breath. 'Let me know what you decide, then, about the column. I'm early with it this week, so there's plenty of time for another. I—' She was going to tell him that she had worked all day on Saturday but thought better of it. He could figure that out for himself, anyway, since she was handing in her work so early on a Monday morning. And the extra work was immaterial. Yet again, she felt herself softening.

'I will let you know,' he said.

She forced a brittle laugh. 'Any chance of a ceasefire around here?'

He smiled, and for once there was no mask. 'That sounds like a good idea.'

She hoped he would move from his chair, but he showed no sign of doing so, and she prompted gently, 'Great! Then I'll get on now.' The words came easily, though she still felt anything but at ease.

'Get on with what?'

She shrugged. 'Oh—this and that.'

'No this and that around here, Clare. I've got another much better idea.'

'Yes?' She knew she sounded unsure and was afraid he was thinking that the ceasefire might extend into a lunch-hour together. If that's what he wanted, he could think again.

'About your next column,' he began. 'I've got a tip-off for you.'

She remembered what she had promised herself about writing something more light-hearted next time. 'It had better be good.'

He was regaining his usual composure and self-assurance. 'My ideas are always good,' he laughed. 'And this one certainly is. I think it's got all the elements you like, and Boston will eat it up: intrigue, culture . . .'

'You're winding me up,' she jibed.

'What better way to put a good journalist on the trail of a good tale?'

'Tell me more.' Like Pete, she was relaxing now, enjoying herself almost as much as if she were back in *Women Today*, in conference with Andy and Dave.

He put his hands together. 'There's some risk involved, but it could be a plum. You're equal to it, I'm positive. Wait— are you any kind of a music buff?'

'Yes, but not as well informed as I'd like to be.'

'What about *I Giocosi*? Ever heard of them?'

She shook her head. 'That's an Italian name, but who are they?'

'A small arts orchestra. Appeared out of nowhere, like a comet across the sky, if you'll pardon my language. Not well known yet, but my gosh they're good. And people who count are noticing them. A couple of people left the Boston Philharmonic and joined them. There have been accusations of sharp practice.'

'Overcharging? Plagiarizing? What kind of thing?'

'No. Headhunting with big pay-offs, so my sources tell me. The Philharmonic is upset. And it gets more lively yet.' He stretched his legs and beamed at her. 'There's talk of mob connections.'

'You mean the Mafia?'

'Sorry—yes. I forget sometimes that you're a limey. You fit in so well.' He was turning on the charm again, his eyes raking over her.

'Pete—'

He winced and dropped his eyes. 'No, that's not allowed, is it? Excuse me, back to business. Where was I? Yes, the outfit. I doubt it, myself. Just because everyone in the orchestra has a name from Italy or Sicily needn't mean a thing, you know. But how'd you like to find out?'

She hesitated. 'Is this a job for me, or for someone with much more experience?'

'Baby, you've had plenty, I'm sure.' He winked.

She blushed and laughed. 'You're incorrigible.'

'And you love it.'

'Not sure I do. But the Mafia—there's nothing too romantic about gangland killings and loan sharks, is there? You need a man on the job, surely.'

'Oh, I wish I could print that in gold letters and hang it on your door!' He creased with laughter. 'You're right, after all. You're not like the other women here. I'd never catch an American woman making such a confession, not to me, at least. Ah well—' He heaved a huge mock sigh. 'No, you're the one I want on this. It's right for your column. You've hit the yacht club set and the McEnroe clan. Now it's time to sound a little sweeter and hit the concert scene. Only you might find a few discords in there, I guess. Get the concert schedule from the information office, and go for it. Tickets to all the concerts you want are on the house, OK?'

'Fine. I'll do it.'

He cocked his head knowingly to one side. 'You'll do it well, I know. Just be careful. Very careful.' For a moment his face was serious. 'I don't want to lose you. But hey, listen, no one knows you yet, and won't, either, because of the alias—so no one'll have a contract out on you.'

'Small consolation! But, yes, I'll be careful. Here's hoping there were no Mafia people in that drugs scene at the yacht club.'

'Oh, there probably were. But you were just an anonymous if rather gorgeous long-legged girl on the fringes of the party, I'm sure. Or did you fall into the harbour and attract attention to yourself that way?' He was grinning wickedly.

'Right! Sure, I decided to learn to swim that night as well.'

'And fell into a bucket of champagne.'

'I wish.'

He stood up. 'It's nice having a ceasefire with you.'

'Yes,' she agreed uncertainly, also coming to her feet but making sure she stayed safely behind her desk. 'Oh, something else I keep meaning to mention.'

He was at the door, once again ready to open it. 'What's that, Clare?'

'We spoke about my immigration papers and getting a social security number. What's happening?'

He flapped one hand irritably, and his smile vanished. 'Oh—I'll talk to personnel. Don't worry your pretty head about it, you hear?'

'We-ell—'

'Listen, it's nothing but damn bureaucracy. You'll get paid—that's all you need worry about, isn't it?' He pulled the door open, went through it, and let it swing after him. The last she saw was his retreating back and the thick gold hair grazing the edge of his collar. Something indefinable inside her ached.

She waited until he would be out of Kathy's room, then went straight to the cuttings library. 'I'd like to see everything you've got on *I Giocosi*,' she said.

'What are you up to now?' Virginia Enright asked ungraciously, and Clare was glad that she couldn't possibly have yet seen the McEnroe column she'd written; the hackles would certainly be up if she had.

'A complete change of focus,' she said evenly. 'Mr McEnroe wants a column on the concert scene, that's all.' *That's all!* The words echoed ironically in her head. *Yes, never mind organized crime connections, and heaven knows what else.*

She spent the remainder of the day immersed in reading,

running back and forth between her own office, the cuttings library, and the photo-library. By five o'clock she could almost hear Vivaldi and Paganini in her head as she folded the cuttings together and rode the elevator down to the lobby.

She had decided to risk carrying some of the cuttings home with her for the evening; her cousin Jack was on holiday from Springfield for a few days, and she wanted to talk with him about *I Giocosi*. Ed, who liked only rock concerts, would know nothing about the orchestra, but Jack—an avid Boston Pops enthusiast—probably would.

They hailed her loudly when the screen door banged behind her. 'Hey, Clare! That you?' Ed's voice—from the patio.

'No, it's Cinderella in glass slippers,' she called back, still thinking of Pete. 'What a lot of lazybones you are.'

Jack met her in the front hall, wearing cut-off jeans and a loose T-shirt. 'Hi there! Why shouldn't we be lazy? Hasn't anyone told you real Bostonians don't work in August?'

She laughed. 'Well, you know I'll never be a real *citizen*. Come on, where's the iced tea? I need to pick your brains.'

Ed wandered up behind Jack. 'Lo! The glowing lady herself. Better get those hot office clothes off and slip into something cooler.'

'Oh, Ed, you're so predictable,' Clare giggled.

'Give up, little brother!' Jack said.

'For now I will. Listen, Clare.' Ed's eyes were bright, but his face was serious for once. 'I've got some big news for you. Mom's gone over to the marina earlier than she expected this evening. The drug enforcement guys showed up here today.'

She watched their faces. McEnroe had wasted no time, then, in pursuing the information she and Pete had fed him. 'Oh?'

'Ed's sins catching up with him at last,' Jack drawled.

Clare dropped the pile of cuttings by the telephone, her heart beating a little faster. 'What's happened, then?'

'Stake-out over at the marina,' Ed began.

'The DEA wanted to set watch on the yacht club tonight,'

Jack explained.

Ed added, 'They wanted Mom over there so they could use the marina for surveillance.'

'Great excitement!' Jack beamed at her. 'See what you guys started?'

Clare pushed her hot hair off her shoulders and shook it out. 'Yes, yes.' For a moment she pictured that young woman dead in an anonymous hotel room in Miami. 'Yes, but it's not really exciting at all, Jack—Ed. It's frightening. We're not talking television cops and robbers here, you know. This is for real, as your mother would say. And your mom—she'll be OK, will she?'

Ed's face fell. 'I hadn't thought of that.' He looked quickly at Jack.

Jack nodded. 'She'll be OK. There'll be police protection if she has to testify later, and right now the marina's fairly crawling with police and undercover guys. One of them will bring her home—that was something she stipulated as soon as they arrived. It's bad enough her coming home from late nights down there anyhow, without this. I would have gone for her, I guess, but she'll be fine.' His eyes rested gently on Clare. 'You'd better watch your own tail, honey. You may need police protection yourself if you write many columns as explosive as last week's.'

Wearily she turned away from them into the kitchen to pour a cold drink. They followed her to stand under the whirring blades of an overhead fan. After the brilliance and heat outside, the room was dark and cool. 'If you wrote a column like the one I'm writing,' she said slowly, 'then you'd have to expect potshots. I knew that when I took the job, and that's why I've got an alias. But thanks for your concern.' She gave them a thin smile and shook lemon juice into her iced tea.

Jack cleared his throat. 'Say, I've had an idea—just to change the subject and blow your frowns away. I know Ed's been showing you around, Clare. But it's my turn, if you'll have me.'

She smiled at them both. *So utterly different.* Ed was

scowling ferociously at Jack, but Jack remained calmly detached. She gave him a mock curtsy. 'Your will, fair cousin?'

'Prince Charming wants to escort Cinderella to the ball,' Ed said sourly.

'Well, something like that,' Jack said. 'I've got two tickets to an *I Giocosi* concert tomorrow. I've been wanting to hear them for weeks. Everyone in Springfield's been talking about them. How about it, Clare?'

37

Light sifted through the cracks in the curtains, and Clare rolled over to see that the alarm clock read 5.25. Then everything came back to her.

Tuesday, and I still don't know why I haven't heard from Frank.

Pulling up the duvet, she rolled back towards the wall and screwed her eyes shut. She willed herself to fall asleep again, but it was no use. The clock's pale hands had imprinted themselves behind her eyes. She did not want to be awake or to remember the hollowness of the past three days: first at the station, then in the flat, then at work.

She lay sprawled in the half-light with her left arm thrown across her face to create a false darkness. *Sleep,* she told herself. *Just drift away.*

She couldn't. Her pulse drummed in her right ear, and below the window a flock of starlings started scolding in the trees. A milk float bounced along the brick courtyard beside the flats, the milkman chinking bottles and whistling. But it wasn't the noise that kept her awake; it was the terrible pall of sadness. It enfolded her as heavily as the duvet.

She shifted slightly and sighed. On so many other mornings since late June she had been woken early by hope or happiness—or both—thinking of Frank, letting dreams of him merge into daydreams. This time, however, there was no lightness or joy: only a stifling disappointment.

I've got to get up, she decided. *It's no use lying here thinking of how we might have spent the weekend.* She turned over for the third time. *But if I get up now, I'll probably wake Sandy. And what is there to do at five in the morning on a Tuesday?* She searched her imagination for other explanations of why she had heard nothing further from him, why he had not arrived as planned. Her mind was blank. Groaning, she looked again at the clock. *Five thirty-five.*

That was the last she remembered before full daylight was pouring in around the edges of the curtains and traffic was rushing past on the main road. The phone was ringing.

Her heartbeat lagged and bumped, the way it always did when she was woken by the phone. *Why doesn't Sandy answer it?* she wondered in a daze, swimming to the surface of the day.

With a jolt, she sat up and pushed her hair away from her face. 'Sandy?' she shouted, throwing back the duvet and sitting up. 'Sandy!' Silence except for the demand of the telephone. Obviously, Sandy had already gone to work.

She gathered her wits and ran out into the sitting room. The phone rang again. *Dear God, let it be Frank.* The clock on her work table said 9.15. *No, it won't be Frank. It'll be Dave or Andy to see where on earth I am.*

'May I speak to Clare Hogarth?' A woman's voice, one she did not recognize but felt somehow that she ought to.

Hope shrivelled. 'Yes? Speaking.'

The caller was friendly. 'This is Jill Peterson, from Bristol.'

She pulled the phone cord to its fullest length, tucked the phone under her ear, and slumped into the armchair. 'Oh, yes, Jill. Of course.' Questions buzzed and hammered in her head, but she swallowed them and pressed the receiver close against her ear. She wanted to shout, 'Is Frank angry? What's happened?', but she waited, breath held. 'I'm calling for Frank Bernard.'

'Mmm.' She did not trust her voice.

'I tried—Nigel and I both tried—to ring you last night. We couldn't raise anyone and gave up in the end.'

Clare groaned again. 'Oh—I was working late,' she muttered, stunned. *Nothing better to do,* she thought wretchedly.

Jill murmured sympathetically. 'Poor thing—on a holiday as well! But I was going to tell you—'

She could bear it no longer and felt almost like replacing the receiver. *No, don't say it, don't say it,* she chanted inwardly. Aloud, she cried, 'He wouldn't even ring me himself?'

Jill stammered in bewilderment, 'What? He *can't* ring you, I'm afraid. Too ill.'

'Ah—'

'He's got pneumonia.'

'Is this a joke?' She remembered some of the tales Frank had told her about the ridiculous pranks and jokes that went on even among senior police officers, especially when the pressure of work was too great. She felt bewildered, playing in a game whose rules she didn't understand.

'Good grief, no! He's been ill since the end of last week— probably longer, according to his mother.'

Clare became very still, listening with complete concentration. 'Can you tell me the details? I knew nothing at all. Pneumonia! In the summer!'

'I don't know a lot. Frank's mother gabbles away so fast that I can't remember half of what she said. From what I could make out, Frank went to supper with them on Friday night. He was taken ill then, she said. It was touch and go whether he'd go into hospital for the first night. I knew nothing—no one in CID did—until his father phoned in.'

'How does he look now? How does he feel? Have you seen him?'

'Hey! I don't know if I can go that fast. You're worse than the DIs in an interview!' Clare heard her draw a deep breath. 'Nigel and I went over to Weston last night. He looks terrible—his face is thin and pale. He's got that ravaged look—all blue eyes and beard. Desperately handsome.' She giggled, then sobered. 'But desperately ill as well, I think. He had a high temperature all weekend, and he drifts in and out of sleep all the time, even while he's talking. And coughs so you think he's going to turn inside out.'

Clare guessed that as well as being genuinely concerned about Frank, Jill was in a strange way enjoying the drama of reporting his news to her. She ached for him.

'He needs you to make him smile,' Jill added. 'I'll give you his mother's address and number and you can ring and see about coming down. Or—is that a problem?'

Her head was spinning. 'I don't know. He would have been up here at the weekend. I'd love to go. But there's work . . . and I don't know his family at all. I wouldn't be welcome showing up on their doorstep out of the blue. Don't even know if they know about me.'

'They do. His mother asked me if I knew you. Said Frank had just mentioned you. She's curious as can be about you.'

Clare laughed nervously. 'Sounds ominous.'

'Oh—not at all. She's Irish, very friendly. I didn't meet his father, though. Out fishing, she told me. As usual, she said. They're nice, ordinary people.' Patiently she dictated the Weston address and number.

Clare noted them and stirred herself to move to the edge of the chair. 'Well, I couldn't have had a better briefing. Thanks, I'll have a think about what I do next.'

Jill offered her own telephone number as well. 'If I can help again, just ring, OK? Nigel and I have just—no, never mind, I'll tell you when you get down here. You're very welcome to stay with me again, if you like.'

'You've been so kind. Thanks.' A sudden worm of doubt turned inside. 'Wait—did Frank actually ask you to ask me to come down?'

'No-o. Not exactly. He asked us to ring you, but nothing was specifically said about asking you to come.'

'Oh.' She felt deflated, at the same time aware that she knew nothing about pneumonia and so could hardly presume to understand anything about how Frank was reacting.

'But don't let that put you off. He was falling asleep at the end. Believe me, you'll cheer him up no end.'

She replaced the receiver thoughtfully but did not move from the chair, except to reach up and open the window. *Of course I should go. He'll be glad. But maybe he won't be glad . . . yes he will. Jill just said so, didn't she? But what do I say to his family?* The debate leaped back and forth in her head.

Sighing, she ran a bath and lay soaking in it with the same dialogue bouncing round her head like a Wimbledon tennis ball. *Pneumonia's not that serious these days. Or is it? He'd be in hospital if it were. Not if his mother was skilled enough to nurse Damian with leukemia. But if I go rushing down there now, when we're still getting to know each other, it'll be worse than a story from the magazine.*

She let the water out of the bath and towelled herself dry. 'I'm going anyway,' she told her blurred image in the steamy mirror. The telephone rang again as she was dressing, and she catapulted from her bedroom to answer it. *What if . . .?*

'Clare? Hello! It's Nina.'

'Oh, you gave me a start.' She waited as her heartbeat returned to its normal speed.

'Why, what's up? You sound so breathless. And why aren't you in today?'

'I overslept and didn't even hear Sandy go out. But I'm not coming in, anyway.'

'Andy came looking for you. Said you *were* supposed to be coming in.'

'He didn't know. I can't—and anyway, after yesterday, I need a break.'

'Yesterday?' Nina sounded bewildered.

'Yes, I was in yesterday. Providence, I think! Frank's ill, Nina. I've decided to go down and see him.'

'Oh.' Nina's voice was surprised, faintly irritated. 'But what about the copy for—'

'It'll have to wait. Especially after all the overtime I've done this summer, *Women Today* owes me. And Frank's more important.' The words spilled out before she'd thought of their full effect on Nina. She wanted to bite her tongue after she'd said them, hating the sound of her own apparent certainty about the closeness between herself and Frank: the intimacy her journey today implied.

Nina didn't answer immediately; then, resignedly, she said, 'So do you want me to tell the boss for you?'

313

Clare hesitated. Nina's offer provided the easy way out, but she knew it was unfair to ask Nina to bear her messages. 'No—I'd better talk to him myself.'

'I hope Frank's not too ill. What's wrong?' Nina's voice was carefully neutral.

'Pneumonia. But he's not in hospital; he's with his parents. And Nina, I got your note about another story from Frank.' She inhaled quickly and added, 'Good for you.'

When Andy came on the line he sounded less concerned than Nina about Clare's absence. 'You can pay back the time later,' he said drily. 'There may be some travelling jobs I want you to cover in the next few weeks.'

'Thanks a lot!'

'Go on, Clare Nightingale. Sort him out.'

She laughed. 'I will. And I'll come back as soon as I can.'

In the bustle of the final week of the summer holidays, Paddington was drearily familiar. She ran out of the underground to the ticket office and then straight onto the first Intercity train for Bristol. She would pluck up the courage while she was on the train to telephone Frank's mother from Bristol. Maybe ...

As the miles melted away and the train bore her deeper into the fields and hills of the West Country, she lost rather than gained courage to ring the Bernards' number. *No, it would be far better just to turn up. At least I know I've got a place to stay*. She sat with her head against the seatback and her eyes shut, and tried to imagine Frank's parents. Tried to hear what they would say when she arrived. Tried to picture their faces. What if Frank had told them that he didn't want to speak to her? *What if—what if?*

She smiled, not caring what the other passengers thought of her, listening to the train of anxieties rattling across her brain. Worries wouldn't change anything. *Do not worry about tomorrow*, she reminded herself. *Tomorrow will take care of itself. Each day has enough troubles of its own.*

In Bristol she changed trains for Weston-super-Mare with only five minutes to spare, and certainly without sufficient time to ring Mrs Bernard. The short last leg of the journey gave her a reprieve to think once again about what she would say when she arrived on the doorstep.

'My name is Clare Hogarth, Frank's girlfriend.' And was she? What if he had one or two other girlfriends whom his parents had met before? No, that was too presumptuous.

'Hello, I'm Clare Hogarth, from the magazine *Women Today*. Mr Bernard's written a story for us (she would hold out the new issue triumphantly), and I'm wondering if I could see him . . .' But Frank might not have told them about his story—or, worse still, he might have told them it was a story about himself and a journalist called Clare Hogarth. And *Women Today* didn't generally send journalists—even journalists called Clare Hogarth—to see uncommissioned authors at home. No, that was a silly speech, too.

'Hello. I'm Clare, a friend of Frank's from London. I heard that he was very ill . . .' But what if he were too ill to see her? *Rubbish! Jill and Nigel went last night, didn't they?* Yes, that would have to serve as her introductory speech.

Something Frank had said to her in passing while they were in Coventry suddenly came to mind. She wasn't sure if it would help her, but at least for that moment it brought some reassurance. She had been speaking to him about finding peace with God, and the memory stirred her. She needed that peace now, herself. 'My parents would love to talk to you, Clare,' he had said. 'They speak your language, you know.' She wondered whether she would be strong enough to speak their language now.

The taxi deposited her outside a four-square house on the outskirts of Weston. The house fronted onto the Bristol Channel, she noticed; and at the side of the house sat a grey Sierra she recognized immediately. Her palms began to sweat as she walked between two berry-laden rowan trees planted like sentinels on either side of the path. The walk to the front door seemed at once long and short. She had the feeling of one about to begin a new journey.

Lifting her hand to ring the bell, she saw the curtains by the door move. A woman looked out, a young woman. Too young to be Frank's mother. She heard voices, and hesitated. *Should I ring, or wait?*

Her heart was in her mouth. She tasted the bitter-sweetness of risk.

'Lucy? Are you down there, sweetheart?' Through the open window above the front door lilted an Irish voice. That must be Mrs Bernard.

Who is Lucy? she thought frantically.

'Yes, I'll get it.'

The door opened immediately. A florid woman in her thirties, plump and with untidy dark hair, stood in the open door and ran her eyes over Clare, overnight bag and all. She beamed.

Clare stammered into the beginning of her speech, then left off.

'You must be Clare. Well, how wonderful.' The woman turned. 'Mother! Is Frank awake? It's Clare.' She stepped aside. 'Come in. Oh, I've heard a bit about you already.'

There was a scuffle beside them, and two children burst giggling out of a door to one side of the front hall. Behind her came a breeze off the sea; the house smelled of salt, fresh coffee, and toast. Then suddenly the hall seemed crowded with people, and Clare was overwhelmed.

'I'm Lucy, Frank's older sister,' the woman said. 'Now let's see. These are my two, Susie and Emily. Oh dear, what a squash in here!'

The children giggled again, pushed each other and stared. Clare could hardly keep up with Lucy.

The children nodded and smiled at her, all looking directly into her eyes. She couldn't stand still and silent any more. Their warmth made her laugh and blush with pleasure. 'I'm a friend of Frank's from . . .'

'No need to say a word at all!' An older woman came rustling down the stairs, her hair drawn into a grey-blonde knot at the back of her head, wispy like Lucy's. *His mother.* Like her daughter, she instantly made Clare feel welcome.

'Come on. We've all heard who you are. Sure we didn't know if you'd come or not, that's all. Has Lucy offered you tea? No? Whisht, you kids are making a terrible din. Off into the garden with you, if you please. And Lucy, now, where'd the men get to?'

'Wait, Mother,' Lucy said gently, 'let the poor girl get a breath for a minute. Didn't she come all this way to see Frank, now, and not a pack of people she's never set eyes on in her life?'

Clare wanted to answer but saw that she would have to learn the trick of making her voice heard in this family. The noise rose and swelled around her, billowing over her like the front hall lace curtains Lucy had looked out of. Then, above the hubbub, she heard a man's voice from upstairs, croaky but nevertheless familiar. The babble around her ceased.

'Mother? What's going on down there when a man wants peace to sleep?' The words were peevish, but the voice was full of suppressed excitement. 'Does the whole clan have to hold a meeting in the front hall, right under my pillow?'

Frank's mother looked straight at Clare. 'There's himself. Don't know if he knows you're here, but he'll surely be wanting to see you. Go you up—I'll bring you both a cold drink in a wee minute.'

About the only thing Clare could think to say was a dazed 'thank you' as she went slowly up the stairs and left the children below, tittering and nudging each other while Frank's sister stood with eyes of friendly but undisguised curiosity boring into her shoulder-blades every step of the way.

38

When I heard the front doorbell and all the racket downstairs I thought my father must have come back with a one-stone seabass and a witness to prove it—my unhappy brother-in-law. But when even my mother, usually as unfazed as can be about his fishy stories, left me in a flurry and went abruptly down the stairs, and when I heard the particular note of eagerness in Lucy's voice—I knew someone important must have come. *Not the doctor this time,* I thought ungraciously, by now feeling just well enough to have recovered some of my normal friendliness.

Had someone mentioned Clare? No, that was the fevered madness of a man with a temperature. I subsided under the covers feeling sorry for myself, and comforted only by watching the sea again. For the first time since Friday, I wished I could be out on the sands, taking a long walk or a donkey ride as we had done when we were kids: picking up ragworms to frighten the girls, shells to delight the teacher, and more fishing tales (of fish's tails as big as mermaids and whales) to bedevil my father. Now, however, I could think of other things and other people more interesting than those. Sandy beaches were wonderful places for fantasies—at least if the sun was shining.

I called down—but the house seemed suddenly strangely quiet. Someone was coming upstairs: footfalls I didn't recognize. Not the cheerful humming of Lucy, or the thoughtless thumping and squealing of my nieces, (imported for the day in case I died, though I felt I was more likely to die with them around than otherwise . . .) and not the rustle of Mum's old-fashioned petticoat, either. My door was half closed, so I couldn't even satisfy my inquisitiveness by watching the head of the stairs. A burst of seabreeze lifted the curtains and blew the door a few inches farther open. Then there came a timid knock, followed by an explosion of giggles from the hall below.

'All right,' I said in the gruffest voice I could muster from my crow-croaking throat, 'which of the pests is it this time? Emily, I bet.'

'Guess again,' said a little voice I couldn't recognize at all.

Any game is better, I thought, than staring at the wall or the slow-moving tide. 'Well,' I ventured, 'it must be Susie.'

'Nope.'

'Come in, then, whoever you are. Stop playing coy and show your face, you monster.'

The door opened slowly, and a circlet of red hair appeared, gleaming in the indirect sunlight around a smiling face: it was Clare! She hesitated by the doorway, then seemed to forget herself. With a small sound of concern and happiness she ran straight into my open arms. Her beautiful hair fell all over my face, and her weight across my chest was more welcome than a whole pile of duvets.

She struggled out of my arms after a moment and sat down beside me, pushing her hair back. She was blushing and laughing. 'I'll knock the breath out of you if I do that again,' she said.

'No, don't go away. I'll get cold,' I said.

She leaned back into the same chair where my mother had been sitting chatting my ears off before the all commotion downstairs. 'I'm not going anywhere now,' she said. 'I came to see what you're doing in bed on a brilliant sunny day like this when you're supposed to be out finding missing children.' Her eyes sparkled at me. 'You're a fake, I'm sure. Don't bother playing any hypochondriac tricks on me; I won't pay a bit of attention. You've got your mother and sister and half the population of the West Country dancing attendance on you already, as far as I can see.'

I grinned at her. 'You noticed.'

'Well, it's true.'

I looked her up and down. She was clutching a rolled up

319

magazine in one hand. 'You're the stuff of dreams,' I told her. 'I didn't know whether to hope you'd come, or just try to put you out of my mind so I wasn't driven mad with frustration.'

She blushed again, but her eyes were mischievous. 'I think you're fit as a fiddle.'

'Much better, but still coughing a bit.' I illustrated the point, and saw her face change from laughter to dismay.

She concealed the dismay quite well, however. 'You must be getting better if you can cough to order like that.' She was waving the magazine around as she spoke.

'I'll get better faster if you're here. Tell me—' I reached for her hand and held it. Her skin felt cool against mine. 'Are you going to beat me with that thing, or what?'

She unrolled a copy of *Women Today*, beaming at me. 'Look at this. It's your story—or is it Nina's?' Her eyes were bright with mischief and laughter.

I took it reverently. 'Where do I look for my first magnum opus?'

'Pages forty-eight and forty-nine.'

'You didn't even have to look up the table of contents,' I teased.

'I have most magazines memorized before they come out. And this one's special.'

I looked with awe at the double-page spread that told the world and his wife about how I'd met Clare. Then I pushed the magazine aside. 'Come here.'

She hesitated slightly, so I brushed her hand with my mouth. 'Now tell me how you got here, how you knew.'

My mother came in, then, bossy as ever about seeing that I was propped up on the pillows, but tactful enough then to put down two glasses of something cold and leave us alone. I saw Clare's eyes follow her out of the door.

'I think you've passed my mother's exam,' I said. 'This is all most irregular—women in my bedroom. She must think you'll do.'

'And what about my inspection of *her*?' Clare laughed. 'Don't you think it's mutual?'

'I never thought about that. Well, does she pass?'

She shrugged offhandedly. 'Oh, she'll do.'

I gave her hand a squeeze. 'Go on, you were just going to tell me how you got here. Did you come down in that clapped-out old Fiat of yours?'

'No. By train. Jill rang me.'

'That's good.' I shut my eyes. 'I'm sorry I didn't make it on Saturday, or ring you to say what was going on. Until yesterday, about the time Nigel and Jill came, I wasn't even sure what day it was or where I was, half the time, or why. I think I've battled through the worst of this now, though.'

'But you look so hot.'

I opened my eyes again. 'No, I've been freezing all weekend. It's not so bad today, though. I actually didn't mind the window open and the sea air coming in this morning.' I shifted slightly and drank some of the grape juice. 'But don't let me bore you with sickbed talk.'

'You're not boring me in the least.' She frowned, bending nearer to me again so that I could see clearly the small laughter lines on either side of her eyes, and the beginnings of other lines on her forehead where she so often creased her brow in concentration. 'Your face looks—'

'Thinner,' I supplied. 'Yes, so Jill bluntly told me last night.'

'She was swooning over the phone about how gorgeous you look, actually.'

'Don't gang up with her. I don't believe a word of it.'

'And they say *women* are vain!'

'Come any closer and I'll ask you for the next dance.'

'You can have it, anyway, when you're well enough.'

I let go of her hand and put my arm around her neck to draw her face down. 'We'll have to make do with more kissing instead,' I told her solemnly.

'What a hardship,' she murmured, her lips against mine.

'You'll catch pneumonia,' I teased her.

'I doubt it. I don't even have a cold, and you must be dosed up to the eyeballs with antibiotics. But *you* had a cold, though, didn't you?'

I didn't answer her, and the medicine of her kisses was worth a thousand of any wretched antibiotics. After a while, I told her, 'Anyway, if you catch it you'll just have to get into bed, too.'

She laid a finger over my mouth. 'Shh. Your temperature will go up, talking like that.'

'Yours has already,' I teased, seeing the colour flood her cheeks. I let go of her then, and sat forward. My chest suddenly tightened in the now familiar spasm, and for several moments I couldn't stop coughing. I hated the barking sound I was making.

She said nothing about it for a minute: just offered me more to drink and a tissue from beside the bed. My face burned again, and not because she was in the room.

'Sorry,' I said at last. 'I thought it was about time I practised my impression of a police dog.'

She didn't smile. 'Stop it and get well.'

'And that's an order?' I thought about Nigel, who had said the same.

'That's an order.'

'She barked.'

'Oh, hush. Frank, maybe *you're* talking too much.'

My mother put her head round the door and took in my flushed face at a glance. 'Have a drink,' she advised, then added. 'Clare, I didn't ask if you'd had lunch at all?'

'No, but—'

'You can't live on love, you daft pair. I'll make you something now.' She disappeared again.

Clare's eyes sparkled. 'Is she always like this? I like her.'

'She's fine, except when someone starts talking religion to her. Says she can't stand religion. Faith is what counts.'

'I like her even better.'

I reached up to her face again. 'For the first time in my life, I think I understand what she's been on about all these years. You've taught me a lot. But come here quickly, before she's back in again on some excuse or other, and kiss me.'

She bent and stroked my hair again, smiling, and whispered, 'I hope you get over this quickly.'

'So do I. Then all the better to grab you, my dear,' I whispered back.

'Be serious for a moment!'

'I've never been so serious in my whole life.' And then I was kissing her again so that light seemed to pour over my whole body, the healing running like a river across the bed.

She dropped her head against my shoulder and rested there against me. 'I hope you never go away,' I said.

'I will soon. But not for long.'

The room was quiet for a while, except for the children's voices outside and the breeze fluttering the curtains now and then.

'Will you take the train back tonight?' I tightened my hold on her shoulders.

She shook her head. 'No, Jill said I could stay at her flat again.'

'Good old Jill. But don't do that. Stay here. Mother will find room.'

'I don't think I could.' She pulled away and turned to face me.

'Why ever not?'

'Your sister, for a start.'

'Oh—don't fret about Lucy. She'll be gone by tonight, with the kids in tow. They live fairly near, anyway. No one's here for the night except the three of us. And you.' I could see that she wanted to accept the suggestion. 'Think about it. You'll have to face the gathering of the clans sooner or later.'

Her grey eyes shone steadily into mine. 'Yes, I'll stay,' she said.

323

39

I haven't seen him talking to Bobbie for days, Clare reasoned as Pete walked away from her door. *So why shouldn't I go out with him after all?*

She watched the way he moved, once again letting her eyes rest on the light hair that brushed his white shirt collar, and the width of his powerful shoulders. She felt again the ache of longing, and the answer to her own question came back sharply, *Because you're infatuated with him, that's why. And he's dangerous.*

Just as he reached the production department door, he turned and smiled at her over his shoulder. The smile was for her alone, and in the relative darkness of the corridor it dazzled her. Embarrassed to be caught staring after him with what she knew was such a naked expression of desire, she pulled back into Kathy's office, fled through it, and bolted into the privacy of her own.

'Well,' she said aloud to herself when the door was shut and she was back in the bright reality of a sunny Wednesday afternoon at her desk, 'well, I've burned my boats now, all right.'

He had come to see her on the pretext of showing her the galleys of her column on McEnroe—a column substantially unchanged and already causing a scandalized discussion throughout the building. They had worked through the text together, their heads bent over her desk and their shoulders touching. The scent of his aftershave floated into her nostrils each time she breathed in, and she knew that she had only to turn her head to find his mouth close to her own. But she did not allow herself to turn her head; not even to lift her eyes from the galleys.

If Pete was aware of the strange mixture of pain and

pleasure she felt at his closeness, he gave no sign—until the last moments before he stood up to go. Then he lifted his left hand and touched her face—a gesture she would never have expected.

'Clare.' He sounded gentle for a change. 'You're killing me.' He didn't move his fingertips from her cheek.

She looked down and felt herself redden. 'I could easily say the same to you,' she said levelly—though not feeling level.

'Then why are we wasting time?' he asked—reasonably enough, she thought.

'Bobbie,' she said simply, not trusting herself to do more than speak elliptically; he would know quite well what she meant.

She expected him to jeer again, but he seemed to think better of it. Instead, he said quietly, 'Clare—Bobbie and I— that was a long time ago.'

Remembering her first encounter with them, on the plane, she wanted to argue; but the words would not come out.

'And what else is holding you back? That scrupulous conscience of yours which dictates that you don't date your employer?'

Other objections crowded into her mind: he had been rude to her; he still had not sorted out her immigration papers; he had almost drowned her; and, above all, *What does he want?* She felt dumb, stupid, unable to answer—not at all like herself.

'Is that it?'

She let out her breath in a nervous laugh. 'No. Not now.' She wanted to say, *I'm afraid of you. You're so attractive—but so unscrupulous . . . if we're talking of scruples.*

'Good. Then why don't we talk particulars—like what are you doing tonight, for instance?' He slid his fingers to her lips and brushed them back and forth across her mouth in a way that sent her heart hammering. Her voice came out in a croak. 'I—there was another concert, at eight.' *Damn it! This man's playing seducer, and I want him to . . . don't want him to . . . want him to . . .*

325

'I'll take you!' he said triumphantly. 'What could be simpler? And afterwards a meal, if you're hungry?' His eyes were playing with her, and she felt herself blushing again: flattered, but uncomfortable and still afraid.

'Lovely,' she said, before she could think up any more arguments against him.

'I'll pick you up at seven. At your aunt's house?'

'Yes,' she gulped.

'And Clare,' he added, lifting the galleys from her desk and turning to open the door, 'for heaven's sakes stop looking like no one's ever asked you on a date before. Just relax, will you? We'll have a good time, I know we will. Just relax. Take it easy. We'll have fun.' And with that, he'd left her standing by the door.

She sighed. She'd get no more work done at all for the rest of the day; she might as well be back at Rita's house now, lying with her feet up and half-listening to Jack enthusing again over *I Giocosi*. She wished the time away.

When eventually she stepped out of the lift to cross the lobby and leave for home, Pete was talking and laughing with a group of her colleagues by the reception desk. Bobbie was among them, too, her eyes fixed on Pete's face. Clare remembered what Pete had said to her only a few hours before, '*Bobbie and I—that was a long time ago.*' Looking at Bobbie now, she was reminded once again that as far as Bobbie was concerned, at least, the relationship was still alive—if only as a hope for the future. A niggle of guilt returned, but she brushed it aside and went smiling to sign out for the night.

'Are you going to join us, Clare?' one of the men from the art department asked her. 'We're going across the square for a "happy hour". There's a new bar just opened.'

'Yeah, come on, Clare,' another pressed. 'It sounds like a great place.'

She hesitated, throwing a quick glance at Pete. Was he going with them? He gave nothing away; and, predictably, she felt her face heat up. He was carrying on as if nothing was different; as if he had not talked to her upstairs and asked her out; as if he had not given her that intimate smile. But perhaps everything *was* the same for him.

Her eyes swerved back to the two men. 'Thanks, but no,' she said, shaking her head. She caught Bobbie's eye and wished she hadn't. 'I've got to get home right away.' For her, nothing was the same at all.

'Party pooper!' Pete teased. 'Go on, then. We'll see you, Clare.'

'Yes,' she said, looking at no one but Pete, 'I'll see you.'

She fled out of the doors and onto the breezy street outside. She began to laugh to herself. *The cool nerve of the man!*

He had told her to stop acting as if no one had ever asked her out, but for the next hour she lived in the fever of a fourteen-year-old. Ignoring curious looks from Jack and teasing questions from Ed, she rushed past the usual welcoming committee in the front hall and showered and dressed as if someone with a pack of dogs were chasing her. Nothing in her wardrobe suited her; she flung on one dress after another and finally gave up, reverting to the first dress she had pulled from the closet. She smudged mascara on her cheek and broke a small bottle of lotion in the bathroom basin. By the time the doorbell rang, she was shivering with excitement, her hands shaking and her skin hot even under the cool blue cotton she had chosen.

Glad Rita wasn't home yet to witness her frantic preparations, she snatched up her handbag and checked her watch. *Seven fifteen. He's late.* Then she went dashing down the stairs to open the door.

Jack reached the front door before she did. He looked over his shoulder at her, whistling under his breath as he pulled it open.

Rather too loudly, she called over his head to Pete, 'Hi! You made it.'

Pete gave Jack only a cursory nod, but Jack stretched out his hand to him. 'You're Peter McEnroe, aren't you?'

'Yes. And you—?' Pete's mask of wariness went up immediately.

'Jack Williams, Clare's cousin. Pleased to meet you.'

She watched them sizing each other up and felt glad that Ed was nowhere in evidence.

At last Pete turned to her, his eyes raking over her so obviously that she wanted to shrink back against the wall and away from the quick observations of her cousin. 'Sorry I'm a bit behind schedule,' he said. 'You're ready?'

She gave him a bright smile. 'Quite ready.'

'Let's go, then,' he said. He took possession of her hand immediately and nodded again to Jack. Then, as they went down the driveway together, he said, 'Your cousin looks bright.'

'He is,' she answered mechanically. 'Bright enough to catch that look you just gave me, as well.'

'Sorry.' He actually sounded contrite, and she laughed.

'And you were bright enough to catch it, too?' he added.

'I could hardly miss it,' she returned with heavy sarcasm. 'How did he know who I was?'

'I expect he sees your picture every week on the inside cover of *Citizen*.'

'Oh, of course.'

'Yes, of course. He works in Springfield and never misses a single issue.'

'Since you joined us?'

'No. Long before that. He told me before I got the job with you that he'd always read it.'

'He likes you, as well. I felt like I was meeting your big brother.'

'I haven't got a big brother. It's the "little brother" I have to watch.'

Pete started the car and gave her a sidelong look. 'Why? Fancies himself as something more than a kissing cousin, does he?'

She laughed again. He made Ed's interest in her sound as ridiculous as it was. 'Yes, something like that.' Luxuriously she stretched her bare legs into the air-conditioned coolness and space of his car. 'But I don't want to talk about Jack and

Ed at the moment, if you don't mind.'

'Agreed, then. Much more fun to talk about us.'

She swallowed. She had walked straight into that one, and she told herself to be more careful how she chose her words.

He leaned over and lightly kissed her hair. 'Mmm. You smell gorgeous as well as looking gorgeous.'

She caught a whiff of gin on his breath and frowned. 'Thanks,' she said. Her voice sounded tight and unnatural.

'Hey! I thought you were going to relax. We've got all the time in the world. We won't miss one moment of *I Giocosi*, don't you worry.'

'I'm not in the least worried about that,' she countered. She remembered the 'happy hour', then, and quelled her anxiety about the gin. He was certainly clear-headed enough to be manoeuvring the car smoothly through downtown traffic.

She searched frantically for something else to say, to stop herself analyzing why she was with him and what would happen. 'Er—I went to *I Giocosi* last night, as well.'

'Really?'

'Yes. Different concert, though.' She found she was playing with the strap of her handbag, twisting it back and forth in her lap.

'You'll be sick of Italians by the end of the week.'

'I doubt it,' she said, and Bobbie's face swam up again in front of her mind. 'I like Italians.'

'Fine as long as they're not Mob.'

'Is that what you think—really?' she asked. 'That there's a racket going on behind *I Giocosi*?'

'If there is, we won't be able to ascertain much from their music, will we?' he said drily.

She bit back the temptation to ask him why he had told her to go to as many concerts as possible.

'I told you,' he went on, 'I doubt if there's anything in the least sinister about an arts orchestra just getting started and headhunting some of the good players around here. But I still think it's worth checking things out.' He grinned at her.

'Especially if we can do it together ... Anyway, Ms Nosy Hogarth, did you see anything suspicious last night?'

'Only my cousin,' she laughed.

He didn't laugh. 'You went with your cousin? Which one?'

'Jack.'

'The one who met me at the door.' She nodded. 'And he knows we're going to hear the same group tonight?'

'Yes. Why not?'

'Does he know you're doing a column on *I Giocosi*?'

'Sure.'

He scowled. 'You'd better be careful. We worked hard enough to get you an alias, as it is. Don't go blowing it. McEnroe wouldn't say a word about your real identity. No one in the office would blow it, either—or I'd fire anyone who did. But how d'you know your cousin can keep his mouth shut?'

She shifted and brought her legs up under the seat, suddenly feeling too warm again. 'Jack's utterly trustworthy and discreet.'

'And your other cousin?'

'Ed, or Marie?'

'How many are there, for heaven's sakes!'

'Only the three. And Ed has read the first columns and understands the need to keep quiet, I think—at least for now.'

'I hope he does.'

Hearing the sharp tone of his voice, she wondered again what she was doing with this man. She felt as if she were standing on the edge of a precipice, making a choice about whether or not to jump. Months ago, the jump would have frightened her. Now it looked as appealing as Pete himself with his debonair good taste, magnetic blue eyes, and shiny smile. But she still questioned herself about why, against her scruples, she was sliding into friendship with a man whom in cooler moments she knew she did not and could not trust. There were no answers to that riddle, she realized, except 'Because I feel like it.'

All these debates and doubts melted as soon as they were

settled—barely on time—among the perfumed audience in the small hall where *I Giocosi* were to play that evening. The hall was packed, as another hall the night before had been; Pete had been right about the meteoric popularity of the group, Clare noted.

Overhead, fans turned silently, and as she listened to Vivaldi's music rippling in perfect waves, she watched the lazy blades with a kind of abstracted fascination. The music curled and swept around the hall like so many skeins of silk, and for the first time in days she felt the sort of peace she had known each week at church in London. *God seems so far away these days*. The thought was instantly followed by another that was quickly pushed away. Hadn't she been holding God at arm's length since arriving in Boston? Even her good-natured aunt was plainly dismayed by her new habit of missing church each week. But except at moments like this, when the mantle of quiet descended over her shoulders, she had felt no sense of loss.

She looked at Pete again. Surely this was her world now—*to be with him*; to live, not among cheerful, softly spoken but often boring friends in London, but to be part of the world of the rich and the beautiful in America. This was where she felt she belonged now.

As if Pete understood her thoughts, he gave her the same kind of smile he had bestowed that afternoon. He reached for her hand, too, gave it a squeeze, then turned his attention back to the music as if nothing was different. Clare thought once again, *But everything is different for me*. She ceased to be aware of anything except the pressure of his fingers around her own. And she felt the same curious sense of belonging after the concert, when Pete opened the door to his apartment and showed her in.

'I'm not hungry. Are you?' Pete had asked as they drove away from the concert.

She was too excited to be hungry. 'No, not in the least,' she had said.

'Then I'd like you to see my apartment,' he said.

331

'Not your etchings?' she joked, quite aware that she was flirting with him, but no longer caring.

'Oh, you can see those too,' he purred, 'of course.'

Opulent furnishings and deep carpets met her as she stepped past him down the half-flight of stairs to the open-plan rooms of his apartment. Watercolour prints and reproductions of the Italian masters filled the white walls, and glossy plants billowed in every corner. Yet again she felt that she belonged, though she could hardly explain that feeling to herself. For a moment she remembered that her mother had written to her that morning asking for news; she was behind in letter-writing these days and hadn't phoned her for weeks. What would her mother have thought of Pete's apartment? For that matter, what would her mother have thought of Pete?

She sank into a soft chair. *She wouldn't like him,* she told herself, unsure how she knew that.

Pete was handing her a tall drink. He loosened his tie and suddenly seemed less assured than usual. 'Gin and tonic OK for you?'

She saw that he had cut fresh limes into it. 'Fine as long as that's all I'm getting in my glass,' she teased.

He surprised her by taking her seriously. 'Hey! I thought we had a truce now, you and I? You're mighty trusting, aren't you? All I put in the glass was a twist of lime for her ladyship. I can take it out if you like.'

'I'll have it just as it is, thanks,' she said, leaning forward to take the glass.

He hesitated, as if deciding whether to sit near her or beside her. Then he smiled. 'I'll join you here, I think.'

She felt the warmth of his lean body subsiding against hers in the loveseat, but he made no attempt otherwise to touch her. She recalled, as if it had happened to someone else, the first impressions she had formed of him on the plane to Boston. *I was wrong,* she decided, *to think that he was boorish. He's the most attractive man I've ever met.* And then she added to herself, *You didn't know how to react to him then, and you still don't, Clare Hogarth.*

They sipped their drinks and talked—about Boston, about the magazine, about Bobbie-Ann Rizzo, and about her cousins. Whenever she was speaking, he listened as if with rapt attention; she was unused to such perfect manners and taken aback by them.

'You're very flattering,' she said, 'the way you make me feel as if what I'm saying is interesting. I'm sure it isn't.'

'Oh, but it is.'

'No. I save all the really interesting things for the column.' She widened her eyes to draw his attention.

He imitated her gesture, then broke off to laugh, leaning against her more heavily now. 'And you'll wow us this week with a piece about *I Giocosi*?'

'Sure hope so,' she murmured. They were talking of everything except what she was thinking about; perhaps even everything except what he was thinking about. She darted him another quick glance from under her eyelashes, but his thoughts were veiled behind the mask. She sighed.

'That was a big sigh,' he said, getting up. He took her glass and moved—somewhat unsteadily she noticed—towards the drinks cabinet. 'You obviously need something to cheer you. Another of these for you?'

Her better judgment warned against it, but she was suddenly weary of always doing what was wise and sensible. 'What the heck!' she laughed. 'Why not?'

She forgot now that neither of them had eaten supper. Their conversation became more and more rambling, punctuated by giggles over little things that suddenly seemed desperately funny. She no longer cared about the time. The drinks went straight to her head.

Pete leaned closer, dropping his voice in a confiding, friendly way as if he had known her all her life. He launched into a long speech about Bobbie. Clare no longer felt any compunction about being with Pete without Bobbie's knowledge, and she listened closely to him.

'And she said to me,' Pete was saying from a long way off, ' "You're a no good s.o.b., Pete McEnroe. I'm not marrying you if you're the last man on earth."' He broke into wild laughter. 'Isn't that an original speech, huh? It's so funny it makes me weep.'

Clare stared. 'Bobbie would never talk like that.' She shook her head, and the room swam round her.

He ignored her. 'So I said to her, "Right, well if that's how you feel, I'm not marrying you either, Bobbie-Ann." So we called it all off.'

Something told Clare she'd want later on to remember what he was saying now, but that she might forget. Something told her, too, that there were questions she should be asking. For some reason, she couldn't think what they were.

Pete's arm came round her shoulder. He leaned forward at the same time, with great care and an expression of fierce concentration, to put his drink onto the floor at their feet.

'I've been waiting for this for a long time,' he said. 'I've discovered with you that a man needs to be patient.'

She nodded dully and turned her face towards him.

His eyes were steady, but his lips moved awkwardly, as if he had just come back from the dentist. 'Like when I asked you to consider the job,' he said. 'You gave me a flat no, then look what happened.'

She nodded again now, catching at the tails of his thinking. Her thoughts seemed to float away from her like so much driftwood before she could grab hold of them. Everything except his nearness seemed unreal and disconnected.

He went on, 'And look what happened when I asked you before for a date. Again a flat no.' He smiled into her eyes. 'But now here we are, as cosy as anyone could wish.'

She snuggled against him. 'Mmm.'

'Worth the wait, though, isn't it? Anticipation only sharpens the appetite.'

Her head came up sharply, her nose bumping against his jaw. She heard the slurred sound of her own voice saying, 'Back to your big bad wolf talk, Mr McEnroe.'

'You're fresh! You're just a jumped-up little writer from

little old England. Don't go getting ideas above your station, Ms Hogarth,'

'Then don't go giving them to me, you big old wolf.'

With his free hand he turned her face closer to his. 'Your boss is going to kiss you in just a moment. I just thought I'd inform you of that. Any objections?'

She smiled, for once not blushing. 'None at all.'

'No accusations or complaints of sexual harassment on the job?' His teeth stuck on the sibilants, so that they came out as a series of 'sh' sounds.

'Not at all,' she giggled.

'Good.' His mouth found hers, his lips hard against hers in a kiss that forced her mouth open and her head back. She groaned and reached both her arms around his neck. The ache of longing deepened into an abyss of simple need. She had pushed Ed away, but she would not reject Pete.

His left hand stroked her neck, then came to a stop at the top button of her dress. 'And now, for his next trick,' he said, 'the big bad wolf is going to take off Little Red Riding Hood's cloak.' He fixed his blue eyes on her face, and she met the look with a strange equanimity that betrayed nothing of the deafening drumbeat of her heart in her own ears.

'He can go right ahead,' she murmured huskily. 'No granny to stop him in this story.'

But he didn't unbutton her clothes. Instead he stood up and at the same time lifted her into both his arms. The room dipped and wavered around her, but his face was intent and steady and she felt no fear. His arms were strong, warm around her; and she leaned into the crook of them, her face buried against his white shirt front.

He peered down at her. 'Yes,' he said softly, 'a man needs to be patient with you. One week you're screaming "I hate you!" like a fierce little tigress, and the next you're purring like a sweet little domestic kitty.'

Something unpleasant bubbled to the surface of her memory but was lost. 'I hate you!'—when had she said that, and why? She could not remember.

'Which are you?' he asked, not moving from where he stood but swaying and rocking her slightly.

'Which am I what?' she asked, trying to focus.

'Tigress or kitty-cat?'

'I thought I was Little Red Riding Hood.'

He laughed and bent his face for another kiss. 'Oh, yes. So you are. Come on, then, Little Red Riding Hood. Let's go for a walk in the woods.'

'No picnic basket?'

'Who needs a picnic basket?'

He carried her with a few laughing interludes down another half-flight of stairs into his shadowed bedroom. *Do all the stairs in this place go down?* she wondered vaguely as he laid her on the bed. She had lost all fear, floating on a dream-cloud with an inexplicable sense of ease about all that was happening.

She watched him shed his jacket and shirt. His skin was smooth and beautiful, and she reached up to touch him. At the same time she knew clearly that they were both drunk. She tried to sit up but couldn't; the bedroom turned a somersault, and she groaned.

He fell on the bed beside her. 'In a hurry after all, Red Riding Hood?' he whispered thickly.

'Yesh,' she said, and 'no.' She moved away from him, but at the same time she longed to move closer.

He seemed to see the hunger and doubt in her eyes, for he touched her hair again and kissed her eyelids. 'Don't be a fraidy cat now,' he said. 'I won't hurt you.'

'No,' she said uncertainly. 'No, and I won't hurt you, either.'

That made him laugh. 'You are funny!' He rolled away from her to the edge of the bed and flung off the rest of his clothes. She lay still, watching him, inwardly moaning, her breathing suspended. His muscled body reminded her of a Greek sculpture.

'I'm going to run us a nice long bath,' he said, 'to get the anxious look off your lovely face. Then I'm going to make love to you like no one's ever made love to you before.'

Like no one's ever made love to me at all, she thought, but said nothing, lying passive and disappointed that he had not undressed her himself.

He went staggering through an adjoining door. Then she heard the hiss of water running into a bath. There was a splash, and the water was turned off.

Moving carefully, half afraid she would lose her balance and fall in an undignified and unappealing heap on the marble floor beside the bath, she left the bed and dropped her clothes beside his. In a mirror by the lighted bathroom door, she caught a glimpse of her pale body and huge, feverish eyes. She moved into the light, stiff as a marionette, wanting to cover herself.

'Oh, my beautiful baby,' he said as she came in. 'I could look at you all day long. Come here and get into the tub with me.' He made no move, just gazed at her and remained lying back with his head resting on a froth of bubbles.

'Don't be daft,' she tittered. 'There's not nearly enough room for two.' She sank into a basket chair by the bath and absently scooped water onto his back. His skin gleamed back at her.

'That depends on how the two are situated,' he said.

'Naughty!'

He shut his eyes. She watched him hungrily, let her eyes roam all over him. She had an uncomfortable feeling all the time that something was wrong, but all the luxury and ease around her—as well as Pete's presence—told her that nothing could possibly be wrong. She smiled to herself and let her mind drift. It no longer seemed to matter that she couldn't think clearly.

'Pete?' she said at last.

He did not open his eyes.

'Pete?' she said again, tousling his head. 'Come on, it's my turn in that bath of yours.' She stood up unsteadily and went to shake his arm where it was draped over the side of the bath.

His mouth fell open slightly; she saw that he had fallen

asleep. 'So much for the big bad wolf,' she said aloud, and stumbled back to find her clothes.

Before she left the apartment, she returned to the bathroom and pulled the plug. 'Mustn't let him drown,' she muttered, watching the water drain away. She opened the apartment door to go out again into the cool late August air. Nothing seemed funny any more.

When the taxi dropped her outside Rita's house, and after she'd found her uneven way up the dark stairs to her own bedroom, her head began to ache. The world had begun to right itself now, the gin no longer carrying her on a wave of dreams.

On the writing-desk in the corner she noticed some papers she had set out to take to work that morning. Had set out, but had forgotten: her passport and a letter from her mother. She picked up her passport and flicked idly to the visa page. Her visitor's visa was useless. The wave of euphoria beached on reality. She took the passport and flung it hard against the wall—as hard as if she were flinging it into Pete's face. '*It's your fault*,' she sobbed.

She had already outstayed her welcome in the United States. Perhaps she didn't belong here after all. Still fully clothed, she fell onto the bed and wept.

40

It was Frank's first time out of the small bedroom over the front door that faced the sea. Clare steered the Bernards' family car confidently, pleased that she had him to herself at last. In the morning, while he had slept the time away, she had sat talking with his mother; but now she and Frank were alone on the open motorway.

She knew he was watching her as she drove, and expected him at any moment to begin the stereotypical argument about whether women drivers were worse than men... but he didn't.

'I like that dress of yours,' he said instead, rubbing a corner of the pale blue cotton between his thumb and forefinger.

'Thanks. It's nice and cool.' *'Nice'—one of Mum's favourite words,* she thought unexpectedly. 'Anyway,' she said, 'you can tell your mother I like those Irish tartans you're wrapped in, as well.'

He grinned. 'I'm not quite sure who needed them more—Mum, or me.'

'I'm not sure, either,' she laughed.

'Do you have a slight feeling that you've been this way before?' he asked.

'Not really,' she said. 'This is all new country to me.' She waved her hand at the reed-choked ditches and stubble-dry fields along the edge of the motorway. 'I like it.'

He told her dismissively that she was seeing the boring parts of Somerset. 'This is nothing. Wait till you see the Quantocks.'

'It's farther than I expected.' She frowned, not wanting to fuss over him. 'Are you sure you're up to this?'

'Yes. I've been dying to get out. Don't worry about me.'

'I won't, then. But what did you mean about going this way

339

before? I told you I'd never been anywhere near this part of the world before—except Bristol—a few weeks ago.' She took her eyes off the road for an instant and flashed him a smile, remembering her debate about telephoning him from Bristol on the first day they'd met. *What a long road since then!*

'That's just what I'm talking about,' he said. 'Here you are again driving along the M5, with me watching you all the way, and the wind in your hair.'

She pursed her mouth. 'It was the M6, Frank, you great romantic.'

'Don't quibble.'

'It's not the same at all, silly,' she said gently. 'That tangle of roadworks and motorways around Birmingham is nothing like this. Your parents' car bears as much resemblance to my Fiat as the Severn Estuary does to that grotty little canal just there.' She pointed at another of the wide ditches intersecting the fields.

'You could be right,' he agreed, straight-faced.

'So much for *déjà vu.*'

'Yes, I suppose so. I'd rather enjoy the present "view" of you.'

She wrinkled her nose. 'That's supposed to be funny?'

'Must be slipping. Pneumonia takes a toll in more ways than one.'

Her mouth curled. 'You'll live, you old hypochondriac.' Her eyes went to her mirror, then back to the road. A grey Sierra was roaring along the fast lane with its blue light brilliant in the already bright sunshine.'Here comes one of your colleagues, I think.'

He craned around awkwardly. 'Oh—it's Nigel Sands!'

'I don't think he saw us.'

'No, poor man. Must be on urgent business . . . I wonder—never mind—he has a holiday coming.' Frank laughed, suddenly. 'When you rang her last night about staying with us, did Jill tell you?'

She shook her head. 'Tell me what?'

'They're getting married. In about a month.'

She watched Nigel's car vanish over a rise. *Jill must be happy,* she thought. 'That's good news, Frank. I'm glad.'

'So's the best man—that's me. I hope they let their best man have a best lady, and that I don't get matched up with some old schoolfriend of Jill's—or worse.'

'I hope not, too!' She gave a theatrical shudder. 'You'd definitely better get better. And when you give me the date I'll make sure Andy doesn't send me to Outer Mongolia—or Southern California, for that matter—for the weekend.'

They drove on in relative quiet. Clogged the weekend before because of the bank holiday, the motorway was now almost empty. A kestrel hovered over unseen prey in the reeds at the roadside, and heat rose from the tarmac in glittering waves.

Clare wiped her forehead and glanced sideways at Frank. 'You must be *so* hot.'

He shifted and opened the blankets cautiously. 'Yes, beginning to be. For the first time in days.'

'That's a good sign.'

'I shouldn't be cold at all, now my temperature's staying down.'

'Perhaps we should have gone walking on the beach,' she suggested, and her foot unconsciously came off the accelerator as she wondered about turning around at the next exit. 'You were saying how much you wanted to do that.'

'No, we can see Weston beach any time. This will be better. The view up on the crest will be worth every minute of the drive. You'll be off the motorway, soon, anyhow.'

Leaving the M5 behind them at last, they skirted the northern edge of Bridgwater and wound around villages and streams at the foot of the hills.

'I'm enjoying myself,' he said. 'I don't need a map around here, and I've got you driving me everywhere. I've never gone so far with a woman before—er, a woman driver, that is.'

'Your tongue's sticking out of your cheek fit to make a hole in it,' she laughed, colouring slightly. 'I've been waiting for the women driver jokes.'

341

'Happy to oblige. But you're good with this car,' he said, 'though I hate to admit it.'

She grinned and nudged him with her elbow. 'Don't sound too grudging in your praise! I may not be used to controlling a car at chase speeds on the two-lane race tracks of Bristol, but I'm generally used to the madness of London.'

'That must be why you're so calm.'

'And don't sound so surprised. It's lovely driving these small lanes.'

'You're always full of surprises.'

'And you're full of nonsense.'

'Nothing else to do but talk sweet-talk to you. What a good life.'

She sighed, 'Not bad, I agree.' She wondered, all the same, if behind all the renewed cheerfulness he was turning over and over in his mind the next steps in the abduction cases. If he was, he gave no sign of it, pointing ahead to where the lane bent around two fields and curved under an arch of grey-barked beeches.

'Look, the road's going up now. Watch out for sheep.'

They came to a fork. 'Which way?' she asked, slowing the car.

'Either,' he said serenely. 'They both end up in the same place. Take your pick.'

One lane was narrower and more overarched with trees than the other. 'That one looks less travelled. I'll go that way.' She steered to the right, enjoying every minute.

They passed close to Nether Stowey and kept climbing into the Quantocks. The hills were rich with yellowing beeches farther down, and purple and pink with August heather higher up. Clare tried to see them with Frank's eyes, as if she knew them well.

She slowed the car again, looking at her watch. A small chill bit into her happiness. Frank's father was to drive her to Bristol for the last London train—in only a few hours. She did not want to go. 'Where do you want me to drive, exactly? Shall we stop?' She tried not to think about leaving. There would be other times together.

'If you turn right up here—by that signpost,' he said, 'we'll be in the forest. Not as breezy as on the very top.'

She pulled the car into a lay-by about a mile beyond the signpost, and turned to him. She felt bright with the prospect of dense woodland flowers on high banks, deep avenues of trees, paths branching away into mysteries—and Frank to share it all with her. 'I'd love to walk a bit.'

'Let's, then.' He threw back the blankets, laughing. 'I'll leave the leper wrappings behind. Time to throw off the graveclothes.'

'Your pneumonia *did* make an impression, I can tell.'

They stepped out of the car onto a few dry-edged leaves and crackling sticks—signs of an early autumn after the drought of the summer. Clare took his arm, more for his sake than for her own, and they set off down the lane with the sound of a loud brook running invisible on one side of the hedge.

'So what did you think of my crazy family?' he asked.

'Good people,' she said unhesitatingly, picturing Frank's mother with the two grandchildren hanging on to her and begging for a hug.

'That's not saying much. I told your friend Nina when I talked to her that she'd never manage in a police line-up. Come on, you're a writer,' he teased. 'Describe!'

'You're winding me up,' she said. 'It's not much use making snap judgments.'

Frank laughed, 'All in a day's work for me—every day.'

'That just shows how different we are.'

He squeezed her arm and leaned over to kiss her. When she closed her eyes, the red banks, dusty hedges and overarching beeches disappeared into a golden field of hope for the future. And when the kissing stopped, her head was empty of all but the man beside her.

When he released her, she was off up the lane, running and skipping and laughing. 'See what you do to me?' she called, standing twenty yards away with her arms out.

'The same as you do to me,' he wheezed. 'Only I haven't

got the breath to come running after you—the way I do these days in all my dreams.'

She laughed and waited for him. They went on together again, stopping only to look over a gate, where they caught sight of the stream they had been hearing for half a mile. It was lower than it might have been in other summers, but fuller than Clare expected: fringed with ochre-coloured ferns, tinted red by the earth and flecked blue by the sky. She could not remember ever being so happy.

'We were talking about your family,' she reminded him when they began to retrace their steps.

He was having difficulty breathing again, coughing a little, and still wheezing. 'Yes—they're a chatty lot, aren't they?'

'Everyone around you seems to be chatty . . . even that man Joe Cafferty you introduced me to in Coventry.' She grimaced. 'You're just as bad.'

'Usually, perhaps,' he laughed, then had to stop. 'Sorry. This is embarrassing. There's no pain in my chest any more, but it feels sometimes as if there's a tight band across my lungs.'

She put a hand on his back. 'In a few weeks you'll be running up these hills with the best of them.'

'I hope so. My mother was saying I should see being ill as God's way of making me think. I suppose it has, though I certainly gave my mother a hard time when she said that. But I've thought about you, for a start. About what I want in life. And more about Damian.' He was shaking his head, and Clare watched him warmly. 'It all goes round and round and up and down like the donkeys on the beach, but I get the feeling I'm being told to take stock of my life.'

Her answer came back neutrally. 'And are you?'

He shrugged. 'I'm beginning to, I think. It's like a very bright puzzle. The more bits I put in place, the brighter the picture gets. The more I understand. The things you said in Coventry—they've helped. I'm beginning to see some light where there was nothing but darkness before.'

She was surprised. 'But you're usually so full of laughter.'

He stroked her arm. 'That's a poor way, sometimes, of running away from the sadness.'

'Damian, you mean?' She saw the old hurt in his eyes.

'Yes, Damian. Or the horrors of whatever case I'm on at the moment.' His eyes strayed from her face, and she knew he was remembering the children again.

She kept silent for a moment, then said softly, 'The light of understanding God gives me—when I take the trouble to look for it—is sometimes as blinding as the sun going down over the estuary—the view we had last night from your window. It hurts our eyes. We don't want to look straight into it.'

He nodded. 'I think I wanted a God who was all comfort and nothing else. Light can burn as well as illuminate . . . Oh, just listen to me! Frank, the detective inspector, Mr Ordinary himself, talking about *light*.'

She smiled. 'Remember that picture in Coventry?'

'Christ in the garden—with the gold cup?'

'Yes—that one.'

'I've thought of it over and over again. D'you think that's what the artist was trying to show?'

She darted an anxious look at his face to see if she was upsetting him. 'Yes,' she said. 'That cup looked beautiful, and the light was pouring out of it, into the darkness of Gethsemane. But it *was* a cup of suffering.'

'Thinking of it still makes me uneasy,' he said.

She considered for a moment, kicking at a pebble on the lane. 'It can't have made Jesus very "easy", Frank.'

He shook his head. 'You're probably right—but how can we know?'

She shrugged. 'In the end, all I've ever been able to hang on to when things are going awry, or when someone's in pain, is that he's there with us—God—Jesus—holding us. Going before us. Going after us, as well.'

'You sound so convincing.' He grinned. 'But what do you mean–*following* us? To snoop over our shoulders?'

'Not in the least!' She caught the impish look in his blue

345

eyes. 'No, that's not what I mean at all, and you know it. Following us, and picking up the pieces from the messes we make, the bad choices. That's not all he does, of course, but it's one of the ways he loves us. He pursues us—won't let us go.'

They stopped again, only a few yards from the car, and she put her arms round his neck. He held her close to him and she breathed golden beech leaves, fresh air, and the smell of Somerset earth.

'Talking to you for the first time was one choice I made,' he whispered, 'a good choice. When I think of you, when I look at you, I begin to see something of that love you talk about. You're so open, so straight.'

She blushed, turning her cheek away from him in embarrassment. 'You make me sound far too nice,' she said lightly, wincing automatically as the word 'nice' reminded her of how 'un-nice' she had been to her mother. Ignoring her for weeks. Vowing to telephone her, then doing nothing. 'You're in for some shocks, I'm afraid.'

'Am I indeed!' He roared with laughter. 'Oh, Clare—you make me want to follow this God you say is following us.'

PART FIVE

I took the one less travelled by,
And that has made all the
difference.

41

Clare went back to London on Wednesday evening, and the time dragged. Overnight, Weston had become colourless and dreary. A heavy wind sent wadded clouds skeltering across the sky. There were no donkeys on the beach, and no children playing by the water's edge.

I spent the morning in bed, dozing fitfully. There was nothing to get up for, I told myself. The house was lonely; Clare had gone back to work with promises that she would be down for the weekend if she could take the time off; Mum, humming to herself, was up and down the stairs with trays of juice and reminders about antibiotics. She was happy being so busy, but I felt useless and listless.

After lunch on Friday I could bear my room no longer. 'I'm getting up,' I shouted down the stairs when she came to take away my half-eaten lunch.

She came back into the room, tray still in hand. 'Sure there's nothing to stop you, darling. No use moping and grizzling in here. Get up by all means.'

'Dad's back, is he?'

'He should be after a while—but you know what he's like.'

'Typical!' I grumbled. But I didn't mind; why shouldn't he go fishing if he wanted to? It was better than lying in bed with the last gasps of illness, or changing sheets and cleaning the house. Still, I felt redundant and childishly in want of distraction.

Mum peered at me over the top of her half-moon spectacles. Her blue eyes didn't blink. 'Listen, Frank. Your daddy's only over by the pier. The tide's half up, and it's a warm wind out there. Why don't you walk down slowly on your own? I'm sure you're fit enough for that.'

'You're tired of having me under foot,' I said pettishly.

'Dear God, no! How often do I have you at home at all? Don't be so daft. The air'll do you good. Go on now, or I'll put you in the washing machine with the sheets and peg you out on the line afterwards. That'll blow the bugs away.'

Dressing slowly, still weak enough to have to rest between underwear and top clothes, I knew I was in the awful in-between stage of not quite well and not quite ill. It seemed impossible that in a few days I'd be doing those ordinary tasks, which now took so long, without coughing, and without breaking into a sweat.

I borrowed an old fishing jersey of my father's and went down between the rowan trees, out of the gate, across the seafront road, and along the parade towards the pier. My mother was right, I realized before I'd gone a hundred yards; the cool salt in the air stuck to my cheeks and eyelashes, and for the first time in days I could catch a full breath without gasping, wheezing, or coughing. I was happy to be alive.

But I missed Clare. Half shutting my eyes against the wind, I could almost feel her arm through mine. *Only a hundred or so miles away,* I thought, trying to imagine what she was doing. I wished she could see with me now the humped silhouette of Steep Holme, a dark island shadow hunched on the horizon five miles out; wished she could see the windsurfers bouncing and tacking across the white-caps, the pensioners nodding in deckchairs at the end of the parade, dreaming determinedly of sunshine even in the stiff breeze.

My father saw me before I saw him, and hailed me. He waded out, secured his beachcaster beside the other tackle and came plodding up the sands towards me. 'This is a surprise,' he said. 'I remember when you used to come down on a Saturday and find me.'

I felt even more childishly resentful at that—a sure sign that I was at last on the return to health. 'And you used to give me broken bits of peppermint rock,' I said, grinning in spite of myself.

'What?'

I repeated what I had said, and he laughed as we stepped

through the gritty wet sand to the water line. We stood together facing out to sea.

'What's your mother up to?' he asked.

I told him about the scintillating drama of wash-day and housecleaning, adding, 'I can't imagine what on earth you two do all day when there's no one ill at home and neither of the girls is over with the kids.'

'You know what *I* do, at least,' he said, fingering his line and nodding to another fisherman who was setting up camp about ten yards away. 'Your mother doesn't want for things to do, either. All I ever longed to do before I retired was fish— I couldn't be more content.'

'And I suppose Mum has always poured her life into home and church, anyway. Nothing's changed for her.'

'Just that it's slower, and I'm around more; that's all.'

We watched a boat trip leave the pier, the decks almost empty. 'They'll be packing up that run soon,' I said.

'Yes, leave us in peace,' he grunted. 'Look at them go. Far too fast, as well, and a bit too close to the shore for my liking. They'll drive my fish away.'

'*Your* fish, are they now?' I teased him.

'Not today,' he growled. 'It's a bad day. Too many cloud shadows on the water.' He looked up and down the beach mournfully. 'In fact, if you're going back now, I'll go with you. I've been down here since seven this morning.'

I found I was weak. The steps from the beach to the parade seemed longer and steeper than usual, and when I stopped, irritated with my exhaustion, half-way up, my father's face was all anxious concern.

'Too much of a good thing, Frank,' he muttered. 'First that girlfriend of yours, keeping your temperature up—'

'It's down!' I panted.

'And now you've overdone it again.' He lugged his creel and bait tub to the last step and stood waiting until I caught him up. A single seabass tail—healthily silver and respectably large—hung out of the creel. I kept my eyes on it as I puffed behind him.

'No, I can't bear to sit in bed all day or watch Mum doing the house. I needed to be out . . . but I'll feel better when we're home again.'

Mum greeted us in full flow at the door. 'Frank, I should never have let you out. The phone's not stopped ringing for you. First it was Clare, from the office, to say hello and ask how you were—I had a long chat to her. She's going to ring you later, she said. And then it was a man from the CID.' She frowned at me, stepping aside to let us both in. 'Oh, and you've brought Dad with you, have you? Let me see now . . . it was Charlie Somebody. Not on business, he assured me.'

Dad shut the door with a bang. 'Peggy, love, do let us catch a breath, would you?'

I slumped into the nearest chair in the sitting-room, glad to be out of the wind again, after all. 'What did Charlie say?'

'He's coming down to see you tonight. Sounded very nice, so I said I'd let him in as a big concession if he doesn't worry you half to death with police talk.'

Dad winked at me. 'Better than worrying you half to death with women's talk.'

'Sexist,' I said, but he went out into the kitchen pretending he hadn't heard.

'And there was another call, too, from CID. A Mr Cafferty. Oh, I had a grand chin-wag with him. Soon as I heard that Kerry voice, we could have talked for all the Irish day.'

'I can well believe it. But Joe's in Coventry. How would he—?'

She looked bemused. 'He said nothing at all about that. Mentioned your colleague, Charlie, as well. I gathered they'd be coming together.'

I shrugged. 'Well, that's a surprise. Are you sure you'll let those two madmen in the door?'

'And Charlie said he had a pile of stuff for you—no work, mind, I saw to that! Things from your house, I think.'

I put my head back against the lace antimacassars my mother insisted on keeping over the chairback in accordance

351

with old Irish parlour tradition, and in total defiance of normal modern convention, and shut my eyes. 'It'll be nice to see them,' I said.

She clucked and rustled her way round to the window, drawing the curtains with a swish. 'There, there. That's right. You have a nice doze before tea.'

I must have flickered out like a candle in the wind, blown away on the breath of my mother's sighs and streams of chit-chat, for the next thing I remember was my father opening the curtains with irritated complaints about how it wasn't winter yet, and weren't we to enjoy the daylight while we had it?—before he switched on the six o'clock news loudly enough for the neighbours as well as himself to hear it.

I watched with only half my attention, my mind floating inevitably eastwards, distracted also by the mouth-watering smell of fresh fish cooking in the kitchen. If today had been a bad day for my father's fishing, what was a good day like?

We were in the middle of the meal, plates on our knees in front of the television, when the doorbell rang.

Mum jumped up, frowning fiercely. 'That'll be your friends.'

The door swung open behind her; a draught chilled the living-room instantly.

My mother was oddly quiet in her greetings. I heard a lot of shushing and faint laughter, then the door frame was filled by Charlie Hotchkiss, Joe Cafferty grinning over his shoulder like a garden gnome.

'Well, well,' my father boomed through a mouthful of fish, 'a full house, just for a change!' He winked at me. 'Come on in. Just in time for some tea.' He shook hands with them both, and they dwarfed him: Charlie robust and meat-fisted; Joe gangly and comparatively fresh-faced.

They turned to me, Charlie first. 'Well, you're back from the dead, I see.' He gave me a light punch on the arm. 'A bit pale and puny, still, though.'

'Half-way, at least,' my mother said. She had her eyes on Joe, and I could see that she was convinced he had come to see her, not me, after all. Anyone from Ireland was fair game the minute he stepped through the door.

Charlie's big arm came round my shoulder. 'The place is falling down without you. Here—' He held out a sports bag. 'This is to open after we've gone. A goody-bag just for you, in case you're bored to death.'

'No doggy bags? I've been living on a starvation diet of nothing but local fish,' I moaned.

'Hush, don't you believe it,' Mum said. 'Thinks he can live on love, this boy.'

'Frank, if you can see alsatians lolling their tongues out of that bag at you, you're a sicker man than I thought,' Charlie said with a straight face. 'Though there might be the odd sniffer dog in there to make sure you're on the straight and narrow.'

'And no work, either,' Joe put in, looking in my mother's direction.

'Jill went round to your house and got Tim and Richard to look out some of your clothes. They're in there, among other things.'

'That's a relief,' Dad said crustily. 'He's been wearing mine most of this past week.'

I grinned at him, but Mum was switching off the weather report and hustling him out of the room. 'We'll leave you lads to it,' she said. 'But not too much CID talk, d'you hear?' She had obviously thought better of monopolizing Joe.

The room seemed breathlessly quiet after they'd gone, and we sank into chairs near each other, Joe's eyes wandering over the knick-knacks of two countries and a thirty-five year marriage, and Charlie looking at me the way he looked at someone across an interview table.

'Inspection complete?' I asked him mildly, and he grinned.

Joe gave me a smile. 'I was just admiring your mother's bits and pieces.'

'Go ahead. I was talking to Charlie, anyway. But I'm surprised to see you down here, Joe,' I added.

'I'm a bit surprised meself, tell you the truth. The SIO found out from your guv'nor that you were ill and off the case, and while we were still in the thick of it, he thought it would be good if I came down.'

'Since I couldn't go up again,' I prompted.

Charlie's face twisted wryly. 'What makes you think you'd have gone up, anyway? The guv'nor might have sent me, you know.'

'You're a good copper,' I said sarcastically, 'but not that good.'

'I'm glad to be down here, anyway,' Joe intervened. 'Good to see how the southern half lives.'

Charlie nodded, serious now. He was still inspecting me. 'You've got very thin,' he said. 'When will you be back on the job?'

I rubbed one hand through my beard. 'Not for a while. I was lucky I was here when it hit.'

'We'll have to rub along somehow without you.'

'I'm sure you're managing fine. How's Bill?'

'In rude health.'

'And Sally?'

'Pining away with no one to boss about. She says hurry and get better.'

'Your place,' Joe observed with a sly look at Charlie, 'appears to be held together with shoestrings, sellotape, posters of Angel Avalon—and a lot of romantic goings-on. Don't know how you get any work done.'

'No worse than Coventry,' I said, 'with the pall of pollution that hangs over your incident room all day.'

'Snooty lout,' Joe accused.

'Here's a riddle for you,' Charlie said irrelevantly, looking at the ceiling with an air of innocence. 'What did Frank call the mermaid on Weston beach that he fell in love with during the beauty competitions last week?'

'I don't know,' Joe offered. 'What did Frank call the mermaid on Weston beach that he fell in love with during the beauty competitions last week?'

'You're hopeless,' I growled. 'Miss New Monia, of course.'

'And what was he singing as he walked down the beach at the time?' Joe asked, winking at Charlie.

' "Au *Clair* de la Lune", I imagine,' I answered. 'Pack it in, you two. You're making me worse, not better.' But I was laughing feebly anyway, the warning itch of a cough returning to my chest.

'When do I get to meet the lovely lady?' Charlie asked. 'At Sands' wedding, I suppose. I hear you're best man—though fine best man you'll be, without the breath to sing a hymn and make a speech.'

'I'll manage,' I said tersely, hearing teacups rattling in the hall.

My mother came in with a tray of steaming tea, which she handed round. 'Well, and isn't this nice to have you all here at once?'

'Almost a quorum,' I said.

'Almost a congregation,' Mum said.

Charlie winked at me and stirred three rounded teaspoons of sugar into his cup. 'Shall I preach?'

Joe laughed, 'You!'

My mother turned to Joe. 'What do you think of Frank here? He's looking better, isn't he?'

'Better than what?' Charlie said, pulling a face at me irreverently.

'I am much better,' I said firmly, getting a little tired of them speaking as if I weren't in the room. 'Pain's gone, nightmares've gone, the worst of the cough's gone too.'

'Lots of TLC from your mother,' Joe said.

'And Clare.' I smiled at him, glad he'd met her.

Joe clapped his hands. 'She's made an honest Christian of you, has she?' he crowed.

I gave them all a slow smile as I answered them seriously. 'She's doing her best—and I've definitely called a truce.'

My mother looked at me narrowly, as if no one else were in the room. 'What about Damian?' she said perceptively.

'Have you resolved that old grief?'

I looked at her steadily. 'I'm getting there.'

She stood up suddenly and kissed me, her eyes wet. 'I'll leave you to your friends,' she said, replacing her emptied cup on the tray. The door closed softly after her.

'You made her day,' Joe commented with a grin.

Charlie rubbed his hands together. 'Now then, can we get down to business?'

'Charlie—' Joe cautioned.

'No, Joe. Give me a break . . . sir! Frank ought to know why you're down here and what's going on.'

I watched their faces and waited.

'What chance of you being back on Monday?' Charlie's eyes were glittering. 'We think we're finally going to crack this case over the weekend. You'd hate to miss all the action, wouldn't you?'

42

When Pete did not arrive at work the next day, it was all Clare could do not to phone his apartment and say, 'I'm so sorry. Are you OK? I shouldn't have run out on you like that.' But instead she resolutely asked Kathy to screen all calls, kept her door shut, and clicked away on her word processor to the music of *I Giocosi*.

'The boss called in sick today,' Kathy informed her over a gossipy cup of coffee in the middle of the morning. She laughed and twinkled at Clare. 'I guess he had one too many drinks last night. He was well away when we all left that new bar.'

Clare murmured a non-committal response. Still nursing an aching head herself, she did not want to think about anyone else's hangover, least of all Pete's. Then she went back to her notes and her word processor and began sifting and shaping one of the most intricate and careful articles she had ever written.

For once, even the frosty Ms Enright in the cuttings library proved obliging and pointed her to files she would never have known about. It was becoming clear from interviews with everyone from concert hall doormen to the trumpeter (plainly not an Italian) in *I Giocosi*, and the second cellist in the Boston Philharmonic, that organized crime had moved in on the classical music scene to stay.

'It's laundered money behind all this,' one of the doormen had told her with a sweep of his hand. 'Maybe you ain't been in town long enough to know it, lady, but some of them big construction companies is just fronts for the Mob. I'd swear it. The FBI ought to be in here.' Then the little man had noticed one of the violinists staring his way and had ducked out of sight behind an ornamental column. When Clare followed him, all she had seen was his disappearing back scurrying into a door marked 'Staff only'.

Stories were circulating, she discovered from other similar conversations, that Mafia 'family' members in the city had been hired to infiltrate other orchestras and buy for sums no one could refuse the best musicians in the country. *I Giocosi* was set to outclass every other group of musicians in North America, and Mafia money, Mafia favours, were going to make the wheels turn. There was no disputing the superb quality of their music, but what she wanted to probe was the means by which the orchestra had risen so dizzily to over-night success.

When Pete arrived the following morning, just as she finished running off the last paragraph of her column, she had lost her feeling of anxiety about him and was spoiling for a fight. *I don't owe him an apology*, she told herself indignantly. *He owes me one.* Irritation, fear and shame all sharpened her anger: irritation that he had broken his word and left her without a visa that would allow her to work legally; fear about the danger that her new column might place her in—and shame. If he so much as brushed a hand across her shoulders she knew she would explode. She felt foolish and cheap.

He marched into her office a few minutes later. The only warning of his arrival was the creak of the outer office door and surprised exclamations from Kathy; then her own door jerked open and he stood on the threshold with a rolled magazine in his hand and a murderous look on his face.

'What the heck were you playing at?'

She jumped up, scattering the papers for the new column onto the floor, and cut him off before he could utter a word. 'What d'you want? You can't come flying in here like this.' She heard her own voice: cool, the fury contained now—but nevertheless full of rage. 'Unlike some people who take extra days off midweek, I haven't been *playing* at anything at all. I was in here writing all day yesterday while you slept off your hangover. As if no one else had one! In here by eight today, as well, to finish my week's work.' She wanted to twist the knife in one more small way. 'And can't you shut the door, for heaven's sake? D'you want the whole office to hear this?'

Letting the door go, he went white, the lines of his mouth and eyes setting as hard as her own. 'Well, good for you, Ms Goody-Two-Shoes. One columnist at least who keeps the old flag flying, Union Jack and all. Good for you.' He stooped before she could grab them and snatched up the papers that had fallen on the other side of her desk. 'So this is the much sweated over magnum opus for the week, is it? Well, how noble of you to keep writing even with a headache.'

She began to tremble, her resolve crumbling against the spears of his sarcasm. Why was he attacking her? Because she had run out and left him in the apartment? Because she had stirred up trouble for the magazine with the previous week's column? She had no idea where (as he might have expressed it) he was coming from.

'Yes, wasn't it noble?' She tried to match his cutting voice.

His blue eyes glinted up at her, hard as ice. 'Too bad this copy stinks. It's the worst piece you've written so far.' He tossed it back on her desk as if it were a piece of offal. 'You can damn well think again. And think fast. Your piece on McEnroe came out today. My secretary says the switch-board's been lit up like the Fourth of July since eight this morning.'

She gritted her teeth, leaning forward with one hand resting on the desk. 'And who said it was OK to go ahead with it if we had a legal reading? It was *your* choice, not mine.'

He carried on as if she hadn't spoken. 'And that's not all. Look at this.' He unfolded the magazine he held and pushed it at her. 'What?' she said scornfully.

'New magazine. Scooped *I Giocosi* before we had a chance.' Relief—but also fear—flooded her. 'And that's my fault as well, I suppose?' she said bitterly.

'Every journalist worth her salt keeps tabs on others snooping around at the same venues. I'll bet you knew all the time that someone else was working on this piece.'

She ran her eyes over the glossy cover. *Up Front*, it

proclaimed; clearly a first issue. There was nothing familiar about it. She groaned inwardly, then met his eyes. 'I don't know this magazine at all.'

'Then you should.'

'I suppose *you* knew all about it?' She saw two spots of colour appear on his cheeks. He was caught: if he admitted knowing about the new magazine, he should also have told her about it; if he denied knowledge, then he was in no position to criticize her ignorance. She smiled, knowing she had scored a point, then looked back at the new magazine in her hands, her smile fading. 'It's a good piece, is it?'

'Very good.'

'And they've covered the underworld angle, have they?'

'No,' he said violently. 'Far too smart for that.'

She looked up again in surprise. What he was saying was tantamount to an admission that he should not have asked her to research and write about the supposed Mafia connection. 'What d'you mean?' she asked levelly.

He did not answer her directly but instead savagely punched a number into her phone without lifting it out of the cradle. He shouted to his secretary on the other end, 'Bring your butt in here right now. And bring those letters you showed me a few minutes ago.'

Clare stood facing him, her fingers locked together. *Now what?*

He towered above her, his anger more fierce than her own, and hissed, 'You're a silly b——. You should have fought me before you wasted a whole week and a small fortune of my money on concert tickets with your goddamned *cousins*.'

'Your idea, I thought,' she challenged. 'And, in case you've forgotten, one of the concerts was with you.'

'I didn't hear you arguing. And you should have done.'

Pete's secretary crept through the door with a frightened face, and in the background Clare saw Kathy craning her neck to get a better view of the proceedings.

'You're blaming me for your own stupidity,' Clare shrieked, no longer caring if anyone else heard.

'No, it's your stupidity I'm worried about. For all we know this mag's a product of the Outfit as well.' He turned and took a folded white paper from his secretary. 'Now, get!' he shouted, practically pushing her back through the door.

'You're disgusting,' Clare heard herself saying, easily loud enough for Kathy to hear. 'You treat your staff like dogs.'

His eyes hardened again. 'Read this, damn you. Read it.'

She backed away from him, wishing she could edge towards the door. He looked insane with anger. *Did I ever want this man?* she asked herself incredulously. It seemed impossible.

'Read it!' he roared.

'I'm reading.' Her legs began to shake, but she wasn't going to let him see that. She dropped back into her chair, gripping the arms for support and bending over so that he could not see her face.

Unfolding the paper, she saw that it was covered with crude black lettering cut out of newspapers and pasted together like a child's collage. At first she wanted to laugh. What silly game was he playing now? A threat letter delivered in the clichéd style of old gangster movies! Without looking up, she said, 'What sort of a joke is this?'

'*Joke!* No joke at all,' he spat. 'Someone's got wind of the *I Giocosi* column you're writing and is threatening mutilations and early funerals for a few of the staff here. If I find out who spilled the beans, I'll—' He stabbed at the papers with his forefinger, his nail grazing her palm. 'Your name's on the hit list, see?'

'Touching of you to be concerned.'

'I'm not concerned about your skin, you little fool.' He bent and rattled the papers in her hand. 'It's Bobbie's skin as well.'

She didn't think before she answered, and later she had no idea where the cruel words had come from. 'Huh! Maybe it's Bobbie's family who're behind the whole racket anyway. Mafia all the way, I bet.'

'You little—' He grabbed her shoulders and shook her. 'I

should swing at you for this.' His jaw was clenched, his eyes blazing. 'You're filthy, cheap—'

She let her shoulders slump in his hands. 'And you? What does that make you? We're not really talking about this threat letter at all, are we? What's at issue here is your precious male ego, shattered I suppose when you woke up cold in a dry bath after I'd gone. That's the real issue, isn't it? You were too drunk to get me.' She twisted away from the chair and ran behind him to the door. 'I don't care if Kathy hears, and I don't care if anyone hears. You think you're the best journalist in the state. You think you're some kind of wonderful stud. Just because you're good at pulling women and just because your uncle's a McEnroe.' She wrenched open the door. 'You're as cheap as you tried to make me! But you didn't succeed, did you? Poor male ego. About time someone taught you.'

Her whole body was trembling now. In front of her eyes danced red anger mingled with the black and white after-images of the ugly threats she had just read. She wanted to go on and on screaming abuse at him; wanted to make him look small because she still felt small herself.

He suddenly roused himself and leapt after her. She chased through Kathy's room and out into the corridor where only two days before he had smiled so brightly at her and turned her world upside down for a few hours.

A door opened a few yards away, and Bobbie-Ann came out, closely followed by Clare's sparring partner, Virginia Enright. The smug smile on Ginny's face told a tale, and Clare was immediately suspicious. *Is this some sort of hideous conspiracy?* she thought wildly, but then blinked and shook her head. *Nonsense! That's paranoid.* At the same time, she stopped in mid-flight, shame burning her face and ears. *Of course Bobbie's no part of any leak to the Mafia. I should never have said that.* She bit her lip and felt tears pushing out of her eyes. *Lord, what's happened to me?*

'Leaving, are we?' Ginny asked nastily. 'So early!'

Pete caught Clare by the shoulders for the second time.

'She's not going anywhere, except to write a different column for next week—to replace the one she's messed up on; that's what she's going to do. And she's going to apologize to Bobbie-Ann for what she just said in that office.'

Virginia Enright's eyes gleamed. 'What exactly is going on, Pete?' Under the saccharin of her syrupy voice was the thirst for blood. 'I thought Clare was writing a harmless little piece this week? A lot sweeter, I was persuaded, than the scurrilous piece you let her get away with last week.'

'Come on, Ginny,' Pete insisted. 'I don't need you in on this act. I can fight McEnroe battles myself, thanks.' His fingers pinched the skin of Clare's shoulders as if for emphasis. 'Like I said before.'

She wrenched away. 'Don't you touch me,' she raged, 'or I'll have you for harassment.' She glanced away from Pete's stony face to Bobbie's and saw a look of stricken incomprehension.

Bobbie threw out her hands in a wide gesture. 'Pete? Clare? What on earth—?'

'But I *told* you,' Virginia hissed, glaring at Bobbie, enjoying the fray.

'Virginia—out!' Pete shouted, shoving at the nearest door and pushing her through it with a grunt of angry effort.

Turning her back on Pete, Clare stood defiant. Hands on hips, the short-lived tears drying on her cheeks, she said, 'Bobbie, I'm sorry. I said something awful about you just now—something speculative and untrue. Pete's right. I owe you an apology.'

Bobbie only shrugged and smiled. 'I'm sure it was nothing.' Her eyes swerved in bewilderment to Pete's face.

'She called your family Mafia. Said you let out confidential office information to the Mafia—about *I Giocosi*,' he grated between clenched teeth. He held out the threat letter to her. 'She more or less said your family was behind *this*.'

'I said I'm sorry,' Clare jibbered, 'Of course that's not true. Pete made me so angry—I didn't know what I was saying. It was—'

363

There was a moment's silence. Then Bobbie's face turned flinty, though her eyes were full of fire. She leaned towards Clare, breathless, and for the first time since Clare had known her, she spoke with an excited Italian intonation. 'You accuse my family of being behind dirt like this? A criminal piece of threat mail that says that if we finger *I Giocosi* for Mafia ties we'll meet the real Mafia and find out what sort of music their guns can play in this office?' Bobbie began to quiver. 'And you say my people were behind this?' Her voice rose to a shout. 'You are wrong, wrong, wrong! See, even I would be hurt. *My* name is here.'

Her dark eyes turned on Pete again. 'Peter McEnroe, I'll resign here and now if you don't pull out the column she's been writing this week.'

'I wrote it in good faith!' Clare wailed, at the same time struck with the realization that Bobbie's resignation was pure theatrics. Pete would never print the column anyway; he had already told her to write its replacement. But it was no use saying so.

Bobbie flung the letter on the carpet and ran off. Clare heard her sobbing all the way down the corridor.

'Your thoughtless, thoughtless words, Ms Hogarth. You do damage with that quick, sharp tongue of yours. I don't want to see you in here again until next week. And after that— not at all. D'you hear? Get your ass out.'

Clare didn't move.

'I said get out.'

'I'll have to go for good, then,' she said coldly. 'You never sorted out my visa as you said you would, so I'll be put out of the country anyway.'

'Still harping on about that, are you? How very convenient that I didn't arrange for the new visa.'

'And you haven't paid me yet this week.'

He smiled mirthlessly. 'Nor will I. I don't have to pay an illegal immigrant.'

'You'll be hung in your own noose, then, for employing me here these last few weeks.'

'How will you prove it?' His head went to one side.

'Oh, you are—'

'Yes, an unscrupulous man. So you've said before. Even my uncle tried to warn you, I think.'

'I'll prove my employment here by the copy I wrote, of course.'

'Under an alias?' His eyes were mocking her. 'Any member of staff could claim that.'

'I'll prove it by . . .' She stopped, her brain working frantically. *How will I prove it? I don't even have a pay slip!* McEnroe's advice to her that she get the required papers quickly echoed hollowly in her ears.

'Your uncle will testify that you hired me,' she said abruptly.

His eyebrows rose, and his mouth twisted. 'Oh, will he? Yes, my uncle's an honest man. But you've just excavated a heap of bad memories about my cousin Ellie. How much help d'you think he'll be to you this time?'

Her breath was coming in gasps of fear and anguish. *He's unjust. He's a criminal. I must find Bobbie and make peace. I must get out of here and lick my wounds. I must, I must . . .* She found she had nothing more to say, and leaned against the wall for support.

'This is Labor Day weekend,' Pete continued smoothly. 'Think about what I've said. You'll write a replacement column, so you've got three days. Then you can pack up and get straight out. Book yourself a seat on the plane for Wednesday so that Bobbie and I don't have to look at you again after you turn in the copy.'

She recovered slightly. 'You're despicable! What makes you so cocksure I'll show up next week if you don't pay me, anyhow?'

'Oh,' he said silkily, 'you'll show up all right. Even if I have to send Bobbie's family to bring you in.' He laughed harshly. 'You know—those *gangsters*.'

Her heart plunged sickeningly. *These people fight by rules I don't understand.* Fleetingly, Andy's mild-mannered face rose in her mind as if to taunt her with what she'd sacrificed to this blue-eyed wolf of a man. Then she could no longer think.

She turned away. 'I hate you!'

Blindly running towards Kathy's door, she collided with a well-dressed man striding in the opposite direction. She saw the flash of his silver hair and recognized him instantly.

'Senator McEnroe!'

'Yes, my dear.' Gently he propelled her out of his way. 'Don't you know that love is always stronger than hate?'

Looking towards Pete, McEnroe's face was thunder.

43

'All right, all right!' Andy had repeated, 'I know you worked on the bank holiday. I know your boyfriend's ill, but we just can't let this go. I told you at the beginning of the week that I'd have some travelling work for you—we had no way of knowing how fast it would come up. And I wasn't even thinking of your child abductions when I said that.' He was grinning wickedly at Clare, apparently enjoying her discomfort.

Her plans to return to Bristol for the weekend with Frank were disintegrating. Worse, she had brought this disappointment on herself by telling Andy about the phone-call from Coventry. She had known it was a risky choice; she longed so much to see Frank again that she was almost tempted to say nothing. But she couldn't afford to jeopardize all the good work she'd put in on the story thus far. *I have made the right choice,* she kept telling herself.

Things had begun simply enough: a tip-off from a woman in Coventry whom she'd interviewed two weeks before.

'There's a story up here for you, if you want it,' she told Clare. 'I've got friends on the other side of town—nowhere near where the children disappeared, but they say the police are watching a house over there. They had a friendly chat, like, with one of the coppers—and he told them—unofficially, of course—that the detectives they've seen hanging around are after those kidnappers.'

Clare had taken all the details and run straight into the editor's office, where Andy was in the middle of a meeting with Dave.

'You'll just have to cancel with your boyfriend and go straight up.' Andy's mouth formed a firm line. 'But you knew that, I'm sure, when you came rushing in just now. Get one of the girls to book you into the B & B up there—wherever it was you stayed last time. You want to be there when the fireworks go off, don't you?'

Clare caught Dave's eye. He was looking alarmed, and she could guess why.

'Andy,' she began carefully, 'I'm far more excited about this news than I can tell you, but—'

Andy waved a piece of paper in the air irritably. 'I know, I know. You'd like me to say you can go on Monday, I suppose. Sorry about that! And, yes, I do know we're not a tabloid running after a scoop.'

'That's how you're acting,' Dave put in sharply.

'But Clare, your handling of the background to the abduction stories is going to be one of the best human interest things we've run since I've been here,' Andy insisted. 'I'd stake my career on the ratings going up afterwards. So I want you on the spot—right there when they nail the abductors.'

'You'd better get independent confirmation from another source, Clare,' Dave cautioned, 'before you go anywhere. How do we know this woman who called you isn't spinning a yarn herself? It's all hearsay, anyhow.'

Andy heaved a huge sigh of impatience and smacked his glasses so hard on the desk that Clare was surprised they didn't break. 'Dear God! Of course we don't know. And of course Clare will get confirmation.' He leaned forward. 'Won't you? Phone up your pals in CID in Coventry. You met the boss up there, didn't you? He'll tell you what you want to know, I'm sure.'

Remembering the laconic senior investigating officer in Coventry, she smiled a wry smile. 'I doubt it, but I know someone who might.' She would ask Joe Cafferty.

For the next few hours—in fact until almost eight o'clock that evening, she spent her time on the telephone arranging her journey for the next day. Joe Cafferty, one of his colleagues told her, was away on urgent work; no one would tell her where or why. Undeterred, she made other calls to people she had met in Coventry and eventually felt fairly confident that the reports of a major surveillance were true. Her final Warwickshire call was to the senior press officer at the police headquarters.

'Listen,' she said, after identifying herself and explaining what she had heard, 'I'm not asking you to tell me anything, and I'm not going to get onto other members of the press with this story, either, you can be sure. I just want to know if what my sources have told me is even remotely true and whether it's worth our while sending up a journalist—to be on the scene if anyone's arrested for those abductions. You can tell me that much, can't you?'

The press officer was plainly uneasy but conceded that it was at least worth sending a journalist. More than that he would not say.

The building was hushed and most of the lights had been turned out as one by one the offices emptied for the weekend. The evening cleaners were coming round to empty rubbish bins and vacuum the carpets when Clare made her last call of the day—to Frank.

He sounded cheerful and happy to hear from her. 'Charlie and—oops, can't say who else—but I've just had visitors. Anyway, I'm feeling well enough to struggle into HQ on Monday, I think.'

'Frank—' she blurted, hardly taking in what he had said, in her rush to give him the news, 'I won't be in Bristol after all.'

His voice came more quietly now. 'Oh—everything all right? Aren't you feeling well? Your turn to be ill, is it?'

'No, it's not that. I'm fine.' She struggled with the desire to pump him—especially now that he was talking to his colleagues again and must have news from the CID about what was happening in Coventry. He was certain to know, but she decided it wasn't fair to use him to get her story, or to persuade him to divulge information she couldn't have obtained without him. She went on, 'I'm afraid I've got to go up to the Midlands for a few days. I can't argue with Andy on this one, particularly after taking Tuesday and Wednesday off with no notice, and—'

'*And* working on the bank holiday,' he interrupted indignantly.

'Yes, but . . . Andy's right, I've got to go. It's my choice, anyway.'

'I see.'

'No, you don't see at all!' she wailed. 'I'd love to tell you, but I can't.' She would never be able to travel to Coventry again without thinking and dreaming of him, and she longed to tell him that. 'Oh, don't sulk on me.'

He laughed. 'Don't worry, love. Just tell me you haven't found some other hunk and decided to go running into his arms for the weekend. That's all I want to hear.'

'*Other* hunk?' she giggled, relieved he was teasing her, 'So you think you're a hunk, do you?'

'Decide for yourself.' He began to cough, and she waited.

'Frank, I'm not chasing after anyone, I promise,' she assured him after a moment. 'Just a story.'

'Sounds like a good journalistic line, anyway. When will you get back?

'I'm not sure. Sunday, or Monday perhaps. Longer if it takes longer.' She felt miserable again. 'I'll ring you if I can.'

'I'll be here in Weston until Sunday night. Back to Bristol then, and into HQ first thing Monday. Probably extremely early.' He sounded distant now, almost cheerful again.

'OK.' Her voice had dwindled to a sigh.

'There's next weekend, Clare,' he said. 'And wherever you're going I'll be thinking of you.'

'Me too—thinking of *you*, I mean,' she gulped.

Saturday morning found her on Euston Station waiting for the 9.40 train to Coventry. The train hadn't even been announced when she arrived, so she browsed in the bookshop, looking idly at the magazine rack as she waited for the platform number to show on the board.

A magazine she had never noticed before caught her attention, the glossy front cover and tiny stars and stripes proclaiming its American origin. She picked up a copy with the resigned sense that a journalist was never really off duty. 'UP FRONT' shrieked the masthead, and 'Welcome to the introductory issue of a dazzling new music rag.' Below the bright lettering was a sharp photograph of an olive-skinned drummer—or was he a timpanist? She looked more closely. His long hair and dreamy expression were familiar, but the black bow-tie and the vivid white tuxedo were not. 'Lorenzo Marti', read the small letters under his portrait, and she shook her head. *Sounds more like an opera singer than a drummer.*

She turned the front page. *Never heard of this one ... or have I? They're brave,* she thought, *starting life without a pic of Angel Avalon on the front!* Mentally she made a note to ask the cuttings librarian to order *Up Front* for their collection. Then she flicked to the list of contents, straight to the line that announced the cover story: '*I Giocosi* take Boston by storm.' Something sizzled in her mind—something faintly familiar after all, but she had no idea what. She stared at the cover again. *Don't be silly,* she told herself. *This is a brand-new magazine, and you've never seen it in your life.*

Inside, a double-page spread, all in stark black and white, showed a small orchestra in performance. Immediately she thought of her cousin Jack, remembering how much he enjoyed classical music and wondering if he had already heard *I Giocosi*.

Sitting on the train later she read the article, one minute amused at the polished, witty coverage of a group that had evidently annoyed some of the more established musicians in America, and the next wishing she could hear the arts orchestra for herself. Then, in the rush to get to the address she had scrawled on her notepad—Rosemount Road—she forgot the magazine again. What mattered now were her own articles for *Women Today*.

Saturday afternoon and Sunday passed in a blur of boredom as she waited outside the house on Rosemount Road in Coventry. None of the police who watched near her would tell her the names of the suspects, though she found out from two children dawdling on their bikes behind their grandfather that the young couple under observation were called Bennett. She wanted to ask more questions, but something in the children's eyes stopped her; she didn't want to seem too curious.

For about the hundredth time, she looked up at the house. There seemed remarkably little about it to arouse suspicion: an ordinary, neat suburban house in a row of other ordinary, neat suburban houses. Borders of drooping rose bushes flanked a closely cut lawn that had parched in the summer's heat. White net curtains hung at all the windows. No sign of movement within the house until the lights went on at twilight and a small window was opened in a bedroom at the front. *What are we all expecting?* she wondered. *How do the police know to watch here? Do they really know anything at all?* She stared alternately at the house and at the concealed policemen, at least one of whom was eyeing her with irritation. Doubt set in, and she actually found herself wishing she had brought her Fiat, so that she could at least sit in relative comfort as she waited. As it was, she was doomed to wander up and down the street as if she were a passer-by, only occasionally diverting herself with a short walk to the nearest corner shop for a drink or tasteless sandwich.

At last one of the plainclothes men spoke to her, clearing his throat self-importantly and narrowing his eyes. 'Is there something you're wanting? I could have you for loitering, you know. You've been up and down here at least twenty times.'

She felt like retorting that he was loitering as much as she was, but her knowledge that he was probably one of Joe Cafferty's colleagues—perhaps even acquainted with Frank—kept her tongue in control.

The detective pulled out his ID card, and she winced, remembering Frank even more vividly.

'I guessed who you were,' she said levelly. 'I'm sorry, but I'm on a job, too. I'll move to a different place if you can suggest one. I'm not exactly enjoying myself here.'

He looked her up and down ungraciously. 'Try going

home, if you want my advice,' he said nastily. 'We don't need anyone else nosing into what's going on here. It'll be dark soon, what's more.'

She pulled out her press card. 'I'm sorry,' she said, 'but I have to be somewhere near here, myself. Press, sir.'

He scrutinized her face, then in the failing light minutely examined her card. 'All right,' he said eventually. 'All the way up from London, hmmm? Well, stay if you must. I don't like it, though.' He gripped her elbow firmly and led her to a garden shed apparently belonging to the neighbours, but close enough to the Bennetts' property to give her a good view. 'This'll do you, and the owners have given us clearance to move freely around as we need to. But for goodness sake keep yourself out of sight of the house.' He turned away, then swung back again. 'Incidentally, how many other baying press hounds are we going to have up here before the day's out? Once you people get wind of something, you make our work a damn sight harder, you know.'

She gave him a dazzling smile, beginning to enjoy herself after all. Far too often her job was a mechanical exercise behind a safe desk. *On the spot reporting,* she reflected, *is a bit livelier.* 'We don't mean to make your work harder, of course,' she told him.

'Of *course* not.'

'But no one else in the press knows about this operation, to my knowledge, outside *Women Today.* If anyone else *does* know, it's not because I've told them. I'm not answerable, though, for members of the local press called in by the neighbours.'

The detective looked annoyed. 'Oh, no, I'm sure you're not.' Then he sneered, 'Well, enjoy yourself. It'll be a long vigil, believe me.' And with a glance at the house he ducked down the street to an unmarked Sierra parked about fifty yards away.

For a while a small dog barked monotonously from someone's back garden, and she stood or sat uncomfortably, inhaling the scent of creosote from the slatted walls of the

373

shed. A black and white cat came and wound its body round her legs, purring. She stroked it absently, sighing. The day hung between dusk and night: a magical time. *What if . . . Frank were on the job here now?* she thought dreamily. *Would things be any different?* She stretched to ease the stiffness in her shoulders and legs. It was pointless to dream about him; he would be chatting to his mother in Weston, packing up to return to Bristol for work the next day. *I hope he's well enough . . .*

Darkness fell at last; dew was beginning to rise on the grass around her. Then, just when she could bear to watch no longer, the sound of a woman's crying split the quiet air. She leaned forward, craning to identify the source. An unseen hand slammed the window at the front of the house, muffling the sound.

Curiously, she looked around to catch the response of the detectives watching with her, but they were now so well concealed that she had lost sight of them in the cobalt nightfall. No one and nothing moved, and she held her breath.

In the house, the crying was renewed. It was louder now, even with the window shut: a jagged, awful weeping. A man's voice sliced across it—anger and anxiety mingling. 'Shut up, will you, for God's sake!'

A stab of sympathy made Clare groan softly, and for the second time in ten days she had a strong sense of having gone through something like this before: not Mrs Drury in Bristol . . . but another woman weeping over someone or something lost to her. *What was it? Who was it?* The memory evaded her.

Footsteps rang on the path that linked the Bennetts' house with their neighbours'. A stout woman had left the adjoining house and was marching straight to the Bennetts' front step. If she was aware of the many watchers in the bushes and nearby cars, she did not betray them. Clare shrank back into the shadows of the shed, hating the suspense, yet longing to know the outcome. She heard the muted ring of the Bennetts' doorbell. Immediately, the weeping ceased. The world was hushed. Still, no one answered the door.

The woman rang the bell a second time, this time stepping back to peer at the lit windows of the upstairs. In the dim glow that spread from the curtained squares, Clare could see the woman's expression of concern, the flicker of doubt across her features. The woman hesitated for a few more moments, then returned more slowly to her own house.

Rosemount Road lay quiet again. Clare saw two of the policeman flit like ghosts across the lawn, confer in inaudible whispers, then change their observation posts. Two cars cruised by and parked, and other plain clothes men took up stations behind branches and in shadows.

She shivered and pulled her jacket more closely around her shoulders. Her legs felt leaden, and her head ached slightly. She wanted to go back to the guest house, but felt somehow that if she did she would miss the important moments. Then common sense took over. She was too tired now to do anything but sleep.

44

A marked change had taken place in the incident room since I'd last stepped into it. Gone were the expressions of resigned boredom or forced cheerfulness, gone the chatter of fruitless phone-calls about information irrelevant to the puzzle. Instead, there was a sense of purpose and cautious hope.

Bill briefed me first. 'Inspector Cafferty may have told you unofficially,' he began. 'Warwickshire had been watching one area for quite a while.' He heaved a deep sigh. 'Then several people from the area phoned in with the same story: about a woman who keeps crying and crying but who's going at it worse than usual, by all accounts. They've been keeping an eye on the place—as I said.'

I felt slow-witted and out of touch with the case. Ten days away seemed a long time, though not long enough to be fully well again. Yet certainly far too long for me to remember the details of the Midlands end of the case.

'One of the neighbours got upset last night and went round. Says they often won't answer their door anyway, especially at night.'

'Who, sir?' I was still ten paces behind him.

'At the house where the woman cries all the while. Young couple, apparently. No kids. In their late twenties, married very young. Well, this time the crying stopped abruptly when the doorbell went, but no one would come to the door. The woman who phoned in had found out about the police obs and was worried, they told us. Joe Cafferty's colleagues've heard that story before, from other neighbours, but this woman seemed to know a bit more than most about the couple concerned.' His eyes wandered to the door, then back to my face.

'Wife-beating, is it?' I asked. He shook his head. 'No, no

one thinks so, thank God. And it wasn't that kind of crying, she said—though they'll have to look into that as well, of course. But no, more like the sound of someone grieving for something—unable to stop.'

For a split second—but no more than that because the governor plainly had more to say—I thought of my mother after Damian died, of how long and sad the mourning for him had been—of how she had gone walking and walking on Weston-super-Mare beach to cry the pain into the sea. I said, 'You don't think there's *another* Coventry child missing, do you, one we didn't know about?'

'No,' he said patiently. 'I told you, these people don't have kids. In fact, there's the rub, our informant thinks. There was a time a few months ago, it seems, when young Mrs Bennett broke down and wept about having no children. It was just the once, the neighbour reported, and since then the girl has avoided her. Mr Bennett keeps strange hours and is gone a lot, too. Keeps everyone at a distance.'

I thought how typical that sounded—a woman who wanted to communicate with her neighbours but could not; a man who went on as if he didn't need to communicate with anyone—but who in the end wore down his wife by expecting her to carry all his emotional burdens for him. But I was finding it hard to work out where the governor's account was going. *Surely,* I thought, *this is more a case for the social services?*

He took up the story again. 'This weekend, the Coventry SIO started by sending a couple of men round to the street in question to talk to some of the other neighbours. The same tales kept coming back—oh, why don't people realize how even something small, something unimportant, may be just what we need to hear about? All the neighbours said they saw Bennett driving off early on several occasions. He's out of work, so no one could account for it. And coming back after a couple of hours—just for a few minutes each time—with someone else inside the car. The wife would run out and look into the car for a moment, then the husband would drive

377

away again. There'd be no more crying for a while. The husband would come back very late the same day—by himself.'

'Did anyone say who else was in the car on those mornings?'

'No one saw anything close up. Someone small, they said.' He leaned back in his chair. 'With me now?'

'Yes. But why isn't Joe up there nailing that couple if it looks so certain his colleagues are onto the right people?'

Bill snorted. 'Oh, he's working on it. They'll be busy all right, don't you worry. But there's a Bristol dimension to all this, and I'm glad you're back in.' His face broke into a wide grin. 'We've looked into our old friend H.O.L.M.E.S. and found out the Bennetts' car's been sighted in Bristol more than once.'

I was all ears now.

'Yes—and what's more, near that old fellow our mob have been watching since before you were ill. In Blagdon, remember? Name of Lomax.'

I nodded. His excitement was almost tangible.

'*Parked outside his house,* no less.' He paused for effect. 'Not recently, mind, but you can see what I'm getting at now, can't you?'

I sat down—he hadn't invited me to do so—and studied him. 'You think we're dealing with a ring, sir? You think the kids are down here? That Bennett may have brought them down into a sort of "safe" house?'

'Down here, yes. But not a ring, Frank. Ordinary people, I should think. Ordinary people who wanted kids so badly they had to grab someone else's. Perhaps also simple people who might imagine that after a while we'd forget about those kids and that it would "all blow over", as they say.' He scoffed again. 'Not on my patch! Not on Joe's either, or I'm a circus ringmaster.'

It all made sense. I stood up again. 'I'm sure they've got everything under control,' I said, 'but I'd like to go out to Blagdon and have a good look myself at what the lads are doing.'

'Yes, of course. You do that.' He stood up and shook my hand. 'Welcome back. We've missed you.'

I beamed at him. 'Only half here, yet—but just you look out when I catch up.' I was thinking fast now, my eyes on the stained matting on the floor of the office. 'I still don't understand a lot of things, but at least we're moving.' I looked up. 'You were on the phone to Coventry all week-end, I suppose?'

'You suppose right. And to the other forces, as well. And the office manager's getting something into the teleprinter. It may be early, God help us, but it's all happening.'

For a second I thought about the words he'd chosen—*God help us*—and realized I heard them in a different way now. They would never sound the same again. God *was* helping us. It was a small miracle, for a start, that I was back on duty again.

'All happening!' he repeated.

'Sounds like it,' I agreed, breathless. 'But haven't there been *any* other developments here while I've been off? Charlie Hotchkiss says you've had the Lomax house under continuous obs . . . the whole time I was ill.'

'*Was* ill?' Bill quirked his eyebrows as he echoed me. 'You're still not a hundred per cent, though, are you?'

I didn't want to get side-tracked. 'I'm coping, sir, thanks.'

'That's what I was afraid of.'

I disregarded the bait. 'I'm not going to miss this—not for anything.'

'Suit yourself. Oh, I grant you Detective Sergeant Hotch-kiss does well enough, but I *have* missed the Bernard brains, Frank.'

He knew how to rub me up the right way, and I grinned as I passed him to open the door. I should have known better, though, about becoming complacent with Detective Super-intendent Bill Longley.

'By the way,' he added casually, propping up the doorway, 'I gather there was a journalist who had an appointment with my counterpart in Coventry a couple of weeks ago, and that she's a friend of yours.'

I hesitated in the middle of the passage outside his office and tried to work out what he was expecting me to say. His expression was neutral. 'Yes,' I told him carefully, 'the tom-toms have drummed out the right message thus far, at least.'

He smiled. 'He tells me there's a lot going on under that ginger mop of hers. He didn't like her.'

I felt defensive. Or was it protective of her? 'We first met in June. I didn't see her again until a fortnight ago.' I stopped, suddenly wondering why I felt I had to explain myself. When and how I knew Clare was not Bill's business.

'Well, you keep your eye on her, d'you hear?'

'She'd never publish anything that would impede our work,' I said hotly.

He clicked his tongue and gave me a lazy smile. 'Now, now! Don't jump so fast, Frank. All I said was, "watch her".'

'With pleasure, I assure you.' I grinned at him. *Checkmate,* I thought, but I knew I was bordering on being cheeky, so I sobered up and looked him right in the eye. 'It's much more likely, I think, that she'll help our work than impede it.'

The corners of Bill's mouth twisted. 'Don't get me wrong, Frank. You're a sharp young copper. We can't manage without men like you. But you're still running in the marriage stakes, and you'd better watch the hare doesn't run off the rails with the prize and leave the greyhound panting somewhere on the track. Could be rather embarrassing. Try to keep business and pleasure apart, will you?'

I felt put in my place. Did he just want me to be on my guard? Perhaps I hadn't been—not enough. I met his eyes. 'I take your point,' I said levelly.

He measured me with his eyes. 'Right,' he said, and backed into his lair, shutting the door.

Charlie had driven out to Blagdon after the six a.m. briefing, but Joe had waited to keep me company. He was tactfully silent as we drove out of the city, and I was grateful. In spite of everything the SIO had said, I wished Clare were with me instead. Abstractedly I watched as Bristol passed us under the luminous dawn of an early autumn day. The streets were empty still: a beat policeman's dream.

To the unpractised eye, nothing around Harold Lomax's house looked out of the ordinary. No tell-tale line of unmarked grey or white Fords; no faces peering out of bushes. Nothing like that—of course not; my colleagues knew their business. Several men would be comfortably holed up with one of the curtain twitchers. ('Mind if we use your front room, love?' 'Oh, no, sergeant, do come in. Tea and toast all right for you while you're watching?') They were the lucky ones. A few others would be almost invisible in unmarked cars. One or two others would be crouching in the shadowed bushes, well out of sight of the house and driveway.

'What's on your agenda for the rest of the day?' Joe broke the hush as we circled the village looking for a place to park, some distance from the house.

Coughing, but hardly conscious of the noise of my own bark any more, I tried to remember the notes in my diary for this first day back in harness. 'It depends on what happens here. But I've got to spend some time with the systems supervisor and get myself reorientated. That's all.'

He guffawed. 'That's enough, surely!'

'How long will you be around, Joe?'

'Not long if my lads are doing their job properly up there, and even less time if they aren't. I'll see what develops here this morning, then I'll push off up the motorway.' He sighed. 'Wish I had wings some days.'

'Or a helicopter, at least.'

When we opened the car doors a stiff breeze off the Blagdon Lake struck us full in the face, but it was a warm wind. It carried with it a tang of autumn from the Mendip Hills beyond, and I remembered again my walk with Clare through the yellow woods.

I checked my watch. *Still very early*. I thought of Clare sleeping quietly under a soft duvet in London—or wherever she was. I wondered what she was dreaming about; whether she usually fell asleep straight away, or whether, like me, she

381

lay awake every night thinking of the times we'd had—and wanted—together. I even wondered whether she slept on her right side or her left, and whether she was curled up like a warm cat or stretched out in a gentle line like the sleeping Somerset hills. I sighed, then replayed yet again the conversation we'd had in the old cathedral.

That God who was Clare's friend and guardian—was he watching over us as we were to watch this darkened house? And was he also watching the six children where they slept—whether here or somewhere else? *Yes,* I thought, *that's what he's doing. What he was doing when Damian was dying, and just what he's doing now—watching over us all.* It was a new and happy thought.

I shook my mind clear; I would need full concentration.

We strolled nearer to the oak trees and the six-foot fence that obscured what was anyway an out-of-the-way house. Perhaps Joe understood, in spite of all the encouraging signs that we might be on the point of making an arrest, that I still felt detached and rather useless. At any rate, he turned to me as we were ducking into a clump of bushes that marked the corner of the fence and said, 'Listen, mate, Charlie's got this all wrapped up. It's only a matter of time. It doesn't matter whose case this is now—yours, or mine, or your guv'nor's, or Charlie's—'

He was right, of course. 'No,' I said quickly. 'All that matters is getting those kids out safe if they're still alive.'

He saw through my bluff to the disappointment that I hadn't been in on the last two weeks of the case. 'You're here now, at least.'

I grinned at him. 'Yeah, and all we have to do is watch the show unfold.'

'The kids'll be fine, I'm certain of it.'

I looked at Joe's freckled face in some amazement. 'Fancy yourself with the second sight, do you?'

'Not at all. But why wouldn't they be fine, now?'

Was Joe stupid, or just making some kind of sick joke? 'A thousand reasons!' I told him in an irritated whisper.

'Doesn't the good Lord himself watch out for the little ones, Frank? Sure he does!'

I opened my mouth, then shut it again. Who was I to argue with the combined faith of Joe, my mother, and Clare? I shrugged and settled into the crackling twigs and leaves to wait.

At the general briefing Charlie had told everyone he would signal for the men to close in as soon as he knew that I had arrived in Blagdon—unless something broke before I got there. Silently, training my eyes on the house and on the corner of the garden where I knew he was hiding, I thanked him for his understanding.

Sunshine angled palely through the tarnished oak leaves, and though I could still almost smell the Mendips, the Lomaxes' garden felt airless. The place wasn't sinister, just oppressive. *No wonder they burned so many electric lights,* I thought, remembering the reports that had come back from the first observations on the house. *And if they are in there— dear God!—what a gloomy place for kids to be holed up in for weeks on end!*

After a few minutes, a slight movement made me look through the criss-cross branches to the back of the garden. Charlie and two of the others had come out of hiding and were walking purposefully towards the side entrance of the house. Charlie touched his personal radio to indicate that he wanted to talk, and Joe and I stood and showed ourselves.

'We're off,' he whispered, when I reached him. His excitement was barely concealed. 'Just got a fascinating little message. Joe, your lads in Coventry are closing in on the young couple—the Bennetts. Looks like we'll sew it all up today.' He beckoned one of the other men. 'Come on, hop to it. Let's get this show on the road.'

Joe grinned at me. 'Better look out when Charlie starts chucking his great weight around.'

Charlie was not grinning. He caught Joe's eye again. 'That woman your chaps've had under obs—it turns out she's the daughter of this old couple here.'

Joe looked as if he wanted to clap or dance. 'So that's it! Oh, I'd give anything to see the end of the stake-out in both places at once.'

For an instant I smiled to myself, recalling Clare's mad philosophizing, the first time we'd met, about being in two places at once.

'Wake up, Frank—sir!' Charlie exclaimed. 'Can't stand here gabbing all day.'

I tried to pull myself together. 'Right, they're all yours.'

'You sure you want me to go in there? I thought you'd want to.'

I was tempted, but decided against taking over from Charlie. 'No, I've been out of this too long. Let's not stand on ceremony, for pete's sake. You do it. Joe and I'll be right behind you.' Why shouldn't Charlie enjoy the glory for a change?

We signalled to the others to cover every exit from the house, and Charlie lifted the brass knocker. It was polished brilliantly, I noticed absently.

I dropped my eyes to my watch. *Seven fifty-five,* I noted automatically. I could see the scene already—the formal words of arrest, the rush of anxiety and excitement as we pushed into the house for the first time . . . and, please God, found the children.

Nothing happened quite as we expected. From above the door came the groan of rending wood. A shower of large splinters burst onto our heads, followed by the sound of nails protesting their way through wooden planks. Not stopping to think, all of us leapt backwards. A metal chair leg protruded through a barred window above the door. Someone was pushing it, frantically driving it through the slats that had been nailed across the window.

'Stay where you are!' Charlie cautioned. 'This is the police.'

The chair leg stilled for an instant; then the frantic motions were renewed. A hand was visible now, wrestling the metal up and down in the cracks between the splintered wood.

'Wait,' I wanted to shout, 'you'll cut yourself to pieces.' But everything was happening too fast.

From just inside the door, I heard the voice of an old man cursing whoever was pushing out the window above. 'Quiet, you little fool! D'you want to be hurt?'

Then a woman's frantic crying. 'No, Harold, no—for God's sake, open this door. It's all up now.'

'Shut your face and stop that idiot upstairs. I'll deal with them out there.'

'Open this door,' Charlie shouted. 'Open it at once.'

'Don't you open it!' the old man's voice rose to a shrill squeak and cracked.

A struggle began behind the door: grunts and thumps—and Joe and I exchanged glances. It would be premature to break the lock.

Suddenly the door jerked half open, slammed again, then juddered open once again. Panting, gripping a pale floral dressing-gown around her bird-like body, her eyes staring frightened and enormous out of a white face, stood the old woman of the house. Behind her, staggering backwards into the twilight of oak shadows, her husband reeled and fell to the floor.

'Annie!' He was hysterical, cursing her, flailing on the polished floor. 'You pushed me! You—you old—' Joe passed me to help him up, and Charlie stepped forward to hold the door wide. 'Mr and Mrs Harold Lomax,' he began, 'I'm arresting you in connection with—'

Annie Lomax's already pale face turned ashen. She fell forwards suddenly, and just in time I caught her in my arms. My own breath was coming now in ragged coughs and gasps, but I led her gently to a wooden settle just inside the door. 'Get your head down over your knees,' I wheezed, taking her shoulders to steady her as she lolled like a rag doll against me. Half-winded myself, I wished I could join her on the settle.

Joe held Harold Lomax firmly by the arm, but the old man was no longer struggling. 'Heart attack, Frank?' he called to me anxiously.

385

I shook my head. 'No, Joe. Dead faint.' I was watching Mrs Lomax's face, and I ran my hand over her forehead; it was clammy to the touch. 'She'll be all right.'

A low moan escaped the old woman's throat. 'Oh—oh!'

Charlie tried again. 'Mr and Mrs Harold Lomax, I'm arresting you in connection with the abduction of six children in Bristol, Cheltenham, Birmingham, and Coventry. You're not obliged to say anything unless—'

A crash at the top of the stairs stopped him. A child's voice shrieked, and simultaneously the metal chair came through the window above the front door and smashed onto the step we had just crossed. The next minute, three children—a girl of about ten and two younger boys—hurtled down the stairs into the front hall. First down the stairs was the red-cheeked girl, a streak of blood running across her hand.

'I done it, mister!' she crowed. 'I broke that window for you. That's 'ow you knew we was in 'ere, right?' Hands on hips, her face radiating with triumph, the girl stood foursquare at the foot of the polished stairs. Our colleagues had gathered around the side entrance and now followed us into the hall. The two little boys halted by the newell posts, then cringed back behind the girl when they saw so many strange faces at once. The smaller boy began to weep.

'I want my mummy!' His thin voice rose to a broken wail of despair, and one of the WDCs went forward and knelt beside him. 'You're safe now, darling,' she said. 'We're going to get your mummy here just as fast as we can.'

The boy couldn't take in what she was saying, and three other children now straggled down the stairs: altogether three boys and three girls, some still in pyjamas, some halfdressed in spotless white vests and pants. Their hair was tousled from bed, their faces blank with surprise and bewilderment.

A wave of revulsion against the Lomaxes swept over me. The children were all safe, but what had they gone through in this strange place?

During the next few hours I might as well have been

suffering from jet-lag. I suppose because I was still not fully well, I was dogged by the persistent feeling that what was happening around me was happening to someone else: as if I was watching a film in which another man called Frank Bernard was going through the motions I knew I should be going through.

Yes, I was there when Joe told the Lomaxes to get their coats and asked them where the electricity could be switched off. I was there when Charlie enquired whether there were any pets to be fed, and when Annie Lomax handed him the keys of the house. I was there when the WDC came back down the stairs with all six children fully dressed and clutching an assortment of teddy bears and other cuddly toys. I was there when the Lomaxes were charged and remanded in custody. (They were refused bail, of course— 'Likely to abscond' the magistrate said simply in a court appearance that was over before we knew it. He recommended psychiatric reports, as well.)

I was there, too, later, when the children's parents were brought in, first from Bristol and Cheltenham, then two hours later from Birmingham and Coventry, with a police escort. There to witness the weeping, laughing reunion of six broken families. But I still didn't feel as if I were truly present.

When at last I had a few moments at the end of the day, I crept into my little box to see if I could reach Clare on the phone. I needed to 'touch base' with the normal world again.

The clock on the wall said 7.40, so I knew that if she'd returned from her mysterious trip, she'd also have left *Women Today* hours before.

I dialled the flat. 'Hello? Clare, it's Frank.'

'Sorry—she's gone away.' I didn't recognize the voice, but the woman went on helpfully, 'Frank Bernard, is it? Oh—this is Sandy, Clare's flatmate.'

My tired mind vaguely registered the name. 'D'you know when she'll be back?' I longed suddenly to hear her calm voice.

'She won't be coming back tonight, I'm afraid. Her boss sent her off with hardly any notice. She went on Saturday.'

That much, at least, I already knew. 'But—?'

'I got a message from one of her colleagues tonight that she wouldn't be back for a couple of days.'

So she's still away! I slumped into my chair. 'Oh, that's bad news. D'you know what's going on?'

'I thought *you* would know. Nina said her trip had to do with the child abduction cases she's been working on, and—'

'Well, that's news to me! So—is she in Coventry, then? Or Birmingham?'

'Yes, Coventry, I think—wait a minute.' Paper rustled by the phone. 'Nina gave me this number. Said Clare would probably be in a B & B. It was something to do with Coventry.'

My head was whirling now. The Lomaxes were safely in custody in Bristol and, according to the teleprinter, the Bennetts in Coventry. But we hadn't even issued a press release yet. How could anyone possibly have known at the weekend that Joe's colleagues in Coventry would be arresting someone there today?

'How–? When—' I started several questions, gave up, and thanked her. After I hung up, I realized I had forgotten to take down the number of the guest house where she was staying. I presumed it would be where she had stayed before, but I was too tired now to remember the name of the place. I would have to wait at least another day to talk to Clare.

I pulled on my raincoat. My in-tray was overflowing with message forms from the front office. Normally, even after a fifteen-hour day, I would have flicked through them. That night, however, I was too exhausted. I turned off the light and went straight down the stairs to drive home.

45

Apart from a long-haired girl walking her alsatian and a couple of small children innocently digging for clams at the end of their boardwalk, the wide beach was empty when Clare and Ed came over the rise of the dunes. A strong breeze off the blue-grey water hit them full in the face. Clare shivered and drew her sweater more closely around her; bare legs, tanned and comfortable the week before in the late August heat, now felt unseasonal and prickled with goose-pimples.

'I must be crazy,' she shouted over the breeze to Ed.

'You must be. We should have come up last weekend while it was still hot. But I can't stand to miss the last weekend of the summer.' The wind caught at his knitted cap, and he pulled it down over his ears.

They stepped off the end of the Williams' boardwalk and out onto the shifting dry sands at the top of the beach.

'In a few weeks you wouldn't recognize this place,' Ed said. 'It'll be choked with dead black seaweed and flotsam from the summer—from one end of the beach to the other. The dunes travel all over the place, so we have to dig out the boardwalk every spring. And I won't be fishing until then. The place gets empty—and lonely.'

Clare let her eyes drift to the slow-moving water. Since her night out with Pete on Wednesday she had found it hard to focus on anything; her mind stubbornly drifted back to the anguish of Friday, in the office. *I won't be here to see any of the winter here*, she answered Ed silently. *I'll be back in England—almost certainly without a job*. Depression settled over her like a cold cloak.

Ed caught her mood. 'Hey? Why the long face? You've been looking so down since Friday; I thought a trip here would lift you up.' Ed stopped, bent to drop his bait bag and tackle onto the sand, and put one hand under her chin. 'Come on, little cousin, don't look like that. Do me a favour—it's my last weekend before college, and I want to squeeze every last drop of fun out of it. Labor Day comes fast enough, heaven knows. Go on, Clare. If you won't tell what's bothering you, at least smile.'

She turned her head slightly so that he wouldn't see into her eyes. Ed saw too much already. She couldn't tell Rita or Jack or Marie—and least of all Ed—what had happened with Pete; or that she would be on a plane back to England by the middle of the week. *Not yet, but I'll have to tell them soon.*

She wanted to weep and was afraid Ed would see that, and that her summer-long resistance to his siege would crumble.

'I'm OK,' she muttered, swallowing hard.

He let her go, and they went on walking, now across the wet, ridged sand, towards the water's edge. 'Jack didn't think you were OK.'

'Oh, Jack's always analyzing everyone,' she said with a half laugh of dismissal. 'He really ought to leave his analysis for the state economy and for lobbying sessions with men like Julius McEnroe.' As soon as the name was out, she pursed her lips. *Why did I have to choose him as an example?* Her cheeks began to burn, so she stooped to pick up a marooned sand dollar, and to hide her face from Ed.

If Ed noticed her discomfort, he chose to ignore it. Hoisting his rod from one shoulder to the other, and shifting his bag to the other hand, he said cheerfully. 'Yeah, well, big brother's going to be down here a little later. Did he tell you?'

'No.' Still she didn't look at him.

'Said he'd come up this afternoon, later on, and give me the pleasure of helping him put up the storms. Big Brother is watching us! We'd better make the most of the day, don't you think?' He leered at her.

'Put up the storms?' she queried.

'The storm windows. Local hobby this weekend. You'll see them all going up. Hear them, too, if the wind changes.

Hammers going. Essential here if you want any glass in the windows come next spring.'

'Oh, I see.' It was a ritual quite foreign to her.

'It's part of what makes this weekend depressing for me. I remember when I was a little kid—'

She couldn't resist it. 'Oh, what an ancient old man, Ed!'

'No—I mean only about fifteen years or so—everyone used to have a big Labor Day cook-out on the top of the beach. Only after that would the storms go up. But these days everyone works so damn hard they're back in the city before the end of August.' His eyes swept the beach. 'Only the odd fishermen left.'

'Very odd.'

'Or kids digging in dry sand—*dry* sand, I ask you!—for clams.'

'Never mind,' Clare said vaguely, unable to identify with the grievance, 'we've got it almost to ourselves.'

'No one else I'd rather be with,' Ed said. He stopped again. 'In fact, come to think of it, you looking so cold and all, maybe we should just turn right around and wrap up in blankets and light a fire and drink cocoa for a while before Jack arrives. What d'you say?'

She sized him up. It sounded like a comforting way to spend her last Sunday in Massachusetts, but she knew he had other things on his mind besides wood fires and cocoa. 'I think that's a nutty idea,' she said lightly. 'You're a fisherman. Fishermen should fish.'

He scowled. 'All right. But don't say I didn't offer. Time flies, and offers like that may not come again.'

She forced a smile. 'Too bad, I guess. In any case, you'll never live it down if you don't come back with at least a couple of big bass for supper.'

'Don't get too cold, then, will you—or Mom will have me for bait. You gotta say if you want to go back up to the house.'

She nodded. 'All right. I wasn't going to sit meekly beside you anyway. I thought I'd walk a bit.'

'Good idea. You might frighten the fish away, anyhow.'

'Oh, thanks!'

'I'll catch the biggest bass ever, in your honour,' he said.

She set off away from him towards a line of rocks about half a mile distant. On the few weekends when she had come with her cousins to the family beach house, she had always meant to explore the rock pools. Now was her last chance. She walked fast, the wind beginning to warm her as her blood moved faster and the surge of exhilaration she always felt in sea-air rose up like the waves on her right.

The tide was still running out, the water far down from the end of the boardwalks where they had held a barbecue, weeks before, under the stars. She remembered the conversation: that first mention of the McEnroe family, the bitter-sweet memory—now grown double in her imagination—of Pete on the transatlantic flight. And now here she was, washed up on her incomprehensible emotions about the same man; as high up on the sands of her own uncertainties as the bladderwrack already left in untidy, scalloped lines by the real tide below. *How strange!* Her life had taken on an air of complete unreality: as empty and uncertain and hard to understand as the empty beach and the sudden change of season from summer to autumn. As empty and unreal as some of the surrealist paintings she had seen in a Boston gallery at one of the openings she had been obliged to attend a few weeks before. She felt bereft.

For a moment she tried to look at the beach, and even her own feelings, as she might have viewed them with the fresh eyes of the Clare Hogarth who had made a plane journey to Boston for the funeral of her Uncle Bert. *Have I always been as jaded as this?* she asked herself. *No—it was once I'd met him, that's when the troubles began.*

She tilted her face to the huge sky—slate-blue melting to a white haze on the horizon, and grey cloud massing in the north, beyond the rock pools. *I've lost my bearings since I got on that plane,* she thought. *I chose to leave God out of the equation. He won't want me now. I've flirted too long with Pete, and I'll be flirting with Ed again before the day's out, no doubt.*

And I should have expected every bit of grief I got. Bitterness twisted her mouth down at the corners. There was no internal voice to contradict that new conviction, and she shrugged hopelessly.

Below the rocks she paused and took off her sandals. The sand was now so cold that she felt it right to the marrow, but when she climbed onto the biggest rocks, carefully picking her way between sharp edges and weed-slippery planes, they were warm; in spite of the cold wind, sun was soaking the rocks.

She made her way around an outcrop and found a crevice shadowed by a wind-and-wave-worn pinnacle. The crevice was full to the brim with water, about two feet deep, and alive with small fish, clusters of bright weed, and barnacles that looked as dead and grey as the rocks themselves. She eased herself onto a shelf at the side of the crevice and found herself quite sheltered from the wind. From that perch, the beach was invisible—her only view the pool in front of her and the sky above. She huddled there, warm at last, and imagined Ed casting out into the surf, perhaps already with one fish in his basket; imagined Rita driving home from church, perhaps thinking about the last groups of summer tourists she would be guiding across the marina; imagined Jack leaving home after lunch, perhaps with Marie, to travel Route 128 and board up the windows for the winter.

Everything is ending.

Usually she thought more about beginnings than endings. She imagined Pete walking arm-in-arm with Bobbie out of the *Citizen* offices. Another ending—for her at least. *But not for them. I should have stayed out of that friendship.*

She gathered her rambling thoughts together; gathered her culottes about her legs, then climbed back down to her sandals.

Walking across the beach towards Ed, she saw that the light was changing. The haze of morning was giving way to a sharper, crisper sky. Deepening from soft grey to ice-blue, the tide was returning. The breeze, too, was changing, beginning to drop; and a few more beach walkers, shell collectors, clam diggers and fishermen were dotted across the sands. Ed himself had been joined by two older men. Where they stood with their backs to her they had left a confusion of tackle, overturned canvas stools and bait bags.

Ed turned briefly, saw her, and waved.

She knew she shouldn't shout in response, but mouthed 'hello' and waited a few yards behind them to watch.

Ed turned again, pointing to his basket. She moved forward quietly until she could see the contents, then smiled at him. Two large bass lay lifeless at the bottom, their mouths gaping, their gills wide open in a way that made Clare herself want to gasp.

One of the other fishermen was threading a thick piece of mackerel onto his hook. She watched him arch backwards slightly and cast it in an easy, accomplished movement. Then Ed's stance suddenly changed. His line went taut, the rod bowing towards the low waves on the shoreline. The other men turned to watch. Without hurrying, Ed waded a few steps forward, wound the reel a little, then waded farther. In the shallows, a few minutes later, he lifted a struggling silver-grey fish and turned again to smile at her. His face was full of sharp pride, but the bright trickle of red blood across his hands, and the painful gulping of the fish's frantic mouth and gills, hurt her.

'I got another bass,' he told her softly. He spoke barely above a whisper, the sound losing itself in the waves behind him.

'Yes,' she said, knowing how pleased he was, but unable to share in his joy.

'I'm quitting now,' he told her. 'Can you give me a hand?'

She went forward, glad to be distracted from the painful sight of the fish, and folded his stool. After that, she didn't know what to do and simply watched as he bagged the tackle, shouldered it again, and picked up his basket.

'I did well this morning,' he said, wanting her approval.

'Three fish!' She didn't know what else to say.

'That's enough. I'll clean them up, and we can cook them for supper.'

'Jack would like that,' she said. 'And your mother.'

'The heck with Jack and Mother,' he said tersely. 'I'm hoping we'll have some time on our own before Jack comes charging in.'

'Ed,' she said wearily, 'you don't give up, do you?'

'No. Come on, Clare! Give a guy a break, can't you? I'm off to college co-eds on Tuesday. So immature and boring!'

'Three fish is enough of a catch for one day, you said,' she laughed.

'We'll see,' he said grimly.

Back at the top end of the boardwalk they left the fishing gear on the patio. Clare brushed the sand off her legs and feet to go inside, while Ed peeled off his fishing-boots and emptied water at his feet with a childish delight as the drops splattered everywhere. The screen door banged behind Clare, and she suddenly felt tense again, wishing Jack or Marie had come straight to the beach with them, instead of going to church as usual. Or that she had stayed in town with Rita and gone to church as well.

'I think there's some lager in the fridge,' Ed called carelessly. 'And Mom said we'd find a few tomatoes out front, if you want to look. Is there any bread around, or cheese?'

Clare rummaged through cupboards and opened the refrigerator. Then she bent to look out of the front window to where a row of tomatoes grew in the sandy soil in the lee of the house. There was a line of lettuces, too, wilted by wind and sun, outgrowing their strength. She fled back outside to pick tomatoes just as Ed was coming in. He reeked of fish.

'What's the matter with you, Ms Nervous?' he jibed.

'You stink,' she said, not looking back.

'Thanks. I'll soon see about that.'

In the deep-freeze she found a loaf Rita must have made at the beginning of the summer and left for later. Wondering about hacking off the frozen bread, she remembered the microwave and then made sandwiches. All the time she stood in the kitchen with the scent of fresh tomatoes on her hands, cutting cheese and buttering thick wedges of bread she wasn't sure she would eat, she could hear water running in the upstairs shower. At last Ed came down, wearing a T-shirt, shorts, and flip-flops. He grinned wickedly. 'I'll bet you thought I'd pull some low trick on you like last time,' he said, 'and show up with nothing much on but a smile. But you've been looking as fit to bolt as Mother's pathetic lettuces, and I haven't the heart to pursue you too hotly. Poor Clare.'

Unaccountably, she felt her chin start to tremble. Pete swam up before her eyes, and she turned away before Ed could see the tears gathering. She didn't want his kind of sympathy. It was as dangerous as any such offering from Pete. Between her teeth, she bit out the word 'thanks', and began to pour lager into glasses with a shaking hand.

After Ed had gutted and cleaned the fish, they sat in the back of the house watching the wind ruffle the grains of sand on the crest of the dunes. Ed ate hugely, pleased with himself, chattering expansively about fishing and about his plans for the senior year at college. She let him talk on, determined not to falter in her guard, barely tasting the bread and tomatoes.

Outside the window, the sun disappeared behind a ridge of cloud. 'Time for blankets and cocoa,' Ed said. He put down his plate, leaned out of his chair, and took Clare's hand. 'Relax, sweetheart,' he said. 'I'm not going to eat you as well as all that. You look so wretched. Can't you trust your own cousin?'

She heard her own laughter wavering towards tears again and angrily drew a quick breath. 'Ed, I can't even trust myself these days, never mind *you*.'

He seemed to think it would be a better tactic to put distance between them, and he shuffled off to make cocoa in the kitchen. He went on shouting to her, however, through the open doorway. 'Your trouble is that you're too uptight about everything. Just relax, can't you, like I said? Life's too short.'

'No, you don't understand.'

'Probably not.' He gave a deep and exaggerated sigh that she could hear from twenty feet away. 'Fallen in love, have we?'

She knew he meant 'have you?' 'Yes, no. Well—I suppose I have.'

'It's that guy McEnroe, isn't it?'

She examined her fingernails, then looked back out of the window. 'What makes you think so?'

'The way you acted that night he picked you up.'

'Oh.'

'So transparent, Clare. The light could shine through you.'

'I doubt it.' She felt anything but full of light.

'He hurt you, did he?' Ed was standing beside her, holding out a cup of cocoa.

'No. I could have hurt myself, though. He's hurt someone else much more than he's hurt me.' She thought of Bobbie and sipped the hot drink. It was made just the way she liked it; he had not even had to ask her how she drank it. 'But Ed, I don't want to talk about it.'

'Are you sure?' He sat down close to her and left his mug on the floor. 'Listen, I know you think I'm just another wolf on the prowl, but what do I have to do to convince you that I care an awful lot about you?'

His look of appeal was hard to ignore, but she did so, resolutely returning her eyes to the dancing sand outside. 'The best way you can convince me that you care is to stop trying so hard all the time to make me like you—or want you. I won't be around much longer to talk to you, and I'd rather remember you in a different way.'

His face went cold. 'What d'you mean, "won't be around much longer"?'

She saw fear in his eyes. 'No, no. I'm not going to do myself in, silly. I mean, Ed, that I'm going back to England this week.'

'That's ridiculous.'

'No, it's true. I didn't mean to tell you, but, well, there you are.' She waved her free hand. 'My visa's no good if I'm working. And Pete McEnroe's interest in his society columnist has run out. Another fast-burning freelance bites the dust.'

Ed was frowning, pale with indignation and disbelief. 'He's scum, if that's the case.'

'Yes and no.' She looked at him with a challenge in her eyes. 'I wouldn't sleep my way to the top in that magazine of his. That was the real problem—nothing to do with visas or controversial columns I wrote—no matter what stories go flying round the city after I've left. You remember that.' She bit her lip, hearing the moral indignation in her own voice, and suddenly embarrassed because she knew she was trying to lie to herself as well as to Ed. She *would* have given herself to Pete that night—had he not fallen asleep so ignominiously. And she would have done it again—had he not humiliated her in front of Virginia Enright and Bobbie-Ann Rizzo. And if she hadn't realized that the only person Pete wanted— whether he knew it or not—was, in the end, Bobbie.

She swallowed all these thoughts with her tears and looked away again.

'Oh, Clare.' Ed was out of his seat and crouching by her knees with one arm round her waist and the fingers of one hand knotted through hers. 'I don't like to see you like this.' He was whispering now. She felt a tide of warmth roll through her body, felt herself sinking under it as she had almost sunk that night in Pete's apartment. *I can't go on saying "no" for the rest of my life,* she thought miserably. Yet she knew all Ed's posturing was just that: part of the same game Pete had played with her. And Ed was even more persistent— perhaps even more skilled—than Pete.

She pushed him away. 'Go on. You'll just make me feel worse.'

He reached up and stroked her hair. 'No, I'd like to make you feel better. Clare, I'm your cousin.'

'Precisely,' she said drily, gathering herself to jump past

him to the other side of the room. 'And I'm not into cradle-snatching.'

He snorted. 'Cradle-snatching! I'm only five years younger than you. What's five years, for goodness sake?'

'Nothing in ten years' time, maybe. Everything now. You're just an oversexed kid, Ed.'

He drew his hands away sharply and stood up, his back to her. He laughed scornfully. 'Well, lots of girls would fall right into my arms at this point, if that was what they thought. And I know what you'll say, "I'm not lots of girls." Yeah—as you said a minute ago, yeah, exactly. You're different, Clare.'

'Not at heart.' she shook her head unhappily. His kind of consolation would be so easy. 'But at least I know my limits when temptation's staring me in the face. You're making it so damn hard, Ed. *Please* give over.'

'Suit yourself, then.'

He moved away, and she heard the slam of the screen door and thumps out on the patio. She turned and ran to the door to see him jerking on the wet wading-boots.

He looked up angrily. 'Might as well go back down to the shore,' he snarled. 'When Jack and Marie show up, you can tell them where I am. I'll come right up and do the windows when they arrive.'

'But—'

He picked up his empty basket. 'You didn't want me, Clare.'

Tears spilled out before she could stop them. 'Oh, Ed, this is horrible. Friday was hell, and now this, and on Wednesday—' She broke down, hating herself and confused beyond all thinking.

Ed's face softened. He left the basket quietly outside the door, pulled off the boots without effort, and came back in. As soon as he had stepped through the door, he gathered her into his arms. She smelled soap and tomatoes on his skin, not fish now, and his arms around her neck were young and strong. He wiped her face with the edge of his shirt. 'Hush,' he murmured, speaking to her like a child. 'Hush, I'll kiss you better.'

He led her upstairs to the same view of the dunes, but higher up, where they could see also down to the beach and the tide rolling in again. Clare felt as if she had lost all will to do what was right, longing only for comfort, however short-lived. He took her top off first, stroking her back and murmuring words of comfort into her ears, and pulled her down onto a sofa bed near the window. Aching and still weeping, but without any of the shame she had felt with Pete, she let him touch her as he wished, kissing him hungrily. In turn his kisses sent fire through her whole body, and she arched towards him, crying as though the whole world were lost.

Somewhere, dimly, she became aware of a car's engine ceasing not far away, and of doors slamming and voices in the front of the house. Ed paused, pulling away from her, his eyes dilated and his mouth as red from kissing her as it had once been from eating strawberries, as in the photograph back in her flat in Ealing. 'Ed,' she moaned. 'What's going on?'

He was pulling on his T-shirt. 'Put your shirt back on,' he ordered. 'It's Jack—already. *Damn*.'

He left her on the sofa bed. She was still crying, now with bewilderment and frustration, shaking so much that she could hardly make her fingers fasten the two buttons at the top of her shirt. In a few more minutes, she realized, he would have had all her clothes in a heap on the floor.

She shuddered. *Is this your idea of a joke?* she asked the ceiling. 'Twice in one week! I don't believe it!'

'Clare? Clare, where are you?' Marie called.

She was filled with shame, suddenly, hearing the innocent gaiety of her cousin's voice from below. She rustled the curtains and felt her face turn scarlet. 'I'm—I'm just up here.' She looked frantically at the windows. 'Ed asked me to take down the curtains so we could—'

Her ridiculous excuses were lost on Marie, who bumped cheerfully up the stairs and apparently hadn't heard a word of her reply. 'Hi!' she called. 'Looking at the view? Isn't it great?'

She turned away gratefully and stared blindly at the beach again. 'Yes, great.'

Marie came and stood beside her. She sighed. 'I wish we didn't have to shut this up for the winter. I wish it was summer here for ever. It's been wonderful having you here and at home this year.'

Clare would usually have turned and hugged her, but for the moment it was all she could do to mutter something inane and walk slowly down the stairs to Jack and Ed.

Jack stared at the runnels of tears on her face but said nothing untoward. 'Hi, Clare. Ed's gone out front to open up the store closet. Are you girls going to help?'

'Sure,' said Marie.

Clare couldn't look at Jack. 'Yes,' she said quickly. 'Yes, of course.' In a daze, she followed him outside. Nothing seemed real.

'We'll have to go fast, anyhow,' Jack said as they started heaving storm windows around to their respective places. 'By the way, you got a call, Clare, after we came back from church.'

'Oh, yes?'

'Senator McEnroe, would you believe,' Marie piped excitedly. 'Said he had to speak to you personally.'

Jack looked hard at her again. 'Is it about that column, Clare?'

She turned away from him to lift one side of a window Marie had begun to lift on her own. 'That's probably the least of my problems,' she said.

'You are being cryptic!'

'No, Jack,' she said wearily, throwing a glance at Ed to see how he was coping. 'Just careful. A lot's changed in the last few days.'

'Mom and I noticed that,' Jack answered, also glancing at Ed.

'Oh, leave her,' Ed growled.

Jack narrowed his eyes at Ed. 'Anyhow, Clare,' he said, 'you've got to ring the senator as soon as we get back. I told him I'd come get you earlier than we'd planned, and that seemed to appease him. Said he'd probably drop by on his way back from church this evening if he didn't see you sooner.'

The four of them worked mechanically. Even without any knowledge of this annual beach ritual, Clare was glad of the unthinking sweat of the job. One by one the windows were heaved up, wedged into place, and the catches tightened or banged in. All the time they worked, she turned over in her mind the particular words Jack had chosen. 'Ring the senator as soon as we get back . . . that seemed to appease him . . . if he didn't see you sooner.' A sick feeling squeezed at her stomach, made worse every time she looked at Ed and saw the same look of frustration and desire on his face as she felt herself—in spite of herself.

They drove back to Bedford as they had travelled north—in two separate cars. To Ed's annoyance, Clare elected to travel with Jack, leaving Marie to keep Ed company; she diverted Ed by telling him under her breath as they separated outside the locked beach house that she would tell Jack about her return to England. Then they went to their respective cars, Ed with a glum, angry face, but Marie blithely unaware of any heartache.

Rita was heating coals on the barbecue when they drove in. Clare watched Ed swing his basket of fish out of the car and drop it onto the patio beside her with a grin. She saw Rita hug him; then he said something to his mother that she couldn't hear, threw a look at her over his shoulder, and disappeared up the stairs towards his room. She felt like an intruder, even in the house that had made her welcome for so long.

'You'd better call Senator McEnroe,' Jack reminded her. He followed her eyes to where Ed was turning at the top of the stairs.

'Yes,' she said vaguely, taking the note from him with the number on it. 'Thanks.'

'Clare—you look anything but happy. Is there anything I can do—or Mom?'

She hadn't said a word to Jack about going back to England, after all. 'Yes, there is. Just don't ask too many questions.' Her face crumpled. 'Sorry. I don't feel like talking.' And she fled up to her own room.

A few minutes later she heard a light tapping on her door. Thinking it must be Ed, she called churlishly, 'Go away.'

'Clare, it's me. Rita.' Her aunt's voice was uncertain.

She got off the bed and wiped uselessly at her face. Opening the door, she said, 'Sorry. I'm a wreck.'

Without an invitation, Rita sat down on the edge of the bed. 'No you're not. You've just had a long few days and too much pressure at work, for all I can see. And now Mr McEnroe . . .'

'That's only a fraction of it,' Clare said. She thought she would go mad if she heard the name of McEnroe again.

'Has Ed been bothering you again?' Rita asked sharply. 'If he has, I've told him—'

'No,' Clare lied. 'He's never been more of a bother to me than I have to him.' *Well, that's true enough, at least,* she told herself.

This seemed to amuse her aunt. Rita looked at her with a wry smile. 'He's always had a thing about you, you know. Since you were last here.'

She followed a swirl in the design of the carpet with her eye. 'Yes, I've noticed. But, to be honest, Rita, I've been much more bothered by—' She stopped. *No, I can't dump on Pete like that. It was as much my fault as his.*

Rita's mind was evidently travelling in other directions altogether. 'Is it still some problem with your passport or something? You mentioned it a while ago, and I'd forgotten.'

'Sorry.' Clare wiped her face again. 'Maybe I can talk more when I've spoken to the senator.'

Rita stood up. 'Have you phoned him yet?'

She shook her head unhappily. 'No.'

'You do that, then. Use the phone in my room if you like.' She gave Clare a bright smile. 'Listen, try to get that chin up. I want to enjoy tomorrow, honey. One of the few days of total

403

rest around here. It seemed like a good idea to barbecue Ed's fish tonight. Whatever your problems are, d'you reckon you can put them on the shelf for a few hours?'

It was hard not to say yes to an appeal so simple and direct. She nodded. 'Yes. Sorry. No more wet weekends. I promise.'

The McEnroe phone rang ten times. She knew the senator lived only ten or twenty blocks away, in a wooded part of suburbia; could still picture quite clearly the wide lawns, the palatial rugs inside the house . . . and the fateful swimming-pool. But no one lifted the receiver.

She dialled again, letting it ring even longer. At last a woman's voice answered. 'The McEnroes' residence.'

Clare didn't recognize the woman—certainly not Marianne. 'I'd like to speak to Mr McEnroe,' she said. 'He left a message for me. I'm Clare Hogarth.' She paused, adding stupidly, 'from England.'

'Oh,' the voice returned blankly. 'Well I'll tell him. They're all at church.'

'And you are—?'

'Mrs McEnroe's housekeeper.'

'Ah—thanks.' She hung up. She had left the call too late. Now the senator would—if he carried out his promise (or was it a threat?) come past the Williams' house on his way home. She trembled inwardly.

She went out onto the landing and listened at the top of the stairs. From the back of the house she could hear her cousins talking in low voices to Rita out on the patio. Ed was downstairs with the rest of the family now; she wouldn't have to face him alone. Then, from the front of the house, she heard a large vehicle of some kind crunch over the gravel and stop nearby.

She rushed headlong down the stairs, eager to get it over with . . . to hear whatever the man had to say . . . without the rest of the family in attendance. She opened the front door and waited as one door of the Oldsmobile opened. Through the windows of the car she could see another man—vaguely familiar—in the front passenger seat. Younger than the senator, he gave her a half smile and turned to speak to the others in the back of the car. Their faces were shadowed from her view, but she thought she might recognize other members of the McEnroe family from Marianne's many photographs.

The senator strode towards her. His neutral face gave nothing away. 'May I come in?' he asked, offering her his large hand. 'It's just for a moment. I don't want to spoil your family weekend.'

She stood aside to let him pass. 'Yes, come into the dining-room,' she said. 'This way.'

They sat facing each other across the table. 'One way and another,' McEnroe began, 'I'm not bringing good news. But it's probably not what you're expecting, my dear.' He looked at her with an expression she interpreted as pity. 'In case you're thinking I've come to tear you apart for the piece about my daughter, God rest her, you're wrong. I'm through with all that already—had my say to Pete before.'

Clare swallowed. The old man's piercing blue eyes seemed to bore into her; but they had none of the hardness of his nephew's eyes, and she took a quick breath to steady herself. 'Thank you,' she murmured, though not quite sure what she was thanking him for.

'I don't care what Pete said to you,' he went on. 'And, yes, you needn't think I don't know he's been giving you a hard time—however you look at it—' The senator's eyes narrowed. 'The whole family knows Pete well. We love him, but we don't have too many illusions about him. Anyhow . . . I'm not here to rake you over the coals for any copy you've written or to read you a lecture about messing with Pete.' His look absorbed her stricken face. 'It seems as if you've had enough grief already. No, it's what I thought would happen. And I'm very sorry for you, honey. Very sorry.'

From anyone else, the words might have sounded patronizing, but the old man spoke gently, and his eyes were full of fatherly concern. 'Sorry about what?' she said weakly.

He looked away from her to a basket of flowers on the

dresser by the window. 'That you've been caught in a nasty little bureaucratic game. And that you weren't in a position to follow up my advice about arranging your papers. I've come to warn you, in fact, that the district attorney or—more likely—the US Immigration and Naturalization folk—will be serving you with a voluntary departure notice within the week.' He cleared his throat. 'That's a polite way of saying that the INS will throw you out of the country if you don't leave of your own free will by the date they specify. I wanted to warn you in advance. My son and daughter-in-law think I'm out of my tree to come tell you. Is that the expression these days?' His bushy eyebrows quirked. 'That's them out in the car now, with the kids—here for the weekend.' He jabbed a thumb over his shoulder in the general direction of the Oldsmobile. 'Don, my son, was all for having you thrown on the next plane home tomorrow, Labor day or not. My daughter-in-law, too—Eleanor's best friend all those years ago. But I calmed them down.'

Am I supposed to be reassured? She didn't know what to say, and looked down at the polished grain of the table.

'You're a naive young woman, Clare Hogarth,' McEnroe pursued. 'Pete was well aware of his power to intervene on your behalf and get you the right visa. He could have filed a third or sixth preference petition on your behalf, and your immigration status could have been adjusted that way. Pete knew that, but it's too late now.'

She struggled to keep up with the legal language and gave up, shrugging helplessly.

'You'd better leave others to fight the ugly battles here.'

She wondered suddenly if he could see through her and read all the ugliness in her heart after the last few days. She shook her head wordlessly.

'Bobbie-Ann Rizzo was talking to me after church just now.'

Her head came up. 'Yes?' She knew she sounded querulous, and she remembered with anguish the sight of Bobbie running in tears down the corridor, crying because she had speculated about the Rizzo family's connections with the Mafia.

'Bobbie said there was a threat on all your lives—from the Mafia. Pete hadn't told me. I'm going over to see him tonight after I drop the family off.'

She waited, wondering where the words were going, not wanting to betray even more of her own part in the events of the last week at *Citizen*, and lose the good opinion of a man she respected and who seemed—however surprisingly—to like her.

'I understand it was because of a column you wrote. So Bobbie said.'

And what else did she say? Clare wondered bitterly, looking at the same vase of flowers. 'Yes,' she said numbly.

'Pete wouldn't have told me anything on Friday, I guess. I was too mad at him for printing that other column you wrote.'

'I thought you were,' she said quickly, almost relieved that he was at last owning his full feelings.

But he brushed her away with a wave of his hand. 'No. That's not the point any more,' he said. 'The grievance there was between me and Pete. He—not his staff, no matter what he lets them think—and he alone controls what goes in that magazine of his. I had my say in private to him, and there's an end of it—though I'll certainly support him over this Mafia business. Meanwhile, honey, I've got no quarrel with you.' His eyes crinkled at the corners. 'Don't you remember what I said that afternoon?'

Her mind was in overdrive after the emotional tangle of the day. 'What, specifically?' she asked, dreading the answer.

'Love is always stronger than hate,' he said gently. He leaned back and looked down at his hands. 'It took an old man many years to learn that. Too late for my daughter, I'm afraid. But God's ways aren't ours.'

A lump grew in Clare's throat. 'That's for sure,' she said unsteadily.

'You go home,' he said. 'You don't belong here, in my opinion. Leave Pete to someone else—Bobbie if she's fool enough.' He stood up. 'The Mafia—well, we'll take that seriously, of course, and I'll get the FBI onto that threat letter when I get my hands on it. Meanwhile, if you ever come back here—' He winked at her. '—with the right papers, of course, I hope you'll look me up. I like you. And my daughter-in-law Maggie—she would have liked you—whatever she thinks now.'

Clare watched him walk away from the front door towards the car. A small woman stood by an open back door of the car and smiled at McEnroe but seemed not to notice Clare at all. Watching them crowded together—even in the big car—she felt an ache of something like homesickness. Julius McEnroe was right. She didn't belong in Boston.

46

When Clare woke, her body felt heavy, her mind drugged by a deep sleep. She lay unmoving for a moment, savouring the luxurious warmth of the bed, then turned over in a rush as she remembered where she was.

Monday! I've got to get over to Rosemount Road. She pushed her hair out of her eyes and sat up in a daze. With a groan she registered the time: seven forty-five.

From a small booth in the front hall of the guest house she telephoned *Women Today* to leave a message describing her progress on the story. *Progress!* she thought irritably. *Hardly the word for it!* The thought of a third day outside the Bennetts' house was almost more than she could bear, and the alluring smells of a rich breakfast tempted her to further delay in the dining-room. Resolutely, she turned her back on them and swung out of the front door to hail a taxi.

Deposited at the foot of the hill, she walked past the corner shops towards the Bennetts' house. *What if there's still no arrest today?* she wondered. How long would Andy expect her to wait for the story? *Until there's snow on the ground?* She smiled— almost giggled—relieved at her own change of attitude.

It was almost nine o'clock when she turned the curve below the Bennetts' and saw a roadblock of police vans. A crowd had gathered outside the house, and a man with a loud-hailer was warning everyone to keep back. Cars that had queued impatiently behind the roadblock were directed back along another route; they were sweeping in U-turns right in front of Clare as she came within sight of the house. On the pavement a local television crew was filming everything, reporters swarming like flies round a dead cat. Suddenly, she felt sickened.

She pushed forward, her heartbeat picking up in her

determination to discover what had happened. For a moment a chill passed over her. What if this house had nothing whatever to do with the child abductions and she had instead been watching the conclusion of another case altogether? What if someone had been murdered—one of the children, or the woman who had been weeping?

She pushed the fears away. *Dear God,* she thought breathlessly, *whatever's happened here this morning, please keep those kids safe.* She wanted to pray for the Bennetts too, but the prayer wouldn't frame itself in her mind; she felt certain only that God loved them and that they needed God's love—as she did herself.

'Can't go in there, Miss,' a constable told her. 'Won't be long now.'

'Press,' she hissed, edging forward.

'That's what they all say.'

She fumbled for her card but couldn't find it. 'Press,' she repeated. 'Please, I need to get through.'

'You were up here last night, weren't you?'

'Yes.'

'I saw you.' He swept his hand over the crowd. 'You responsible for bringing this lot down on us?'

She shrank back. 'No! I told one of your colleagues, I wouldn't dream of blowing the whistle on you.'

The constable looked at her contemptuously. 'Just wanted your scoop, did you?'

She saw that it was fruitless to speak to him. 'Excuse me, please.'

Backing away from him, she skirted the crowd until he could see her no longer. She would try to approach the house from the other side.

A babble of Coventry voices washed around her.

'Always thought there was something funny about 'em.'

'Mrs Smith said she heard her crying half the night some nights.'

Heads nodded knowingly. 'No children, poor girl.'

' "Poor girl" nothing,' a louder, more censorious voice

intervened. 'Children or not—it doesn't entitle you to go kidnapping other people's kids for your own. Wicked, I call it.'

A scuffle on the doorstep drew the eyes of the crowd. The front door had opened and was filled now by one female and two male detectives. Between them, bowed down and with their faces hidden by blankets, two people were nudged forward. Clare saw the glint of metal handcuffs on their wrists.

No children. No children. The words echoed in her head like a knell. She longed to see the Bennetts' faces, forgetting for a moment the anguish of the parents she had interviewed in Bristol and Coventry. There was another story here, surely: the pain of the childless.

Suddenly a soft swishing sound sent her spinning round. Someone at the back of the crowd had thrown a tomato. It splattered on the wall of the house, the pulp oozing red onto the step. Another tomato followed it, and Clare turned to see a woman not far behind her whose face was suffused with blood.

'Scum!' the woman was shouting. 'Dirty scumbags!'

Several detectives made a dive for the heckler and, when Clare turned again, the Bennetts had been led away from the house towards one of the white vans waiting in the road.

Two men in the crowd took up a chant. 'Where are the kids? Bring out the kids!'

Soon everyone had joined in. Yes, she thought, where *are* the children? The same shiver of apprehension passed over her, intensified as she watched one detective pulling the Bennetts' front door firmly shut.

No children, she repeated to herself. *And no one else's children, either. Then what's happened to them?*

A tall woman fought her way towards the house and tried to wrest the blankets from the Bennetts' heads.

'That's the auntie,' someone near her said, clucking in sympathy.

'Whose auntie?'

411

'You know—auntie of the one that went missing in June. Enough to make you weep! If I was auntie or mother to that child, I'd scratch their eyes out.'

'No,' Clare said vehemently, hardly thinking what she was saying.

The two women turned on her. 'No?' One of them swore at her. 'Oh, listen to her! Who d'you think you are, then? Mrs Bennett's sister, are you?' The voice rose to a venomous shriek.

Blushing in indignation and bewilderment, Clare held her opponent's eyes steady. 'No.' A thousand other answers clamoured in her brain: that she was from the press; that there was always another side to the story; that if the Bennetts had taken the children they would be punished enough without all this public castigation now. But the look of hatred on the faces of those standing near took her quite by surprise, as if all Coventry's anguish over the missing children was to be projected against her—for a mere glimmer of compassion for the Bennetts. She stammered, 'But no one knows what the Bennetts did or didn't do. We can't—'

A roar of fury drowned her, and one of the women swung a punch at her that sent her notepad flying. Another shoved her hard against the people behind her. She fell backwards with a grunt, one of her shoes flying off and disappearing into the mêlée.

Somewhere in the distance, a male voice boomed instructions to everyone to move aside and return home. Tomatoes and oranges rained heedlessly down from the back of the crowd.

Half-winded, she scrambled to her feet, her face still red with shock. She knew she would have defended the children just as fiercely as she now felt the need to champion the doubtful cause of the Bennetts in a mob apparently determined to mete out judgement before any charge was made or trial held.

Two tall men elbowed through the crowd and grabbed her.

She recognized one of them as the detective constable who had spoken to her on the first night of their vigil.

Her emotions were strung so tight that she began to laugh uncontrollably. *The police.* Everything seemed funny, suddenly: even the bumping of her own feet over the kerb as they pulled her towards the now-familiar unmarked Sierra; even her own laughing protests that she'd walk peacefully if they'd let her.

Beside the police car, one constable abruptly jerked her round to face him. 'You're nicked!' he said. Gasping for breath, she still wanted to laugh, noticing irrelevantly that he was slightly shorter than she was.

His chest was heaving, but she began to feel utterly calm; detachment set in.

'This way,' he said gruffly, not releasing her arm.

She realized dully that her arms were bruised where they had held her and that her shoeless foot was cut. Then she saw one of the white vans draw up behind the Sierra. *Any minute now,* she thought, *I'll wake up . . . But what if I were Mrs Bennett?* She started to laugh again, but this time she was shaking, as well.

'Show me your teeth so I can hit 'em,' someone called harshly to her.

The constable who held her swung her round again, this time to face a police photographer. 'Go on,' he said abruptly, 'he wants your picture. Smile for the bobbie with the polaroid, will you?'

Instinctively she grimaced and went to cover her face, but they took her photo anyway, pinning her hands behind her back.

'Name?' someone snapped.

'Clare Hogarth,' she said dully, then watched as he wrote her name and the time on the back of the picture. Beside the time, he scrawled 'obstruction'.

Then, before she could think what was happening, she found herself bundled without ceremony into one of the tiny cells inside a van.

She stared at the cell wall in disbelief. *What have I done?*

Someone in the cell beside hers began banging on the wall and crying out in protest, but she was too dazed to do anything except crouch against the wall and try to remember how she had got there.

The banging from next door ceased a few minutes later when the van's engine roared to life. Then the vehicle bounced and bumped its way over the pot-holes, carrying her in some unknown direction. The constable's sharp words, 'You've been nicked', circled dizzily in her head. 'I've been arrested,' she thought incredulously, wanting to laugh again.

She was still smiling to herself (*I'm going mad as well*, she thought) when the constable took her out of the van and led her into a cramped room where a tall police sergeant stood behind a desk.

'The charge room is where you meet god with the stripes on,' the constable hissed to her.

She tried to concentrate on what she would say. Nothing seemed funny now.

She was nudged forward to stand in front of the custody sergeant and caught her breath in anticipation of her chance to explain that—of course—she was meant to be outside that house and had gone with no intention whatever of obstructing anyone.

But they gave her no time to explain anything. 'I was on duty at the surveillance on Rosemount Road,' the detective constable began stiffly. 'Things were getting a bit out of hand. This young lady, Miss Clare Hogarth, was on the fringe of the crowd, and people began lobbing things around when the suspects were being escorted from their residence. The crowd wasn't dispersing as instructed. Miss Hogarth was shouting and seemed to be in a spot of bother with some of the other bystanders. I arrested her to get her out of the way and allow the other officers to get through. It was quite a crush, sarge.' He cleared his throat.

Clare heard anxiety in his voice. She opened her mouth to

tell them that she was with the press, but the sergeant was saying something now, and she bit her lip, waiting for another chance.

'Miss Clare Hogarth—' The sergeant's voice was formal, clear even over the hubbub of other voices in the room. 'You have been arrested in connection with obstructing a police officer. You are not obliged to say anything unless you wish to do so, but what you say may be given in evidence.'

She listened as if transfixed, then swallowed, her eyes darting uncomfortably from one man to the other. In them she saw no answering spark of pity or understanding. They made her feel like a criminal. *Of course I'm no criminal,* she said to herself.

'You have a right to have a solicitor present, if you wish,' the sergeant went on.

She almost laughed again, until she saw the severity of his face and reminded herself afresh that an arrest was serious. She shook her head quickly and murmured, 'No, thank you. I don't think that'll be necessary.'

'Then is there someone we should inform about your arrest?'

She fumbled in her handbag, forgetting for a moment that her notepad still lay on the pavement outside the Bennetts' house.

'My boss—I'm with the press,' she answered, but she knew her voice sounded unconvincing.

The sergeant looked sceptical. 'The press, eh?' He exchanged glances with the officer beside her. 'What newspaper?'

'Not a newspaper, but—'

'Then?'

'A magazine.' His laconic way of questioning intimidated her, and she found it hard to speak at all.

'Which magazine, Miss Hogarth?' The sergeant's voice made a mockery of patience, and Clare cringed. His disbelief was apparent in the twisted lines at the corner of his mouth.

'*Women Today,*' she gulped. Then inspiration struck. 'I've

415

got my—my press card . . .' She searched frantically for it and felt their eyes burning into her as she delved into her handbag. *The press card was not in her purse.* She remembered with dismay that she had left it by the bed at the guest house, and she groaned, 'I can't find the card.' She wondered stupidly if she should add 'sir'.

'Your boss will vouch for you,' the sergeant said, 'will he? That he sent you to cover this surveillance—er, these *arrests?* At least, he'd like to be informed—is that right?'

'Yes, I'm sure he would,' she answered. *And Frank would vouch for me, too,* she thought, *but I can't possibly drag him into this!*

'Your boss'll be there now?' the sergeant asked.

'Yes.' But she shook her head miserably. 'But—

The sergeant gave her a narrow look. 'You want us to inform someone else, after all, of your own arrest?'

It was useless to wish that Joe Cafferty could step through the door and come to her rescue; he was away. Instead, Frank's face returned immediately into mind. 'My friend— I have a friend down in Bristol who's a detective inspector.' She spoke quietly, but her words seemed to electrify the listeners. Both leaned towards her simultaneously. 'He can't vouch for the work I was asked to do today, but he can vouch for me as a person and for the job I do. I'd like him to know what's happened.'

'Your *friend* in Bristol—his name?' the sergeant rapped out. His expression was sarcastic.

'Detective Inspector Frank Bernard.' Even saying his name brought a little comfort to her.

The sergeant and constable exchanged glances. 'Which force—Avon and Somerset?'

'Yes, that's right.'

'Look him up in the almanac, will you Jarvis?' the sergeant said without removing his eyes from Clare's face. 'The jailer will ring him later for you. We're too busy just now, I'm afraid.'

'Do you understand why I arrested you?' Constable Jarvis

asked her.

The words 'obstructing a police officer' echoed in her brain, but for the moment they meant little. 'Not fully,' she said.

'We'll outline it for you, then,' the sergeant said, his voice soft but sneering. 'There was a police surveillance of a house in Rosemount Road, Coventry, was there not, Miss Hogarth?'

It sounded like a summary, but she felt suddenly that it was more like a trap. 'Yes,' she said steadily. 'And there was a big crowd of onlookers and other members of the press.'

The sergeant leaned forward. 'You were fighting with others in the crowd, were you, Miss Hogarth?'

'No.' She couldn't forget the shock of being punched and pushed.

'But you were shouting, weren't you?' the constable pursued. 'And blocking my colleagues' passage as they brought out the suspects?'

She flushed. The same indignation she had felt before rose to her face. She hated the way she was being bullied. 'Yes, along with a hundred other people.' What point was there in explaining that she had never meant to stand in anyone's way—just to observe and get her story.

'Well.' The custody sergeant's mouth twisted at the corners. 'Well, we do want to keep you out of harm's way when there's a scrimmage going on, don't we?' He stamped a piece of paper in front of him with the words 'detention authorized'. 'You'd better put all your things on the counter for inspection, I think.'

Another surge of resentment rose in her, but she did as she was told.

'Your handbag, please. Shoes. Pens—anything.' She emptied everything onto the counter. A tube of lipstick rolled onto the floor and was retrieved. They separated her nail file, a pen, her money and credit cards from her other belongings and dropped them into a bag with her remaining shoe.

'Only one shoe?' the sergeant asked quizzically. He shot a

glance at Constable Jarvis, then looked back at her again. 'Lost your shoe, have you?'

'Yes,' she said bitterly.

'Now we'll do a routine body search, Miss Hogarth.'

A woman police officer lightly ran her hands over her. Clare felt her face turning pink again and became more and more miserable.

'Sign here,' the sergeant said harshly, pushing a form towards her on which he had listed all her property. 'These things'll be kept safe for you while you're here.' He sealed the bag and passed it to another officer. 'You'll go down with the jailer now.'

As she was brought through the door, she heard scuffles behind her and caught a glimpse of the Bennetts being dragged into the charge room by two other plain clothes men. Then she was led along a narrow corridor and locked in a dimly lit cell. It struck her suddenly that she had no idea where she was—or for how long she would be there.

'What next?' she wanted to ask, staring at the pitted wall as her eyes grew accustomed to the dinginess around her. The only adornments in the small room were black graffiti on the shiny cream-coloured walls and a stained blanket and mattress that masqueraded as a bed. In one corner stood a steel toilet bowl with half a wooden seat on it and a roll of what looked like school tracing paper hanging beside it.

She slumped onto the bed and looked down at her feet resting on the dusty floor. Where her bare left foot touched the floor she felt the stickiness of blood. She mopped at the small cut with the hem of her skirt, then thought of Andy's commission and groaned. She could lose her job for this. *But why?* she demanded of herself. *All I did was witness an arrest— as part of my job.* Then another internal voice answered her, *Ah, but how can I say I wasn't obstructing the police? I wasn't sent to be arrested myself.*

She lay back, then, and gave up trying to puzzle everything out. *The children,* she thought. *What about them?* Her own discomfort meant nothing in comparison.

47

Sleep. I was becoming obsessed with it again, but every time I lay down to rest (a snatched moment here and there between interviews), my head swarmed like a hive of bees. Since Monday morning I had been running on coffee and the exhilaration of the arrests in Bristol and Coventry, and I knew I couldn't go on much longer. A foggy sensation like jet-lag, and the rasping cough, wouldn't leave me alone. Even after a few hours' broken sleep on Monday night I still felt dazed; the novelty of being back in my own bed in Bristol had worn off fast.

Nor was there was time to think about sleep on Tuesday. Now that the children's parents had all been brought to Bristol and the police surgeon had examined the children, Charlie and I were fully taken up with interviewing the Lomaxes, briefing the office manager so that the H.O.L.M.E.S. could be updated, and working with the press office on a formal press release.

Early on Tuesday, I found the typed press release on my desk on top of an ever-growing pile of message forms.

> Four people have been detained in connection with a series of child abductions and are at this moment being questioned by officers of this and other forces. They will appear before the Bristol magistrates' court this afternoon charged with offences in connection with their detention. At this time the children involved have been medically examined and found to be physically unharmed. They have been reunited with their parents.

I stared at the neat type on the release and thought how straightforward it all sounded. Words like 'detained',

419

'appeared', and 'charged' reduced a complicated and emotional process to something flat and painless. I sighed. Unless the governor had any complaints, the statement would go out as written anyway. We'd be besieged by the press soon enough. *The press.* I thought of Clare, glanced at the telephone, and contemplated calling her. Had she managed to get more of her story in Coventry? I was longing to talk to her, but I knew it would be unprofessional—until the press release went out—to ring her and pass on the extra news of our arrests in Blagdon. In any case, she worked for a magazine, not a daily paper; and her own story would (as I now knew from personal experience) no doubt be written and rewritten several times before finally appearing in print weeks later. I remembered, too, Bill's sobering words: 'Try to keep business and pleasure apart, will you?'

I knew I should tackle the messages first, but Charlie hadn't arrived yet to give me a hand, so I leafed through them quickly, planning to pend all but the most essential. One immediately stopped me: from the jailer of one of the Coventry stations. I stared at it, completely unable to take in the words; Clare Hogarth had been arrested on Rosemount Road in Coventry for obstructing police officers. *Arrested!* Sweat broke out over my whole body, and inwardly I cursed the dogged, still-wagging tail of this pneumonia. Angrily, I pushed the paper away. *Why didn't anyone tell me before?* The answer, I realized, was all too obvious; yesterday had been a maelstrom of activity. A message from a jailer in Coventry, apparently quite unconnected with the abduction cases, was hardly likely to warrant my attention—or so the downstairs office staff must have concluded, especially as a subsequent message form reported that she had been freed without charge.

Arrested! my tired mind bleated at me again. I felt stupid. I wanted to ring Clare immediately and find out what was going on. Or was this all some crazy hoax cooked up by Sally? I wouldn't have put it past her ... Well, I would have to wait until later to find out. I was frustrated with myself for not recording the telephone number of the place where she was staying. *Nothing I can do now, I suppose, except get on with gathering the evidence on the case.*

After stopping at the press officer's desk, I plodded round to the incident room. The smoke in the room might not have been as thick as in Coventry, but it was enough to start me coughing again.

Charlie met me just as I was resigning myself to sitting down for a few minutes with the systems supervisor in front of the H.O.L.M.E.S. terminal. 'Frank! You ought to get a medal for being here on time this morning,' he said.

'Really? You must be joking! I was in *early!* And this is the stuff of real detective life, I thought.'

He looked at me with a frown of concentrated observation, and I knew he would make a pronouncement. He tutted at me. 'You still don't look well.'

'Never felt better in my life.'

'Hung over, then.'

'I wish.'

'Late night on the tiles with Clare? Or is it someone else already?'

'Don't be so nosy.'

'It's my job to be nosy.'

'She's away, anyway.'

'Is she indeed!'

I thought to myself that Charlie was getting bossy in his old age. Or perhaps it was that, in my absence, he and the office manager had run the show very nicely, thank you, without Frank Bernard. I sat down, so I wouldn't have to look him straight in the eye. 'The heck with it, Frank, you *do* look ill.'

I rubbed at my forehead and looked at the carpet. 'Yeah, well, I don't feel brilliant, if you must know. But with all the action around here, perhaps it's not surprising.'

He put his hands on his hips. 'Look, let's leave this lot to stew for a while. What's next on your agenda?'

'Interviews—as you know—later today. Somehow I need to find some time with the systems supervisor, as well. And you've got the court appearance, haven't you?'

421

'Yes, but not this minute. Let's get out of here—take another peep at the house in Blagdon.'

The prospect of a few minutes' fresh air made me feel better immediately. 'All right. You're on,' I said. 'After the briefing, if all goes according to plan, OK?'

An hour and a half later we pulled up outside the Lomaxes' house in Blagdon. We pushed the gate open and went up the path and round to the side entrance. 'Yesterday morning was my best moment ever as a DS,' Charlie was saying. He positively swelled with pride as he went on, 'When we saw that brave little girl breaking the window with a chair; then when they all came down the stairs—I almost wept for joy. I'll never forget it.'

I grinned at him, nodding in agreement. Too much of our work was grim and ended in bad news. 'Charlie, I'm glad I was here, too.' I turned the key in the lock, and in we went.

'Right!' Charlie was cock-a-hoop. 'It's more or less as we left it. The forensic chaps must have finished off yesterday. Those poor children, Frank. It makes me ache.'

I switched on lights as we went around. The SOCOs had opened desk and kitchen drawers looking for letters, photos, and further evidence that would link the Lomaxes with the Bennetts, but otherwise there was scarcely a pin out of place. The old lady had been an immaculate housekeeper, and all the furniture was polished to a high gloss. Even in the two big bedrooms that had been set up as dormitories for the children, mirrors gleamed and floors glowed. Only the six unmade beds gave any clue to the strange goings-on in the house.

I stood by myself in the doorway of one of the rooms. *The girls' room,* I thought. Dolls, dolls' prams, dolls' clothes—all new—lined the shelves and filled the windowseat of another window which had been barred shut so that no child could be seen from it. Every attempt had been made to make the children feel that they were wanted here; but judging by the clean appearance of the dolls, the little girls had not been happy enough to forget their parents, as the old couple and their daughter had obviously so naively hoped, or even to pick up the dolls and play. And I certainly couldn't imagine the little tomboy, Jennifer Drury, playing with dolls, anyway! Still, I marvelled at the effort that must have been made for weeks before to prepare the house to receive the children that Lee Bennett would abduct. After all, I reminded myself, the children were eventually supposed to be moved north and accommodated in Coventry. I shook my head. They must all have been stark mad to think they could follow through on their plans for a family of six children that they did not have— six children that belonged to other families.

'Frank! Come and look down here.' Charlie was calling me from somewhere in the bowels of the house.

I turned away, following his voice past the window Jennifer had at last managed to force open and down two flights of stairs to a sort of pantry. Low timbers outlined the entrance, and I had to duck. The room was chill; I was surprised to see my breath white in the beam of the torch I had flicked on to see my way down the cellar stairs.

'Will you look at this!' Charlie exclaimed. 'This explains a lot. I didn't see it when we moved in yesterday, but the SOCOs obviously didn't miss it.'

I shone the light around the pantry. The floor was laid in grey flagstone, the walls lined from a height of two foot right to the ceiling with shelves sagging under row upon row of tins. Canned fruit, tinned meat and tuna, boxes of cheese and jelly, jars of jam and marmalade (all neatly labelled), pots of honey and peanut butter, bags of sugar and flour . . . enough food to feed the Bristol police for six months at least.

Charlie and I whistled simultaneously. 'Well,' he said, and 'well,' again. 'D'you reckon this lot's been here since the war, or what?'

I leaned forward to get a closer look at the labels. 'Course not. She and her daughter must have been saving this for a long time, though. This is more than a couple of old pensioners could afford in several months of state benefits. What a store!' I stared. Charlie had said that he ached for the children. So did I. But I ached for the old people as well. So much care . . . and so much desperation.

We went back up the stairs and out of the house. The light hurt my eyes as we passed through the outer door and into the garden, but the Mendips air was welcome. The old house might have been clean, but it smelled stale compared with the tree-lined freshness of the garden. My breathing seemed to be easing at last.

'Interviews, here we come,' I said, wanting to put the Lomaxes' house out of my mind. Something about it made me deeply sad. A couple of pensioners playing at Wendy houses and dolls.

By 4.30 I was having trouble breathing again. It was also getting harder and harder to think straight. *Sleep,* I kept thinking. *I've just got to sleep!*

I set a notepad and pen on the empty table, checked the tape machine, then rang the custody sergeant and asked him to bring Annie Lomax up from the cells for another interview. After the first round, she was the one who had puzzled me the most. One of the women officers joined us as an observer, and we were ready to start.

We began quite routinely with a record of the date, time, and people present: Mrs Lomax, Charlie, one of the women DCs and myself.

'Can we get you something to drink, Mrs Lomax? Or a cigarette?' I asked her as usual.

'Don't smoke,' she said gruffly when Charlie nudged the ashtray towards her.

'Do you require a solicitor?' I asked. So far so good; all routine stuff.

'A what, dear?' she asked me vaguely. 'I don't know if I do or not. I want my husband, that's all. Where have you taken him?' Her voice was quavering already, and I exchanged glances with Charlie.

'Please don't distress yourself, Mrs Lomax,' I said. 'Your husband is safe and well cared for.'

'We didn't mean no harm,' she pleaded. She had said the

same words the day before. Then she broke into tears. 'It was our daughter. Our son-in-law, I mean. They wanted, they wanted ...'

'I know,' Charlie said gently, and I was glad of his sympathy, for I could as yet feel little. 'They wanted you to help them.'

'Yes. Yes, that's true enough.' She wiped her eyes.

'How were you supposed to help them?' I asked her.

'Look after their children for them. They were busy, you see.' She sounded weary.

'Their children, Mrs Lomax? You said yesterday they didn't have any children.'

'Not their own, they didn't. We were just helping, that's all. Like you said.' She nodded towards Charlie, and I saw that even though he was the one who had brought her before the custody sergeant, he had managed to win her trust. 'They were fostering children.'

Charlie glanced at me. We both had in front of us typed notes sent down on the computer from Coventry. In separate interviews the old woman's daughter and son-in-law had admitted that they had wanted to foster children but been turned down—'for reasons they claimed not to understand', the reports said.

I looked at the watery blue eyes of the old woman on the other side of the table. I thought of a phrase the guv'nor had used yesterday, and how apt it seemed: 'silly innocents'. Yes, this poor old woman certainly was that. But 'mentally unfit' might have been a more accurate, if less compassionate, description.

'Didn't you wonder,' I said steadily, 'why your son-in-law kept bringing the children to you one by one? Didn't that make you suspicious at all?'

'No.' She wouldn't meet my eyes.

'And what about all the food you have stored in your pantry in the cellar? Why was that there if you weren't planning to feed those children for a long time?'

Her eyes flickered over me like pale flames in a dying fire.

'I've always made lots o' jam and marmalade and the like,' she said sullenly. 'Ask me husband. He'll tell you the same.'

'But it wasn't just jam and marmalade, was it, Mrs Lomax?'

She wouldn't answer, and I decided to take another tack. 'You told us yesterday that you have just the one daughter, Carolyn. Is that right?'

'Yes. Just one.' A heavy sigh.

Charlie leaned forward. 'This is a painful question,' he murmured, 'but were there ever any others? Were other children born to you?'

Her eyes filled again, and she began to sniff. 'Yes. We lost one before our girl was born. Another girl. That's all, honest. You can ask the old doctor. He'll tell you the same.' She threw an appealing look at the WDC.

Her words were sounding a kind of refrain, and I felt as if in asking these questions we were trespassing on very private territory. Still, I knew we had to probe further if we were to make any progress.

'You hoped for more children, did you?'

'Yes.' Her voice was wistful.

'And your daughter—when was she married?'

She gathered a little confidence then. 'Very young, she was. Only eighteen. In 1979.'

I looked down at the notes in front of me. 'Your son-in-law, Lee Bennett, is he the same age?'

She gave me a wan smile. 'No. Older. He's a bright lad, too. About seven years older than our Carolyn.'

'You were happy when they got married?'

She gave me a piercing look. 'Yes, though I don't see why you're asking all this. What business is it of yours?'

Charlie glanced at me, and I opened my mouth to speak, but the WDC beat me to it. 'The inspector's trying to find out why you hid those children for as long as you did—what was behind your co-operation with your son-in-law and daughter.' She glanced at the tape machine. 'With Lee and Carolyn Bennett . . . Mrs Lomax, this isn't easy for any of us.'

I shot her a grateful look, then returned my gaze to the old woman. 'Your daughter had no children of her own.'

'I told you she hadn't, didn't I?' There was anger in her voice.

'Yet they've been married ten years.'

'That's what I told you.'

She must think we were stupid, repeating questions and apparently going in circles the way we always had to in these interviews. 'But your daughter wanted children badly, didn't she?'

Her head came up sharply then. I saw all the pain of her daughter's childlessness in her eyes, as well as the love that had gone into the jam-making and neat labelling and stacking of food. For the first time in all the police interviews I've conducted I wished I could take the question back—even though I'd been right to ask it.

She stared straight at me with such anguish that I felt tears prick my own eyes. I thought of my mother and Damian. I thought of all the women I had ever known who had loved enough to make sacrifices for others, take risks for others. My chest convulsed again, and I began to cough so hard that I knew I couldn't go on with the interview. I scraped my chair backwards and stood up to leave the room.

'Excuse me,' I panted. 'Charlie, I'll send one of the others in here in a minute. I'm not really fit to—'

Charlie's face was instantly full of the same concern he had shown earlier in the day. 'Yeah, I know you're not. Go on, then, Frank.'

Before I left the room, I looked back at Annie Lomax. For a moment I saw her as if she were my own grandmother. We hardly needed a psychiatric report to see that she was slightly deficient mentally ('kangaroo loose in the top paddock,' Nigel would have said caustically). But what I saw as I looked at her was a tiny, shrivelled, confused old woman caught in something she didn't understand, trying to do something she did understand—mothering. I wondered if I should ever have been a policeman. I wanted to take the old woman in my arms and hug her. Not exactly standard police procedure.

Nigel and Jill were coming in for the late shift as I made my way down the stairs to go home.

'Frank, for goodness sake! You're white as a sheet.' Jill took my arm and frowned into my face. 'You shouldn't be here!'

'I'll be OK.' I wiped a thin trickle of sweat off the side of my face and gave them a falsely bright smile that ended in a cough.

'No.' It was Nigel's turn to look worried. 'Jill—can you whip up and tell Bill I'll be an hour late? I'm taking this man home.'

I laughed. 'Don't be daft! I'm quite capable—'

'Yeah—of driving into a tree. Come on, you're shivering. First stop your house. Second stop Weston-super-Mare. No arguing. This is ridiculous.'

I gave in and let him take me home.

'Your case is wrapping itself up nicely,' Nigel said comfortingly as we raced down the M5 with blue lights flashing. I could see he was enjoying himself.

'Yes. But I wanted to be there to—'

'Why? Charlie's doing all right.'

'I know it's nothing to do with you,' I murmured, 'but do me a favour and keep an eye on Annie Lomax for me—would you?'

The car swerved slightly as Nigel gaped at me. 'Frank, you're nuts. The welfare of the kids is far more important, and you've seen to that.'

'Yes, and they'll be fine. But—'

Nigel scoffed. 'What is this? Candidate for adopt-a-granny? Adopt-an-abductor, more like. You're getting to be a softie since you met Clare.'

'No,' I wheezed. I wanted to rib him about Jill, in return; in the old days he would never have taken time to drive me home when he was supposed to be going on duty. But I was now so short of breath I had to content myself with saying only what seemed most essential. 'I can't explain,' I began. I thought of the pantry in the Blagdon house and tried to describe to Nigel how I'd felt. 'It was the way it was all laid out. All those jams and marmalades! She made them all, I'm sure, last year. And she and the old fellow must have gone shopping two tins at a time every day for months to get all that stuff laid in. If there had been more light in that place, it would have made a gorgeous two-page spread for Clare's magazine. A picture of housewifely organization. Oh, I can't tell you, Nigel. It upset me to see it all. Something so loving twisted into something so wrong.'

Nigel stared at me again. 'Clare's really had an effect on you, mate,' he muttered. 'That or the pneumonia.'

A quarter of an hour after Nigel had left me at the house in Weston, I found myself once again bundled in a tartan blanket and ensconced in front of the television. Wretched as I felt, I had to know what was going on. While Mum made supper, Dad kept me company as I watched the evening news.

It wasn't long before the newscaster mentioned the all-too-familiar cases.

'Harold and Ann Lomax, arrested and charged recently in connection with six cases of child abduction in the west of England, have now been put under the care of their local authority for a programme of psychiatric treatment. The Lomaxes were remanded for psychiatric reports before they were charged, and police spokesmen say that the reports are now complete. A date for the trial is not yet fixed as the cases are complicated by cross-county investigations involving the Lomaxes' daughter and son-in-law, Carolyn and Lee Bennett, currently remanded in custody in Coventry.'

'There they are,' I shouted at Dad over the crisp voice. 'Look.'

Cameras panned in on the anguished faces of the Lomaxes as they were brought out of one of our buildings and into a waiting car. I remembered watching the cameramen at work.

'And there *you* are,' Dad said, hunched forward with as

much interest as my own. 'See? Standing over by that door?'

It was odd to see my face on the screen and relive those moments. Even allowing for the distortions of a television screen, my face looked thin and preoccupied, drawn with lack of sleep and illness. I was shaken. No wonder everyone was clucking and fussing over me.

'Sick as a dog,' Dad commented. 'And look—who'd have thought it? Such a sweet-looking old couple.'

'But slightly unhinged,' I said. 'Very sad.' Annie Lomax's pale skin and watery eyes loomed larger in my mind than the pathetic, bird-like figure on the screen. I couldn't forget the interview with her, the stricken, wrinkled face.

·48·

Standing in her aunt's front hall, Clare hugged the telephone close to her ear, hungry for the familiar tones of her mother's voice, and for words of comfort. Passing her on his way out to the car with a pile of packed boxes, Ed gave her an inscrutable stare. She looked away uneasily. The tension between them since the previous day had been almost unbearable.

Far away in Barking, her mother's telephone rang four times, then stopped.

'Mum?' Her voice sounded small, like that of a little girl, and she shook herself.

'Clare! Is that really you, love?'

She laughed, relief breaking over her like a wave. No reproaches that she had not rung or written for weeks. 'Yes. And I'm coming home.'

There was silence except for the faint crackling of four thousand miles.

'I said I'm coming home.'

'Yeah, I 'eard you the first time. What's up, then? I thought you was all set over there. This is a bit of a shake-me-up.'

Her mother sounded so normal, so *ordinary*. Clare wanted to be in Barking now, *now*, and not have to endure the rushed goodbyes, the awkward questions, and the pain of one more day in the office writing a final column she didn't know how to write; facing Bobbie and Pete for the last time. 'Well,' she said, 'I thought so too. But there's been—I've got—anyway, I need to get home.'

Her mother sounded bemused. 'Well, you 'ave taken me up short. But, of course, I'm delighted. You coming 'ome 'ere, or straight to Ealing?'

She knew her mother wanted her to go back to Barking first. 'I'll try and make it to you,' she said doubtfully.

'I'll come out the airport, shall I? 'Ere, which airport? When's the plane landin'? Just you wait a tick—I'll get a pencil.'

She heard the shuffle of slippers and the gasp as her mother dropped into the chair by the phone.

'There. That's better—get the weight of me feet for a bit. I bin out in the garden all day.'

Clare had been outside all day, too. To her embarrassment, Rita had insisted on holding a farewell barbecue with a few of the neighbours and family friends who would have been barbecuing anyway, because of the Labor Day break. Now that they were gone, and Ed was packing for his return to college the next day, she felt even more conscious of the ending of everything. 'Outside all day?' she murmured. 'But it's only mid-afternoon with you, isn't it?'

'Yeah, well, that's quite long enough for an old body to be digging up earth as 'ard as iron. Oh, it's bin a shockin' summer 'ere. We need rain so bad. P'r'aps you'll bring some with you, Clare.'

She didn't want to be diverted into talking about English weather so she began abruptly reading out her plane times. 'But don't you worry about coming out to the airport to meet me. You can expect me—oh, around eleven in the morning, I suppose. It's a long haul for you from Barking, Mum, and expensive, as well.'

'Maybe I will, and maybe I won't meet you,' her mother said. 'You leave that up to me, dear. But, Clare, ain't you going to tell me why you're leaving in such an 'urry?'

She took a deep breath, fighting back the tears that had dogged her for five days. 'No,' she said shakily. 'But I'll tell you later.'

'All right then. I'll see you on Wednesday. What a treat! I'm so pleased, Clare.'

'Thanks, Mum.' She tried to match her mother's excitement.

'Oh—by the way, there's one bit of not so good news for you.' Her mother's voice had become anxious, placating.

'But you mustn't think it's my fault. I was keeping an eye out, honest.'

'*What*?' she begged, wanting—but not wanting—to know.

'It's your car. I 'spect you've forgotten 'ow it broke down when you left.'

Her memory scrolled back. 'I had forgotten—completely. You're right. Why?'

'It's gone—that's what. A copper, a bit snappish 'e was, brought it back with an invoice from the garridge. I paid up for you—it wasn't a lot. The car sat outside for weeks. Then just the other day I went out and it wasn't there. I would've told you if you'd rung me up since then.'

Clare's shoulders slumped. One more thing to sort out when she returned home. 'Look, Mum, I can't cope with all that now. I'm too pushed. I'll see to it when I get home. I hadn't given the car a thought for weeks. It'll have to wait.'

'You don't want me to report it's bin nicked?'

'No. What do the police care about clapped-out old Fiats stolen from Barking? I told you—' She heard her voice rising impatiently, and stopped herself.

'You sound so funny, Clare. You all right?'

'Yes, fine,' she mumbled. 'Not long till I'm back now.'

'How's Rita and the kids?'

'All fine, too.' She suddenly saw a way out. 'D'you want to speak to Rita before I get off the line?'

'No, love. This ain't a cheap call for 'er. Just give 'er my love, will you? I bin thinkin' ever such a lot about 'er since Bert passed on.'

'She's a brave lady, Mum. I think she'll be OK.'

Her mother sniffed. 'Yeah, I'm sure she will. Now you get off of 'ere and let me make a cuppa. Get yourself some sleep, as well. You sound bad to me.'

'I told you, I'm fine,' she said with dwindling conviction.

'No you're not,' Ed said, passing her with another load. He grinned.

She turned her back on him. 'Goodbye, Mum. Until the middle of the week.'

'All right, Clare.'

'You're telling lies to my Aunt Edith,' Ed hissed, stopping beside her as she put down the phone.

'Oh, Ed, leave me alone, can't you?'

Jack appeared in the kitchen doorway. 'Hey, you guys, it's getting dark already. Ed, why don't you let me give you a hand with that junk so we can sit outside together and relax over a last drink?'

'I thought you had packing of your own, Jack,' Ed said warily. 'You're heading out to Springfield at the crack of dawn, you said.'

'Yes, but I've only got what I brought for the week. It won't take me five minutes to get myself together. You've got a whole semester's junk to move.'

'OK, then. Help yourself. The *junk* is all on my bed or my floor.'

Grateful to be out of the discussion, Clare slipped past Jack up the stairs and shut her door. While her cousins were preparing for separate journeys, she might as well do the same. She couldn't face Rita, Marie, and the visitors out on the patio until she absolutely had to.

It was easy enough to pull out everything she owned, everything she had bought since her arrival, onto the spare bed. More difficult was getting it into the one travelling bag she had brought in her hasty trip to Massachusetts ten weeks before. Some of the American things, she decided, would have to stay in Rita's spare room until her next visit—if she ever came again.

She heard Ed and Jack plying up and down the stairs, joking and shouting to each other about boxes of 'trash' and 'priceless' audio equipment which Jack seemed bent on convincing Ed he was going to jettison down the stairs at the slightest provocation. On the one hand relieved to hear them chaffing each other, she felt at the same time uncomfortable that there was unfinished business between herself and Ed. There was no question of her *loving* him, except as a cousin. And yet . . .

Why did I get drawn into that impossible situation yesterday? She let a dress she was folding slide out of her fingers and back onto the bed, groaning with dismay. *Because you were desperate, Clare Hogarth,* the answer came back to her. *Certain no one cares about you, perhaps not even God.*

She sighed. *But Mum cares about me. I just don't appreciate her care. And Nina, and some of the others at* Women Today— *no, it's no use thinking about them! I don't even know if I have a job to go back to.*

Her mind went chasing itself in ever tighter circles until she could bear it no longer. *Lord,* she found herself praying for the first time in weeks, *please give me peace. I'm so sorry for the mess I've made of everything since I came here.*

There was no audible reply, just the wind lifting the light curtains that hung behind her. The house fell quiet; Jack and Ed had evidently stopped work and gone out to the back of the house with the others. She stood utterly still and waited. All she could picture was McEnroe's gentle old face the night before, watching her with those wise blue eyes and saying, 'Love is always stronger than hate.'

'Clare!' Rita was suddenly calling her from the stairs. 'Are you coming down?'

She pushed the muddle of packing to one side and opened the door. 'Yes,' she said, and went down to the beginning of her long journey home.

That journey brought her into the *Citizen* offices early the next day after an almost sleepless night. Almost inevitably, the first person she saw as she let herself into the suite was Pete McEnroe.

He was standing at Kathy's desk as she walked through, and he gave her a hard, cold stare.

'Nice weekend?' he said, without any apparent interest in her answer.

'Not really,' she answered.

Kathy looked from one to the other with puzzlement.

'I'd like to see you as soon as you've done the new copy for the column. My uncle came to see me last night—'

435

She didn't see why she should let him hold the reins of this conversation all by himself. Quickly, she said, 'Me too. Before he came to you. He told me he was going to your apartment—after he left my aunt's.'

Pete's eyebrows went up. 'Did he indeed? Well, then, perhaps you know that the FBI's looking at that threat letter this morning. And perhaps you also know that I arranged late last night—totally disrupting my holiday, of course—for a stop press to go into several of the papers so that the Mafia would know we've withdrawn a planned feature on *I Giocosi*. And perhaps—' His voice was cuttingly sarcastic, 'You'll know in addition that I said it was because the story about that amazing group had already been scooped by a very successful new magazine called *Up Front*.'

She looked at him dumbly, hating his cynicism, his aggressiveness.

He glared back. 'I want you to write a completely innocuous column this week. Write about anything you like—I don't give a damn. Your aunt's pet goldfish. Your dear cousins' golf handicap—anything that won't give offence to anyone. Is that clear?'

She gave him back all the frost he gave her. 'Perfectly.'

'Good.'

The phone on Kathy's desk pealed. She grabbed it with an anguished look at Clare. 'For Mr McEnroe? . . . Yes, I'll tell him. Yes.' She looked up at Pete. 'Your secretary called. She says there's an official letter for you from the Immigration Office. It's—er—'

'About me, no doubt,' Clare interrupted. 'Well, don't worry, Pete, I'll get out of here as fast as I can. I shan't even wait to be served notice.'

'Good.'

She wanted to hit him, saw in her mind's eye her own arms pushing him into the swimming-pool at McEnroe's house. Hate rose up again, and only McEnroe's words kept her from falling yet again into the trap of it, screaming and lashing out at him. She shut her door as quietly as she could, controlling

436

her features until Pete and Kathy were firmly on the other side of it. Then her face crumpled, and she dissolved into tears. Irritation with herself, exhaustion, loneliness, failure—all washed over her.

At last she dried her face and wrote the most superficial piece she had ever written as a journalist. She wrote about the ritual of hanging storm windows on a beach house at the end of the summer, speculating as she did so about the social significance of Ed's comments that there were no end-of-the-summer parties on the beach any more; that beach summer house life was probably changing as families moved out and overworked yuppies moved in. Half of it, she knew, made no sense at all. Tapping the words onto the screen, she didn't care.

Bobbie's face came round her door during the lunch break when she thought the offices were empty.

'Hi,' Bobbie said, looking uncertain of her welcome.

Clare stood up and ran to her. 'I'm so sorry.' Tears began to push out again, but to Bobbie, who knew nothing of the past few days, she thought they would look like crocodile tears. She sniffed them back.

'I'm sorry too. I know Pete's been like a bear to you. Kathy was telling me.'

'Oh.' She felt outmanoeuvred, at the same time dismayed that Pete would have said nothing to Bobbie about their other escapades—the closeness between them that would have injured Bobbie far more than any ill-timed, thoughtless words about the Mafia.

'In fact he's been like a bear to everyone except me,' Bobbie was saying.

Clare was shaking. She sat down again. 'He'd better be kind to you, Bobbie. At least you go on believing in him.'

Bobbie sat down beside her and gave her an odd look. 'Do I? Oh, Clare, you don't know the half of what's gone on here the last few years.'

And nor, thought Clare, *do you know half of what's gone on here the last few days*.

'We were engaged.'

'I know you were,' Clare said quickly. 'And he let you down.'

Bobbie shook her head. 'No, whoever told you that story got the wrong rumour.'

Clare frowned. 'Then what happened? I mean—oh, it's none of my business.'

'It is, though, a little. Everyone's been aware how attractive he thinks you are. It's been electric in these offices since you came.'

Clare flushed. 'I'm sorry, I—'

'No, Pete does that, you know. It wasn't you—at least, not at first.' Bobbie glanced away, then back again. 'People get so twisted up about him. I was, too, when we were engaged. But it was I who broke it off, Clare. Not Pete. He was drinking himself to pieces because he thought that was how he was going to keep up with the other top-flight journalists. Senator McEnroe had to salvage him more than once. I wasn't so patient.' She chuckled. 'I handed him back his ring and told him to wait until he grew up, and that I would wait too. No one ever did that to Pete, and he's back to me now, still growing up.'

Clare watched Bobbie's face in fascination and disbelief. 'You're generous to tell me all this.'

Bobbie shook her head again and looked at the carpet. 'No. I love him, that's all. Always have. It's silly, but there you are.'

'Bobbie,' Clare said, 'I hope he learns to love you, one day.'

For the second time in three weeks, it was the phone that woke Clare. This time, however, the flat was bathed in the light of early morning as she stumbled across the room to answer it.

'H-hello?' She was breathless with jumping out of bed, straight from her dreams, to the phone's shrill insistence.

'Clare, it's me, Frank.'

Before Clare could answer, the alarm clock began to ring furiously from her bedroom. Still drowsy, she tried to summon her wits. 'Oh—just a moment and I'll—'

She ran back into her bedroom, shut off the alarm, and returned to the telephone. She felt dizzy with a mixture of relief, surprise, and sleep.

His voice was warm. 'I'm not sure I should be talking to a brazen woman who gets arrested for obstructing a police officer.'

She laughed uncertainly. 'Then why *are* you?'

'My mother would have talked my ear off, if not.'

A chill rippled through her. 'You're ill again?'

'Not so sick I can't check up on obstructive journalists.'

She found she was smiling. 'At this hour?'

'Why not! I'm back in Weston, and fed up already. I wanted to hear your voice.'

She thought about her own longing for him and melted inside. 'It's lovely to hear yours.'

'Listen, I wanted to catch you before work. Any chance you could get away again? I'm stuck here for I don't know how long, and—'

She could hear the wheeze in his voice and wanted to tell him to stop talking. 'Frank, I—'

'Clare, there's so much I want to say to you. And not on the phone, either. I had a speech planned in the middle of the night. So how about it—could you come down?'

'To explain how I got arrested?'

'No, you ninny. To see *me*. You've got arrests on the brain. Why don't you tell me what happened if it's bothering you so much—so we can get on with the rest of our lives.' He began to cough.

She waited, then took a deep breath and began her tale. 'Getting arrested upset me. The minute the words were out of my mouth to the custody sergeant that I wanted you to know what was happening to me, I was afraid I would cause you problems.'

'No, Clare. I had enough problems already when the message got lost in my tray. Then I thought it was a hoax. It doesn't matter.' He sounded reassuring.

'And it didn't make life difficult for you at work?'

'No—I've hardly been back. And I'm the only one to know. Not that it matters, anyway, as I said. Except that I might blackmail you some time—you never know.'

She laughed. 'Then *you* might have to arrest me.'

'With pleasure. And permanently, if you like.'

'I do like.'

There was a breathless pause while she realized what she—what they both—were saying.

'Do you suppose, Miss World Journeyer, I could keep you in one place long enough to make the custody official?'

'My custody of you, you mean?' she said pertly. She could feel a wide smile spreading over her face.

'We'll settle that dispute when you get down here. But it's a deal. I won't be flat on my back with pneumonia for ever, so look out. When Lazarus gets out of his grave we'll have a great party!'

Happiness bubbled up in her. She was hungry, now, to see him. She wasn't going to catch a slow train, either.

'I'll think of something. Of course I'll come, as soon as I can.'

She hung up and rubbed her eyes, then absorbed the wonderfully disconcerting fact that she wasn't dreaming.

Sandy staggered sleepily out of her room as Clare turned away from the phone. 'What's the matter? Is it Frank?'

'Oh, sorry I woke you.'

'That's all right. Just don't do it again.' Sandy grinned with the amiability of someone only half awake and shut her door again.

Clare's head was spinning, but she didn't allow herself to think about what she was doing: only to keep moving. She scrawled a note to Sandy saying that she'd be away again for a few days. The phone rang a second time, just as she was pouring herself a glass of orange juice in the kitchen. She picked it up after one ring, puzzled, and concerned for Sandy.

'Sorry.' It was Andy, her boss. She recognized his voice after the first word.

'So am I,' she said drily.

'Weren't you up?'

'I was. My flatmate wasn't.'

'Sorry about that. But it's just that I won't be in the office today, and I remembered something I meant to tell you yesterday.'

'About the arrest?' Her heart sank.

'Heavens no! Though that probably put it out of my mind.'

'Andy, I won't be in today either.'

He brushed away her words with a sweep of his invisible hand. 'Never mind—just *never mind*. Listen, this is more important—whether you're there or not. It cost me a bit of sleep on Monday night—I can tell you. Don't panic, and I certainly don't want to hold you up—but you ought to know.'

'What? Andy, I said I wasn't coming—'

'We got a very strange fax Monday evening. Most people had left the office. I was working late—so what else is new! It'd come from somewhere in Italy, I think. No identifying mark at the top.'

Clare frowned. 'No fax number to show the sender? That's odd.'

'None. It was a nasty bit of work, as well, and I've got the

441

serious crime squad onto it, I'm afraid. I didn't get out of Blackfriars until after eleven. The wife's fed up with me. Another reason I'm so damn tired.'

She murmured a few words of comfort. 'But tell me I'm dreaming. First you didn't seem too concerned when I was arrested, and you don't mind when I can't make it into work *again*; then you tell me you've had Scotland Yard crawling round the offices after dark!'

She expected Andy to chuckle, but he didn't. 'The fax was a threat—against the magazine as a whole. The men from Victoria Street thought it might be a hoax, but better to be on the safe side. I can't read a word of Italian.'

'Nina can.'

'I know. Dave got her to translate it before I rang Scotland Yard. It was some incomprehensible gibberish about an arts orchestra in the States, warning us off doing a feature on it. *I Giocosi*. Never heard of them myself.'

'I have—just recently. Are we doing a feature, then?'

'Of course not; you'd know if we were. Dave's never heard of them, either. But it *is* rather unnerving; they said they had information that one of our staff writers was taking a special interest in the orchestra. Gave no names, though. The whole thing's ridiculous. Either someone's got his wires crossed, or it may even have been a mass fax sent to a number of magazines at once. Scotland Yard's investigating that at the moment, but I don't suppose anyone'll get very far until . . . Clare, listen, we'll talk about it when you get back.'

Though Andy had done all the talking, Clare was still breathless when she hung up. She dressed mechanically, threw a few clothes into a bag and small suitcase, then decided impulsively that she would rather fly standby to Bristol than drag all the way west on the train. Pleased with the idea, she phoned for a taxi.

As she waited outside, she was overwhelmed by a sense of *déjà vu* far more real than when she and Frank had travelled the M5 together a few weeks before. *Surely I've done this before, and recently?*

The taxi swept her away into streets empty of all but road cleaners and early schoolchildren. The air smelt sweeter than usual: crisp with the edge of autumn. She watched suburbia slide away, then the miles of chainlink fence, lines of lights, and open land that bordered the airport.

At the terminal entrance she fumbled for her money. As she did so, the same feeling of repeating herself overcame her. She paused, her fingers still around the notes and coins.

'You all right?' the taxi driver asked her, peering through the smeared glass window behind him.

She shook herself slightly. 'More or less. It's just that I'm making another unexpected trip, that's all.'

He rewarded her with a broken-toothed smile. 'You was sleepy last time I brought you, too.'

She stepped out of the taxi, even more bewildered by the conviction that she had gone through almost the same motions a few weeks before.

'Going far?' he asked, returning some change to her hand.

She stared at him in confusion, then remembered where she had heard those words before: from Frank. Standing then on a faraway bridge over motorway traffic, she had said, 'A long way, I hope.' Now, she simply said, 'Not far this time.'

In the main concourse she checked the board for the first plane to Bristol. A flashing red light announced that a flight from Boston had just landed. In a heady moment of fantasy, she pretended to herself that she was flying to Boston, not Bristol. *What if . . .?* But then she made herself come fully awake, running to the flight desk to secure a cancellation seat to Bristol.

Delighted she would be there in less than an hour, she nevertheless felt hot and flustered. There was just time to buy a bright bunch of dahlias for Mrs Bernard, then to rush to the ladies' room and pull a comb through her hair.

A large mirror faced her as she pushed through the swing door. Coming towards her was a woman very like herself: pale with fatigue, eyes huge from the surprise of lights so harsh, the dark pupils accentuated by the dark suit. She smiled vaguely, and the woman smiled back—a brittle, fixed smile. Hesitating, resting her flight bag on the ledge, she leaned forward over a basin. Then she groaned, shut her eyes, and stood still for an instant.

When she opened her eyes, the same woman looked back at her, grey eyes clear and unblinking, this time unsmiling. They looked at each other for perhaps twenty seconds; then Clare dropped her eyes and reached to turn on the taps.

Plunging her hands into lukewarm water, she felt a surge of relief. *What if he were waiting for me at the airport?* she thought fancifully. *No, of course he won't be. But next time, when he's well, he'll be there for me.*

Thoughtfully, careful not to catch the other woman's eyes again, she dried her hands and retrieved the bag.

She turned away just as the other woman on the other side of the line of basins turned away also. For a moment, her eyes betrayed her. The other woman was not now dressed as she was—in a simple navy suit—but in a garish jacket and skirt, American style. It was just a trick of the light. She frowned back at her, over her right shoulder, walking away from her, away through a door at the far side of the room.

Blinking, she turned her head again and moved forward. When she went out again into the main concourse, she did not see that other woman again.

Instead, as she hurtled across the concourse towards the departures area on the far side of the terminal, she ran almost slap into the last person she was expecting to see in the airport—in any airport: her mother.

'Clare!'

'Mum, what on *earth*?'

Her mother was beaming with delight, though there was no look of surprise on her face. 'I *told* you I might come and see you.'

Clare blinked and shook her head, still dazed. 'What? But here—?' She could make no sense of what her mother had said. 'Well . . . it doesn't matter.' Time pressed on her. If she asked too many questions, she'd have no hope of catching the plane to Bristol. Still—she told herself breathlessly—she could hardly rush away after neglecting her for so long. With a shock, she knew she did care about her, after all. There would be time, later, to ask what her mother, of all people, was doing in an airport.

She searched her mother's face keenly, noticing that she was thinner than she remembered, her clothes hanging more loosely on her broad shoulders. She was more stooped, too, and much greyer. Then Clare dropped her flight bag and folded the old woman into her arms.

'I do believe you're taller, love.' Edie Hogarth's voice, muffled against the soft stuff of Clare's suit, was full of pride and amazement.

She laughed. 'I can't be, but you've shrunk, Mum!'

Her mother stood back, her shiny forehead and cheeks turning pink. Clare saw that her eyes were wet, caught the quick swipe of fingers to face, a gesture almost of shame. 'Well, and maybe it's not 'alf surprising, with all this 'eat, and your Uncle Bert, and one fing and another.'

Clare danced unhappily from one foot to the other. It was like being in the playground at school again: loving her mother, yet needing to escape from her, as well. She knew she should ask what brought her mother to the airport, and what she'd meant about Uncle Bert; but she became newly conscious of a light flashing on the board above them, right below the announcement for the Boston flight; LAST CALL FOR BRISTOL FLIGHT 023, NOW BOARDING GATE 31. The light was as searing and intense on her tired eyes as blue police car lights on a motorway.

Her mother followed her eyes to the board without any apparent understanding. 'What's up, then, love? Shall we go straight 'ome? Where's all yer baggage?'

'Baggage?' Impatience mounting, in spite of herself, Clare looked at her blankly. 'Somewhere between here and the plane, I imagine.'

'Oh, that's all right then. You can get it in a minute, I s'pose.'

445

Again Clare stared, a bubble of amusement rising in her throat. Of course, her mother knew nothing about how airports worked. *Perhaps she even thinks I have to carry my suitcase onto the plane!* She smiled softly. 'Mum—you don't—'

'But you do look all of a fluster. Tired out, are you, after all your doings?'

Clare laughed, hoping her exasperation wasn't showing. 'You could say that!' *And what did Mum mean about going home?* She inhaled quickly. 'Look, I certainly didn't expect to see you here now. We need to have a good old chat. There's so much . . . but—' She pointed up at the board. 'My plane's not going to keep. That's why I'm—'

Her mother's face fell. 'But you've only just—we've only just . . . You mean you're off somewhere else again, *already*?'

'Mum, please—I'll explain it all, I promise. But I can't now. Frank's ill. You don't know about Frank, and there isn't time . . . but you will, and oh—' She felt as if she were in the eye of a whirlwind that sent the random flotsam of her life spinning around her without sense or sequence. Then inspiration struck, and she thrust the flowers into her mother's arms. 'They're not much, but here you are—dear Mum.'

Edie Hogarth's face lit up. 'Oh, Clare, what a treat! How *nice*. Are you sure they're for me?'

Clare wasn't sure at all, but was touched by her childish excitement. 'Yes, for you,' she said affectionately. 'For being someone who goes on loving me even when I don't ring you and hardly ever write . . . but I will now, I promise . . .'

Her mother took the flowers and buried her nose in the red petals. 'Mmm, autumn. That's what I like to smell.' She looked up, her face sharpening from soft pleasure to sudden practicality in a mood swing that was as familiar to Clare as her mother's Cockney accent.

'But listen, Clare, don't you make no more promises. Just you catch that plane, 'specially if it'd mean otherwise you don't catch that man of yours.' She grinned, enjoying her own little joke. 'You tell me all about 'im when you get back, that's all I ask. Frank, you say?'

Clare backed slowly away from her. Rarely had she felt so uncomfortable in her mother's presence, but rarely so certain, either, that she would in future love her more than she had in the past. 'Yes—Frank. Frank Bernard.'

Her mother's mouth fell open. 'But isn't 'e the one what kept calling for you? You know—the one 'oo gave us both the creeps that weekend?'

There was no time to understand—let alone answer—such questions, though some sort of faint echo resonated at the back of her mind. She tried to remember, but couldn't. She was going to see *Frank*. 'You'll meet him soon. I love him, Mum. I'll ring you when I come back. And I love you, too.'

Her mother was shaking her head. 'You young people! Well, you do that. Don't forget, now.'

Clare turned and fled. Outside the security checkpoint that led into the domestic flights area, she turned to catch a last glimpse of her mother's broad face in the crowd. Instead, she saw the splash of scarlet that was the bunch of dahlias she had given her: a small vermilion beacon threading through the crowds away from her. *I have promises to keep,* she told herself, thinking as she ran at last to gate 31 that even though Frank was uppermost now in her mind, she could never again leave her mother so long out of her life.

Two once branching paths were running together. Clare knew that God was drawing straight with her own crooked lines and with Frank's slow searchings on the pathways of pain and unknowing. The way through the woods ahead was lovely, dark, and deep. But she did not mind, now, how many miles she had to go before she could sleep. Neither she nor Frank would ever be journeying alone again.

A selection of top titles from LION PUBLISHING